FOREVER SHALES

DEBORAH BERKELEY

Deborah Berkeley

Published by

MELROSE BOOKS

An Imprint of Melrose Press Limited
St Thomas Place, Ely
Cambridgeshire
CB7 4GG, UK
www.melrosebooks.com

FIRST EDITION

Cover designed by Deborah Berkeley

ISBN 978 1 907040 71 9

Printed and bound in Great Britain by:
CPI Antony Rowe. Chippenham, Wiltshire

MIX
Paper
FSC FSC® C013604

This book is dedicated to my late, great uncle,
Frederick Richard Comyns Skinner Berkeley.

*The past is a foreign country: they do
things differently there.*

L. P. Hartley

CONTENTS

Cast of Characters

Herbert Bowyer (b.1851), youngest son of William Comyns: nephew to Augustus; chemical manufacturer; photographer: lived at Cotheridge Court, and later, Glengowan, in Shortlands, Kent.

Harry (b.1851), Harry Douglas: son of Comyns Rowland; solicitor and brother of Algernon Cecil.

Jane – wife of William Nichols: sister-in-law to Mildred and lived at Newbury House, Cotheridge.

Julia (b.1858), daughter of Augustus: unmarried.

Jessie (b.1852), daughter of Augustus: devoted companion of Shales; unmarried.

Lucy (b. 1853), daughter of Augustus: unmarried.

Maud (b. about 1860), in Norfolk: Maud May Allen Diggins; married Thomas Rowland; daughter-in-law of Augustus; mother of Mary Matilda; dressmaker.

Mary – wife of William Augustus: daughter-in-law of Augustus.

Mary Matilda (b.1882), Mary Matilda May Comyns: daughter of Thomas Rowland and Maud.

Mildred – wife of Rowland Comyns of Butts Bank Farm.

Philip – son of William Augustus and Mary: resided at The Bear Hotel; grandson of Augustus; cousin to the Philip below.

Philip – son of Charles Clement and Amy: grandson of Augustus; cousin to above.

Rowland (b.1845), Rowland Comyns: eldest son and heir of William Comyns; nephew of Augustus; farmed Butts Bank Farm; married to Mildred; inherited Cotheridge Court.

Stanley Tyerman (b.1855), distant relation: Victorian painter and water-colourist: illustrated for the *Illustrated London News*.

Shales – son of William Augustus and Mary: grandson of Augustus: lived at The Bear Hotel.

Shales (b.1879), name of the dog that is narrating the story you are reading: a black and white Border collie: an entirely fictitious character.

Thomas Rowland (b.1860), 3rd son of Augustus: traveller (salesman) and worker in the family coal enterprise; married to Maud; devoted to Shales.

William (b.1849), eldest son of Augustus: proprietor of The Bear Hotel, Gorleston-on-Sea, Norfolk; married to Mary (nee Mary Burton Shales).

William Comyns (b.1810), Reverend: eldest brother of Augustus; heir to Cotheridge Court.

William Nichols – second son of William Comyns: lived at Newbury House, Cotheridge: rector of St. Leonard's Church, Cotheridge.

ADDITIONAL CHARACTERS:

Armstrong* – Annie Armstrong: housemaid to Augustus at 64 Cassland Road and 15 Darnley Road.

Charlotte* – nurse to Mary Matilda.

David King Foster – employed as an office clerk in Stoke Newington in the employ of Augustus Berkeley.

Florrie* – female dog, white in colour: lived at the pub on Darnley Road.

Harry* and Jack* – delivery men for a Worcester brewery.

Holmes – Emily Holmes: cook at Cotheridge Court.

Millie Holmes*: cook at 15 Darnley Road.

Horatio Harvest* – a cat: long-time friend of Shales the dog; resided at Harvest Farm, Essex.

Jasper* – beloved hunter belonging to Thomas Rowland Berkeley.

Mary Ann Moore – dressmaker and owner of a boarding house at Shelly Terrace, Stoke Newington: widowed.

Mrs Butterworth* – hotel keeper of the Prince Hotel.

Mrs Hennessey* – wealthy merchant's wife.

Soames* – stableman in the employ of Augustus Berkeley.

Eliza* – cook in the employ of Augustus.

Thomas White – occupation – cutler: married Emily Berkeley.

Toby* – a Border collie living and working at Butts Bank Farm.

Toothless George* – Thomas George: farm labourer-cum-stableman-cum-kennel man at Butts Bank Farm; originally from West Riding, Yorkshire.

Will Stone* – dog trainer, esp. farm dogs.

*Fictitious names and characters, which are a complete invention by the author. All others bear a resemblance in name only.

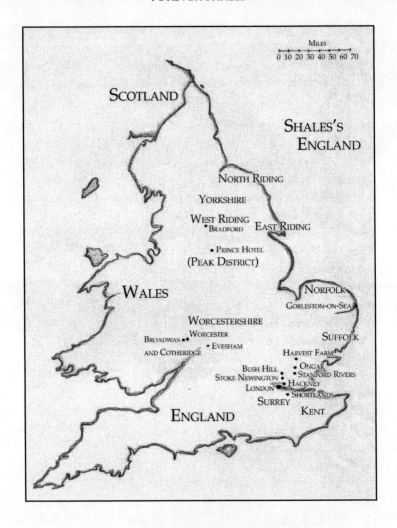

INTRODUCTION

*"What is a life worth, if no one has any
interest in its history?"*

EAR READER, the beginning of my story could very well be the end, or the end could possibly be the beginning, but if you decide to read into my life then I can guarantee you a timely spot – somewhere between the start and the end. You must forgive me for talking in circles – life has been a bit difficult for me; it toyed and goaded me along, but I went willingly, so I don't expect any amount of sympathy from you. But should you come to know my story, you may then at least understand how, during the final two decades of Queen Victoria's reign, I lived my life.

There has been ample time for me to mull over my life, which seems to have been a life as adventurous as that of say, Stanley, or Livingstone. My life is a story worth telling, and if you think not then there was no point to any of it at all, and I may as well have not been born. What is a life worth, if no one has any interest in its history? If you, the reader, shall dare to embark upon the voyage of my life, you shall then be rewarded with laughter and tears. If you do not experience either of these emotions then perhaps *you* require a bit of adventure yourself. Call it a seasoning, such as salt and pepper, of your own life. How is it they say? "Spice it up." Then the spice of life is a life worth living – for one thing, it is never dull. If you can't think of your own past with fondness, then don't think of it at all; for, it is your life – to do with as you wish.

During my life I have had great difficulty communicating with people, but that is a burden all animals are destined to carry, and it is a weighty one. So, I shall try my best to relate to you the exciting adventures of my past in a way you can understand me, and just as long as you are interested.

Dear Reader, I must apologise for my bad manners. It seems I haven't introduced myself: I'm a sheepdog; well, a long time ago I was, when I lived on a farm. My coat is black and white, and my Christian name is Shales, which is easy to pronounce – it rhymes with tales.

Oh, dear. My thoughts are getting a bit deep, and my head feels like it's spinning like a top. It's a bit like rounding up and dividing invisible sheep and then forgetting how many sheep there are supposed to be, and then – they all run off in different directions.

I shall have to start the story of my life at the very beginning, which created itself quite a long time ago, or perhaps just miles and miles away. You may need to get comfortable and have yourself a pot of tea on hand, and don't forget – help yourself to some biscuits. I highly recommend ginger snaps, or perhaps some Scottish shortbread, or if you find the biscuit tin empty, then a lovely cream cake. One more thing – you'll need to sit in front of a warm, cosy fire, especially if the weather outside is cold and damp. *Shales.*

THE FOOL

BOOK I

I

GETTING TO THE END

"A tug can set you free."

5TH NOVEMBER, 1901

I T HAPPENED ON AN AVERAGE MORNING, on what should have been an average day, considering the house oozed emptiness – not empty from the lack of furnishings, but empty from the personal scent and tobacco smoke odours of my late master. The house smelt empty of him; my heart ached for him. I mourned him deeply. On this particular morning my heart actually pained for him, physically, as my chest cried out in anguish to the point that it frightened me. I lay stretched out in front of the warm coal fire, but try as I might, I could not move a muscle. I was paralysed. My mind screamed, "Jessie! Come quick!"

Busy fussing over who knows what, someplace in our large house, she never heard me in my plight. As I lay waiting for her, the already darkened room dimmed to an inky black, and the sense of panic I had experienced eased off into a delicious feeling of sleepiness, and the pain in my chest seemed to be not so painful after all. My sleepy mind played tricks on me, and I imagined I heard farm sounds: the sounds of bleating sheep and, above that, the impatient moo of a milch cow. I felt light and feathery, as if I was about to float away, but then I felt a tug, and I heard Jessie say, "Oh... Shales. Shales... love." Her voice was husky and it croaked with emotion, but she was too late, and then the tug let go, and I was free.

3

II

THE FARM

"This was my home, my life, and my farm,
and it was the whole world as far as I was
concerned; no other place existed."

AUGUST, 1879

I T'S NICE TO BE ALIVE ON A DAY when the sun is shining and the sky is blue and there is warmth to the sun, and also, there is a gentle breeze that tickles your hair, making you feel relaxed, and all the worries that live in the caverns of your mind tend to disappear. A day such as this often reminds me of those early farm days, at my home, in a little place called Broadwas. This is as far back as I can remember: being taken there as a small puppy and not knowing anything at all about the outside world. I was just a babe in arms, a tiny puppy: black with white markings, and very cuddly. Bless my little cotton socks. I had a white muzzle, two tiny white eyebrows above brown eyes, a white chest, four white legs, and a little white splash on the tip of my tail; not that you would ever notice it hiding amongst my thick, black tail hairs. Even to this day, I still have those two peculiar white eyebrows, which move about whenever I frown or scowl.

One day in particular, when I was just a few weeks of age, some people came to see me. They were ladies, and there were just two of them. At their behest I was placed inside a deep wicker basket, which held a lid, and this they closed on me, and it all went dark – leaving me feeling confused and lonely. Then the basket, with little me inside it, was whisked away and placed on the seat of a carriage by Heydon, the coachman. It was safely wedged in-between the two ladies, and off we went. All I could hear was the clip-clopping of the

4

horses' hoofs and the laughing and chattering away of the two ladies who were my escorts. What strangeness to my ears! I lay curled upon a very thick blanket and wondered what was happening to me, and because my mind was so young I couldn't imagine very much beyond when I would be getting my next meal. Every once in a while the lid was raised, as if by magic, and bright, warm daylight spilt in on me, and I momentarily basked in its soothing warmth.

I heard a musical voice ask, "Now what is he doing?"

A voice answered, as if surprised, "It's just sitting there, looking up at me." Then, sounding doubtful, "Oh, I wonder if it misses its mother? What do you think, Mildred? I confess I don't know much about puppies."

"Jane, wouldn't you miss your mother if you were a child and were snatched away from her?" Through gaps in the wicker, I saw she tilted her head as she whispered in a conciliatory tone, *"I think it's the same for puppies."* Mildred had obviously been taken by surprise at the innocence of Jane's question.

"Yes, I would," answered Jane in a pouting voice, barely heard above the loud sound of the horses' hollowed clip-clops. "Poor thing! You'll just have to coddle it and give it lots of love."

"I suppose we should refer to him as a 'he', and not an 'it', because I can tell you now, I wouldn't like anyone referring to me as 'it'. Jane, I would be most offended, and I'm sure the same goes for you." Mildred continued to complain to her travelling companion. "Rowland has paid good money for this puppy, and he is going to be trained as a herding dog. Rowland won't want it spoilt, and I just know he'll take charge of the puppy and I won't see much of it at all. He'll give it over to George, like he has said he'll do, and it'll, I mean to say, *he* will be locked up with Toby, and I'll never see him again. It's a wonder that Rowland even allowed us to collect the puppy today, in his stead, and that's only because he had to go to Worcester."

Jane sadly confessed, "I wish my William would allow us to have a dog. When I was a child we always had dogs, and now it just doesn't seem right living without them. One would think a rector would enjoy the companionship of a dog, or a cat, but not my William. He thinks they belong outside, in kennels, but I disagree with him. I think they make wonderful companions, and there should always be a dog in the house." After a thoughtful pause she suggested, "Perhaps one of those small dogs, a little terrier. I wonder if William would consider us having one of those?" Her voice expressed hope, and then, as realisation dawned, it faded away into nothingness.

Butts Bank Farm

As I listened, the conversation went on like this between the new sisters-in-law, and occasionally the wicker lid was lifted and I would see one of the ladies' faces, or at times, perhaps both of them, face, bonnet, and all, peering down at me, and a delicately gloved hand would carefully reach down and stroke my little ears. The lid would be lowered again, darkening my new world. I was beginning to miss my mum, but something told me that I wouldn't ever be seeing her again. I decided to be brave and to embrace this new world, hoping that I would get my dinner soonish, as I was already feeling quite peckish. I yearned for my mother and her delicious-tasting milk. However, I quite liked the company of those cheerful ladies, and I would have willingly gone anywhere with either of them.

Eventually, we ended that noisome journey of clip-clopping sounds and endless chattering. Once again, my basket was carried along in Heydon's arms, with me inside it, and I felt it sway about gently until it came to a final stop. I whined and scratched at the rough wicker, hoping for the lid to be raised and for daylight to fall upon me once again. I was desperate to get out – longing for something familiar, such as the scent of my mother.

The very next time the lid lifted, I was collected up into the arms of one of the young ladies. Which chatterbox was she, I wondered? It was Mildred. She was darker than Jane, and her voice was slightly deeper. She held me there against her chest, to calm my whimpering, and lightly stroked me until someone suggested I be put down, outside on the grass, in the event I would have to relieve myself. I was carried in her gentle arms to an outside area that had a grassy lawn. That was my first experience of grass; I had only ever walked upon straw before, which tended to be dry and sharp on all its ends. The experience of walking upon grass was magical, as it moved about when I walked upon it and it seemed to have a life of its own. I loved it: the feel of the moist, green grass against my paws, and also, its deeply delicious smell. It was incredibly soft and inviting, and filled with strange, new, pungent scents and little crawling things. With the memory of my mother momentarily forgotten, I then looked up at the young lady, Mildred, who was smiling down at me. She was very nice to look at – dressed from head to toe in a blue the colour of the sky, and her brown hair was pulled back, away from her pretty face.

From out of nowhere, I heard a different woman's voice politely announce, "Mistress, your tea is ready."

Mildred picked me up and held me against her chest. She stroked me soothingly while saying wistfully, "I believe George is coming. He will look after you now, my little one." She kissed the top of my head and then set me back down upon the grass. I didn't know a George; I was confused. Mildred looked back at me with sadness as she walked away in that blue dress, all the while making a strange rustling sound, and I cried out and tried to follow her across the lawn.

I didn't get very far, just a few wobbly steps, when a man reached down and picked me up, swung me through the air and said roughly, "Tha'll be us

7

new sheepdog. Yon mistress will 'ave to spend time wi' 'er 'usband, your new maister, so tha'll come to us, and *we'll* learn thee thy job. What mistress needs is a babby for her own. Then, she'll as like leave thee alone."

This must be George, I thought. He then smiled at me. I noticed he had a front tooth missing, and that the rest of his teeth resembled crooked, brown stumps, and his lips were stained brown – but it was a friendly and honest smile. Later, and for the rest of my life, I would always think of him as Toothless George. He didn't smell anything at all like the ladies, as he worked with farm animals all day long, resulting in his strong odour, which followed him about like a cloud, and his clothes were always baggy and covered in dust, or manure, or something else equally as dirty and smelly. I knew I was going to like Toothless George, so I wriggled about and licked his face. He laughed and was gentle with me.

"We mun go an' find Toby. Now, 'e'll show thee round, and tha won't miss thy mam so much – if tha'll keep company wi' 'im."

Whatever did those words mean? What foreign language did Toothless George speak? I soon learnt there was a difference between George's way of speaking and the way the master and the mistress spoke. She spoke differently from him, and the others on the farm, they spoke differently, yet again.

* * *

TOOTHLESS GEORGE was correct in his assumption that the mistress wouldn't have much time for me, though she did make a point of seeing me each and every day. Even Master Rowland came to see me, though he usually spent the time discussing my future with George, who I had noticed had begun to discourage my master from entertaining me during those visits. Toothless George warned him of spoiling me – it would affect my character and ability to work. I craved companionship. It seemed the more I asked for it from George, the less I received. My home was in the kennels, and he kept me there with Toby. I didn't get to go to the house at all, not even up to the back door for a quick peek inside.

The mistress had been allowed to choose my name, which according to Toothless George was highly unusual and practically improper. He did not like my name, and he moaned and groaned about it; he preferred names such as Fly, Rex, or Dan. *Shales*, the mistress had named me *Shales*. It was a name that she had taken a liking to, but also, a little cousin of Master Rowland's was named Shales. Of course, I didn't understand any of this naming business at the time – that would come later. Mildred was good to me, and she was very affectionate, but whenever Toothless George happened to see her coddling me, he always came along and took me from her arms and put me back in the kennels with Toby, or carried me off somewhere, tucked under his arm – I would be kicking and squealing at the injustice of it all. I would feel so sad whenever I watched her walk away with her back straight, but knowing full well that there was genuine tenderness in her gentle, watery blue eyes. There were times when I wished Mildred would carry me off in *her* arms and take me into the house, leaving Toothless George behind, for a change.

Later, as I grew older, I still didn't get to visit with the master and mistress in the farmhouse as I had hoped I would do, and this disappointed me. As I had grown older, I had harboured a secret hope that I would be able to go inside the rambling farmhouse, which was to my young eyes enormous. I was quite curious about it, as there were other people living in there as well; there were several women from what I could see, and Toothless George referred to them as *servants* or sometimes, *maids*.

The kennels were situated at the far end of the yard, beyond the stable block and long barn, where us dogs' loud barking and baying wouldn't disturb the household, and it was there I lived with Toby. We had our meals there, and we slept there day in and day out. There were other dogs on the farm – hounds, but their kennels were separated from the one Toby and I shared, although we could see them easily enough through the barrier of iron railings. We never, ever, got to hobnob with them. They thought themselves better than Toby and me, as they got to hunt foxes and run in a pack ahead of the horses and riders. They were a noisy lot! They bayed non-stop and created a fuss from daybreak until sunset. Even at an early age, I learnt one thing: hounds and sheepdogs don't mix; they are as different as chalk and cheese.

Toothless George lived above us; he had a large room to himself over the dog kennels, but I preferred the kennels to his place, as they were cleaner.

George was forever being told by the master that standards had to be kept, because he was famous for having a dirty and cluttered room, as well as an appallingly rakish appearance.

Toby was an elderly sheepdog with peculiar bluish eyes, and when I first met him he had already started to go blind. He had lived at the farm his entire life, but as he got older he was beginning to slow down – this more due to his failing sight than anything else. I knew that he would be retired, eventually, and would live his last and final days as a dog of leisure, but that, I hoped, would be far away into the future. That was the reason why I was at the farm – to eventually take Toby's place. Until then, he still had to work with Toothless George and the sheep or the cattle, even though, at times, it was an effort for him to do so.

As the weeks passed and the days grew shorter and much colder my mistress, Mildred, continued to come to the kennels and visit with me, but Toothless George severely frowned upon it, which caused a rift between them – mistress and servant. I could tell, because there was a difference in the tone of his voice whenever the mistress coddled me, thus causing me to sense a certain amount of unease and dislike within her. This confused me, because I really enjoyed the attention she gave to me. I could tell that she liked dogs, and I wasn't the only one to be on the receiving end of her affections – Toby also felt the gentle touch of her hand, and he always looked forward to seeing her. Our mistress was but a new bride, and she was only trying to make herself at home and establish her own way of doing things, but Toothless George was stubborn, and he would not budge an inch when it came to us dogs.

I remember one particular time, when he angrily bawled at me: "Yer'll be nay good fer doin' yer job. Sheep'll be awl ower the place!" He angrily spat upon the ground, wiped his wet, tobacco-stained lips, and sneered, "Ladies! Nay better thun the rest o' us!"

It was a lucky day for Toothless George that I was the only one who witnessed his angry outburst. He could have been sent packing for it. I didn't understand his attitude. What harm could happen to me if the mistress visited with me and doted on me? Why did it matter to him that she was a lady and not a servant? Why couldn't he let *me* be happy? After all, wasn't I the master's dog, when it was all said and done? I thought about it long and hard, and came to the decision that I would be lonely without her and the master's visits. Sometimes they came to admire us dogs, together, arm in arm, as they strolled about the property in a casual manner, but on those occasions Toothless George behaved politely and with deference. He would even give himself a wash and tidy himself up, if beforehand he knew they were coming. He was ever watchful of the master, especially when accompanied by Mildred.

Toby informed me that a mistress should not hang about the farm buildings, not at all. It simply wasn't done! It was improper! Ladies kept to the house and gardens, and didn't wander about the kennels, hobnobbing with the workers. They had babbies to look after. It was the way things were. I wondered, what on earth was a babby? According to Toby, things shouldn't ever change. He also said that George believed a sheepdog should know only one world, and that was the kennels, and the sheep, or other animals in the fields; anything else would fill a dog's brain up with a lot of uselessness, and that would take up too much space in there – leaving little room for herding thoughts.

Incredible!

Who would believe that rot?

I certainly didn't. I could hold lots of different thoughts in my head, and when I thought about them they would always be there, just *waiting* for me to think about and sort them all out.

Eventually, a time came when I had to learn the ins and outs of rounding up animals. At the start of my training I didn't learn anything that was too strenuous: just the basics of being able to sit and stay, respond when my name was called, and fetch a stick, and so on. It was easy-peasy. The master spent quite a bit of time with me, and he took me for long walks round the fields; then, I would practise my running, and he would do so with his whistling – if I got too far away from him. I would eagerly follow him about as he inspected the fencing and hedges or the trees in the various orchards. He didn't look at all like Toothless George. I noticed a striking difference between the two of them. Our master was clean, well-dressed, and confident, and on nice sunny days he rolled up his white shirt sleeves, allowing his arms to become browned from the sun. His legs were always encased in shiny leather boots, which smelt rich and luxurious to me, and when he walked it was with an air of authority. His darkish hair was slightly wavy but was kept short, and he had a moustache as well as short, thick sideburns. His manner was sharp with me, and I found I had to be obedient or I'd hear the lash of his tongue – but he was never cruel or rough with me. Above all that, he spoke an entirely different language than Toothless George.

Speaking of Toothless George, now *he* smelt odorous of a combination of unwashed body, farm odours, and stale tobacco smoke, and his clothes were always baggy. His trews were too large for him, so he had his wide belt buckled tightly around his waist to keep them up, that of which he was always making adjustments. In other words, he was forever tugging at the waistband of his trews, which appeared to me as if he was performing some sort of a wild dance. I had been known, at times (when I was in a silly mood), to grab hold of the seat of his trews when he performed one of his dances, and to tug ferociously, resulting in yet again another strange dance as they slipped to his knees, leaving his grubby shirt-tails to flap about in the wind, and resulting in my being severely scolded – if I didn't receive a good hiding for it. His greying hair could never be tamed, and it was rather longish at the back even though it was short on top. He always had the look of being 'dragged through a hedge backward ways on'. It was evident, even to little me, that one was master and one was servant, and as the saying goes, 'The twain shall never meet'. I didn't dwell upon such differences for long. Never mind. I loved to run like the wind upon the green grass, and take in all the smells that wafted about in the air and upon the ground.

At that tender age I was busy learning where every tree grew, and where every stone lay hidden, and where every rabbit warren lay hiding, as well as what animals we had for livestock, and whom we had for people. This was my home, my life, and my farm, and it was the whole world as far as I was concerned. No other place existed.

* * *

ONE DAY, when I was about six months of age, I received my first serious taste of herding sheep. Toby had told me what to expect, so I had looked forward to it, hoping I would do well and impress the master. A man named Will Stone came to the farm that day. He worked on another farm in our village, and had a reputation for training animals, especially farm dogs. To start with, we went into a small field (beyond Scatter Brook), which held just a few sheep; they were huddled together in a small flock with their backs to the cold, northern wind. Patches of snow lay in the shaded parts where the sun could not find them, and the ground was stiff. It was frozen – winter had come early that year. There were about five sheep – ewes, and at that time I couldn't count, so to me their quantity seemed like lots and lots. When I say *we* I mean the master, Toothless George, Will Stone, and me. Stone's job was to teach me the very basics of herding – rounding up, and what the verbal commands and whistles would mean to me; otherwise, I wouldn't know my lefts from my rights. George knew it all, but Will Stone, now, *he* knew how to *teach* it to young dogs like me, and Toothless George didn't.

That cold afternoon, I was permitted to run circles around the sheep, and I actually managed to keep them between Stone and me. As much as learning about rounding up sheep, I also learnt lots of new words from Stone's local dialect, which was rather broad and different from Toby's, Toothless George's, and mine. Toby and I tended to sound like Toothless George, who came from somewhere in Yorkshire, and not at all like the Broadwas locals. I understood I had done quite well, as afterwards Will Stone called out to me, "Yer". That was his dialect for "here", so I eagerly ran over to him. Then he said, "Good dog." He then gently stroked my face and fondled my ears for a few minutes. He was gentle and affectionate when it was necessary. I *knew* he was a good teacher, and I wanted to please him. I eagerly thumped my tail in response to his affectionate stroking – a soothing show of affection, which was something Toothless George always lacked in doing.

"'E ezn't bad," said Will Stone slowly. Looking up at Master Rowland, he said thoughtfully, "'Ims done all right fer izz first time. I'll cum back Friday... same time, same field. I don't want ta wait too long between teachin's, and it should all be done in the same field, and slowly. We'll move um sheep from field ta field, and slowly increase the size of the flock." He looked up at the sky. "If we're lucky, then we shan't get any more snow."

His dialect was so strange to my ears that I have translated it into better English for you. At the time, I didn't understand what came after "'E ezn't bad."

While stroking my head, my master said to Stone, "It's nice to know he shows promise. George thinks the dog is a bit spoilt. I take him for walks through the fields, and I'll even throw a stick for him to fetch. I find him eager and willing to please, and I don't think shows of affection will ruin him."

Stone pushed back his greasy-brimmed tweed cap from his brow. It was a brown, grimy thing that had seen many years of wear. He slowly scratched the sparse hair on the top of his head. He then spat carefully, with much intention, and a glob of spit hit the frozen ground with a splat, before he replied, "Well, zir. I reckon I doan't knows wot to say ta that. Thur's sum folk who think a dog's just another farm animal, and then thur's others who thinks different. My very own opinion regarding working dogs... is that they're working dogs, and should be treated as such. Doan't pamper um, I says."

My master just looked at him. So, in a hopeful voice, Stone then said, "What say first we'll give 'im a few weeks, and then see ow 'e comes along?"

Master Rowland seemed to be satisfied with that reply, and he agreed to have him continue my training. Stone came to the farm two or three times a week for a few weeks, until Toothless George was satisfied I had understood my instructions and I could work alongside Toby and himself. Eventually, we moved from pasture to pasture and the herds and flocks of animals became larger. I had to practise on pigs, cows, horses, ducks, chuckies, geese, and sheep – and in all sorts of weather. Sometimes these farm animals spoke back to me, taking me by surprise. I could only understand a selected few of them, as the rest spoke gibberish, another language that I did not understand. I would hear odd words and phrases, such as "Ouch!" or "Watch my heels you little so-and-so!" or even, "Nasty dog; you're all the same! Just another farmer's pet!" I thought this was perfectly normal, and so it was.

You might not know this: some animals communicate with words, such as a spoken language, and others solely with pictures, all of which they put into your mind, whereas others do a bit of both. The thing is, not all of them could communicate (talk) in any way, shape, or form, and I often wondered how they got on with each other, such as pigs talking to pigs, and chuckies talking to chuckies, or better still, pigs talking to chuckies!

I was better at understanding them than Toby was, who once said, *"They're all as daft as moggies. The lot o'them. Thick as two short planks, and rightly so. Now moggies, theer's a wasted animal if I ever saw one! Thur'll actually sit theer, wi' a full stomach, and let t'mice run about int full view, then later on when they're 'ungry, thur'll ask in a pathetic little voice, 'Wut's t'eat? We're starvin'.'!"*

It was obvious to me that Toby didn't hold any high regard for the feline species.

So, there it was – my life, as simple as that. I was a working dog; I was a sheepdog. My name was Shales, and I had a purpose in life, of which I took enormous pride in. As for the future, I didn't really understand what the concept of that word was. I thought it simply meant *tomorrow*, and it took me a long time to understand what that was all about – having to think beyond the borders of that particular day. It's amazing when one fully realises there is always another tomorrow – coming up after tomorrow, and so on, which means that life is full of tomorrows. My life at the farm was lived day to day, and my hopes and fears were day to day, as well. For me, the future simply did not exist, as I did not dwell upon the tomorrows.

* * *

TOOTHLESS GEORGE HAD ME WORKING EVERY SINGLE DAY, except for Sundays, and Toby, he would still come with us to the pastures, but he could only do so much because of his failing sight, which got worse as the weeks went by. At times he would become frightened as, without seeing it, he would trot into a hedgerow, or even a fence, and then becoming confused at the sudden obstruction he would startle himself, walk backwards with blinking eyes (the result of being poked in the eyes by the twigs in the hedgerow), and then head off in the wrong direction, and Toothless George would have to shout for him to come back. The sheep would take advantage of Toby's miscalculation of distance and would try to change direction on him, or slyly slip past him. At

15

times like this I thought Toothless George was also going blind, as many a time he shouldn't have let Toby get that close to the hedges or fences. Toby was only obeying Toothless George's calls and whistles, and when George knew Toby was in danger he should've changed his instructions. Without me the sheep would not have moved from pasture to pasture, and the cows would simply have reclined in the fields – and roared with laughter – until tears came pouring out of their eyes.

I loved the farm and everything about it. It was my home, and I felt like I was a part of it, such as the grass belongs in the fields and the leaves belong to the trees. As the months passed, one running into the next, as they invariably do, I, at times, saw Master Rowland, who took me for long, friendly walks throughout the orchards, or fields full of hops or beans, though he left the care of me to Toothless George, who looked after me rather well and fed me my meals, and so on. George even looked after the horses as well as the hounds, and did lots of other things on the farm, though he had plenty of help. There were two other men as well as the two boys who worked at the farm, and also there were female servants who worked inside the great farmhouse. It seemed to me as though Toothless George made the world go round at the farm, as he knew ever so much about it, and everyone seemed to like him, although I noted they always stood downwind from him and pinched the tips of their noses, in protest at his manky smell.

Mistress Mildred occasionally came to administer her affections, but Toothless George would always speak up after she had left, and would often say, "She'll spoil thee, un' then tha woan't be any good t' us." I used to spend a lot of time wondering what he meant by that, as I lay upon the sweet-smelling straw while Toby snored during his afternoon naps. Also, I learnt that he could be harsh, as well as unloving. Sometimes I craved for a gentle cuddle, or just a little scratch about my ears, but I wouldn't receive it. Toothless George was not affectionate with us dogs, and he rarely, if ever, stroked us. A simple "good boy" just wasn't enough to make me feel loved. There were times, when after I'd successfully driven the sheep from pasture to pasture, that I felt I deserved praise – but he didn't give me any. Toby told me that I would have to learn to live without getting any affection from George – now that I wasn't a small puppy any more. After giving it much thought, I decided that I would grow out of wanting to be the centre of attention, and it was just a young dog phase I was going through. Still, there was something emotionally undefined that I felt whenever a person touched me with genuine affection.

Nevertheless, I still looked forward to the mistress's visits and my walks with the master, but there were days when I didn't see them at all, except from afar. Sometimes they would have their baby with them, she who had arrived late in the year of 1880. I had finally understood what a babby was. It is a little person, sort of like a puppy. The little bundle, named Evelyn, was always swaddled in an abundance of lacy clothes, and her mother, Mildred, would stand holding a parasol over them to keep away the bright sunshine or the nipping breeze. Evelyn was the smallest person I had ever seen, and she couldn't walk (a human oddity which I've never got used to), so she was carried about in the arms of her nurse or the master. Even from a great distance I could hear her babby words of gibberish blown afar upon the wind. She would shout out to the sky, and I found all of this to be so odd. Later in life, I came to realise that babbies grew into children, and children into grown-ups, and then they became either masters or servants, unless they were unlucky and were neither of these, and were so low they were subservient to no one. But these latter sorts of people oft-times were homeless, or they lived in hovels – not even fit for a dog to live in.

17

III
THE BEST DAY OF MY LIFE

"If you don't know what's out there, then
you really don't know anything at all."

1880

I REALLY DO BELIEVE THE MASTER HAD A SOFT SPOT FOR ME, because one summer's day that year, before the arrival of baby Evelyn, when the air was hot and sunny and flowers were in bloom everywhere – he came for me. He whistled a merry tune as I followed him from the kennels, through the courtyard and along to the drive, where I was placed in the waiting carriage with himself and Mildred. We set off down the road, driven by Jenkins, who was one of the male servants; amongst his various household duties was to be the coachman when required. My mind returned to that very first carriage ride taken just less than one year previously, when I was confined to the dark, small interior of a basket. It was not Jenkins who had driven that carriage, but another man named Heydon.

This time, I could see what was going on around me, especially the countryside, which passed us by at an alarming rate – we were going at a trot, and I thought that exceptionally fast. I must impress upon you that up until that day I only knew of *our* farm, as I had never before ventured beyond its borders, and *that* farm was my entire world. I had not even questioned if there was anything of interest beyond its tree-lined borders, except for the neighbours, and I had thought that *they* and *we* were the entire world and nothing else existed. Oh, what a little mind I had. But isn't that the case with everyone who stays in one small geographic area, and never ventures beyond its boundaries? If you don't know what's out there, then you really don't know anything at all.

My master was dressed rather smartly: a summer-weight suit of light brown, and an embroidered waistcoat in shades of delicate creams and browns, adorned with black-enamelled buttons, a well-starched collar with a lovely brown necktie, brown shoes with a shine that gleamed *well done*, a beautiful gold watch tucked into his fob, and to finish off his attire a brown felt hat and cream-coloured gloves. I dared venture to imagine what Toothless George would look like dressed as the master, and seated in the carriage as if it were *his* rightful place. I shook my head and squeezed my eyes shut to forget *that* image! Toothless George was better off as himself, and I was better off not thinking of him as being anyone else.

Now Mildred, she looked quite elegant and delicate, and the perfect picture of a mistress. Her beautiful brown hair was piled up with ringlets, framing her face, and her dress was a shade of the loveliest pale green, which reached to her toes and spread upon the seat either side of her, as well as taking up a lot of the spare leg room within the carriage. Her long sleeves were made of a lace the same shade of green, and her hands were encased in soft silk gloves – white to match her parasol. Around her neck she wore a small locket on a filigree chain, and across her lap she held onto a folded-up parasol made of the whitest silk. Its stock was enamelled in dark green and was decorated with little pink roses. From her left wrist hung a stick, which was attached to a white silken cord. I had thought it was a stick – you know – a small branch or twig off a tree, but a short and stubby one, stripped of all its leaves. Well, as it happened, it was an article called a *fan,* which happens to be something that ladies use to cool themselves down when they feel they are too warm, or as Toothless George would say, "ower heated" or "mafted".

It was a very hot day, and all of us were feeling the intense heat inside the enclosed carriage. My feet felt sticky and I panted heavily, but I didn't care; the excitement of doing something different made it bearable. As the carriage gently rocked and swayed, the master sweated profusely; his face was flushed, and he kept wiping his damp brow with his handkerchief. I was intrigued when I watched Mildred unfurl her fan into what looked, to me, like a bird's wing, and vigorously start fanning herself with it. I watched with increasing horror as the flapping thing tried to attack her, and thinking it was *bird*-related, I became rather excited. I wanted to kill it! Suddenly, I lunged at it, grabbing onto its delicate, shapely wing, and a tug of war ensued within the confined space of the swaying carriage. My teeth sank into the flapping wing, and as my mistress instinctively pulled it back, to keep possession, I emitted a low, deep growl, and I tugged back even harder. I was not about to let that winged stick get away! The bird was mine! All mine! Mildred emitted a squeak and her eyes grew to the size of saucers, but she firmly held onto it with both hands – in stubbornness her lips were pressed tightly together. I growled again, showing her all my teeth as I pulled at what I held within my mouth, and in doing so, my bottom hit the empty padded seat behind me, with Mildred being yanked forward – she was nearly torn from her seat.

The master cried, "Oh, my! Mildred, dear, I think you had better let go and allow the dog to have it!"

He quickly shifted to the empty seat behind me and clapped onto my collar. As he pulled me backwards with alarming strength there was what resulted in a loud tearing sound as my sharp teeth shredded through the silk and lace, allowing the skeletal whale bone tips of the fan to protrude, thus causing me to reluctantly relinquish the now *dead bird* to Mildred. I desperately grabbed at the receding bird; my teeth merely gnashed empty air, resulting in a loud snapping sound. My bottom hit the floor of the carriage with a firm thump, nearly bruising it. Amazingly, I did not receive a telling-off for this palaver. Mildred, in my defence, stated she had enticed me with the wagging of her wrist, and that I was still *in training*. My master snorted in agreement, but continued to hold onto my collar as we continued on our journey.

"Poor Shales thought he was defending his mistress." She first removed a glove before she reached out and patted my head. In uncharacteristic fashion she started to giggle, and she hastily dabbed at the corners of her eyes with her fingertips, obviously finding the incident somewhat humorous.

I glanced at Rowland as he smiled back at her. He wagged a finger at her in a naughty fashion. "Just wait until I tell the others what happened to your fan," he laughed deeply. "You should have seen your face! Oh, Mildred! It *is* rather funny."

Mildred giggled back. She held up her shredded fan and examined its damage, then carefully laid it to rest on the seat beside her. Her voice was full of wonder. "I've never had anything such as this happen to me before." She giggled once again.

I thumped my tail in response, happy that I hadn't frightened her, and happy that I was forgiven.

The dead wing-thing sat motionless on the seat beside Mildred as she carried on conversing with her husband. No longer interested in it, I sat and gazed out of the open window, mesmerised as the countryside passed us by. Through the dusty haze kicked up by the feet from the carriage horses I saw there were more hedgerows, trees, fields, and orchards than I had ever imagined existed, and occasionally, to my surprise, I saw houses.

I wondered where it would all end.

After a while, though it wasn't a very long journey because I could've walked it, we came upon a large house known as Cotheridge Court. Now, as you very well know, I had never before been to this manor house. I didn't even know of its existence, though it was only about one or two miles in distance from our farm. I had no idea of what to expect; remember, I was only young and had not experienced much in life, although I thought I knew it all. Apparently, there was a huge family gathering, and there were family members from different parts of England in attendance. Some were from down London way, and others were from a county west of us, and some were from a county north of us. At the time, I didn't know what London was let alone where it was. I was amazed that so many people existed in the world, and that this London was so far away that these people stayed for many days at the large house.

It was beautiful, much larger than the farmhouse and lovelier to gaze upon. The approach was astounding. We travelled up a lane with trees growing on either side, and through the gaps of the trees I could see that part of the house looked ancient – one end was black beams and plaster – and yet part of it looked new, as if a brick-built addition had recently been constructed. Even for a dog, I was impressed; I was awed. I swayed back and forth within the carriage with my head hanging out through the opened window, both enjoying the gentle breeze upon my face and admiring the scenery as we trotted up the drive.

Disappointingly, I didn't get to go inside the manor house. Heydon, the coachman at Cotheridge Court, ordered the horses to be stabled until they were otherwise needed, and he and Jenkins disappeared into thin air, as duties awaited them. Rowland bade me stay by the carriage, which had been parked near the stable block, to the right of the house – so that is what I did. I understood this to be a part of my training, and that it was important I obeyed him. Mildred had forgotten her fan. It remained left behind on the seat of the carriage, looking very much like a bird with a broken wing. Of course, I now understand, as I tell you this story, that the fan wasn't fit to be seen outside the vicinity of a bonfire, let alone a fancy party. At that time – in those years when I was so young – I did not understand anything at all about the value and care of property.

To the soft, soothing tones of the many stabled horses, I watched intently from my vantage point, and saw everything that was going on outside the grand house. I could see many people from where I was placed, as I lay there in the shade cast by the many carriages, which were all parked in a long, double row. Though later I crept forward a fair bit, and with my chin on my paws, I watched beautiful ladies walk about in the distance. They were all elegantly dressed; well, I thought so at the time, but I *can* say one thing which is true, and that is they walked about elegantly as they held parasols overhead to keep the sun off themselves, and sauntered about as if they had the entire day to do so. I quietly contemplated the difference between them and Toothless George; it was too great for me to bother going into details. I tried to sort out who these strangers were by listening to their conversations. I didn't recognise any voices. Sometimes I would hear only bits and pieces of sentences, barely snatches of conversation, which had drifted across to me, carried by the warm breeze. I strained to hear it all, but nonetheless it was all very interesting and new to me.

As the afternoon wore on my master came to fetch me. He led me away from the vicinity of the stables to the far side of the house, where some gentlemen were seated in lounging chairs, in the shade of some large and ancient trees. The grass, there, on the south side of the house, was lush and green, though closely cropped, and the coolness of the shade was appreciated by not only me, but, I think also, the gentlemen. He was showing me off to these gentlemen, both highlighting my handsome appearance and my fine ability to herd sheep and other livestock. I received plenty of attention from them, and as a result my tail made lots of windmills as it wagged in happy motion. This was wonderful! I was the centre of attention, and I loved it. I was stroked and petted and talked to like never before, and the feel of their hands against my body calmed and soothed me. The men were all quite taken with me, and I basked in their friendly attentions. It was canine social bliss. Oh, what had I been missing all my life?

Cotheridge Court .

These people were also quite interesting in themselves, as they were all different from each other in some small way, and they smelt abundantly exotic of previously unknown scents and smells. They too, like my master, spoke differently from Toothless George, and I had to listen carefully to fathom what was being said. There were a great many eloquent words I didn't understand, they being new and foreign to me.

Their many names confused me, many of which were the same or similar, and the relationships between these gentlemen were also confusing to me: brothers, cousins, fathers, sons, uncles, and nephews etc. At first, I understood none of it, but being a quick learner I soon began to sort out who was related to whom.

I heard my name, Shales, mentioned in discussion, but they weren't talking about me; it was something to do with a little boy who shared my name. I wondered, *"Who on earth is he?"* Somebody else had my name! Was that fair? Of course, at the time of this garden party, I didn't know about that little boy who shared my name. I did not even know that little boys existed, as I thought the whole world was filled with grown-ups. Later, when the men got bored with me and focussed their attention upon the discussion of other worldly things, I laid myself down upon the lush grass, which had been cut short – resulting in its delicate softness – and I started to doze off whilst contemplating my own name.

Suddenly, a voice startled me from my gentle slumber. I lifted my head to look about.

It was a woman. I first saw the hem of her gown, and then I looked up at the rest of her. She bent forward so that she could reach down to me. "What's your name?" she asked, ever so gently, and reached out and ruffled my ears with tenderness. "Aren't you lovely? Oh, your ears are so soft and silky."

I thumped my tail; I liked her right away. She had a lovely face, framed with light brown hair, which was pulled back in the usual style, but it had a slight tendency to wave. She started to walk away, but my master, who was seated nearby, spoke up rather friendly-like, and said, "Hello, Jessie, he's *my* dog, and his name is Shales. Do you like him?"

"Oh, Rowland, I didn't see you hiding there! Yes." She reached forward and they politely shook hands with each other. "Yes, Rowland, I do like him," she said, and then stepped back to look at me. My master got up out of the chair he was lounging in, and then gave the lady a generous hug.

"You must forgive me for my bad manners," he said. "The day is hot, and I'm afraid I've taken to lounging in these lovely chairs – I think I was nearly asleep."

Jessie, the pretty, young lady, laughed at my master with obvious familiarity. "I feel like taking a Spanish siesta myself, but that wouldn't do." She then commented on the lovely view beyond the ha-ha, where obedient cattle lay chewing their cuds with the Malvern Hills in the hazy blue distance, and then steered the conversation back to me. "He's very

24

handsome. I suppose he *is* a working dog?" She smiled down at me, and in return I gazed upon her with awe. I was conscious that my tail was thumping to a regular rhythm.

"Yes, you're right there," replied Rowland, "he *is* a working dog, but I thought I would bring him over today to show him off. He likes people. I thought it would be good for him to be around new people, though George, my stableman-cum-shepherd, disagrees. He says the dog will become spoilt. I just want to show him off and get him acquainted with meeting strangers. And, I think I've got a bit of a soft spot for him. I do confess I'm hoping he's going to become my pride and joy."

"I rather like spoilt dogs," whispered Jessie, bending down to stroke me again. I felt incredibly marvellous, as if all my breakfasts had come at once.

"Yes, I know you do. And, Jessie dear, this one is incredibly intelligent, and I am hoping to breed him next year and produce a good litter of puppies. They *can* be quite valuable, and the Americans will dig down to the bottom of their pockets to own a trained herding dog boasting a fine lineage. I have an old friend over there, and for an ample amount of money he is willing to purchase all the trained young dogs I can provide. I admit I'm doing it more for a hobby than anything else, but after saying that, I could earn myself an excellent reputation if he wins some trials. It'll be good for the estate."

"Trials?" she asked. "What are they?"

"Well, they are a competition of sorts, for sheepdogs. They recently started in Wales – in Bala, and now they are becoming a popular thing – to prove who has the dog with the best herding capabilities. The puppies fetch more money when they've been sired by a champion dog, and, increasingly, these working collies are fetching large sums of guineas."

"Oh," she said. "I didn't know this. So what does this have to do with your dog Shales?"

Rowland was pleased that Jessie was genuinely interested. "For starters, I want him to become good enough to be entered in a trial; he's nearly ready now. Then I'll start the breeding programme, and you can then have one of his puppies."

"Oh, yes. I see," she said, looking a bit perplexed.

"And this is where the Americans come into it."

"Americans?" wailed Jessie, sounding shocked right down to her toes. She looked down at me again and said, "It's a crying shame to send them out of the country! That frightful journey, and all that way on a horrid ship. I should think they would not travel well. Oh, Rowland, are you sure it's the proper thing to do to a dog?"

Casually stood with his hands in his trouser pockets, my master stared at her and thoughtfully replied, "Goodness, Jessie. I hadn't thought about the voyage. The dogs *will* have to get to America somehow, and I don't know of any other way than by sea. Do you?" He developed a smile at the corners of his lips, which ended up in a loud but pleasant laugh.

Jessie lightly punched him on his arm, and then said, "You always were a teaser!" She smiled at him, and he lightly hugged her again.

"I tell you what, my dear. I shall ask Herbert to fetch his camera and you can have your photograph taken with Shales. I'm sure that today he is being kept very busy taking pictures, as he takes his photography hobby seriously."

"Yes, I know," answered Jessie with a nod of her head. She smiled. "We're all so proud of him, and we all know it isn't just a hobby with him. He makes work of it, and he is striving for future improvements with the developing processes." And then she added in a surprised tone, "To think he is actually a member of the Royal Photographic Society!"

"Actually, he's been dabbling with the developing fluids and he's made some sort of a breakthrough, or has created something of better quality. He's published his findings, and that he's done just recently."

"Yes, I know. I've read two articles of his just this year." She gazed about as if hoping to see Herbert lingering somewhere close by. "I would love to have a portrait of Shales, as long as Herbert doesn't mind taking a photograph of a dog." She continued to scan the faces of the distant men and women, but it appeared she couldn't find who she was looking for. With an obvious reluctance to leave me, she quietly said, "I would really love to have a dog again. Perhaps you could let me know when he sires a litter?"

Rowland nodded his head. "First the trials – next year."

26

Ending the conversation as if in a hurry, she said, "We'll talk again on this subject, but now I must seek out our Auntie Emily, who is proving to be either elusive, or simply well sought after; I'm not sure which. Rowley darling, I shall see you later on." She excused herself as she kissed him on his cheek, and I watched her slim form stroll away as she twirled her parasol about in a leisurely manner and the hem of her dress lightly dragged upon the grass, as she quested for someone named Auntie Emily.

I thought to myself, *"Crikey! What a lovely, lovely lady."* I hoped I would see her again, and I tried to see where she walked off to, but the trees and the other people milling about had blocked my view of her. I had lost sight of her, but I hoped she would return – if not to speak to my master, then to speak to me.

The remainder of the afternoon happened exactly the way I'm going to tell you. Rowland had *not* bidden me to return to the stable yard, and he had not tethered me either, so I wandered about the property at leisure. I had no intention of running off, as there was simply too much going on about that great place and I was deathly afraid of missing something. Many of the men and women strolled about, or they gathered in small groups under the shade of the trees or the large umbrellas, all of which provided ample shade from the hot sun.

* * *

LATER ON THAT AFTERNOON a small army of servants carried out from the house many large plates of food, and these they carefully set upon tables, which were covered in white cloths. The tables had been set out under the shade of the trees to protect the food from the heat of the sun. There seemed to be lots of food, more than I had ever before seen. I hadn't known that so much of the stuff existed, only ever seeing what Toothless George provided for us dogs. The delicious smells drifted across to me, and I could hardly resist them. These food aromas were unrecognisable, and I was dead curious as to what delicacies were there, heaped upon the large platters, and simply waiting there – for some hungry person, or persons, to come along and help themselves. I fancied myself walking casually up to one of the tables, leaping upon it with ease, and helping myself, my snout buried pig-like right up to my eyes in unimaginable tastes and textures. I wondered if that would be a good or a bad thing to do. I looked about and saw that nobody else was crawling across the linen-covered tables in hog-like fashion. Something in my consciousness told me that it would be an unforgivable crime if I attacked the food-laden tables in any manner. I sensed that I would never be forgiven, and would be sent away in shame, and that it would be many times worse than attacking Mildred's bird-fan-thing. I had actually started to salivate as the delicate aromas wafted appetizingly across to me upon the afternoon breeze, and I found it difficult to resist attack. I was saved, just in time, from an eternity of shame.

The lady named Jessie had returned to me, and she set upon the grass in front of me a bowl of cool, fresh water, and a generous plate of food. It was practically *heaping* with delicacies! Oh, what a kind person for her to do this for me. There was some sort of cooked meat. I don't know what, but there was lots of it. It was summertime, so if I remember rightly, it was probably chicken, and my, oh my, it was delicious. There were other bits of food as well, which I later learnt to be potatoes and crusts of pastry. I was grateful, and I ate quickly, slaking my thirst from the bowl of water. When I finished I casually burped, and then proceeded to clean my front paws and wrists in a leisurely fashion.

Jessie watched me eat, and then afterwards she spoke directly to me. A gloved finger wagged in my face. "Don't you dare steal any food from those tables! Nooo. Stay away from them, and don't touch."

Well, Jessie had answered my question regarding the helping of myself to the buffet. I felt guilty, simply because I had *considered* conducting a solo raid upon the fully laden tables. I took heed of her advice, and I bowed my head in shame.

Jessie returns to Shales.

With a full belly, and feeling sated, the urge to raid the picnic tables had departed. Then, feeling a bit drowsy, I wandered off to a quiet spot; there I slumped down upon the cool grass, and nodded off beneath the soothing shade of the trees, with the gentle hum of voices and laughter fading away into the background. Not far from where I lay was a lengthy, low-lying dip, with a mound behind it. This ha-ha ran for quite a distance, and below and beyond it, in the large field I later came to know as Stockhull Field, was an unobstructed view of grazing cattle.

I was at peace and without a care in the world, and I had descended into a gentle sleep, and had entered the land of Nod.

* * *

As I NAPPED, children played in the far-off distance. To me, children apparently were a small but interesting sort of person, who ran about and played like fools, and did not take life seriously, such as all masters and their servants did. I thought about joining in with them, but I thought they were too many; they outnumbered me by a lot. There were others who seemed to me to be in an in-between stage, between child and adult. I shall tell you now about that sort: they weren't small children, but young men, and I am sure they thought of themselves as grown and mature – the reason which is probably why one of them got himself into a heap of trouble. One lad, named Algernon Cecil, helped himself to a saddle horse from the stables and rode away without permission, or anyone noticing him riding off. It was only later that the stable boy, who had been caring for the many visiting horses, had noticed the empty stall of a valuable hunter, and as well, its saddle and bridle missing. The alarm was raised, and eventually, after a lot of fuss, Algernon's whereabouts were questioned. The hunter, to state it plainly, was a horse that apparently was liable to have temper tantrums, depending on who was riding him. The horse was a mad stallion belonging to William Nichols Berkeley, and required an experienced rider, having frequently thrown riders in the past, resulting in their serious injury. Because of that, Algernon's safety, and also his sanity, had come into question.

I dozed on and off, drifting along on pleasant dreams, and later awoke to a rather noisy fuss. It was a discussion about the wayward Algernon. Whilst I had slept, a large group of middle-aged gentlemen had gathered nearby; they were either seated or stood in relaxed pose. Tobacco smoke wafted about, drifting over to me, and one of the men, obviously fuming and hot under his collar, cried, "That lad never stops when it comes to horses! I tell you, all he wants to do is ride, ride, and ride!" Then the masculine voice continued on in a huff, "He's even just this afternoon taken his cousin's horse without permission, and we know not where he is or whence he shall return. He did not ask because he knew full well his cousin would refuse him, the horse being a trifle mad, so instead he's become a horse thief! He'll be jumping over every gate he comes across, and one of these days he'll have himself a bad fall! It'll be the death of him, I say. It'll be the *death* of him!"

Another gentleman said knowingly, "He also talks about becoming a soldier. All young lads talk about this, but they seldom follow through." The voice then dropped to a more serious tone. "Though, Comyns, you'll have to consider purchasing him his commission, if that is what he really wants."

"He's got his mind set on it," replied the one named Comyns, who was the same man who had woken me with his tirade. He sounded less angry as he continued, "He's sixteen years old now. Being a part of the wine trade or being a solicitor doesn't seem to interest him at all."

As I watched and listened with interest, this man named Comyns then tightly gripped the arms of his chair, and said harshly, "He won't even consider going to Cambridge or Oxford. I suppose if I can get him to agree to continue his education, then I'll agree to buy him his commission, if that's what he desires." He let out a long sigh, as if he was tired of talking about his son. "At least I don't have to worry about Harry Douglas – *he* isn't horse mad. No, Harry will soon be working for me."

"Algernon can always come into the coal trade with me, though I suspect he would laugh at the proposal," remarked another gentleman. His name was Augustus, and he was a brother of William Comyns, who was the owner of this grand estate. Augustus was seated in a relaxed position; his legs were crossed and he was smoking a pipe. Its aromatic fumes wafted over to me on the breeze. After puffing on it again he then paused before saying lightly, "I suppose being a gentleman farmer is out of the question for him. Young men, these days, always want to go off and live an exciting life, leaving the rest of us to do the honest work. I only just read, recently, that farming is becoming less popular, and more and more young men are flocking to the cities for employment. It seems it is no longer popular – to not have any sort of employment and to live a gentlemanly life of leisure. Gentlemen are becoming a rare and dying breed, and our sons and grandsons are endangered."

"We can always use another clergyman," said the white-haired William Comyns. He was also the rector of Cotheridge, and either the brother, father, or uncle to most of the men there that day. Everyone smiled at his suggestion. One son had followed in his footsteps and that was William Nichols. Few, if any, of this William's many nephews and cousins had shown signs of wanting to become ordained ministers.

Comyns Rowland sounded more than slightly disappointed. "I somehow don't see my son as a rector. It'll be a bit of a let-down after wanting to battle heathens by the sword. No... I may have to consider purchasing him his commission, if he refuses to become a solicitor." He looked over at his older brother as he continued, "Nothing against you, William. It is a family tradition, and all that, but it won't do Algernon any good to be writing sermons and Christening babies. He has too much 'go' in him."

"Here, here," responded Augustus, the coal merchant. All attention turned back to him, as he said, "Meanwhile, Thomas will find his cousin, and he'll fetch him back before the lad gets himself into any more trouble. He, too, loves to ride, and as well enjoys a good hunt. All of you know that about Thomas, and as well, that Edmund used to follow the hunt." He waved his pipe about and laughed. "As long as Thomas works for me he can spend as much of his spare time as he likes riding about the countryside. We all did it at that age; it's only because we're much older now, getting on in years, that we don't take to the saddle any more." There were quiet grunts of agreement as the group of men reflected upon their lost youth.

Someone said wistfully, "Oh, those wonderful Essex days with the long summer nights. I wonder what Coopersale Hall is like these days?"

Augustus replied thoughtfully, "It's still standing – it was empty there, for a while. The lads ride over that way now and again. They say there's work been done to it over the last few years."

Thomas, the young man whose ears must have been burning, suddenly strode up to us bearing a grin on his handsome face. When he saw me, he didn't hesitate for a moment but knelt down in front of me and ruffled my ears. "Is this the dog you've been bragging about?" he asked of my master.

Rowland replied with a nod, and young Thomas said wistfully, "I wish he were mine; he's marvellous. I say, I do envy you, Rowley."

"He's not for sale, but you can have one of his puppies next year. I'm on the lookout for a bitch, but I haven't found one yet – and *he* still has to prove himself." There was a short pause when Rowland glanced at me. "Jessie is quite taken with him, as well."

I liked this Thomas, but sadly he couldn't stay with me, as he had to find and fetch Algernon. Yes, Thomas Rowland *was* sent off to find and return his cousin – when I met him he was booted and ready to go. He went willingly, borrowing a good horse from the stables. Algernon's father urged him to find his son and return before dark, and Thomas wasted no time in doing it from the sounds of the disappearing hoof beats heard cantering down the drive. By then it was early evening, and the sun was already starting to lengthen the shadows, and the heat of the day was beginning to cool down just a bit. As I lay listening to the men's conversation, which was no longer about Algernon, but instead about something to do with their railway stocks, I wondered where the lad had ridden off to, as I simply could not imagine there was any more land in existence, other than what lay between my farm in Broadwas-on-Teme and the manor house known as Cotheridge Court.

The world was getting bigger. It worried me.

The subject quickly changed again, as it is wont to do whenever large groups of people converse in a friendly manner. My master had been asked by his uncles as to why he hadn't yet moved to London and taken up a second residence there. I was intrigued by their conversation. What about this London? What sort of place was it, I wondered? I observed and listened from a short distance, fully entertained by the men's various topics of discussion. I learnt lots.

"I say, Rowley lad. Why don't you come down to London sometime?" asked George Brackenbury. He slowly preened his thick moustache as he spoke to his nephew, my master.

"We will soon, just for a visit, mind you. Mildred, she won't want to go to London in this stifling heat – not with her carrying. We will have to wait until later on, either around September, or early next year, after the baby arrives."

George Brackenbury urged, "Be sure to let us know when you do decide to come. We'll celebrate and throw a party for the family, for the baby – one to be remembered."

There was a short pause, and then the conversation was steered back to my master's possible employment with his uncles. "We could always use another hand in the firm," urged his uncle Comyns.

"Not as a solicitor," answered my master in a serious tone. As he flicked the ashes from the spent tip of his cigar, and ground the stub into a small tray designed for that sole purpose, he stressed, "I'd rather go into the coal trade with Uncle Augustus, and I certainly don't want to do *that*. No, I'm quite happy farming for the moment, and besides, there'll be this place in the future, and it shall need managing and looking after if it's going to remain in the family. Our ancestors have always farmed in a big way, and all of you know that I enjoy managing Butts Bank Farm. This place will soon become my responsibility."

"Coal trade," said Augustus, "yes, that's my area of expertise, as well as farming." He squinted his eyes as if remembering something far off into the past. "I didn't want to be part of the legal firm, and I enjoyed farming, though we had quite a few bad years of it." He shook his head in remembrance of something bad. "The forties were hellish years for farmers and the fifties weren't much better. I had to do something; I saw an opportunity in coal and I went after it. Besides, it's better if one owns one's own firm, and if we'd all become solicitors then it might not have worked out for the best. We might have fallen out with each other, such as happens quite often within large families."

The other men nodded and mumbled in agreement as he continued, "We merchants have got to supply all the steamships and the railways, as well as every house and factory in the country. Coal is in great demand now, even more so than twenty years ago, and what's more, there is *money* in it. I preferred farming, though, but one can't both live in London *and* be active on one's farm. Besides, I'm too old to be farming – tied to a farm, that is. The children don't like being out in the country all the time, especially in the winter. It is 'devoid of any social life', or so they tell me, and I happen to agree with them." The others again nodded in agreement and strongly praised the many benefits and opportunities of living in and around London.

"I didn't have any choice in the matter," said another gentleman. "Dad said to me, 'Charlie, I've decided that you're going to be a lawyer – you're up to it, and there's little chance you'll inherit – so, it's all settled then,' and I didn't have a say in the matter."

"What else would you have done?" asked Augustus. His eyes no longer on his brother but on his pipe, which had stopped smoking. He reached down and tapped it against the leg of his chair to rid it of its spent ash.

"Well, I don't know. I haven't the foggiest idea," answered Charles Clement. "I really don't know. I did consider the ministry – I remember thinking about it, but I knew Dad would find something for me to do and he'd give me the money to get started, like he did with William, Comyns, and George."

I had begun to realise who these people actually were. My master was a nephew of this Augustus. The gentleman, William, who was master of this large manor house in Cotheridge, well, he was brother to Augustus, as well as to some of the other gentlemen here, such as Comyns, and George Brackenbury, a London wine merchant. My master, Rowland, was a *cousin* of the young men, Thomas and Algernon, who both were off galloping about the countryside. On that day of the garden party, I had started to realise that there was more to life than what I had ever had on the farm: mostly, that there were more people than I had ever thought existed, and they, at least these ones, were all related, or were at least in some way, one large family.

* * *

MEANWHILE, I HAD, YET AGAIN, ANOTHER NAP, and then entertained more thoughts about helping myself to some of the food. The tasty smells of the various foods that drifted across to me were so tempting and inviting that I again began to question if I could take some and nobody would say anything to me; I didn't, though. Jessie had said not to, but I was so tempted that I did give it serious thought. I was actually saved from that mental torture of indecision when a man sat down next to me, stroked my face, heartily patted my sides, and spoke kindly to me as he offered me a piece of chicken, which I gladly accepted. After tossing a blanket upon the grass he made himself comfortable. He then started drawing my likeness upon a thick pad of paper, with quick and confident strokes.

35

Speaking to me, he said he was going to *paint me*. I knew what paint was, and I also *knew* I didn't want to get covered in paint. Earlier on in the summer, Toothless George had painted the doors and window-sills of the kennel, and out of curiosity I had stuck my face into the pail of white paint, thinking it was milk, and I had ended up all wet and white, which had dried hard and crusty, and had taken days and days to come off. I now had thoughts of being covered from head to toe in paint, and wondered what all the farm animals would think. What would Toothless George think? Oh, dear me, what about Master Rowland! However, I obediently stayed where I was whilst this man drew my likeness. I had absolutely no idea what he was doing, and happily, in the end, I did not get covered in paint. His name was Stanley, and he had spent most of the afternoon sketching people's likenesses. He had with him a little box that contained several different colours of paint, and with a dab of water and a swish of his little brushes he, that day, turned his little sketches into works of art. Later in life, I came to realise that it had been an honour to have been sketched and painted by Stanley Berkeley. He later became famous for his paintings of dogs, and also for great battle scenes portraying soldiers on horseback wielding swords. Later, I understood that to become *painted* was to have one's likeness created, framed, and hung on a wall inside a house, preferably in an ideal location where it can be admired by all and sundry. I, Shales the Sheepdog, am hung on a wall in a house somewhere in England. I find it sort of strange, yet quite pleasing. It makes me want to thump my tail.

Other happenings of interest went on that afternoon and into the evening. I shall now tell you more about what went on: some of the ladies had gone to one of the large fields and had set up large, round stuffed things they referred to as targets. They then flung sticks at them (the targets). These sticks travelled at a dizzying speed, and the women called it *archery*. I say! They *were* deadly with their aim! I understood, by instinct, that it was dangerous to be near the targets, so I observed safely from a distance, not wanting to get an arrow shot into my lovely bottom. The gentlemen, not in the least interested in the archery, or perhaps they were just being wise and were keeping their distance, had a debate about God and His infinite wisdom. Of course, this was all gibberish to me at the time, but now, as I tell you this, I *can* understand it – what it was all about. There were other men of the cloth there, as well as William. The dispute was whether or not the common people, those who could *both* read and write, were more faithful and honest than those who could neither read nor write at all.

William Comyns got hot under the collar. Red-faced, he nearly shouted, "If everyone, man or woman, could read and also write, then the whole world would become a different place. It doesn't mean they'll stop believing in God." He glared at the rest of the group, as if challenging them to go against him.

"I say it does," said another man. He was small and fit, and he looked ready for a fight. Spittle flew from his mouth. "If they could all read and write, then they would have no reason to come to church. Why, they could stay at home and preach to their families from their own Bibles. They'd just sit around their kitchen tables on a Sunday and not even bother to go to church, and they wouldn't have to cough up any of their hard-earned wages, either. And in that, we would be as poor as them before long. If they have to come to church to know the Bible, then they have to pay their tithes, or contributions, or if you prefer to say – donations."

William Comyns cried, "Nay! I disagree with you. There'll always be those who'll attend church, and they'll come because they love God."

Someone responded to this by saying, "If you could be here in a hundred years from now, *then* you'll know whether you're right or wrong. Perhaps a literate society *will* enable a better understanding of the scriptures. The government is saying that everyone should have the opportunity to learn to read and write, and when it happens, then life as we know it will change."

One of the gentlemen interrupted, by saying lightly, "There's Herbert talking to his brother. I suggest we ask him to join us in this exciting debate. What say all of you?"

William Comyns brusquely replied, "Please, not Herbert. He's the last person I want to debate with today. Obviously, you gentlemen have not experienced one of my son's arguments."

To this, the man said, "Oh, I do love a good argument," and then said, "I've heard that your Herbert enjoys long debates."

"Not with Herbert, you don't." Such was the advice from William Comyns, Herbert's father. "He's such as a terrier that won't let go of a rat. I suggest we keep our little chat civilised, because if my son comes over here, he'll get you more hot under the collar than you already are, and no matter how trivial the discussion, you'll be kept here till bedtime!"

* * *

A LITTLE FURTHER OFF TO THE SIDE was another group of gentlemen. Their talk was about horses and gambling. A strong smell of liquor pervaded the air about them. This strange smell was not new to me, but I wondered if it was responsible for making them act so silly. They had laid on a bet: would Thomas and Algernon return, sober or not, and as well, would they return at all, before dawn? They guffawed loudly; their laughter was in half-sober tones. Shivers went down my spine, as I was momentarily taken by surprise by their lewd behaviour – it was ungentlemanly. They reminded me of Toothless George, when on Sunday nights he eagerly attacked his small bottle of rum, which he received as part of his wages. Sunday nights were a good night to keep quiet in the kennel and not rouse George's wrath, which was wont to strike out at any moving animal, and with little cause.

The gentleman who liked to take photographs noticed me, and spoke kindly to me. It is only now, years later as I tell you this, that I realise he had had a camera with him, and that he took my picture – without Jessie, as she was nowhere to be found. I recognised him right away as being a visitor to our farm. He was my master's brother, Herbert. He was another one who lived in that far-off place called London. Herbert Bowyer seemed pleased to see me, and spent a lot of time getting me to sit or stand without moving. He was a very handsome man, with dark, short-clipped hair and longish sideburns, and like his oldest brother Rowland, looked fit and tanned from the summer's sun.

I liked him; he was genuine.

I began to feel more comfortable amongst these people. Rowland didn't seem to mind if I moved about on my own, so I continued to trot about the estate and mingle at leisure. I soon found the doorway to the kitchen. It was situated at the rear of the residence; that, which was built of black beams and plaster, and it being Tudor-like, unlike the front and the newer south wing, both of which were brick. There, in the kitchen, I found the cook. Bless her! She was nice and friendly, and she fed me some meat and vegetables with gravy. It had been freshly cooked and flavoured with herbs, and it was much better than anything George ever fed to Toby and me.

On a full stomach, I then trotted off to the large parterre garden and found some ladies at the far end, seated around a lace-covered table. It hadn't yet got dark, so they were enjoying the last of the warm evening sunshine, filtered through the trees' leaves lest they should burn their pale skin, though the sunlight was diminishing quickly and the shadows had begun to lengthen. Behind them, another very large pasture, Church Field, created a gentle backdrop. The ladies welcomed me with much affection, and served me tea and cakes. I had never had tea before, and I readily lapped it up out of a delicate china teacup. The tea was tasty and it slaked my thirst, and from that day onwards I had a taste for it.

"Shame, isn't it?" said an elderly lady with greying hair.

"What is that, Emily?" asked another elderly lady, seated at the same table.

"The *dogs*. I'm talking about *dogs*. The men always want them to be kept outside or in the stables, but we women would like to have one in the house as a faithful companion. Isn't that correct, Anne?" said Emily.

"Dear Emily, I agree with you wholeheartedly, but men *always* take charge. What do *we* really do? What influences do *we* have in our own homes, other than telling the cook what to prepare for our meals?" replied another lady named Julia. She was much younger than the greying Emily.

"Oh... Please let us talk about something else," said Jane impatiently. I knew who Jane was, because she visited Mildred at our farm all the time. Their husbands were brothers.

Emily fanned her face with rapid movements of her wrist, looked at Jane, and responded wisely, "If you haven't discovered *this* by now, then you soon *shall*. Your William may be my nephew, but he is still a *man*. I'm sure we can all agree around this table, that *all* men don't like women to get the better of them, even when it comes to having a dog or a cat as a pet. I have noticed *you* don't yet have a dog as a house pet, nor a cat. I remember you saying, just last year, that you were going to get a cat and keep it as a pet. Every time you have mentioned it William has changed the subject, and now you don't even bother about it. You haven't mentioned it in months."

I ran up to Emily in excitement and sniffed her fan – it was just a fan and not a bird of prey. My immediate interest in it waned. She reached out to stroke me with her free hand. "Well, hello there. You must be Rowland's dog, Shales," she said affectionately. She offered her fan for me to sniff. "It's just a fan; it isn't a bird," she said humorously. Her hand lingered; she continued to caress my ears.

"William says they make him sneeze," answered Jane petulantly.

"You need to be more cunning," replied Emily, as she once again fanned her face with vigour. "And they *don't* make him sneeze! He's my nephew. I ought to know."

The ladies' various conversations carried on and on. They were mostly about subjects I had no knowledge of. It had been a champion day, so interesting and entertaining. I had become exhausted from all the activity and I wondered when it would be time to return home to the kennels. I was also very full. Full to the beam, and I didn't think I could eat another morsel of food without bursting at the seams. The sweetness of the cakes had settled a bit heavily on my stomach – I desired, yet again, another nap.

* * *

EVENTUALLY, IT BECAME DARK, and everyone went inside the large house, and a short while later the servants came outside and cleared away the remains of the food and clutter. There were discarded plates and wine glasses everywhere, placed upon tables, chairs, or on the grass by the partygoers – wherever the opportunity had arisen. I had woken up feeling better, my stomach having settled, so once again I sought out the aromas of the party food. I searched for the discarded plates and glasses in a mad dash to get to them before the servants could whisk them away. They were mostly clean though, as I had already gone round and made sure no food was left on them. Their smooth surfaces gleamed from my washing up – clean enough to put back in the cupboard. There had been no sign of rain, but even so, the servants had removed all the tables, chairs, and umbrellas to the safety of a building near to the stables. I followed them about as they tidied up, merely out of interest.

Afterwards I sat down upon the soft grass beneath an ancient tree, just across from the main entrance to the house, and waited patiently for my master and mistress to emerge. Still, I felt so full that I could barely move. I'd had what I considered to be a very busy and exhausting day. My brain was nearly filled to bursting point with the knowledge of new experiences, and my stomach felt overstretched from my culinary indulgences. The sounds of music and laughter poured out into the night, and through the large windows I could see people dancing within the bright, candle-lit interior of the house.

Shortly later, our carriage appeared, driven by Jenkins. Its lamps cast a golden glow upon the pink gravel as it was driven out from the stable yard and around to the front of the house, alerting me to the fact that we would be leaving before very long. I continued to wait in anticipation, not wanting to be left behind.

After some time they emerged into the warm night air, and my master whistled for me. Mildred spoke excitedly as she walked from the house to the waiting carriage. Her voice carried upon the night air and the smooth gravel crunched noisily beneath their feet. I ran up to them in greeting, and they were pleased to see me. It was a lovely summer's night, and both warm and light; lit from the moon and stars in a silvery glow that happens only in the countryside.

Thomas and Algernon had not returned by the time we left. I heard my master telling Mildred that more bets had been wagered as to the time of day or night they would return.

As our carriage made its way back to our farm upon the lonely, narrow highway, she spoke to her husband in a quiet but serious tone, "They are not boys any longer; even Algernon has grown out of boyhood, and I think his father should send him off to some place such as the army. It *will* do the boy some good." My master nodded in agreement, but before he could say anything of importance, she continued, "As for Thomas, well, he is not yet

41

of age, but he is so charming and handsome, that it is as if he has already had all the experiences of life."

I listened to their words, not fully understanding their meanings, nor knowing anything about whom they were talking. I simply wanted to soak up every word I had listened to, like a sponge, and file it away for future use.

Rowland knew his younger cousins well. "They're both full of life, the two of them. Even if I were a bit younger, I don't think I could keep up with them. I certainly can't ride like they do. They're both either very brave, or very stupid."

Mildred laughed, and as I glanced across at her I could see her eyes glistened with wet tears of mirth. "My dear, the lads are true gentlemen, and whether they be brave or stupid, I think they are very attractive, and I assure you they shall break many a young woman's heart before long, if that hasn't already happened."

* * *

I HAD TO TELL A LIE. No two ways about it. I did *not* have the heart to tell Toby all that he had missed. When he asked me about my day out, I told him it had been very long and weary, and that I was ignored and went hungry, and I even had to beg for a few paltry morsels of food. I did say, though, that with more outings like that, one would eventually get used to it, and the boredom could be looked upon as a form of relaxation. I had not wanted to hurt his feelings by telling him all of what he had missed. As I spoke to him, I secretly hoped that there would be more days such as this. Sadly, he believed me, and I felt rather guilty for having enjoyed what was up to then the best day of my life.

IV

A TEMPEST COMETH

"Hey up! Int the wind strang?"

EARLY 1881

OW COULD I HAVE KNOWN THAT THE FEELINGS I HAD OF LOVE, security, and happiness would not last forever? It had all been too good to be true. How could I have foretold that horrible day that was yet to come? I did not know that such things could happen, and yet I knew sheep went to the slaughter, and that the farm cats killed and ate the rats and mice, but I didn't understand what that meant for the dead. I had no concept of death. I had rather suspected, that a few days later, they somehow returned as little ones, and grew up all over again in a continuing cycle. I had not had any reason to question death on the farm, as I had only experienced its life – the living animals, those live ones that I saw each and every day.

It is still, to this day, a difficult part of my life to talk about. I prefer to hide from it, but I shall tell you what happened on that dreadful day. We had driven the entire flock of ewes into the farmyard, just Toby, George, and me. The sheep had required moving from the pastureland, which was across the highway and quite a distance from where the house and barns were. The pregnant ewes, being more exposed to the elements out there, needed to be moved into the safety of the barn, which stood at the side of the farmyard, near the house. A second barn, the oldest one, was attached to the house. I had known that a storm was coming, and so had Toby. We always knew when the weather was going to change, in the way that animals seem to know, but what we never knew was how much rain a storm might bring, nor how hot the sun might shine on any given day.

That particular day the sky was a horrible, frightening dark colour, and all had gone still as in the dead of night when there is neither moon nor starlight, nor any hint of a breeze. There was not a bird to be seen nor heard – they had all disappeared. The ewes were heavily pregnant, every one of them, and they had been out pasturing on the delicate green grasses, which had become exposed after the January snows had melted; lambing season was nigh upon us.

Master Rowland had ordered Toothless George to move the sheep to safety, and to do that quickly. As the men stood outside the ancient long barn, looking up at the sky, my master spoke fearfully, "I don't like the look of that sky. There's a tempest coming! If we get a lot of lightning we could lose some sheep, and they're exposed, even in the low fields. They must be moved to safety before lightning strikes. I hope I'm wrong, but I think the heavens are coming down upon us, and there'll be damage done before the day is over."

"Aye, I'll fetch'm down t' Butts Field, un after that they'll 'ave shelter in t'barn," replied Toothless George. I looked up at him, and he said, "We'll ger 'em home, woan't we, Shales?"

In answer, I woofed and yipped in happy anticipation of the round-up. I ran off a few feet and then returned to sit by him. I waited for instruction; I was ignored.

"At this time of the year thunder and lightning are rare, and I've never before heard of a summer storm in the middle of winter. There! And again! Did you hear that?" My master tensed his shoulders as he looked at the ever-darkening sky.

I could hear the storm somewhere off in the far distance, but thunder never bothered me, so I wasn't the least bit concerned. There had been a very low, deep rumbling sound far off into the west, which made the horses nervous. In the paddock behind us they snorted loudly and stamped their feet. I sensed the horses' fear, but my mind was on the job I knew I would have to do. I was happily anticipating an exercise in driving sheep, something I loved to do. A deep rumble erupted from the western sky. I wanted to hurry up – there were a lot of sheep out there just waiting for Toby and me to round up!

A dull 'clap' sounded in the distance. "That was thunder! I don't want the ewes dropping their lambs early. It's unusual to have thunder and lightning in

February." My master still contemplated the distant horizon in wonderment. It had gone quiet again, but the greenish black sky moved in closer.

"That sky is one of the strangest I've ever seen." His voice was filled with awe as he gazed at the eerie sky, which was momentarily silent once again.

Just then, the stillness abruptly broke and a terrible crack of thunder was heard, but it was still a few miles away, west of Broadwas. The calm before the storm had ended, and a stiff breeze started up, announcing the tempest's arrival. Dead, brown leaves, wet, soggy, and half-rotted, wafted about in the air, and the trees started to sway and noisily rub their leafless branches together. George set off for the kennels; we had to collect Toby. Finally, we were on our way!

The master stayed behind with the other men to see that the horses and other livestock were safe. We set off. We crossed the old road and cut through Butts Field, then crossed the highway, and hurried through the orchard towards the nearest grassy field, and then continued along through the middle orchards towards the eastern fields, in the direction of Cotheridge Court. Over that way the fields were wide and open, and the trees in the hedgerows always had a wuthered look to them. With the wind behind us, I couldn't smell the sheep, but I knew they could smell us, thus they knew we were coming for them. I wondered if they remained together as a flock, or if they had scattered and any were lost.

"Hey up! Int the wind strang?"

45

"Them ewes're mekking some queer sounds," said Toothless George, though the wind rived the words out of his mouth as soon as he had said them. We had found the ewes huddled together. A small part of the flock were packed tightly for safety beneath a solitary, low-branched oak tree, and there, close by, remained the rest of the flock. All were in a right nervous state, with the whites of their eyes showing. George sent me away, keeping Toby steady, behind him. I ran off with my body low to the ground. My chest hairs dragged in the cold grass as I deftly crept to and fro, and I began to circle around the bleating sheep. Between Toothless George, Toby, and me, we started moving them down from the pasture and through the middle orchards. As we drove them towards the highway, the wind whipped up with a viciousness I had never before seen, and masses of old leaves and even small twigs and grit blew about. We had to bow our heads in order to walk into the strong, gusty wind, and I could hear the ewes' agitated voices blown about, bleating and sounding to be on the verge of panic.

The magpies and jackdaws, which were normally noisy as they daily flocked about the trees in the nearby orchards, were unusually silent, and their silence was in itself an ill omen. The entire sky was now a dark, sooty black, with that peculiar greenish tinge to it. It hung low and heavy, as if nightfall was descending, and I felt the stinging spit of rain upon my face, signalling more to come. The thunder came closer and closer as if it was galloping along, and its violent cracks and the bursts of brilliant lightning terrified the ewes. They complained loudly, and Toby had to help me keep them together as it was a large flock of about one hundred or more. They baahed and threatened to trample Toby and me, not understanding we were helping them to safety. I could see fear in their eyes as well as smelling its strange sourness upon the air. Through the many orchards' rows of trees we funnelled, and the branches of the apple trees were straining and whipping about, as if they had become alive, and were reaching out to grab us as we struggled to pass them by. It was hard going. All I could think about was getting the sheep into the large barn, as I was actually becoming concerned for their safety.

* * *

THE FINAL GATE AT BUTTS FIELD was held open by Toothless George as he struggled to remain upright; the wind threatened to rive the rails from his grip, and his winter clothes noisily billowed and flapped about him amid the tempest's roar. His flat hat blew off his head, and quickly became trampled beneath the ewes' many cloven feet. Butts Bank Farm was within sight, right across the road from us. I was driving them through the gate well enough, with Toby's help, and they funnelled quickly but politely up the bank and towards the farmyard. I thought to myself, "Nearly thear lad; we'll soon be in t' barn."

Everything seemed to be going all right, considering the state of panic the ewes were in, except the thunder above us was quite deafening and it even made me feel edgy. I didn't like it one bit. My skin felt prickly and I felt my hackles begin to rise. It felt as if the entire storm was right over top of us, as if the clouds had come to ground and we were up in the sky. The wind was nearly gale force, and as if to prove it so, a very large limb from a nearby oak tree gave a terrible 'crack' as it broke away from the tree's enormous trunk, landing very close to me with a solid thud, and just missed landing on one of the ewes. The tips of its branches slapped against my side, severely stinging me as if I had been whipped in punishment; intent upon the job, I did not cry out. The severed limb was large enough that it could have crushed anything it had landed upon. Luckily, it had only struck the ground.

Suddenly, the sky opened up and the rain came down in sheets. It immediately plastered my hair to my body, and nearly blinded me as well. I had never experienced rain like this before! It siled mightily, creating rivulets of cold water, which before my own eyes began to flow in all directions and to merge into huge puddles. The last of the wind-blown flock was through, across the road and into the farmyard, and there, behind me, was Toothless George struggling to close Butts Field gate. Rapidly rising muddy water tugged at his heels as it followed a downhill course. The force of the wind rived the gate from his hands, but he managed to fight the tempest for it, and eventually he pushed the gate back against its post, fighting to ram the bolt home, but not without a fierce struggle. Through blurry vision I saw him hang onto the now closed gate for what looked like dear life. He fell down, or was blown down, and for a few paces crawled on his hands and knees. Toby and I managed to keep the flock together in the farmyard as we constantly circled around them, back and forth, back and forth. I needed Toothless George to open the barn doors. No one else was about, and I wanted him to do it quickly. I could hear roof slates shattering as they hit the ground, and one flying missile struck a ewe, the force knocking her to her knees. I felt sick with horror.

I was nearly picked up by the wind when my feet actually came off the ground for a moment, and Toby had a difficult time as he himself was nearly blown away. The torrent of cold rain created a blur through which we couldn't see, and with half-closed eyes I used my senses instead of my sight. Flashes of lightning surrounded us in brilliant bursts of pinks and blues, and loud thunder clapped and boomed just above our heads. Somehow, Toby helped me to keep the terrified flock together, while Toothless George finally rammed the bolt home on the last gate he'd been struggling with, the farmyard gate, and then it happened: I felt myself lifted up into the air, and then it all went deathly quiet. The tempest had suddenly come to a grinding halt.

I thought to myself, "Hey up! Int the wind strang?" Looking down, beneath me, I could see the farmhouse along with its outhouses, stables, and barns, and there was Toothless George, a little, bedraggled, bareheaded speck, far below me, crouched over something. I wondered what it was, as his body obstructed my view. I was concerned he was getting too wet and that he too would be blown away. I then wondered why some of the ewes were lying down on their sides, and the rest of the flock was beginning to scatter to the furthest corners of the yard; I worried about the downed ones being trampled by the unruly ones. "Rig-welted" is the word Toothless George would use to describe them when they lay like that – with their legs sticking outwards and unable to get back on their feet. Simultaneously, as I travelled even higher into the sky, I realised it was not any longer blowing a gale, and there was a bright light coming towards me; there was such a feeling of calmness over me, as if it wasn't at all real. Then it all went black. I wasn't aware of anything, not until I woke up in front of the fire inside the farmhouse kitchen.

* * *

WHEN I FINALLY AWOKE, after apparently several hours of unconsciousness, I felt sick to my stomach as well as very tired and weak. I could barely move my head. It felt too heavy to be my own. My left side was sore. There was a small patch of my hair missing where it had burnt, and I smelt rammy, as if I'd been on fire. I was in the kitchen on a pile of blankets inside the large inglenook fireplace. Chilled to the bone, I felt both femmered and nithered.

I found out later that I had been in that limp and nearly dead state for several hours, and that Toothless George had carried me to the farmhouse, which was not far from where the lightning had struck. He had barely managed to carry my limp body, as he had suffered from the shock of it all, and had fought against the strength of the storm. He had thought his own heart was going to give out on him that day, whilst he struggled with my heavy weight. One of the kitchen servants had seen him staggering towards the back of the house; his struggling to carry my limp body had been barely visible through the blurry, rain-spattered panes of the kitchen windows. She had run outside into the torrential storm to help carry me inside, and had then run off in search of the master.

Master Rowland had been in such a state of despair – if I didn't survive he'd have to find another young sheepdog and have it trained. That would take time. He did care for me, though, and his concern was later obvious. Apparently, he had kept me wrapped in blankets to keep me warm, and he himself had rubbed my body to keep the blood flowing. I lay there, warm but dead to the world, and he had feared I would eventually pass away before ever regaining consciousness. His concern was evident when later, after I had wakened, he stroked me at length and coaxed me to eat and drink. The house servants hovered about in the background, and behind his back they criticised my demise with sad whispers and silent gestures.

* * *

HOURS LATER, I LAY THERE UNMOVING BUT QUIETLY CONSCIOUS OF MY FUTURE. I had heard what the servants had whispered about me, and as well, about my master. As Grace May had cooked the daily meals and did other kitchen duties she openly discussed my demise with sadness and what Master Rowland might do with me. I lay there in the farmhouse kitchen amidst the normally delicious smells of cooking food and the aroma of smoked hams, hanging on hooks deep inside the chimney above me, all of which did nothing to whet my appetite. I understood enough of their words to question my future. That word, future, was more than a word. It was my life and everything that would happen after all of the tomorrows had gone by. It looked glum for me, and I didn't want to live; I wanted to die if I couldn't work for my master and for Toothless George. I closed my eyes and became very sad. I whimpered. I didn't like not being able to move about, nor eat without help. I was frightened: frightened for my life, frightened for my future, and frightened of everything I didn't know, and that included all the tomorrows that had yet to come.

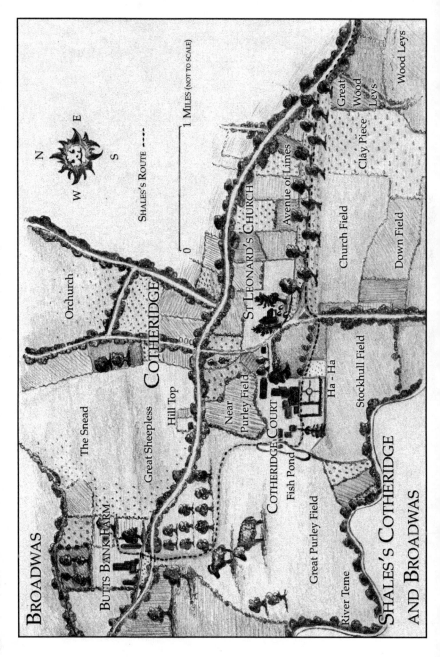

BROADWAS

Orchurch

COTHERIDGE

The Snead

Great Sheepless

Hill Top

Near
Purley Field

BUTTS BANK FARM

COTHERIDGE COURT

Fish Pond

Great Purley Field

River Teme

St LEONARD'S CHURCH

Avenue of Limes

Church Field

Down Field

Ha - Ha

Stockhull Field

Great
Wood
Leys

Clay Piece

Wood Leys

N
W — E
S

SHALE'S ROUTE ----

1 MILES (NOT TO SCALE)

0

SHALE'S COTHERIDGE
AND BROADWAS

V
THE FOOL

"How can one imagine a star, if one has
never before seen the night?"

MARCH 1881

I DID GET BETTER. The horse doctor said it was a wonder I was alive. He'd never before known of any other living animal survive being struck by a bolt of lightning. I was the talk of Broadwas! So *that* is what had happened to me. Six ewes had also been struck and *they* were dead; another two ewes dropped their lambs early from the shock of it all, and one lamb died, but amazingly, the other survived. There had also been a great flood, and the pasture where the sheep had been grazing, as well as all the low-lying land, had been submerged beneath a couple of feet of water. My friend Toby was fine. He had been far enough away from me that he hadn't been struck by the lightning.

Afterwards, about a week later when I was back on my feet, I moved back into the kennels. Toby related to me his memory of the horrific incident. *"It wor the most frightening moment of mi life, Shales. Ah didn't know what wor happening. Ah cud hear all, and that wor mos'ly the wind a raging, and ah heard a loud bang, an' then ah cud smell burning; but, because of the darkness, ah cudn't see what wor happening. Ah heard all the sheep scatter, an mi foot got trod on in the panic. Then George shouted for mi to stay put, so ah did. Ah 'uddled up against side of t'barn not knowing what to do – ah felt absolutely useless."*

I told him that I was just glad *he* had been unharmed, except for a bruised and tender foot. When you think about it, it could have been him or even Toothless George, instead of me, who had been unlucky that day.

Just because I got better didn't mean things were quite the same way as they had been before the tempest had struck: I found I was now terrified of loud sounds. The very next time I heard thunder (in another unusual winter storm) I ran for cover and cowered, something that I had never before done. In gusty weather when the wind sounded loud, and the trees noisily rubbed their branches and twigs together, I was barely able to herd the sheep, as my nerves would become frayed and I would lose my concentration. The sheep began to *know* this; they took advantage of me, and everything began to crumble.

Toothless George was sad. He kept shaking his head. "Maister's goin' t' let yer go. Tha's nay good t'us any langer. Tha cannit compit int' trials if yer doan't buck up."

I became frightened for myself, and questioned the tomorrows. What would happen to me, where would I go, who would feed me, and where would I sleep?

In fine weather I managed quite well, and I'd nearly forget that I had any sort of a problem with losing my nerve, but then when it rained, or became windy and the trees' branches made those horrid clickety-clack sounds, I became edgy and couldn't concentrate, and all hell would break loose with livestock scattering in all directions. When this happened, Toothless George ended up throwing sticks or stones at me, out of sheer frustration, as I ducked and ran for cover from my imaginary doom. I had become *unreliable,* which was a word that injured my dignity like a festering wound.

* * *

A FORTNIGHT WENT BY, and then a delivery wagon pulled into the yard. I was nearby, relaxing beneath a tree and watching the goings on with quiet interest. They were unloading wooden barrels when, after a bit of a struggle, a large barrel filled with wine got out of hand, tipped, and rolled off the back of the wagon. It fell about four feet, hit the cobbles with a tremendous thud, and cracked open, spilling wine like fresh blood, which teemed all over the cobbles and flowed away in small rivulets. I tell you, I couldn't help what happened next. I jumped with surprise at that horrific sound of the smashing barrel, and started to yelp uncontrollably. I yelped and yelped out of fear as such a great fright had come over me.

One of the draymen angrily shouted at me, "Shut thy gob, ya mangy dog!" He then picked up a small piece of wood that happened to be lying on the back of the wagon, and he threw it at me. His aim was off. It hit the cobbles close to my feet, and bounced and landed without hitting me. This angered me, and I thought to myself, *"How dare he!"* So I charged at him and barked like a wild dog gone mad. I created as much noise as if the hounds of hell had been loosed, and the dray wagon's two draught horses stomped their enormous feet and snorted loudly, not liking the commotion. With their nerves already frayed due to the thunderous crash they now neighed and started to struggle and strain, and their large, iron-bound, feathery feet ground against the cobbles. Their heavy shoes made a loud ringing sound as they scraped against the hard stone, and the wagon creaked dangerously, threatening to release its brake.

I put my head back as far as it would go and started to howl, and even to this day I still don't know why I did it. As I released that very loud and long-sounding howl the two draught horses tossed their heads and rolled their eyes. Their frightened neighs and loud snorts turned into throaty gasps of panic. One of them tried to rear up, upsetting its partner, and *he* kicked out viciously with his dangerous hind feet. The two draymen held onto the horses' bridles, and were both nearly swung off their feet as they tried to console their frantic horses. Master Rowland had heard the commotion from inside the house, and he came storming out into the yard to sort it out.

He angrily shouted at George, "Come and drag that damn dog away from those horses, before I put it out of its misery!" He didn't like what he saw. "Get that smashed barrel cleared away; if those ones aren't damaged then shift them to the cellar!" With a thunderous expression upon his face, he shouted this to one of his men, who had been standing there silently observing the commotion but had done nothing to help.

The barrel lay upon its cracked side with a constant stream of wine gushing forth. Its aroma tainted the air unpleasantly.

I then felt a hand clap onto my collar, and I was propelled backwards with great force. It was Toothless George pulling me along with all his might. "Cum on lad... Cum on!" Then he cried, "Ger agate!"

He dragged me along, and this he did roughly as I desperately tried to dig my toes into the cobbles. He yanked me by my collar across the yard to the harness room, which at that moment was closer to us than the kennels. He heaved me in there and shut the door on me before I could escape. With my tail tucked between my legs, I found I was shut in with the saddles, bridles, and harnesses. I could still hear the commotion going on outside, and it sounded as if one of the men had had his foot trampled by one of the horses; he was swearing and sounded to be in a lot of pain. My master was very angry – a drayman was injured *and* a large barrel of fine wine was wasted. A generous supply of European wines had been shipped to him from London by one of his uncles, George Brackenbury Berkeley, the wine merchant. But *I* wasn't responsible for the barrel falling off the wagon! I admit that I had made things worse with my bad behaviour, and I should've known the horses would fret, but I hadn't caused the barrel to roll off the wagon and smash open, releasing its liquid contents upon the stone cobbles. That wasn't my fault.

The harness room smelt nice. The leather saddles and harnesses were deeply aromatic, and there was fresh straw upon the floor. I settled down, and not knowing how long I would be in there I stretched out and waited to be let out. One small window emitted light, and particles of dust floated about amidst the narrow beam of sunlight, which poured in softly, creating a small amount of warmth. I could hear the voices of the men, still agitated, coming from the courtyard. My master was admonishing the deliverymen, and those same men were calming their team of horses. I pondered my life: who was I, and why was I here, and finally, what was to become of me? It seemed like hours and hours went by, and darkness began to fall, and still nobody came to let me out. I began to worry that I'd be in the harness room forever. Eventually, I fell into a deep but troubled sleep.

* * *

GOD CAME TO ME IN A DREAM. He came as a cat. He was an orange and very stripy cat. He said to me, *"Shales, do not despair. You were struck down by the hand of God, but survived for a very good reason. You, Shales, shall have another purpose in this life."* The cat blinked its green eyes. He then said to me wisely, *"Go forth; leave this place and head east. Go east in the direction of the rising sun and you shall find your salvation. There is another family waiting for you, and you will know them when you find them, as they already know you, and they will embrace you with their love and kindness."*

I awoke with a start. I nearly thought there had actually been a cat, a moggy, talking to me, but I knew better – it was just a dream. It was just a silly, silly dream – especially since moggies couldn't talk like that. Wasn't it just a silly dream? God didn't speak to me, did he? Who is God?

Just as I awoke, the dream conversation with the ginger moggy quickly faded away, and it soon became a dim memory. But the idea of leaving the farm, my home, remained behind. I mulled it over, and wondered if I really should leave my farm on my own and venture forth into the unknown world. I pondered what the master would do with me, if I remained: sell me, simply give me away, or retire me from farm work and let me live in the house? I was hopeful about this last thought, but something in the back of my mind said it didn't think that would happen – I was pushing my luck. I didn't want to be sold off to strangers, but would he do that to me? I supposed that would be a terrible thing, and I would be very sad if that happened; thinking about it simply frightened me. My small knowledge of the world and its ways was no comfort to me, because deep down I knew my life was going to change forever. It had already started to change. I had a sense of knowing that I had come to a crossroads in life, but I didn't know which way to go. In an attempt to make myself feel better I thought really hard, and hoped that something or someone would help me.

* * *

IT HAD BECOME DARK AND QUIET OUTSIDE ON THE FARM, and I wondered what was happening out there. I couldn't see out of the window, which was high up, and small at that, so I didn't know what was going on regarding Toby and Toothless George. I tried jumping up and down, and although I found I could then see out through the small window, there was nothing revealed to me but perpetual darkness. After what seemed like an eternity the door to the harness room finally opened, and good ol' Toothless George let me out. I wagged my tail and greeted him affectionately, feeling relief in being released, but he ignored me, and I received no words, nor any touch of affection, nor even a slap to the backside. I cowered at his lack of affection, not knowing how to behave.

He took me back to the kennels and fed me, roughly setting my bowl down in front of me. I dared to thump the tip of my tail in the hope that he would look kindly upon me.

He glared at me, after he set it down. "This 'ere could vera well be thy last meal 'ere at this farm. Maister is deciding what to do wi' thee. I reckon 'e'll like as sell thee t' someone in Worcester or thearabouts. Whatever 'appens, you've done it to thissen."

He slammed the door on his way out.

Those words of doom only resulted in my feeling more depressed than ever. My meal, which was meat, potatoes, and barley, wasn't going down very well, even though I was hungry. My appetite had started to wane due to the depressing news. I understood what he meant when he said I'd brought it all upon myself; it was my own fault, and no one else's – all of it. I had obviously done something wrong when I was out there in that storm, driving those ewes to safety – a place they never all got to.

I wondered, that if I left on my own, I could choose my own family. I could watch a house from a safe distance until I was sure the family would be suitable for me. Would such a family take me in and look after me? This idea started to take form in my mind; it was an escape route. The seeds of doubt about remaining at the farm I called home had been planted, and if I chose to not stay, I would then have to leave. I felt I had to make a decision, and soon: stay and await the master's plans for me, or run away and take charge of my own future. I decided upon the latter. I would do a midnight flit. I would miss everyone terribly, especially Toby and Toothless George, and I would miss Master Rowland and his lovely wife Mildred. They had been very good to me, but what use was I to them now? I felt I had to leave; I now knew this to be something I had to do. The question was, when? Tonight? Tomorrow? I decided that when the first opportunity arose, I would then go, and the sooner, the better.

I glanced over at Toby, wondering if I should discuss the matter with him, but he was fast asleep and had not even stirred with the slamming of the door. I left him alone and did not wake him.

* * *

LATER THAT NIGHT, Toothless George let me out of the kennel to stretch my legs, and I wandered off into the little side field behind the kennels to do my business. He walked away and busied himself with other things, leaving me on my own. It was nearly bedtime, so the farmyard was quiet, as nobody on a farm stays up late at night when they have to be up at the crack of dawn. When he went into the stable to look in on the horses and the young stable lad I wandered off towards the long, single barn at the side of the larger farmyard. I stopped and looked back – nobody was there to watch me, and it was pitch dark, so I didn't think anyone would see me from any of the buildings. The night was deathly quiet as I turned and trotted over to the road. I'd never been past this spot before, not without Toothless George, except for when I went with the master and mistress to Cotheridge Court, and that had been the previous summer. After crossing the road I crept through Butts Field and then, further beyond, I crossed the highway. I slipped through the bars of the gate, which led into the large orchard, and I travelled alongside the hedgerows and simply trotted off in the direction the sun rose each day. In the cold, inky darkness I hopped, I jumped, and I skipped my way cross-country, until I soon found myself at the manor house known as Cotheridge Court.

Because I had arrived after travelling cross-country, and not by the highway, I approached the estate from behind, from Great Purley Field, near to the huge fish pond, instead of from the direction of the church. That pond was like no other pond I was ever going to encounter again – it even had an island! If the time of year had been warm-with-buzzing-flies, I would have taken a dip and had a right good swim, and perhaps tried to catch a few of the large fish that swam enticingly close to the surface; instead, the pond held a skim of ice. The weather had been cold and overcast, threatening snow, or at the least a cold drizzle. Also, my mind had been concentrating on getting to London. I knew from my listening to the people talk at the garden party, the previous summer, that London was in that general direction, and according to them, London was the place to be. Worcester also lay in that direction, and the master talked about Worcester quite often, and also, the Londoners had come to Cotheridge along the road from Worcester. There, my mind was made up. I would go to London and find a family that would love me and feed me, and in return, I would be their protector and companion forever, however long that would be.

I'd already had my evening meal and it was now hours after dark. I skirted the groomed gardens and ancient trees of the estate. Nobody saw me, as the house was in complete darkness, they all being in bed. Within sight of the house, I settled down for the night beneath the old yew hedge that grew alongside the parterre garden. It was sheltered and dry beneath there. I decided to wait until morning before I would get concerned about finding any breakfast. For now, I was going to enjoy my first night of freedom. Although the ground was as hard as stone and the air was frigid, I slept like a log.

Morning came as the cold sun slowly rose in the sky. A little red-breasted robin pecked at the frozen soil a short distance away from where I lay. The birds were awake, as all about they sang and twittered; they were in a right cheery mood. It was time for me to get up, so I yawned and stretched. I had a right good scratch and wondered if I was ridden with lops, as I felt rather itchy, then I set off for the kitchen. The grass was cold to walk upon and it was heavily crusted with a silvery frost. It sent early morning shivers through me, and I could see my breath upon the frigid air; it spewed outward in silvery clouds, skimmering brightly as I walked towards the house. I hoped to find something warm to eat, although I realised that I might be shooed away. I knew where the kitchen door was, at the black-beamed rear of the house, and I also knew it would be frequented by servants, and very friendly and sympathetic servants at that. After a very long time of waiting and of willing for someone to emerge, the door finally opened and the cook stepped out into the cold air. I thumped my tail in recognition and greeted her with obvious affection.

"Ooh. Thee be that lovely dog that master Rowland has." She was surprised to see me, but she bent over me and stroked my head fondly. "Ow bist? Thee just wait yer, and I'll find thee something tasty to eat. Don't go. Stay thur... Stay."

Cotheridge Court on a cold winter's morning.

Emily Holmes, the cook, went back into the house and quickly emerged with a bowl of porridge, topped off with a generous dollop of cream and some scraps of meat called bacon. She set it down, and then stroked me gently as I devoured it. I was ready for that. It was a champion breakfast, and I licked her hand in gratitude. She left me to go back inside, but yet again returned quickly with a bowl of something to drink. It was warm and sort of milky. I lapped it up. Of course – it was tea. I remembered drinking some the previous summer, and I hadn't had any since, until that moment. I then thought it would be best to get a shift on; be on my way, before she told on me and someone decided to tie me up and send for my master.

I thought to myself, *"Well, I've left my farm, walked out or run away, whichever you prefer, so my master, Rowland, isn't really my master any more.*

Shales the Sheepdog – you're a free dog." I was free. I was now beholden to nobody but myself. I puffed out my chest and decided that I was going to have a good day, and be a brave dog, and not let anything prevent me from continuing my journey.

In fine fettle, and with frosty breath puffing about me in a silvery cloud, I left by way of the long front drive, the avenue of lime trees, passed by the church, which was a short distance off to my left, and at the end of the avenue of limes, some three quarters of a mile later, I turned right and continued along the road to Worcester. After just a short time I became thirsty, so I had to resort to drinking ditch water. It was covered with a skim of ice that I had to break through before I could retrieve the icy, murky liquid below. Every time I heard horses coming along the road I ducked off into the hedgerows and lay low, hoping that I wouldn't be seen. I did this so many times that I was starting to get tired of it. I was pricked and poked by stiff twigs so much that I was starting to feel sore all over. I nearly put my left eye out when I had to quickly dash for cover when a horse and rider went cantering by. Getting fed up by all the hiding, I wondered how long it would have to be before I could stop looking over my shoulder. At this rate it was going to be a very long journey to London. I reckoned it was still early morning, but I was a good distance away from the farm, and I didn't think Rowland would search for me this far along the road, and perhaps he wouldn't search for me at all, and he would think "good riddance".

I soon came to a junction. The decision to follow the road to the left or to turn to the right so astounded me that I became rooted to the spot where I stood, looking for all like a dog completely lost and out of his realm. As I dithered about which way to go, I decided to have a rest, and watch and see which way the traffic was bound. I would follow the traffic, thinking it obvious it would be bound for Worcester, and then on to London. I curled up into a tight ball in order to keep warm, and I waited. Eventually, a large dray pulled by two draught horses and fully laden with barrels, or what Toothless George called tuns, passed me by and turned to the right. I'd nodded off beneath the safety of the hedgerow, and the heavy, hollow clip-clopping of the huge hoofs had woken me from my peaceful slumber. As it slowly passed, I saw my opportunity to catch a ride and to save my legs. I ran and leapt upwards, landing smartly in a small, empty space between two large barrels. This was going to be easy if I could ride all the way to London! It was exciting, as I was on an adventure. I could see the road behind me disappearing away into the distance, so I made myself comfortable at the back of the wagon. There was barely enough room for me there, but there I stayed, curled up, and I watched the road as it passed by, with Broadwas and Cotheridge ever retreating further into the distance, and into the past.

* * *

IT TOOK JUST OVER TWO DAYS TO GET TO WORCESTER, even though we were only a mile away when I first jumped aboard that wagon. The heavily laden dray pulled into several roadside inns and unloaded heavy wine and beer barrels, and replaced those with lighter, empty ones from the premises. Each night, the two men took rooms at an inn and spent their evenings at the bar supping tankards of ale. On the first night, I found food scraps in abundance outside the kitchen door, at the back of the inn. They were just tossed out through the door and onto the flagstones, at random intervals. I was there to receive this lucky bit of charity, so I generously helped myself. As I ate, several scruffy-looking moggies came along and also had their fill. I tried to ignore them, as they smelt strong, their feline stink making me uncomfortable, and I fought down the urge to put chase to them. They only spoke with odd words here and there, and as they ate they emitted a strange sound, which to me sounded like a barrel of ale being rolled back and forth across cobbles, which confirmed my opinion of them. I thought they were odd, stupid, smelly creatures, and were only good for one thing, and that was a right good chase.

In the morning I waited until the wagon pulled out into the road before I jumped onto it and hid amongst the barrels. As long as the draymen didn't know I was there, hiding behind them, then I felt safe. It was another cold day, so I curled up tightly to keep warm. The second night, the wagon once again pulled in at an inn where it unloaded a supply of the beer-filled barrels we had been carrying, and I went around to the rear to where the kitchen was to get my dinner. Silly me, I had assumed the kitchen scraps and collops would be tossed out through the door, like at the previous place, and I would be the only dog there on the receiving end. This time, to my surprise, there were several other dogs there! They had come running as if from nowhere, and they barked, snapped, and growled as they descended upon the property, and what they took to be *their* evening meal. Manners did not matter to that lot; it was every dog for himself. They ate amid loud snaps and snarls, and they half choked as they swallowed their food nearly whole.

One very large brindle-looking dog ran up and spoke to me in the local dialect. *"Be quick! Don't chew but swallow. I'll keep an eye out on this lot for ya."*

What titbits and collops I'd managed to grab, I swallowed quickly before they were ripped out of my mouth by one of those other dogs, and I'm sure that would have happened if they had been given half a chance. Two of them got into a fight, and their vicious fighting sounds brought people out from the bar. As the dogs fought, snarling and snapping at each other, a small group of men cheered and emptied mugs of ale onto them; the men thought it a right entertaining moment. Fearfully, I ran and hid, not liking the tone of the men's voices, which frightened me as much as the savage dogs' behaviour. It didn't seem right; this human behaviour seemed out of character, and I was alarmed by it. The dogs then stopped their fighting to lap up the ale that was spilt over the cobbles, and from their wagging tails they obviously had a taste for it. The crowd of men soon got bored with the now peaceful dogs, and with the excitement being over they went back inside the inn, preferring the companionship of the smoke-filled bar, and they smoked their pipes and drank their ales until late into the night.

I settled down in a secluded spot, behind the manure pile at the back of the stable, and slept lightly. A short while later I was awakened by the large brindle dog. He had apparently come over to introduce himself, and although he could speak very well, his Worcestershire dialect was heavy and burry. At first I had difficulty understanding him.

"Ow bist?" he asked me, but didn't wait for a reply. In a deep voice, he advised, *"Stay clear of that lot."* He leaned close to my face, and said unblinkingly, and in an even deeper, slow, low voice, *"They have killed before when I haven't been around."*

I swallowed deeply, before asking, *"Killed what exactly?"*

63

"Dogs!" He pulled his head back as if surprised at my question. *"And cats!"* His eyes were enormous.

This large, handsome brute of a dog sighed, *"I tries t' keep um under control when I'm about, but when I goes off home they be more vicious, and even kill and eat the cats when they can catch um."*

"Oh, so you don't live here?" I asked innocently.

"Nay, I live just over thur, at that house in the far distance, but I'm not always allowed t' come over 'ere. When I do come 'ere, I try to keep this rabble under control. Um two that fought tonight, well, I'd be glad if they killed each other. Ums little terriers is nasty and dangerous! Ums a menace to the 'osses whenever a coach or rider goes by, and that's many times in a day." To my surprise, he said, *"My master says ums should be shot!"*

I told this large, brown, handsome dog of the Alsatian variety with ears that stood straight up on his head, which gave him a rather important air to his character, that I was grateful for this little titbit of knowledge. I would have to remember it, because this tale of dogs fighting dogs and dogs eating cats was shocking news to me. I could never have imagined in my small mind that they could do such things.

Schooner tries to keep the pack in order.

64

We introduced ourselves to each other, his name being Schooner. When I asked about the origin of his name, he said his master had been a sailor and was now retired. I didn't know what a sailor was, but I didn't want to let him in on how ignorant I was, so I didn't comment. It was just another reminder of how little I knew about life. Schooner wished me luck on my journey, and then went off to his home, a warm place by the fire, and a meaty bone.

* * *

I WAS GLAD WHEN MORNING CAME. Those other dogs weren't about, and I didn't want them to be, so I lingered about the yard within sight of the dray. When it pulled out into the road, I once again leapt on board and settled down to watch the world go by – this time on an empty stomach. I did not find anything to eat that morning, and as the day wore on I got hungrier and hungrier. I was cold. My fur was wet, as it had drizzled, and I hoped that it wouldn't turn into heavy rain. I was also worried because we were returning the way we had come. I wondered if we would turn down another road, a different one, but we did not, and I soon saw the junction looming up before me where I had first caught my ride. Happily, we turned in a new direction and did not turn towards Cotheridge, and as my stomach complained about its emptiness, and as I shivered with cold, I wondered where I would find myself by evening. A short time later, I realised I was not to be disappointed, and I found myself gazing upon my very first city.

Worcester was a huge place unlike anything I had ever before seen. With the Malvern Hills behind me we crossed over a bridge, which spanned a river called the Severn, and then entered the city and continued towards the eastern end where the railway station was. Now, as I tell you this, at that time I did not know what a train was or what railways were, or even the name of the river. I didn't actually see a train when I was there, but I did hear its hissing, rumbling, and tooting sounds from a distance, and I could not imagine what I was listening to, not even if you had described to me what one looked like. It is only from my later years of worldly experience that I am able to fill in the gaps with explanations as I tell you my life's story, though, I swear, I am only telling you the truth and nothing is made up – dogs' honour.

The city was all hustle and bustle. It was crowded with many people and horse-drawn wagons, carriages, and drays, all going to and fro as if they were in a hurry. I had not realised before that so many people could exist; was there no end to this England? Also, there were plenty of dogs and cats, as they too roamed the streets freely. I wondered if they had homes or not. Were they like me, free, and without any master, but on the hungry side of tomorrow? And what did they do with themselves all day long? And were they gentle animals, or were they tyrants?

Worcester also smelt different than the countryside. Its strong odour was of man and of refuse, as if every house had a stinking midden in its yard; but, there were other strong, indefinable smells as well. I was awestruck at the immensity of the place. After passing through the city, which at that time appeared to me to be the largest place that could possibly ever exist, the wagon eventually trundled into a large, paved courtyard surrounded by a high, red brick wall. I jumped down and ran over to the far end of the yard, conscious of being conspicuous. There, I sat beneath a large and ancient oak tree, and tried to get my bearings. The drizzle had ended, but the weather remained depressing. I was wet through and I shivered with cold. A little red-breasted robin flitted about and kept me company as I waited; its bright red breast was a cheery contrast to the dismal gloom of the day.

The draymen from the wagon had disappeared through a large door set into the front of the enormous warehouse, and simultaneously two different men came out, unhitched the horses and led them away. Presumably they led them to some stables where they were both fed and watered. Two more strange men came out and proceeded to unload the empty barrels from our wagon onto a small handcart and to trundle them, one at a time, into the warehouse where they too disappeared out of sight. There were other drays in the courtyard receiving similar attention, though some of them were having barrels loaded onto them, instead of being unloaded. What was in those barrels, or tuns, I wondered. Was it wine or ale? I couldn't read the words painted on their fronts. It really didn't matter to me, because I knew that sooner or later one of those wagons would set off in the direction of London. I felt rather confident about that. In fact, I was sure of it. London was such a talked about place that of course some of those barrels would be going there.

Of course they would. Last summer I had heard some of the gentlemen at the garden party say *London is the place to be.*

There was one particular wagon that was fully laden and looked like it could be leaving shortly. I decided I would follow it on foot if I couldn't find room on it to lie down – that is, if it was going to London. How would I know if was going to London or to some other city? Were there any other cities besides Worcester and London? I didn't know, but I was beginning to wonder where the world ended. After some thought, I decided that if it turned down the way I had already come, I would follow it for a short distance, then, if it didn't turn towards Cotheridge, I would follow it and hope it was heading towards London.

Two strange men were stood holding the huge heads of the harnessed draught horses, which were chomping at their bits and snorting loudly. The men were chattering away and sounding more like Toothless George than the locals from Broadwas. I wondered where they were from. The enormous horses tossed their heads and whickered, impatient to be off. Their breath burst forth in puffy clouds, and I wondered if the horses were feeling cold from standing still.

"Jack, we'll set off shortly if that's all right with thee," said the short, heavy-set man. "London's getting anxious."

"Aye. Fust let mi get us bait for the day," answered the slimmer one as he hurried away. "It's a fair way to go on an empty stomach!"

"Aye. It is, Jack. 'Urry up, though. 'Osses ur getting very impatient."

The one called Jack returned a few moments later, carrying a large package, and clambered aboard. The horses leaned heavily into their shafts and started forward, and I ever so quickly leapt onto the wagon and kept my head low. There was just enough room for me at the back. Nobody seemed to notice me as I blended in with all the barrels. The man had said "London", so I *was* on the right wagon. London, here I come! Eeh! I *was* proud of myself!

* * *

AFTER A COUPLE OF DAYS I realised we were, in fact, travelling in the wrong direction. Oh, woe is me! It was the position of the sun that gave it away, as well as the little fact that I found out that one of the horses was named London. I'd finally cottoned on to what a daft error I had made; all done in haste. I was annoyed with myself, and vowed to be much more careful in the future. Eeh! I could've bitten m' own tail off, so frustrated was I! After much contemplation, I decided that as long as we weren't on the road and heading back to Cotheridge, I would remain with my travelling companions, who had no idea, at all, that I was living in the back of their dray cart. What puzzled me, though, was where were we going. How many places could there be? I had no idea how large the world was, and was I still in England?

I felt propelled along as if an invisible hand was behind me, pushing me along a little bit further as each day went by. Days came and went and the countryside changed in appearance. I did manage to eat, but I wasn't getting as much food as I needed, and I felt hungry and thirsty all the time. The hedgerows evolved into stone walls, and the gentle fields and the many orchards changed into wild-looking open areas that were very high, and were spotted with equally wild-looking sheep, wuthered trees, and gorse. The wind blew stiffly with a northern bite to it. There were plenty of sheep, but not so many people. There was the odd night when the men didn't pull into an inn, but instead camped at the side of the road like gypsies. They would have a large bonfire to keep them warm and to cook over. I envied them their comfort, but still kept out of sight. In the night, when they slept huddled beneath blankets but lay close to the dying fire, I would sneak about and eat the food scraps they had left lying about, the ones they hadn't tossed directly into the fire. These men were very untidy, leaving empty tins tossed about to poke up between the tuffets of grass. They still didn't know I was there, so I felt safe to remain with them as a secret travelling companion.

* * *

"**DOG STILL WITH US?**" asked the shorter man, who I now knew as Harry.

"Still hiding back there," answered Jack. "'E'll jump off someplace and we won't knows he's gone 'til later. Yer knows these sheepdogs are valuable. Someone paid good money for 'im. 'E'll be worth a few guineas."

"Well, he's no good t' us," said Harry. "We doan't want t' feed 'im or else 'e'll *never* leave us. Not 'less you want to catch 'im, and then see if we can sell 'im? Might make a few bob."

"That's risky." Jack continued to speak knowledgably. "Thur'll be questions asked, an' we cud be accused of stealing a valuable dog. They 'ang sheep rustlers all the time, so what's the punishment fer stealing a sheepdog?"

"I doan't know, and I doan't want to know," spat Harry as he poked the fire with a short stick, causing sparks to fly. He glanced at his mate, "We'll just pretend 'e doesn't exist then. As long as we don't put a rope on 'im, he's loose and free t' cum and go. Then, we can't get accused of stealin' 'im."

Jack replied curtly, "I suppose so. Let's hope 'e knows weear 'e's goin', an' gets off at the right stop."

So, I had been discovered! Blast! Blast, and more blast! Here was me thinking I'd been so careful and wouldn't be found out. They said they wouldn't feed me, but they didn't say I couldn't continue to ride in the back of the dray and save my legs. I decided to stay with them until the end of their journey, then, once there, wherever that was, I would decide what to do next. I kept my distance from them, because I didn't trust them – I thought they might change their minds, and try to sell me to some strangers for a pocketful of change.

The very next day we came to the end of our journey. We pulled into a yard outside a small hotel that had a brightly painted swinging sign hanging off the front of it. The place was like a small city with many streets, buildings, and people; it was, in fact, a small town. The painted sign said it was called *The Prince Hotel.* I didn't know what a hotel was. It just looked like a large, well-kept public house, or an inn, and I wasn't really far off. Was I? I had learnt that those colourful swinging signs, hanging outside certain abodes, meant that food and drink was served to people, and that scraps and kitchen waste were usually tossed onto a compost pile outside the rears of those places, unless the cook was a lazy sod, and then tossed them right outside the door and onto the cobbles, for the rats and other vermin to clean up.

I could hear people conversing as they walked past us, along the street, and I noted they had a northern way of talking, even more like Toothless George than Jack and Harry. They didn't at all sound like the few people I knew from Broadwas and Cotheridge. I thought it odd how the local dialect had changed in just a few days of travel.

"Well, you've finally arrived," said a middle-aged woman wearing a white apron over a dark blue dress, and beaming a toothy but friendly smile. She stood there with her hands on her hips and spoke roughly, "We've bin expecting thee any day now! We're nearly down to us last barrel o' ale! Would it not be better fer this area if i' twere on a branch line?"

The men nodded their heads, and Jack replied, "Aye. Tha's reet." After thinking this over for a moment, as he casually scratched his bare head, he said, "But then we'd be out of a job if tha cud get supplies fetched up 'ere by railway. Tha'd only 'ave t' have a dray come from the station t' 'ere. At least we're needed t' deliver goods t' towns an' villages not on t' line."

The woman nodded her head and her commodious mob-cap threatened to fall off. She hastily righted it upon her head and then said in a commanding tone, as she nodded towards the hotel, "Mi' 'usband is inside. 'E'll attend to thee shortly, but first unload that thear dray, and when yer done, cum inside and slake thy thirst. Then, we'll settle up."

I thought to myself, *"Where on earth am I?"* We were nowhere near London! Oh, what a mess I was in. It was quite a mess, indeed! Blast!

Jack smiled and said to the kindly woman, "Pardon me, Missus Butterworth, but cud you spare any scraps for this 'ere dog?" I wagged my tail in acknowledgement, but stayed where I was, on the back of the dray.

"Is it thine?" she asked back, surprised. Putting her hands on her hips she accused, "Tha's never fetched a dog afore now! Are ya sure its thine, or 'ave yer pinched it?"

"Aye, you cud say it's ours." Harry slyly glanced at me, then greedily rubbed his hands together.

"Give over! You've nivver even *mentioned* 'aving a dog up till now." She had that look about her that said she wondered if I was indeed stolen property. She then said matter-of-factly, "Well then, I'll see what there is in the kitchen. Tha mun bring dog round back. I don't want it eating in the 'otel's bar; I'll lose all mi custom. We're an 'otel; a proper one, and not a public house."

So that was how I received my first proper meal in days. I was starving, and hadn't been feeling at all well. I was so hungry and thirsty that when I saw the generous plate of food, which was only vegetables and gravy with some stodgy pastry, I thought all my birthdays had come at once. I ate every piece of potato and every carrot, every bit of grease and gravy. It all went down my hatch rather quickly. It was the best pastry crust I'd ever had. I filled my belly to bursting point, and then drank deeply from the bowl of fresh water someone from the kitchen had thoughtfully set down for me. Feeling fully sated, I crept away to find a safe place to sleep. I didn't want to go too far, as I wanted to stay with the dray, hoping it would return to Worcester. I found I had to wander quite a distance from the hotel before I could find a place that was hidden from the general eyes of the public, and also gave me a feeling of security. I settled down behind a brick wall, and even though I was cold, and there was no soft bed, I slept well.

* * *

EARLY THE NEXT MORNING I sleepily navigated my way back to the hotel. I had to sniff my own trail more than once to make sure I got back there and didn't get lost, and once I nearly set off in the wrong direction. Many of the streets and buildings looked alike, and it was all very confusing; it wasn't at all like being in the country where one travels through fields and farmyards. When I arrived at the hotel there was an abundance of activity in the yard, and I was relieved to see the dray that I had travelled upon was still there. The same horses were there as well. They were standing lazily in their shafts, as both had a foot in the slightly raised position that horses do when they are resting.

Jack and Harry were walking towards the large dray cart. "What'd I tell thee? That thear dog is 'ere waiting for us. Thee owes me a pint!" boasted Harry.

Jack replied, "Alreet. Tha's won bet. Doan't tha think thou shouldst feed it? Maybe then 'e'll stay 'ere." He stopped in his tracks – he had a brilliant idea. "I know – they cud take him in." Harry looked doubtful as his mate said, "This 'otel cud probably use a good dog round place. A bit of a guard dog, if you know what I mean." He then said hopefully, "We'll talk to 'er nicely, un see what she says."

Harry answered roughly, "Will you give over! This dog'll follow us. That's why it's 'ere this morning – it's not wanting t' be left behind."

Harry went back into the hotel by way of the kitchen, and shortly later returned carrying two bowls. He set them down and called, "Cum on, dog." He looked over his shoulder at his mate. "I wus right! I told y'so. She said t'make sure we take dog wi' us or doan't ever cum back, or she'll 'ave brewery onto us."

I was hungry, and I now knew these men meant me no genuine harm, but I wasn't about to trust them further than I could throw them. I gladly accepted their generosity, and I ate with relish, but I kept both my eyes on them and not the food. The second bowl contained water, and I appreciated this, as I was still so very thirsty. It seemed to me as though I hadn't eaten any food or drunk any water the previous evening at all, even though I had eaten until bursting point. Chances were that I wouldn't receive any more food or water at all that day, so with one eye on the men, I filled my stomach to capacity, and hoped it would all stay down.

* * *

OUR JOURNEY BACK TO WORCESTER was reasonably uneventful. The sun shone, it rained, the north wind blew at our backs, and we saw some fresh snow. The closer we got to Worcester, the warmer it seemed to get. The nights were too cold for a dog to be sleeping outside, so I would tuck my nose under my bushy tail and curl up into a tight ball for warmth. Many nights the stars were out in their spangled brilliance, and in the mornings, after those cold nights, the grass would be stiff and frozen, glistening with the breath of frost. The effect was beautiful, though, as the frosts made everything look skimmery, as if we had woken up in a strange, new world that would once again disappear when touched by the rays of the rising sun. I found the hoarfrosts more beautiful than snow, as if we were in a world-between-worlds, where every tiny branch tip and blade of grass had been magically dusted with a shimmering, powdered glass that slowly disappeared by midday.

Jack and Harry fed me, but it wasn't a lot of food, just occasional scraps or the odd mouldy heel of bread – not enough to keep a moggy alive. The few inns or pubs we stopped at didn't always toss out their kitchen scraps and plate scrapings, as it was all fed to the pigs, if they had any. At times I had to fight other dogs for just one small mouthful. I didn't like that at all. Many of the other dogs were quite mean and savage, resulting in them being the winner, and my limping off to lick my wounds – I simply wasn't a fighting dog. They didn't seem to know anything else but to fight for their food and then to scarper off until they became hungry again. I deemed these dogs dangerous to society, and it was a wonder to me that humans had allowed them to roam about like that, at all.

I had the opportunity to listen to Jack and Harry's private conversations, and I judged them to be untrustworthy men. They meant me no harm, but I didn't trust them to not change their minds about flogging me. I didn't think either of them fit to be anyone's master, but merely lowly servants of a sort. It was my opinion that if they worked for my old master, Rowland, then he would have sent them packing a long time ago. I did not enjoy their company at all, but yearned to get back to Worcester, where then I could again begin my journey to distant London. I would get there, to London, even if I had to walk all the way there, and if it took me forever; however long that would be.

* * *

IN THE END we made it to Worcester sooner than I thought we would, but, of course, the many barrels that filled the wagon on the return journey were empty ones, and because of this the horses travelled at a quicker pace, and so, therefore, we had made better time. I was so relieved to finally see the cathedral, and, as well, a tall spire, looming in the distance. It was almost a familiar sight to me, and my heart burst with joy as we approached the city.

Meanwhile, unbeknownst to me, my old master, Rowland, had placed a *lost* advertisement in the newspaper. I found out about this later, but at the time I had no idea he had advertised me as being missing. The *Worcester Journal* advertised my plight, and amongst the columns of various lost articles, Rowland's words said:

> *Lost: in Broadwas, Worces., trained sheepdog (Working Collie) wearing black leather collar engraved with name 'Shales'. Black and white dog, and farm-trained. Dog possibly run off, or was stolen. Handsome reward offered for safe return of the dog. Write to: Rowland C. Berkeley Esq., Butts Bank Farm, Broadwas-on-Teme.*

Rowland had also written a letter to his cousin Edmund. I found out about these communications much later, but I want to tell you now what was written about me:

> *Butts Bank Farm*
> *22 March, 1881*

> *Dear Edmund,*
> *I am looking forward to seeing you and the family this summer. I might possibly be coming down to London sometime soon, and if so, I shall take the opportunity to stop over for a visit. I should also mention, in passing, that my dog, the one Mildred named 'Shales', has gone missing. I suspect he has run away from the farm, or, that possibly, he was stolen, and it has only been a few days so I hope the dog will return of his own accord. Meanwhile, I have placed an advertisement in the Lost section of the Worcester Journal. The dog did survive being struck by lightning, though I did lose a number of ewes from said lightning strike. I think that has deeply affected his behaviour, and there was a calamity here on the farm the day he went missing. One of Uncle George's barrels of imported wines from Italy rolled off the dray, and the impact of it against the cobbles created a loud sound, causing the dog to create a disturbance and terrify the horses. That same night the dog disappeared, but was then fed its breakfast*

at Dad's house, by his cook. There has been no sight of the dog since. Mildred is worried that either the dog is injured, has been taken by a dishonest person since leaving Dad's, or worse off, is dead.

The weather here is continuing to be cold and damp, but at least we don't have any deep snow; spring seems to be late in coming this year.

I wonder if you have been to Westminster to visit Herbert, at his lodgings? I have not, so, therefore, I hope they are better than anything imagined in a Dickens book. If I come to London, I shall have to visit him and see for myself.

I shall let you know if I'm coming before the summer begins. Please tell Jessie about the dog, as she was taken with him. I know she will be severely saddened when she learns he has disappeared.

That's all, for now, and I'll let you know if I find anything out about Shales.

Your cousin,
Rowland

If I had known that Rowland and Mildred were going to be so concerned about my well-being, I would not have run away; but then, my life would have been so very different, wouldn't it? Later, when I overheard the details of this letter being talked about, I wondered if I should have stayed, but then I wouldn't have led such an adventurous life. There would never have been any reason for me to travel further than Cotheridge Court, and I would have missed out on so much.

Edmund had replied, and his letter went something like this:

64 Cassland Road,
Hackney, London.
31 March, 1881

Dear cousin Rowland,

I was sorry to read about your dog. My sisters were nearly in tears when they heard the sad news. They would like to have a dog again, but Dad is forever saying "no" to them, but I think it is only a matter of time before Jessie, Lucy, Emily or Julia brings one home with them. I just hope it won't be one of those longhaired lap dogs that old ladies are partial to.

Thomas wanted another dog after our last one died, but Dad bought him a hunter, instead, and that was the end of that. Thomas rides his horse so much that the shoes wear down ever so quickly! (ha ha).

Incidentally, I have been to see Herbert. He seems quite happy and contented at his work, though I did sense he is impatient to make improvements. He says it is only a matter of time before more improved cameras and photo-graphic papers will be commercially available. He is also impatient to move house, and is looking for a house of his own – lodging with others is not his forte.

We hope you do come to London, and then come out to Wayletts to visit with us, if we are there. If you are to be detained in London then we may not proceed to Wayletts, as is usual for late spring, and shall remain at the house in Cassland Road. We do hope you'll bring Mildred and Evelyn with you.

Your cousin,
Edmund

Shales, always at home in the fields.

VI

SOLDIERS OF THE NIGHT

"... the night was moonless – I wondered
where it was, and if it had abandoned me."

AFTER LEAVING THE WAREHOUSE, IN WORCESTER, which is where Harry and Jack came to the end of their journey, I set off in the direction of the afternoon sun glinting off my right ear. I started off, on foot, down a very long and busy street, and after I jogged over a short bridge that spanned a smallish river, I left the city limits. The river was full of strange things that I later discovered were called barges, which floated atop the water, and they were done up in all sorts of bright colours. Some even had dogs wandering about on them. I sat and watched one or two go by, and I then realised they were in fact some sort of a boat. Being so taken with them, I wondered if there was a way to get to London while reclining atop one of those lovely, brightly painted boats. I decided I had better not try, as I didn't want to end up in a place that was not London, and would then have to return to Worcester, yet once again. I thought, that if that happened, it would be too disappointing to cope with. I just hoped I would find the place called London, before too long, and that it wasn't very far away from Worcester. Suddenly I remembered a bit of the dream when the Orange God Cat had spoken to me, and had said for me to find a family, and that I would know them. I held onto this belief that all would turn out well for me in the end, whenever that would be. Not wanting to linger, I set off down the main highway and blended in amongst the fast-moving carriages and slower, heavily laden wagons – ever careful to keep safely out of the way of their iron-bound wheels, as well as from beneath the dangerous flying feet of the horses. To put it bluntly, it was a very busy and dangerous road.

That night, I tiredly came to a town called Evesham. There I found the locals spoke differently than what I was used to, as their dialect was strange to my ears and sounded as if it were a foreign language. In that place I crept about the many pub yards looking for food. It wasn't easy, but I did find bits of meat and pastry that had been tossed out the backs of their kitchens and onto their middens. I cannot repeat enough times that the competition for food was stiff, what with the local population of rats, dogs, and cats on the prowl. I never fully sated my appetite, which always burnt like a hot fire in a grate, and kept aglow even in my deepest sleep. I had even started having dreams where I was looking for food, and invariably, a dream dog would be lurking within the dream's shadows, and would snatch the food away from me with snarls and snaps of its sharp, white teeth.

A couple of days after leaving Evesham the road led me to a place called Edgehill. It was after dark, and getting quite late, and I was, as usual, looking for food. I had once again gone all day without eating, so I was very, very hungry, and I did not want to give up my search for sustenance, thinking surely there was a scrap of food somewhere along this route. The road was quiet at that time of the night, everyone being in bed, and I walked along at a weary pace. The night was moonless – I wondered where it was, and if it had abandoned me. Every once in awhile the hoot of an owl would remind me that I was not alone, and then the inky darkness would once again become deathly quiet, except for the soft sound of my feet upon the dirt of the road. Suddenly, the quiet of the night ended as I realised I could hear horses coming along the road from behind me, and it seemed as if they were running at full gallop. It sounded as if there were many of them, not just one or two. I wondered who it could be at that time of the night, and what was so urgent.

As I thought about getting out of the riders' way, I suddenly realised they were close upon me, so I started to run, not wanting to get trampled beneath the horses' powerful iron-shod hoofs. As I ran I looked for a place to hide, but there were thick hedgerows either side of me, barring my way; in the dark of night it seemed there was nowhere for me to hide, not even a roadside ditch. Feeling trapped within the confines of the narrow road, I ran faster, my knees nearly hitting my chin, but the sounds of charging horses and shouting men were nearly upon me. My heart was beating fast, and as

I fled I dared to look over my shoulder to see just how close they were to me. To my horror, they came just two wagons' lengths away – a large force of mounted horses catching up to me, and they completely filled the narrow road. Their riders wore coats of metal, and I took in the sounds of creaking leather and jingling armour. I could hear the horses' heavy breathing and loud snorting with their every stride, and in fear for my life I quickly jumped to my left, regardless of the consequences, and flung myself into the winter's dead foliage of the hedgerow. With tightly closed eyes, I hit with such force that I actually sprang backwards into the air doing a half a somersault, and landed on my side with a heavy thud. I nearly screamed with terror, though I was severely winded, and could not make a sound nor move. I waited to be pummelled into a pulp by the horses' hoofs, and I braced myself for the impact. The pain of being trampled did not happen, and for a brief moment I actually thought that the pain would hit me later. Then I realised the sound of charging horses had stopped! I dared open my eyes, expecting them to be impatiently standing there – both horses and riders gazing down upon my prone body – but they weren't. They had simply disappeared into thin air! Nothing! Just dead silence, and a cold, inky darkness!

It was as if it hadn't happened, and yet, there I was lying prone, in the road, and sore all over my chest from the stabs of the sharp twigs of the hedge. I gasped for air as I tried to fill my lungs. I had knocked the wind out of myself, and my tongue, swollen with thirst, hung out of the side of my mouth. I was so terrified that, moments later when I could get onto my feet, I skulked off with my tail tucked tightly between my legs, and eventually found a place to lie down, in a nearby orchard, and there I stayed put for the rest of the night. I barely slept a wink – the fright of it all remained burnt into every nerve of my body. I didn't understand what I had experienced, but years later I realised that I had witnessed a haunting, of mounted soldiers, from a couple of hundred years before, who haunt that area around Edgehill. I had seen ghosts! I was never gladder to see the sun come up the next morning, and bask the world in its cheery daylight.

* * *

LUCKILY FOR ME, I didn't have to travel very far to the next town, Banbury, which sits only a few miles from Edgehill. In that place I spent the entire day in exploration, and as it was evidently market day, I hoped that sooner or later I would find my fill. Around midday, as the vendors were packing up at the end of their market day because their stalls were empty, I found lots of trimmings of fat and meaty scraps scattered about the cobblestones. These fat and other meat trimmings had been tossed onto the floor and out of the way by impatient, busy butchers' hands. I quickly scoffed them down – they were delicious, and I realised my body was craving meat and fat. I wasn't alone; the squeak of rats and the smell of cats was but a short distance away. As I wandered about the empty market I ate what I could find, such as turnip and potato parings, stuffing myself like a greedy bird until I could eat no more. That night I slept peacefully beneath an ancient yew hedge, even though the weather was cold and drizzly. Although I wasn't warm, I kept dry beneath its thick foliage, and with my hunger finally sated, though my stomach roiled, I slept.

One thing I was beginning to notice was that every village had a church, and the larger places known as towns or cities had several of them, and some of these churches were absolutely huge; these I now know are usually cathedrals. Also, my suspicion that English was an ever-changing language was confirmed, as I noted the dialects and accents continually changed from village to village. At least I already knew I could understand Londoners from my experience of listening to them at the garden party. I learnt to follow roads, but also to cut across fields to keep my heading true. I knew ahead of time when there was a populated place coming up, because I could either see the church spire, or tower, or hear its bells ringing out the time of day. I had long since learnt that five bells was the signal to arise and wait to be fed – it was the only number I knew. Now that I wasn't living on the farm, but was a tramp, I used this knowledge of time to know that people would be getting up at about this time, if not a bit later. However, this little bit of knowledge didn't always help me to find two square meals a day, or to keep me from starving.

As I continued on my journey the days began to feel just a little bit warmer, and I noticed patches of yellow flowers in the front gardens of cottages. Even some churchyards were filled with these lovely sprays of brilliant yellow, called daffodils, which danced about whenever the wind blew. The birds sounded more cheery, and they flitted about happily as they prepared their nests for the arrival of those miniature eggs, which would eventually hatch into their offspring. There was a change in the air, which signalled that winter was over with, and I could only look forward to warmer days and shorter nights.

It wasn't easy travelling on an empty stomach. At times my energy would lapse, and I would feel drowsy and would require a long nap. After Banbury, I wasn't so lucky at cadging, and a few people threw stones or other things at me in their attempts to chase me away. Sometimes I felt very hungry, and other times I was, simply, just tired. The less I ate, the harder it became for me to go on, and I seemed to require more and more sleep, resulting in my travelling less and less as each day passed by. The pads of my feet were wearing thin. They were filled with small cuts and were frequently sore, thus causing me to limp. I wondered how far they could carry me before I completely wore them out.

Terrified, Shales runs for his life.

VII

HORATIO

"Life is Full of Tomorrows."

FTER I HAD BEEN ABOUT FIVE DAYS WITHOUT FOOD (I had not been successful in scavenging at any of the pubs or inns I had passed), I spent an afternoon devoted to sleeping. I had found a nice tree, with lots of character in its sweeping branches and twisted trunk, growing at the edge of a field, and because the sun was shining it felt nice and warm where the sun struck the grass beneath it. There, I curled up against the warm tree and slept. It sprouted tiny, green leaves, as it was now spring, and the tree would soon be in full bloom. I had become very weary and depressed. I didn't know how much further I had to go, or could go. London was out there somewhere, waiting for me to arrive, and I would find my new home there. The walking and running from sunup to sundown had taken its toll on me; I was in a state of despair. What was in my future? What happened to dogs like me? How did stray dogs and starving dogs live without humans to care for them? I thought about all those canine scavengers I had encountered along my journey, and hoped I would not spend the rest of my life living like them. I couldn't live like them. I'd rather give up living completely, than live a life devoid of human contact and regular meals.

Also, I thought about the town I had passed through, called Hertford. I had been unsuccessful in finding food there, and I even tried begging, but the people in that place shooed me away. Whilst in Hertford, I had actually wondered about the possibility of sneaking through an open doorway into the kitchen of a house, and pinching whatever food I could find there. The door to one particular house had been propped open by an umbrella stand, inviting me, or anyone else, to go inside. I watched from across the street like a criminal planning a robbery. The house was on the busy High Street, both sides a continuous row of shops and houses, with lots of traffic and pedestrians. It blended in with the rest except for its opened door, and like the others, white lace curtains hung in the first floor windows. I questioned what would happen to me if I got caught. It was a calculated risk, and I'd never done anything like that before. Eventually, I came to the realisation that it was a bit dodgy, as I might have found upon exiting the place the door suddenly closed shut on me, and then I wouldn't have been able to escape, resulting in my being trapped. The risk had been far too great for me, even in my desperate state of starvation. I had left Hertford on an empty stomach, and there was no point now in thinking about what I hadn't been brave enough to do.

Feeling the hardness of the tree behind me, I was aware that my bones were protruding, and that it was probably why I didn't feel so well. Also, I didn't know where I was in relation to London, which resulted in my feeling woefully lost. As I was thinking those depressing thoughts, I decided to think about more pleasant things and to forget all the bad ones – anything to make me feel better. There was the warmth of the sun to think about, and the sweet smell of the new, green grass. Then, I imagined myself living with a nice family, with a friendly cook who would feed me all day long. In my imagination she would prepare special meals, just for me. Oh, such good thoughts! Such lovely thoughts! I imagined bowls of porridge topped off with dollops of cream, and warm, loving hands stroking my hair and gently caressing my ears with genuine affection.

My reverie became strangely disturbed. Eerily, I felt the sensation that I was being stared at. You know what I mean. It's that feeling one gets. Uncannily, I felt as if I wasn't alone, and my hair started to twitch all along my spine. Surely, someone was watching me. I glanced about, but didn't see or hear anyone, but then, at that moment, I became aware of a smell. It wasn't a foreign smell. I sniffed the air. It was rank and definitely feline. Moggy. I had smelt moggy. I was aware of my deep hunger, and I wondered if I could possibly catch and eat a cat. The thought, such a tiny

Shales realises he is not alone.

one, had started to grow in my mind, and my belly responded immediately by sending me hunger pangs. Then I remembered how I had felt when Schooner had told me about the dogs that had killed and eaten dogs and cats. I was appalled then, and was now also appalled at myself, for even considering such a barbaric thing.

"*Ah... Hullo. Hullo there,*" said this soft, feathery voice from nowhere. "*Pardon me misther... but yer a'e in my field, an' a'e trethspassing on my family's land.*"

I turned my head, and there, stood in front of me, was this unusually large moggy. It was the colour of baked pastry, and it had a white chest, and its hair was very long and shaggy. It took me a moment to realise that it was this cat that was speaking to me. I had expected to see a human standing there. The moggy was still talking to me; something about trespassing and mithe and that I was ruining his day. I was so shocked that the moggy could speak to me in long, intelligent sentences that I didn't think to answer him back. I thought I was seeing things. It even crossed my mind that I was dreaming.

"*Eeh. Cat got thy tongue?*" It said. Then it laughed and rolled over onto its back, and kicked the air with its shaggy feet. "*Get it? Get it? Cat... got... thy... tongue?*"

I sighed deeply. Then I answered him, "*Yes, ah do fathom the question, but ah don't feel like laughing. T' be honest wi' thee, I don't have the energy t' laugh. I'm absolutely knackered, so doan't bother me 'cause ah want t' go back t' sleep. I want t' kip here in the warm sun, so please, please, just leave me alone.*"

The cat laughs at his own joke.

The strange moggy strolled over to me, with a confidence that only property owners have when confronting a trespasser. It really was quite large and hairy. It peered into my face.

"*Don't larf then. I haven't seen thee here afore now. Thou are not finkink of moving here and tekkink over my territory, are thee?*" It drew circles in the soft ground with its right front paw, as it waited for my reply.

"*Territory?*" I asked in puzzlement.

"*Yeth,*" It replied. "*This field, this twee, this garss... is all mine.*" He emphasized this by waving his right paw about in the air.

I answered innocently, "*Ah was only having a kip. Ah thought it was a safe place to doss down, y' know... get mi head down.*"

"*Right. Right. Jes sleeping. You can do that if you 'ont. I don't mind, but thou'll have to leave when thee is done.*"

"*Why, ta very much,*" I said, wondering why the heck I was thanking a moggy for anything at all. I felt too exhausted to argue.

"*If moy master sees thee, he'll chase thee off. He doethn't like it when other dogs trethspass. I have to warn thee, that he'll fetch his gun an' shoot thee. I'fe seen him do it afore. He bewies 'em somewhere owt there.*" The cat gestured over his shoulder to where a spacious field lay beyond some trees.

I struggled to decipher what he'd meant, and then it dawned on me. The warm sunshine suddenly felt a bit colder, and I shivered at the thought of it. Surely, I was wrong. It couldn't be. His master killed dogs?

"*Well, I'm only sleeping, well planning on doing so, if tha'll leave me alone.*"

I still couldn't believe I was talking to a cat, and I wondered if I was dreaming it all up. His strange way of pronouncing words stimulated my brain, resulting in my feeling less sleepy and more awake than ever. Moggies usually ran away from me. I didn't think they could talk properly, and I thought they were stupid, gormless animals that were here on Earth solely for the reason to keep down the rat and mouse population, and to allow something for dogs to chase. I had always chased them at the farm, and Toothless George never once said it was wrong to do so, though I never harmed any of them. I drew the line at that. They would spit or hiss at me, threatening to scratch my eyes out with their sharp claws, but I never, ever, harmed one.

The moggy cleared his throat. "*I bet thou finks I'm stupid.*" He said this to me matter-of-factly, and not as a question. He cocked his shaggy head as he waited for my answer.

"*Nay. Nay,*" I answered, lying through my teeth. "*Honestly, I know thee not... so why would I think summat like that?*"

Typically cat-like, he changed the subject. "*I know sumpfink thou doesn't know,*" he said, in a singsong voice. "*I know it, and thou doesn't. I know it. I know it.*"

After that, it simply turned away and plodded off towards the field that was filled with the hidden graves of trespassing dogs. I wondered what it had meant by that last reference to knowledge. With the shaggy cat now gone, I settled my head back down and began to go back to sleep beneath the tree. I was too exhausted to worry about any of it, and if the rare cat had gone to fetch its master, then its master could shoot me, bury me in the field along with the other dead bodies, and I would be put out of my misery. I wouldn't have to worry about where my next meal was coming from. Or would I? I started to ponder those dead dogs and if they were still running about, unseen like those ghost riders and their horses I had seen, and I wondered if they still needed to eat and sleep?

I don't know how long I had slept, but it didn't seem to be long enough when I felt something prod me awake. Before I opened my eyes, I knew it was back. The odour of the moggy was strong. There was another smell as well; familiar, but I couldn't place it. Curiously, I looked about and found it sitting close by, watching me. It had a satisfied look on its face. Smug.

"*I know how to catch mithe,*" it said.

"*So,*" was the only answer that I could come up with, because I didn't know what a "mithe" was.

"*So?*" mimicked the cat. "*Mithe equals food, and food equals a full belly. Thou is hungwy. There is a ragged and hawf-starved look about thee. Anyone could see that. I bet thou has not eaten in many a day! So, I thowt, I'll catch some mithe, and thou canst have a meal out of 'em. We'll share, of course.*"

There was a small mound of dead bodies on the grass in front of the cat's paws. The dead mice's arms, legs, and tails stuck out at odd angles. He had been talking about mice! I was astounded. I didn't understand why this cat was helping me, and why I hadn't first thought of field mice as food.

"*Swallow them 'ole and they'll tek longer to digest. Thee'll feel full uwp for longer if thou'll do this.*"

I simply stared back at him. Was I being made a fool of? Was there a multitude of cats hiding in the grass and up in the trees, watching us, and waiting to have a right good laugh at me?

"*Gao on,*" urged the cat. He then tossed a dead mouse towards me with a flick of his paw. It landed in the grass with a little '*plop*'. Softly, he whispered, "*Eat.*"

What words of wisdom coming from a moggy, a cat! Who would have thought that felines were so intelligent? I followed his instructions and swallowed several mice. The moggy delicately helped himself to just one of them. I remembered my manners. "*Ta very much,*" I said.

"*Ith's all right,*" cheerfully replied the shaggy feline. Boldly walking up to me, he said, "*My name is Horatio Harvest, an' this land iths called Harvest Farm. My family owns it, an' we have a vicious dog, and lots of fields, and a house that's falling down, and everyfink you would want to find on a farm, including me, a cat.*"

What an introduction! Mine was equally as good. "*Well, Horatio. My name is Shales Comyns Berkeley. I'm a professional sheepdog, and I am on my way to London to seek my fortune, where hopefully I'll find a family to take me in.*" Then I said, "*Horatio, I am so, so, very knackered. May I stay put until tomorrow and have a really good night's kip?*" I fully expected him to say no.

"*Of corwse thou can. I'll see thee tomorrow. Tell you wot, I'll fetch thee ample more mithe for thy breakfast, an' we'll chit chat, an' you can tell me awl about it. Now, don't leave afore I get here. I promise thee... y'll be safe... as long as thee'll stay owt of sight.*"

Horatio then turned about and slowly walked away through the grass, with his hairy tail held high like a banner. I thought to myself, "*What a marvellous chap.*" I then wondered if he would keep his promise to me, regarding breakfast. I shook my head to make sure I was awake and hadn't dreamt the entire event. I then settled down in a comfortable position and fell asleep in the warmth of the afternoon sun, the ache in my belly momentarily non-existent and replaced with a feeling of satiable, if not furry... satisfaction.

* * *

HORATIO did keep his promise to deliver breakfast to me. He woke me up nice and early, just after sunrise, and gestured towards a pile of little grey bodies.

"*I don't need to eat any of these,*" he said. "*I had a luffly breakfast at the farm. There wath bacon an' lots of cweamy milk.*"

I stared at him. My tongue nearly fell out of my mouth. I had forgotten what bacon and milk tasted like. At that moment I had a great desire to have some, and my stomach started to turn over, reminding me how famished I was. However, I looked at the generous donation of dead mice and appreciated that he had taken the effort to run about and catch and kill them, just for me. I ate wolfishly, and washed them down by drinking from a nearby puddle of murky water.

In a curious voice Horatio said, "*So... tell me how thee got to be in this sorwy state. You look down in the heel.*"

I then told him my life's story, and in return he told me his. I loved the way he talked. He was very intelligent and interesting, and I was beginning to get used to his dialect and odd way of pronouncing his words. He loved to talk, and I think would chat away forever if given the chance, and I found myself absorbing his curious words of wisdom.

According to Horatio, there was food available everywhere – you just had to look for it. Rats and mice live in fields of grass, or in the hay and straw inside stables and barns, as well as near middens, and also, where they can get at human food, such as in a kitchen or a dairy. We both agreed that the best place to find food, when on the road, was outside kitchen doorways, where hopefully someone would toss some out, or the compost pile – but the rats usually got to the compost piles first. He also taught me: "*Never go to the same place twice in a row.*" His reasoning being that the people will think you will move in and never leave, such as what a squatter does.

Here, I'd been thinking I had actually been rather successful in finding food on my journey. After listening to Horatio, I began to feel embarrassed that I had gone those last five days without eating, not to mention all the others. I hadn't even known that I could eat mice, otherwise I would have scavenged the fields and pastures as I'd made my journey. It is indeed frightening to think that I could have starved to death, and there was food literally inches away from me at all times!

Horatio also said that there are many roads in our country, and that they all lead to London, and then on to Rome. Another thing he said was that one could easily just go about in circles, because we have two legs on one side of our bodies, both of which are shorter than the legs on the other side. This causes us to waver from our straight course, and we are never aware of it, and it will happen if one isn't travelling along a road.

I learnt about beds, feathered pillows, and things called carpets. He explained that these things are only found inside houses, and that he had exclusive animal rights to live inside the house at Harvest Farm. He was allowed to sleep in these beds and wander all through the house, and even eat all his meals inside the kitchen. He described colourful walls and soft, coloured floors called carpets. I thought about the kitchen at Butts Bank Farm, as I had thought the rest of the house was a repeat of what the kitchen looked like: floor of wide boards, huge inglenook fireplace with smoked hams hanging from hooks inside the chimney, a work table, and some cupboards filled with an abundant array of bowls and other bits of crockery. Well, I hadn't seen the *inside* of a house before, so how could I *know* what it was supposed to look like? I had been restricted to the kitchen when I was recuperating from my illness, and that was mostly the area in and around the huge fireplace.

Horatio described great and wonderful things in these houses. I was curious to see an upstairs with bedchambers, but the concept of ducks or geese in blankets, known as eiderdowns, bothered me. I mean, wouldn't the quacking and moving about of the birds inside the eiderdowns keep everyone awake? It didn't make any sense to me. He assured me that the duck blankets, or goose blankets, were very soft and good to sleep on, and were extremely quiet and still, literally there being no ducks or birds inside them at all. It was hard to picture this, so I had to believe him because he said it was so. I made myself a mental note of a few things I desired to do.

My List of Things To Do:

1. See the inside of a bedchamber and try the bed.
2. Walk across a carpet.
3. See a… (forgotten what it was now).

Horatio said he knew where the road to London was. It was a fair distance away from Harvest Farm, but he could take me to it.

"*There, on the side of the road, is a signpowst that says it is the London road.*" He said this cheerfully.

I was excited to hear this. A road that actually was signed and directing people, and of course me, to London. This bit of news gave me new-found hope, and I found within me renewed strength. I got up onto my feet and begged my leave.

"*Thlow... slowww... down, Shales; don't hurrwy. Tarry wiff me. Y'll neffer make it there by tomorrow, and thou don't know the way, an' I do. I shall tek thee there myself.*"

This was wonderful news. We planned to set off the next morning, and Horatio would be my guide. He would lead the way; he said he knew all the paths through the fields for miles around and had been as far as the London road more than once. When I enquired as to how long it would take us to get there, he said quite a few days, and that left me wondering just how long I had been on this journey. My sore, worn out feet had badly needed the couple of days' rest, so I resigned myself to wait for morning, and for Horatio to guide me.

* * *

WHEN HORATIO ARRIVED BRIGHT AND EARLY THE NEXT MORNING he came bearing gifts: a single mouse for my breakfast. We had to pass by his farm, so he invited me to finish off his own breakfast, which was on a saucer set out by the kitchen door.

His dog was chained somewhere out of sight but I could hear it barking nastily, announcing: "*Help! Strange dog here! Help! Trespassing dog on the farm!*" It knew of my presence.

Whilst I ate, Horatio stood on sentry duty, on the lookout for his dog-shooting master. Breakfast was milk with clots of cream in it, and there was something else in it as well, which he told me was fish. The meal, though small, was appreciated, and it was heaps better than a meal of dead, furry mice. Don't tell Horatio I said this, but I never, ever, want to eat mice again.

We set off at *moggy speed*, which I found out to be very, very slow. Wanting to remain polite, I didn't comment on the meagre distance we had put between the farm and ourselves by midday. Nevertheless, I did mention to him we weren't going to be too exhausted by the end of the day. Horatio carried on at his slow pace as if he was stalking every blade of grass. We crossed many fields and passed down many lanes; but always, we kept to the same direction, sort of easterly. There were times when I, even in my weakened state, got so far ahead that I lay down and rested, and waited for him to catch up with me.

When Horatio rested we had wonderful chats about things. I found out so much from him about life in general. It was as if *he* had read those great books he talked about, when really he had only paid attention when a person in his family had been reading out loud, and he had remembered it all. All the people in his family could read, but it was all kept hush, as the neighbours would think them uppity. Also, if the neighbours knew they could all read, they mightn't want to sit next to them in church; such is the way things are in the lower classes. His mistress was the kinder one, and it was she who read aloud, even when she was on her own, with just Horatio in her lap. His master, well, he was prone to acts of violence, and didn't get on with his neighbours at all. Hence the elimination of all of the wild and roving dogs which innocently happened upon his land, and that only increased the animosity between Harvest Farm and all the other neighbouring farms.

Early that evening, I watched him do his begging routine outside a kitchen door to a farmhouse. We were wary of the dog that was there, but it welcomed us and said there was lots of food in the kitchen. He was a friendly sort and was pleased to make our acquaintance. I've never before, nor since, seen a dog as large as that one was in size. He was gigantic! This giant of a dog could have had both Horatio and me for dinner, and then had room for afters, but that wasn't in his nature. He told us he was an immigrant wolfhound from Ireland, and he went by the name of Fionn. When the lady there noticed Horatio, and bent down to stroke him, he meowed and lifted one of his paws, as if it were sore. First, the woman just petted and stroked him, but then she took pity on us and went into the kitchen, and returned with a couple of bowls of food for us. That night we dined on roasted potatoes with meat and gravy. Horatio said it was lamb, but I disagreed and said it was pork. I didn't think I had ever tasted anything so good before.

Later, we slept in the stable, confident that the door would be opened the next morning as there were horses in the stalls, and people always tend to their horses at first light. I found myself feeling safe and contented with such wonderful company. The stable was filled with the aroma of hay, and the scent of good hay is one of my sweetest pleasures in life. The sounds the horses made as they settled down to sleep was music to my ears, and I drifted off into a deep, gentle sleep, feeling safe, warm, and cosy, whilst half buried beneath a pile of clean straw.

For Horatio, begging for food came as naturally to him as water running off a duck's back. I soon realised that he only ate mice and moles when he couldn't find food at all, and *that* never happened to him. Like myself, he didn't like the taste of them. He would rather beg at a stranger's kitchen door than eat mice, but this made me appreciate all the more the effort he had put into catching those ones he had generously provided me with. As to his slow pace – it seemed he always walked slowly, then, he would stop and sniff the air and have a listen for signs of danger, and once more he would set off, deadly silent, with his purposeful, if not extremely slow stride.

I told him about my dream. You know the one. I had it when Toothless George locked me in the harness room the day I frightened the dray horses. The *God Cat* dream. Horatio said that without that dream, I might have chased him away and never would have received his offer of mice, and we wouldn't be travelling in the direction of the London road, which, of course, was the proper direction. He explained how I would have denied myself his help, which, as he put it, "*Fatefully, wath direly needed.*"

When I asked him about God, he said, "*All animals are in tune with His presence, but don't understand that it is the same presence that people worship.*" This amazed me. I felt comforted knowing that I was never completely alone, no matter what happened, and that I had a purpose to my life – otherwise I would have died from that lightning bolt. Horatio insisted that my purpose in life would remain a mystery to me, unto my dying day. I then understood that certain incidents would happen to me in my future, and there would be no way, whatsoever, to avoid them. Horatio used the term *destiny* to describe these important events yet to happen to me. He also encouraged me to tell others about this presence whenever I encountered anyone who didn't understand it, or didn't know about it. I realised Horatio was preaching to me, and that the fields and trees about us were our church, and we, too, were God's children, not just God's creatures, even though people didn't readily accept this. He talked of a magical land called Heaven.

"We awl go to Heaven, but thowse who have been family pets gets wings on their backs, an' we ascend into the Eternal Light effer so gently."

"Are you positive?" I asked incredulously.

"Nao," he replied, bowing his head, *"but I'd like to fink it happens this way. We jes' get there, that's awl I knows. Here one day, and there the next. That's the twuth, Shales."*

Then the time came for Horatio to go no further. We were stopped outside a church on a narrow, lonely road. We'd been travelling for five days, but I knew I could have done it in less than one, possibly a half a day at a run, if I was in tip-top shape.

"Thith is nearly the fawthest I'fe ever been, an' the road to London is jes' down there. Gao sowf." He gestured with his head. *"It's twenty miles to London, an' stay on that road down there. After yer get there, y'll have to decide wot to do with yourself; an' I wish thee awl the best, my mate. Think of me, and I'll think of you."*

It was a sad departure. I was going to miss Horatio's friendship. I had enjoyed his company, and had learnt a lot from him. He was a good mate, a true cate, but it was time for him to return to his home. It would've been nice if he could have come with me to London, but obviously he was satisfied with his farm life, and would never leave it. I wished him the best, and watched him slowly plod away down a path until he disappeared out of sight. I felt sad, and I promised myself to never forget him. I had to remind myself – life is full of tomorrows.

Harvest Farm – Horatio's home.

THE FOOL

BOOK II

VIII
WAYLETTS

"They'll look after thee here."

FTER I PARTED WAYS WITH HORATIO I travelled down a long and narrow road until I came to a slightly wider road. This was the road to London, just where Horatio had said it would be. I set off down the road, but being hungry I decided to look for something to eat. Without Horatio I had to rely upon my own talents for acquiring food. I soon noticed a place set back off the road, so there I went, and snooped around the back of the sad-looking, sprawling house, and looked about for a person. It was a farm; pigs populated several sties to my left. It had the usual paved yard with outbuildings, set back at a distance from the road, and at the back of the house, a door, which invariably led to a kitchen. The large, filthy yard was void of both people and animals, but the various scents and aromas indicated recent human activity.

I cocked my head and listened. I heard sounds of movement. Muffled footsteps came from inside the house, so I knew someone was about. I waited patiently by the door, and after a while, when no one showed any sign of coming out, I gave a loud *"Woof"*. I had spoken quite loudly, but still, nobody came to the door. I nudged it with my nose, and then I scratched at the door with my right front paw. Moments later I whined again, hoping to be heard.

Eventually, a man came out to investigate. I wagged my tail and whimpered, then lifted a paw, hoping to gain pity. I thought I had been successful, because upon seeing me, the man grunted, went back into the house and returned rather quickly, carrying a large pail. I eagerly walked up to him, thinking it was filled with milk, because I had seen similar pails used for the milking of cows, and a drink of creamy milk would have suited me fine. I licked my lips in anticipation of the creamy delight.

When I saw his raised arm come down, it was too late for me to jump away. I heard the loud sound of the pail coming into contact with my head, before I actually felt any pain. Then, the pain hit me, searing into my brain and creating a colourful burst of fireworks. There was a loud 'clanging' sound when he then threw the pail at me, missing me. It bounced off the paved stones and noisily rolled away, creating a thunderous, hollow sound as it continued clattering across the yard. This jolted me into action – I thought lightning was going to strike me again. I yelped loudly, as if my tail had been set on fire, and I ran away as fast as I could. The horrific, thunderous sound had rekindled recent memories of doom. I ran past the side of the old house, across the yard and out into the road, skidding and kicking up dirt, and thus continued for a short distance as fast as I could, until I felt safe, and then I stopped to gather my wits. I looked back over my shoulder to make sure he wasn't following me. Oh, my head ached, and I was bleeding. There was blood dripping down my left shoulder and onto my paw. My left leg should have been white, but it was now covered in red blood.

I was shocked! I questioned the man's violent actions. What had I done to receive such a wicked welcome? Couldn't he have thrown water on me, instead of hurting me? He could have ignored me or shut the door in my face, and not inflicted such cruel violence upon me.

I decided to continue along the road for as far as I could go, and hoped that I would find someone who would feed me and give me a drink of water. Sometime later, and still in a state of fright, I passed a large public house on the left side of the road, but I didn't linger there, even though the tempting odour of cooking food and spilt ale beckoned to me, as if to say, "Help is here." Something told me to keep going and to not stop, even though I was beginning to feel quite poorly.

Further on, after a short distance, I heard a voice. It was a woman's voice, low and murmuring. It came from behind some trees, carried by a sudden wind that also swirled last year's leaves into the air and about me. Grit blew into my eyes and blinded me, so I had to stop and wait for it to pass.

With squinting eyes, which stung from the swirling grit, I could see there was a drive leading off to my right, and there was obviously a large farm there, closely situated to the road. From where I stood, I could see the house was quite large and sprawling, as well as there being large outbuildings at the back. Dare I enter and make myself known? I didn't think I had any other choice, unless I wanted to continue my journey on an empty stomach and an aching head. At that moment I was beginning to feel weak and light-headed; my legs felt like jelly. The ground beneath me was beginning to move about in circles, and I felt exhausted to the point that I wanted to lie down in the middle of the road. I was suffering from starvation and loss of blood, and, as well, a sudden sense of hopelessness. I desperately wanted someone to help me, as I was beginning to feel frightened for myself. Feeling even more poorly, I sat down at the entrance to the drive and surveyed the place. Obviously another working farm, from all the sights and smells.

With great effort I managed to walk onto the property. Warily, I stayed out of sight. Off to my right there was a large timbered house with a large yard in the back and, as well, many outbuildings, but also there were groomed trees and lovely flowerbeds filled with those yellow flowers called daffodils. Behind me was a pond, and further beyond grew some trimmed trees such as those in the garden at Cotheridge Court. From where I sat, I could see a woman strolling about. As I watched, she would bend over, admiring the flowers as if they deeply interested her. I liked the look of her. Her hair was light brown and had a bit of a wavy kink to it, and it was pinned up into a bun of sorts – the way most women had their hair back then. She was slim in form, and even from where I lay I could tell she had a kindness to her that seemed to radiate outwards from her. It was the way she moved. I'm sure Horatio would agree with me. I thought to myself, *"If only she is kind to dogs, as well as to people."*

I was so weary that I felt I simply had to try and win this lady over. *Please* let her be nice to me. I didn't want to get hit on the head again. Bravely

I crept up to a large tree and lay down upon the springy grass, beneath its thick, low-lying branches. The leaves were partially out, though not near to full foliage, giving me a sense of protection, though I was obviously in full sight should the woman have looked my way. She was wearing an outfit in a shade of lovely dark blue, which made her stand out against the yellow of the daffodils; they were late in blooming that year. What a pretty picture she made.

She continued to be oblivious to my presence, so I watched her for a few moments longer. I sniffed the air and got a whiff of her scent – amazingly familiar – but that was just me, in a weakened state, hoping to find someone kind and trustworthy. I licked away at the blood that covered my left front leg, its copper taste peculiar to my tongue, but I only succeeded in reducing it to a pink stain upon the white of my hair.

I had to make my move and capture her attention. I whimpered. She didn't hear me. I whimpered again, but this time a bit louder. She turned her head as if hearing something, and then started to walk away towards the house. I whimpered again out of genuine desperation, and then gave a little bark, though it sounded to me more like the croaking of a frog. I lay on my side with a paw stuck up in the air, and I waved it back and forth with what little life I had left in me. This time she heard me, and started walking in my direction. She paused, squinted disbelievingly, then picked up her long, blue skirts and ran over to me. Stopping just a few feet away, her blue eyes became quite large as she obviously took in my sorry state of being.

"Oh, my. Oh, my. Dear, dear dog," said the young lady emotionally. Hesitantly she reached towards me then slowly drew back her hand, obviously frightened of being bitten. "What has happened to you? Who has done this to you?"

I suppose, that to her, I looked as frightening as a scarecrow. She saw a cadaverous, blood-covered dog with a desperate look in its eye, and wouldn't have known if I was vicious or not. But an instant later she knew that something awful had befallen me, and the fact that she cared enough was the reason she shouted for help. I was so relieved to hear her concern; she would not harm me, I was sure.

"You'll be all right," she spoke firmly as she bravely stroked my head, and then started to pull out numerous bits of twigs and leaves, all of which had become entangled in my coat during my long and arduous journey.

"Thomas! Thomas!" she shouted loudly. She looked over her shoulder with an impatient gesture, and cried, "Thomas, where are you?" When there was no response, she then fairly bellowed at the top of her lungs, in a most unladylike fashion, "Thomas, come quickly! I need you!"

I heard heavy footsteps come running from somewhere nearby. I hoped it was a friendly Thomas, and he would help me, because by then I didn't think I could get back onto my feet. I was having thoughts about giving up on life.

"Just look at this poor dog!" she wailed. "Help me get him to the house. He needs some medical attention. Look at *all* the blood! Just look at the state of him. His ribcage is sticking out. He's obviously starving, and if we don't help him, I think he'll die." She started to sob as she rocked back and forth on her knees. I watched as tears streamed down her cheeks.

Thomas just stood there, looking down at the woman who was leaning over me and raining tears of sadness. Angrily, she slapped his booted leg with her right hand. "Don't just stand there! Help me." She plucked at his breeches. "Thomas, I need you to help me with this dog. Please –"

This prompted him into verbal action. "Of course, Jessie. I'm sorry... it's just that... I'm surprised... that's all. I was wondering where he's come from; I wasn't ignoring you. Now, the question is... the house, or... do you think the stable?"

"Oh, I don't know," she was impatient. "What do *you* think?" she asked, now urgently tugging at his shirtsleeve.

Thomas crouched down and gently looked at my head, noting the latest, recent injury, which was still bleeding profusely. I noted his hands were gentle, and I relaxed beneath his touch. Then he patted me gently on my shoulder and said, "We don't know the dog, so I think it will be better if we put him in the stable. He may never have been inside a house before, from the looks of him, and... ah, he might not be very tame." Then, sounding doubtful, "You know these farmers and their sheepdogs." Through blurry eyes, I could see his mind whirled as he wondered where on earth I had come from.

"You don't think Father will mind if we put him in the stable and get him back on his feet?" asked the lady.

"He loves dogs; he just doesn't want us to have another one in the house. And... Jessie, I'm not sure of his reaction to his finding a mangy stray living in our house."

"Stop being stupid," she said sharply. "He's not mangy."

Thomas pushed back his short, dark hair with one swift stroke of his hand and said, "Come on then. I'll carry the dog if it doesn't bite me, and you'll have to fetch a bowl of water and some cloths – he'll need bandaging. I'll put him in the empty stall, at the end, next to Jasper, where he can be kept quiet."

"All right, the stables then, but I think the house is a more suitable place for a dog. Perhaps in a day or so, after he has been cleaned up, we can move him into the house. He'll need a good bath and a comb through his hair," said the lady.

She was still crying, and I was deeply touched that someone could be so concerned for my well-being. I wanted to respond to her kindness and show her how grateful I felt, but I simply could not even lift my head an inch. I questioned how could one stranger, not so very far away, inflict these injuries upon me, and yet another cry tears of compassion over me, all within such a short period of time? It boggled the mind.

* * *

SHE HURRIED OFF TOWARDS THE HOUSE as quickly as her long skirts would allow, and Thomas reached down and carefully collected me into his arms. I couldn't have bitten him even if I had wanted to. I was so dizzy and tired that I wished I could wake up and find out the day had all been just a bad night's sleep. At the same time, I was so pleased that two humans were concerned about me, and were going to help me, which probably meant feeding me, that I would have done anything to show them my gratitude. I didn't mind it at all when Thomas carried me away to the stable, and then set me down upon some fresh, clean straw. I tried to thump my tail in appreciation, but I don't even know if I managed to give it a bit of a wiggle. He stroked me and looked for more injuries, noting the thinness about my ribcage and the sorry state my paws were in. There was something about him that seemed familiar to me. Both he and the lady smelt and sounded familiar, but I couldn't think of a reason as to why this should be so.

The lady returned, carrying a bowl and some cloths. As she knelt down upon the straw next to us, Thomas said to her in a serious voice, "Jessie, this dog is so very thin; he hasn't been looked after very well. He's what we call gaunt, so it's obvious he's been suffering from starvation. His feet are in a sorry state. Look here... the pads are worn down to the pink in places, and they've been badly cut, so that makes me think he's a stray. I wonder where his home is? Not all people look after their dogs, and it wouldn't surprise me to find out that he lives within a few miles of here, but also, he could be miles and miles away from his home. These feet, though; I would say he's been tramping about for weeks." It was obvious he was appalled by my condition, and I wished for him to cradle me in his arms and comfort me.

Jessie added, "I haven't seen him before, so you may be correct in that he doesn't live about here." She then suggested, "Perhaps he's a runaway, or has simply become separated from his master. We'll make him well again, and then we'll try to find his home." She spoke with confidence. "His master will be worried sick, if he cares about his dog at all."

"I'll have a look in the local newspapers and see if there is a notice about a black and white dog being lost," suggested Thomas. He too was concerned someone was missing a family pet or a valuable working dog.

"What about his collar?" she thought to ask. "Is there anything inscribed upon it? Perhaps a house name, or a farm?"

"Let's have a look." Thomas gently unbuckled my collar, and moments later became excited. "Yes! There *is* a name here. It's difficult to read, though. It's coated with some pretty awful grime. I shall have to clean it off in order for the letters to be legible."

He looked about, not finding what he was looking for, and said, "Just a minute; I'll be right back."

As I lay upon the soft straw my wearied mind nagged at me. There was a saying for the feeling I had, one of familiarity that tickled the edge of the mind. Everything about the young man and woman disturbed me. But why?

Thomas left the stable, only to return a few moments later with a damp rag, and with it he rubbed vigorously at my leather collar, using a bit of his own spittle to remove the grime. I hadn't been aware that my name was inscribed upon my collar; nobody had said owt to me, but, apparently, it had been tooled into the leather. I felt relieved that I wasn't a nobody.

He read out my name in awe. "Shales." He continued in the same breath, "Jessie, it says Shales." – More animated now – "This dog's name is *Shales,* and *that* is the name of Rowland's missing dog! I knew there was something familiar about him. I just couldn't quite put my finger on it."

"Are you sure?" she asked, screwing up her face and looking from me to Thomas, and then to my collar. A stray piece of brown hair escaped from her hairpins and dangled near her right eye. Expertly, she tucked it back into place. "That means *this* dog has travelled all the way from Broadwas and Cotheridge Court, in Worcestershire, and has found us here in Stanford Rivers, in Essex." Her voice rose, "It's incredible! It's impossible!"

Thomas shook his head in disbelief. Intelligently, he suggested, "Jessie, that can't be. It just *couldn't* be the same dog. For one thing, you know it is a very *far* distance from Broadwas to here, and for another, there is no reason for this dog to come to us. No. It must be a different runaway, or even a local dog that has been severely maltreated." He sounded deeply disappointed. "Just for a fleeting moment I thought the dog could possibly be cousin Rowland's, but coincidences like this never happen. They don't, Jessie."

Jessie disagreed with him and replied confidently, "I had a close look at Rowland's dog when we were at the garden party last summer, and the markings are about the same. I now think this could be the same dog." With a surprised lilt to her voice she said, "There is this *strange* patch of hair, right here. See here, where it is shorter than the rest? I wonder if that could be where the lightning struck him? Remember Rowland's letter?"

Thomas quickly agreed, "Yes. I do see what you mean." He acknowledged his sister's thoughts. "Jessie, perhaps you *are* correct in the assumption that this is Rowland's dog. Wouldn't it be strange to find out this is actually his missing dog?" Sounding hopeful again, he said with confidence, "It could be Rowland's dog. There couldn't possibly be anyone else with a dog matching the same description *and* wearing a collar with that identical name." He said quietly to his sister, "Wouldn't it be fantastic, if it were true?"

Jessie remembered my unusual name. "What are the chances of someone else naming their dog Shales? After all, it isn't a common Christian name." She stated, "In fact it's a surname – our William's wife's surname."

I was barely conscious as I listened to them converse over me. I fancied I was dreaming when I heard the lady mention the name Rowland. With closed eyes, I drifted in and out of this world feeling as if I was back at the farm – lying wounded, but wrapped in blankets within the warm glow of the inglenook fireplace, with the delicious smells of cooking food upon the air.

Thomas had started to wash the blood from the wound on my head, and all the while I was intent on staying conscious. I was afraid that if I allowed myself to completely drift away that I would never wake up again. I really didn't want to give up, or die, whatever dying really was. Not before I had found my new family and had seen London in all its glory.

The two continued to chatter. I understood some of their words, especially the name Rowland and the house Cotheridge Court, and I now knew, without any doubt, that they referred to my master. They *knew* who I was, and upon this realisation, I felt a great, weighty burden lift from my weary shoulders, as if carried away by unseen beings.

Thomas ventured, "Well, tomorrow morning I shall write to Rowland. If you'll do a drawing of the dog, then I'll put it in the letter. Then he will know if it is *his* dog or not. Meanwhile, we shall look after him and get him back on his feet. It'll be nice to have a dog around the place again." He stroked me gently, but I wished he would hug me to him again.

"Oh, Thomas. I regret, I had the opportunity to have my photograph taken with Shales, by Herbert, but I didn't bother. I wish I'd have done so now, as we'd have the proof needed that he is indeed Rowland's dog."

"Never mind, Jessie. A quick sketch will provide proof. Meanwhile, it'll take nearly a fortnight before we receive a reply... um... so we might as well make the dog feel at home. I'm actually happy at the thought of having a dog around the house again. I'll take him for walks, when his feet are healed."

After they had cleaned and bandaged my head wound, as well as my paws, Jessie offered me some warm milk, sweetened with honey, and I greedily lapped it up. It was delicious, and when I finished I laid my bandaged head back down upon the clean straw. There was a sensation of cottony softness all over me, and I felt as if I was floating upon a gentle cloud. I felt safe, very safe indeed. I fell into a bottomless sleep, and didn't wake until the next day.

* * *

THE FOLLOWING MORNING, WHEN I FINALLY AWOKE, it was to a warm breeze upon my face. It was sweetly scented with grass, and I opened my eyes and came face to face with Jasper. He blew into my face, and with his lips he gently nibbled me.

I was momentarily alarmed, but he calmly said, *"Shush now. I won't hurt thee, lad. I was just making sure thou art still in the land of the living. Thou looked dead to the world. How dost thou feel now, pet?"*

I wasn't used to being so close to a horse. Usually, I had been made to keep my distance from them, because they could easily kill a dog my size, with just one great kick. The enormity of Jasper's head, looming down over me from beyond his stall, was overwhelming, but his manner was obviously friendly. I sniffed his rounded muzzle, and I was amazed to discover its soft, aromatic velvetiness.

"They'll look after thee here," he said gently. *"Thou won't go short of food, and they look after all of us properly on this farm. If thou art lucky, thee'll be able to stay with us, because we don't have a dog on this farm. Not any more. No, siree."*

108

Jasper reassures Shales. "They'll look after thee here."

I loved to hear words like this, even if they were oddly spoken. I wasn't going to be harmed, I was going to be looked after, and that made me feel a whole lot better. I got up onto my feet, albeit a bit wobbly, and I dizzily tottered off outside the stable to relieve myself. My feet felt very strange, and when I looked down, I saw they had been bandaged, and they looked as if I was wearing four huge, white slippers with bows on top. I saw Thomas coming across the yard to the stable, so I met him with a weak but friendly wriggle of my body.

He reached down and carefully stroked my head, and said, "Well, now, it *is* good to see you on your feet. Come on, I'll find you some breakfast. Come on, Shales."

Thomas turned about and strolled off towards the large farmhouse, and then, once again, coaxed me to follow him. I eagerly followed him with awkward steps, even though I could barely walk, but stopped short at the kitchen doorway, where I lay down in the warm sunshine, which felt wonderfully invigorating. The warmth of the sun permeated every bone and bit of muscle, making me feel alive once again.

Within a moment, Jessie appeared with a large bowl of sops: bread soaked in milk, and the food of puppies and invalids. After this I was given a chuckie egg, which had been cooked in bacon fat. Dear Reader, it was so delicious that I'm probably salivating right now, just thinking about it, even though it happened many years ago. To this day, I love chuckie eggs that have been cooked in the pan alongside the bacon and sausages.

Whilst I ate, Jessie said to me, "Shales, today you're going to have a bath; that is if the sun stays out." She looked up at the sky as if looking for threatening clouds. "You can come inside and dry off in front of the fire." She declared, "I shall bath you myself, and then you'll be nice and clean and won't smell so dirty." As an afterthought, she said, "You really do smell rather bad, and your coat is full of grime and bits of twigs and leaves."

I hadn't the faintest idea what she was talking about, but I decided I would go along with it just as long as I was going to be fed and had a warm, dry place to sleep at night. I had begun to wonder if I'd imagined I'd met Jessie and Thomas before. Realising Jessie and Thomas still seemed familiar to me, in some way, it eventually came to me *where* I knew them from. I suddenly remembered, all at once. It was the tea party at Cotheridge Court. I don't know why I had forgotten about it, unless it was because of the sad state I'd been in. Suddenly, I remembered it all so clearly; they were cousins to my master, Rowland. Jessie was the lovely lady I had wanted to see again. How on earth had I been so lucky as to end up here, with them? I thought about this deeply. What if that man hadn't thrown that pail at me in a fit of anger, and had instead given me something to eat? I might have then set off down the road towards London on a full stomach, and passed by their farm, never knowing they were family, so to speak; I would have continued on and left them behind, never knowing their farm was here. Thinking about this really made me wonder about life, and all the 'what ifs' that came along with it.

I had such a good feeling about her and Thomas that I was willing to try anything they suggested. I found out what having a bath meant. It was all done outside, where I was plunged into a large zinc tub that was filled with warm, soapy water, and I was rubbed all over, rinsed with bucketfuls of clean, warm water, and then I came out spanking clean. It was completely different to being caught out in a torrential rainstorm. My hair was combed out and untangled, and Jessie was careful to not tear open the rather large scab, which was the result of the pail injury from the previous day. Afterwards, I felt wonderful and I smelt like a flower. I wanted to tear about in glee, but I still didn't have a lot of energy, and having a bath had tired me out. It was moggy speed for me, for the remainder of the day. She had dried me off with a towel, but I was damp and shivering, so she took me inside the house.

I crept along behind her on tender paws, though they had been generously re-bandaged, each one in a different colour of cloth. I lifted my thickly slippered feet, as if wading through deep snow.

The whole feeling of being inside a house unnerved me; this place was no barn or kennel. I felt I didn't belong inside such a lovely place. She led me into a room where there was a nice fire blazing away, and there, bade me lie down upon the carpet in front of it. I looked about in awe. This place was nothing like the kitchen in Master Rowland's house, nor the room above the kennels where Toothless George slept. This room, with its low, timbered ceiling, was full of expensive furniture, and there were soft, coloured carpets on top of the polished floorboards, and also, there were a variety of pictures all over the walls. It was all what Horatio had tried to explain to me about the interiors of houses, and now I saw and understood it all. I sniffed the air. It was mingled with curious new scents I would later come to know as beeswax, Macassar oil, tea, and coffee.

Hello, hello. I looked about the room. There were even more ladies in here. I was nervous, not knowing what was to come next.

Jessie addressed the ladies, "Julia and Lucy, this is Shales."

The one called Julia said, "Well, Jessie, we shall leave it up to you to inform Father that we have acquired a new dog. Shan't we, Lucy?"

Smiling, Lucy replied, "Yes, but I don't think Father shall mind at all. The dog looks friendly enough, as well as quite handsome. He's lovely, isn't he?"

With this, I wagged my tail, noisily banging it against the fire-guard. Julia came over to me and offered me a biscuit that she had taken from a plate by her side. I didn't snatch when I took it, so she smiled at me and carefully rubbed my ears. It tasted sweet and delicious. I hoped for more, but I could see the plate was empty. I had been given the last biscuit.

"I remember you from last summer," she whispered. "I, too, am sure you are Rowland's lost dog. Poor Mildred has been worried sick over you."

Jessie retold the story of her discovering me. "I was only looking at the last of the daffodils. They're almost finished now; most of them have turned brown. It was then I heard this poor dog cry out. He was in such a state! You should have seen him – it was an awful sight to see. And the blood! He was covered in it. Thomas will tell you so."

The other two ladies agreed that I *was* a poor dog and was lucky to be alive, and that it would be incredible if I had actually travelled from Worcestershire to Essex on my own, as that was a long way to travel on foot, for man or dog.

Another lady entered the room, and her name was Emily. She seemed to be younger than the others, though, in fact, she was older than Julia, and also smaller in stature. I found out that all four of them were sisters, and Thomas was their brother. I began to wonder if this was the family I was meant to live with. I had to think very hard about it all, because I hadn't yet made it to London. My journey was incomplete, and according to Horatio, London was still about twenty or so miles away. I questioned: what if I liked it here and they allowed me to stay? Would I stay, or would I set off one day and leave this place? I decided to take it one day at a time and I wouldn't hurry myself into making a decision to leave. London would still be there, waiting for me, should I decide to make tracks again.

* * *

OBVIOUSLY I *HAD* LANDED ON MY FEET. It was a large farm with a lot of activity, as it was springtime. The days had warmed up and the threat of snow was long, long gone. The leaves were coming out on the trees and there was the buzz of insects in the air; the bees had come out of their hives. There was still even more daylight added to each day, as the evenings continually grew longer. The men were working in the fields, ploughing them and getting them ready for planting. There were horses other than Jasper, and also quite a few sheep as well as pigs and other farm livestock, such as milch cows and cattle. Not to forget the chuckies who laid those lovely eggs I loved to eat.

We were right on the road that led to London, and as the days passed, I sometimes would stand out in the middle of the road when the traffic was quiet, and I'd gaze off far into the distance. Yes, I was tempted. London was calling to me, but somehow, after just a few days, the pull was becoming fainter and fainter. I was content here at this farm, and only after being here just a short period of time. I now wondered if this could be my new home; that is, if I was allowed to stay. Thomas took me out every day, taking time off from managing the farm to walk with me, to where beyond the fields, at the back of the farm, there was a wood. It was called Ten Acre Wood, and I loved to walk through there with him. He would eagerly throw sticks for me to fetch, and he'd laugh at me as I hobbled upon my bandaged feet. He was quickly becoming my friend. The earth in the woods smelt pungent with the rotting of last year's leaves, and rabbits darted about the ground, while chattering squirrels jumped from tree to tree. I was on the mend, and I felt my strength come back to me in leaps and bounds.

* * *

THOMAS HAD WRITTEN THAT LETTER TO ROWLAND, my master, and was awaiting a reply. Being about me, I think you should know what was said. It went something like this:

Wayletts,
22nd April, 1881

Dear Cousin Rowland,

I write to you with the most unusual news. We have had a dog appear on our farm, and it resembles your missing dog right down to the very name. This dog, black with white markings, arrived yesterday on the 21stst of April. Sadly, it was injured, but we hope it will make a full recovery. The dog was very thin and unkempt, as well as having the name Shales engraved upon his collar.

Jessie has made a drawing showing the dog's markings. If this is your dog we shall keep it here as one of our own until you can come to Wayletts. Jessie anxiously awaits your reply. She is nursing the dog back to health... doting on it in her usual way.

On another subject of interest, we are getting ready for planting. The potatoes are already in the ground, but the corn and oats are not yet in – but will be, shortly. One of our men was attacked by our largest and most vicious sow, resulting in his being bitten on the back of the leg, and subsequently, has an illness from the infected wound. I am taking over Wayletts, as the farm cannot manage being short-handed, and with there being no help available from the area due to the great demand elsewhere for extra hands, it needs a foreman.

Also, I can see why Father wants to get rid of the farm – as a merchant in coal, that is a more profitable industry than farming. I would like to be master of both, but he has asked me to choose between them. Alas, I have chosen coal, and along with it the conveniences of London society etc. I think Father is hoping that Charles C. will take over Wayletts – but I wager he will not want to.

The season is over (hunting), and my horse Jasper (the best any man could want) is going to enjoy the summer as being a horse of leisure. Jessie is nudging me as I write – she says to send you her love.

I hope your household and family are well. Enclosed is a letter from Lucy, for you to give to Mildred, as well as a note for Auntie Emily.

Your Cousin,
Thomas Rowland

* * *

I WAS JUST BEGINNING TO FEEL AT HOME, and my new surroundings were becoming less strange, when the master of the house returned. He was called Augustus, and he was the father of Thomas and the ladies. There were also other children of his whom I had not yet met. Two of them returned with him; they were Edmund, who was older than Thomas Rowland, and Charles Clement, who was the youngest of all Augustus's children.

I was outside having a nap, on the grass beneath an old tree, when the carriage rolled into the farmyard. I had been dreading this moment, with full knowledge that the master could send me packing. I wanted to stay, if they would have me. Jessie and the others came out of the house to greet their two brothers and the older man, their father. The well-dressed gentlemen, wearing top hats and holding onto walking-sticks, emerged from the carriage bearing smiles and affectionate greetings, and all appeared to be in a merry mood. This boded well for me, and so Jessie couldn't wait to announce my presence. Immediately, upon greeting her father, my arrival was disclosed, it being the very first topic of conversation, and then I was called for by Augustus himself.

I responded eagerly, just hoping that this gentleman would allow me to stay and be well looked after. Augustus commanded me to sit, and so sit I did, like a proper, well-trained dog. I remembered him; he was the coal merchant who enjoyed puffing on a pipe. I offered him my right paw and he laughed, then bent down and shook it. I smiled by way of lightly wagging my tail, and then I gently jumped on him. He did not admonish me, but instead stroked the back of my neck and shoulders. Luckily, I left no marks on his suit of clothes, as my feet had been freshly bandaged.

"Jessie, I see you've been working very hard while I've been in London. There's no harm in the dog staying for a short while, on a trial basis. Mind you, if he damages anything in the house, *then* it'll be the stable for him." He wagged his finger at her, as if laying down the law.

"Thank you, Father." She was evidently pleased. "Shales *has* behaved himself all this time," she stressed.

She then went on to explain that they were waiting for a response from Thomas's letter, and that I might be only staying with them temporarily. When the entire story was disclosed about my arrival in such a sorry state, the old man gave me a pitying look.

Thomas looked his father in the face and boldly said, "He's a lovely dog. I've grown extremely attached to him." Then he reached down and patted my side, all the while watching for his father's reaction.

That was wonderful, to be spoken of with such affection. Augustus pulled his watch out of his fob, and after seeing the time, changed the subject and announced, "I'm ready for tea. Let's go inside now, and bring the dog in as well. I might as well get used to having him about. Besides, he's terribly thin and needs feeding up; just look at the sight of him."

So, we all went inside, and the maid served us a lovely afternoon tea. At these times, I always received a biscuit or small piece of cake on my own little plate. Jessie had even given me my own tea bowl, and I was allowed to have a small amount of tea to drink, which I enjoyed tremendously. Oh, what a happy environment when I wasn't anywhere near the kitchen.

* * *

DEAR READER, I do *have* to tell you about the cook. We got off on the wrong foot from the very start, so *everything* wasn't all so perfect at Wayletts, after all. I seemed to have either offended the cook, or she simply hated dogs. I'm not sure which it was, but the outcome was always the same. She shouted at me, at times refused to feed me, and would even threaten to hit me with

116

anything close at hand. I was frightened of her. My water bowl and food bowl were in the kitchen, so there *were* times when I absolutely had to enter that dreadful place. If I went anywhere near the table or pantry she would quickly slap me cruelly, across the top of my head, right near my head wound. Her behaviour was like that of the pail-throwing man, and I actually wondered if they were somehow related to each other.

Thomas actually caught her being cruel to me, and he threatened her with dismissal if she harmed me in any way. I'd only been at Wayletts a couple of days, and Jessie had asked the cook, Eliza, to feed me. Well, she led me out of the kitchen and into the yard, and there she slowly emptied the bowl, which contained my meal, upon the cobbles. In doing so, some of the food bounced off my head, as I had started to eat before she had finished upending it, resulting in my clean head being full of lumps of meat and globs of gravy, as well as my having to eat off the ground, and not from a bowl. I knew right away there was something unusual in this behaviour, because I had never before in my life had a bowl of food turned upside down onto the stone cobbles. An insult is an insult – even to a dog. I felt humiliated.

Thomas had witnessed this horrible scene and had berated Eliza for it. He suggested that Jessie or one of the other sisters should become responsible for feeding me, as he didn't trust the cook. Jessie was very annoyed, to put it mildly, when she had to clean me up and remove the sticky gravy from the top of my head and snout. There also resulted another problem – where to place my food and water bowls if they were to no longer be in the kitchen? But that was easily solved. Jessie placed them on the landing, beyond the top of the dark panelled staircase, where the cook was not usually permitted to go. There was a second, smaller staircase that the servants used, to gain access to the loft where they slept. The housemaid simply adored me, so I didn't have to worry about *her* mistreating me. Should Eliza ever have to sweep the stairs, which was not part of her usual cook's duties, she was not permitted to go beyond the top step, where the family's bedchambers were, unless she was asked to do so. The landing became neutral territory, sort of an Eliza-free territory.

* * *

ONE AFTERNOON, about a week after I'd met Augustus, he called me to him. We were having afternoon tea in the front sitting-room, which we always used in the afternoons and evenings. Its spacious size easily accommodated the large family, and was filled with plenty of over-stuffed soft chairs and settees. He commanded me to sit, and sit I did. I offered him my paw in greeting, and he readily accepted it. I was pleased that I was fitting in around such a lovely family. He stroked my head and inspected the spot where the pail had collided with my skull, and then, obviously satisfied with the healing wound, he gently rubbed my cheek with his knuckles. I thumped my tail in response to his show of affection. I liked this gentleman with the greying hair who was fond of his pipe. I remembered him from the previous summer as being one of several brothers. He was a very kind, intelligent man, and he loved his children, and he was kind to his servants, but he also commanded respect, which he received with enthusiastic bobs and curtseys from the female servants, and nods from beneath raised hats from the male farm workers. Jasper had been correct when he had told me that I would be well looked after in this place.

"Well, at least he's friendly," commented Augustus, with an air of satisfaction.

"He's very affectionate," volunteered Jessie, as if it was all that mattered.

"Yes, he may well be, thanks to you and Thomas. I have here a letter from your cousin Rowland, which has just come in the post," Augustus informed her. He waved it about in the air. "If you'll all pay attention then I shall read it to you, and we'll see what my nephew has to say on the matter of this dog."

I was all ears. The letter concerned my situation, and I now knew that I would rather remain with this family than move on or be returned to my previous master. I was happy, and my fondness for the family grew deeper with each passing day. I had fond memories of Master Rowland, but I felt my home, or as Horatio had put it to me, my destiny, was elsewhere, and that elsewhere was with Thomas and Jessie.

> *Dear Uncle Augustus,*
> *I write to you, dear Uncle, and also to my cousins, especially*
> *Thomas Rowland, regarding the dog named Shales. I was*

astounded to read Thomas's letter describing the appearance of the dog. It must be my farm dog that disappeared many weeks ago. The drawing that Jessie did is the spitting image of my dog, the one that is named Shales. Also, the fact that the name Shales was upon the dog's collar also identifies him as my dog and, I'm sure, no one else's.

I have decided that if you are willing to look after him, then, therefore, you may keep him. Actually, I am more relieved that he has come to no harm, than concerned about having him returned to me, and doing trials with him would be out of the question. I know he shall be well looked after, but if he becomes too much for you, please write to me and I shall come and collect him. I now have another sheepdog at the farm, so the return of Shales shall be left up to you. That is, if you are agreeable.

I eagerly await your reply regarding the future of Shales.

Your obedient nephew,
Rowland Comyns

So, there it was, in plain words; my future was up to Augustus and the rest of the family. I just hoped he would allow me to remain and become a permanent member of his family. I didn't want to look for another family. This was where I wanted to live. I thought really hard until I thought my eyes were going to pop, *"Please let me stay."*

Jessie clamped her hands together, and tears ran down her cheeks. "Please, Father, can Shales stay with us?" she begged. "He's good in the house – he doesn't make any messes, nor does he chew the furniture or the carpets."

Augustus strolled about the room, stopping to lift a book here and an ornament there. He glanced at me, and then at the others, all of whom were awaiting his reply. We must have looked a picture. I was at the front, and the rest of them: Thomas Rowland, Edmund, Charles Clement, Lucy, Julia, Emily, and Jessie were grouped behind me, awaiting the verdict. I felt my mouth go dry in anticipation. If he said no, where would I go?

He faced the crowded room. "I think it is about time we had a dog in the house again. Now listen to me carefully; there are dogs and there are *dogs*. Some work the farms and others become pampered pets. I agree the companionship will do us good, but it must be for the rest of his life." He smiled, "I say, William and Mary in Gorleston will be surprised when they read that *we* have Shales." Augustus shook a finger at them. "He will have to accompany us to London, where he will need walking on a daily basis. I won't have him wandering loose about Hackney, because it is just as dangerous a place for a dog there, as it is being at loose in the countryside."

I could not believe my ears. London! I heard him say London! I was moving to London! I wagged my tail and darted about the room, making a fool of myself, but I was so excited I simply had to express my feelings. Thomas rushed to open the door for me, but before he could get there, I jumped the low window-sill – it being a warm day the window was wide open – and I landed upon the grass on the other side. Thomas then opened the door and led the others outside, where I ran about in tight circles at top speed until I became breathless. Home. I was home at last. As I giddily flopped down upon the grass, gasping for air, I vowed I would do *anything* for this family. Anything. Forever.

120

IX

THOMAS ROWLAND

*"I was not going to be the star of the
hour."*

SUMMER, 1881

I SPENT THE REST OF THOSE LATE SPRING AND EARLY SUMMER DAYS basking in the warm, soft Essex sunshine, and I thoroughly enjoyed my new life of leisure, although once in a while my exceptional talent for herding was called upon to sort out the unruly livestock on the farm. The four sisters, Jessie, Lucy, Julia and Emily, lived at the farm all the time, but the men would disappear for the duration of the week, returning only at the week's end. Thomas was no longer required to manage the farm, as the man who normally did that job was back on his feet, after surviving the serious illness due to being attacked by the rather vicious sow. On Monday mornings the men would be driven to the railway station, in nearby Ongar, where they would catch the early train to Hackney, and there, during the week, they lived at the house in Cassland Road. In the daytime they worked at the warehouse and dealt with their business of acquiring and selling coal. They were coal merchants and agents, and had their large warehouse in Hackney, as well as a second, smaller one with an office in Stoke Newington.

Thomas, however, spent more time with me when at Wayletts than the other men did. It was as if I was his dog, and it was he I preferred to romp about with, even though I was terribly fond of all the others. I soon began to know when their carriage would be coming down the road, returning the men for their weekend sojourn, and I would wait for them at the edge of the dusty road, gazing in the direction of Ongar and listening for the tell-tale hoof beats of our horses. Thomas was dark-haired, and he had a swarthy complexion that only comes from spending lots of time outside in the sun and getting lots of fresh air. His hair was short and straight. He had clipped sideburns, and he was fit, lithe without being skinny, and he moved about as someone only does when they spend their entire lives around horses. To put it simply, in looks and manner, he was a younger version of Edmund, but it was Thomas whom I would always greet first. The carriage would turn into the drive, and then I would race with it for the short distance before it came to a stop in front of the house. Thomas would step down from the carriage, saying, "Fetch your stick," and I would fetch one for him to throw. It became a routine we never broke.

Many times Thomas took me for walks through Ten Acre Wood, which was a place such as out of a fairy tale. It was close by, at the back end of our fields, but it wasn't the only wood. No, just beyond, there was Twenty Acre Wood, and even further away was Icehouse Wood, and there was also Knightsland Wood. All were fabulous places to wander about, where old, gnarly trees grew, and footpaths, beaten smooth by hundreds of years of wear from travellers' feet snaked throughout, and the woods were cool and shaded from the heat of the summer sun. Those woods were a paradise never since encountered anywhere else by me again.

Sometimes we would cut across the fields to not so far-off places, sporting names like Coopersale Hall, Toot Hill, and Ongar, thus spending the entire afternoon away from the farm. His late grandfather's house, Coopersale Hall, where his father, Augustus, had lived as a child, was a place he often liked to ride to, though we never called in. We stayed within the shelter of the surrounding pine trees and discreetly passed it by, not wanting to intrude upon the new residents. We would pause briefly, before continuing on our way.

Such as on those adventurous occasions, I would run behind him as he rode his beloved chestnut hunter, Jasper. Frequently we would stop at a favourite pub, and one of them, the White Bear, was only a short distance from the farm. In that place, I would accompany him inside and lay at his feet, as he drank his ale in the darkened interior that smelt deeply of tobacco smoke and spilt ale. At the Kings Head, in Ongar, I always sought comfort near his booted feet, beneath the table or bar, as that place, especially the back room, seemed to have an atmosphere that reminded me somewhat of those ghost riders who had nearly run me over, though, admittedly, it had a friendly and inviting atmosphere. Thomas liked the place, and at times we would go down to the river at the back, ale in hand, and he would sit beneath one of the great old trees that provided ample shade. I would swim about or paddle in the cool river as he drained his tankard, and kingfishers would flit by whilst blackbirds sang their songs in the branches above us.

He was popular. The locals liked him. I admired him, and I would have followed him anywhere, had he asked. He was a wonderful rider, taking any railed fence or gate with the confidence of a seasoned hunter. Jasper would leap over, clearing it by inches, with Thomas low over his neck, and I would follow close behind, my feet springing off the top rail, as I was so agile in those days I could easily jump the height of a five-bar gate. Thomas would always shout out words of encouragement, not feeling the need to use his ivory-handled crop, and Jasper and I would run even faster, and I would try to overtake them, but I never did, always coming in last. What daredevils we were! What love I felt for him!

Also, I loved those excursions into public places, because then I could study people and notice their differences according to their lot in life. Incredibly, sometimes I would know what they were thinking, and some of them I knew were men to stay away from. Others I took to be kind and caring. I enjoyed meeting new people, but most of all, I felt *wanted,* as Thomas obviously enjoyed my companionship, and I was introduced as his "new dog" and then later, I became "*My dog, Shales.*"

Ten Acre Wood was my favourite wood in the entire area in and about Stanford Rivers. In the very early weeks of that summer Thomas spent many hours there with me. I'd follow him around the farm, and quite often he would stop by the group of beehives – a strange place of activity that created something that tasted wonderful, called honey – to whisper soft, encouraging words to the bees. Sometimes he would sit beneath a tree in a relaxed pose, his shirtsleeves rolled up to his elbows, and would read letters that he had collected at the post office, located in the nearby White Bear. Quite often, after reading one of these letters, he would take a short stub of a pencil and he would write a reply, and then we would make all haste back to the White Bear, where he would post it off to some mysterious destination. Other times he would look through his little brass telescope and secretly study the local birds and wildlife, making rough drawings of what he saw.

When we walked I would run ahead of him, anticipating his throw of a stick. He had a good arm and could throw quite a distance. I loved it there. It was like a secret little world completely separate from everyday life. It was cool under the shade of the large old trees with their gnarly limbs, and the air was soothing in the heat of the summer. The aroma of the pungent mosses and peaty soil drove me mad, and there were so many varied scents to follow that it became one of my most favourite places to be, and I sometimes even went there on my own. The leafy treetops always seemed to be full of noisy birds, and it was a favourite retreat for magpies, and at night owls hooted, reminding us that the wood never slept. Large squirrels bounded from limb to limb and filled the wood with their noisy chatter.

There were rabbits living in the wood, and I chased them for hours on end, but I never managed to catch one; they were too quick for me. If I had caught one, I wouldn't have hurt it in any way; I would have let it go. It was just a challenge to outwit them as they zigzagged about, but they always got the better of me, and they would quickly disappear into a small hole in the ground, like water going down a drain. There was even a family of foxes that Thomas kept his eye on. I knew farmers hated foxes, as they could easily decimate flocks of hens and geese. Thomas monitored their den and their activity in the area. If they raided our farm then he would know where to find them.

Shortly after my arrival at the farm I learnt that the family was considering moving to another house in Hackney, from their residence on Cassland Road, which wasn't London City, but I think close enough for them to refer to it as London. Whether it was London or Hackney, I didn't care. I now knew I would go wherever the family went, and that I would never leave them. They only resided at the farm in the summer months, as during the winter months they stayed in Hackney, or London, or wherever it was we were moving to for the winter. The sisters spent the summer preparing for the move, even though they wouldn't be changing residences until the following year. Long

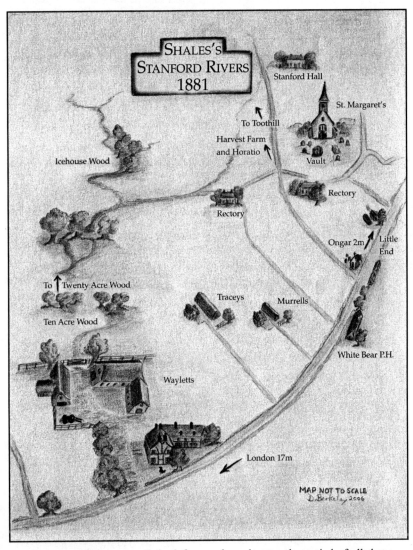

lists were drawn up, and the loft was cleaned out and emptied of all that was ancient and useless. Aged trunks were opened. The dust caused me to sneeze violently as their contents revealed old, musty-smelling clothing that had been packed decades before, which had also resided in the loft at Blakes

Mansion (the family's previous residence), and some of it was so ancient it had come from Coopersale Hall. Most of it was sent away to a local charity; the lovely material in the old coats and frocks that hadn't been moth-eaten was good enough to be reused, according to Jessie, who didn't like anything to go to waste. Old pieces of dusty furniture were sorted through, and what wasn't wanted was sold off. I sensed we would not be returning to the farm after the move in the following year, but I wasn't absolutely sure, it all being a bit confusing and very mysterious to me. It saddened me to think about leaving such a wonderful place, but I kept my hopes up that London would prove to be just as exciting.

For a short period of time, in early summer, Emily went away. She spent a week at her brother William's, on the coast, near Yarmouth. He owned a hotel there, in a place called Gorleston. They didn't see much of William and his family, as Gorleston-on-Sea was a fair distance away. Also, he was the only member of my new family whom I hadn't yet met. What I did know was that William was the eldest of Augustus's children, and that he didn't farm and he didn't sell coal. As for his hotel, I wondered if someday I would ever have the pleasure of visiting it.

One day, as I lay upon the lush, green grass watching the goings on at the farm, as labourers came and went from the huge long barns, and cows mooed amidst the cluck of the wandering hens, I heard a meow, and Horatio boldly appeared out of nowhere. I was astounded to see him come strolling up to me. How did he know I was there? Oh, what a lovely surprise! We greeted each other like long-lost brothers. He rubbed himself up and down the trunk of a tree, leaving wisps of his silky hair stuck to the bark, all the while purring and saying how glad he was to see me.

I greeted him with wagging tail. *"I'm fain to see thee here."* Then I asked him, *"How on earth did thee find me?"*

"Wouldst thou believe I have been awl over Stanford Rivers looking for thee? I have asked evwry cat in the neighbourhood, an' finally, one chap wiff the gift for tarrying and chatting said he'd seen a new dog at this farm. I thowt I would see if it was thee, and that perhaps thou hadn't gone off to London after awl."

He slumped down upon the grass in a furry heap and said, *"I am exhauwthsted! I'm all done in from being chased by a fox. I was afeared for my loife!"*

I thumped my tail upon the ground and gave myself a good long body stretch, as I said, *"I am very glad to see thee, Horatio. Everything has turned out champion. I have been accepted into this wonderful family, who, believe it or not, happen to be cousins to my old master, Rowland. Best of all, they love me. We are all moving to London for the winter, so I'll get there, eventually. You nearly missed finding me at all! I could easily have not stopped at this place, and I'd be somewhere else today, and you would have had a wasted journey."*

"I wath desperate to find thee, but I wath sure thou were still in thith area. I can't explain it, but I knew thee were clothe by. I greatly need to warn thee."

Horatio looked at me, and then very seriously said, *"I had a dream abowt thee, and in it thou were in tewwible danger. It wath more than just a dream. Shales, thou muth be careful! There wath a man wearink a long coat and a top hat, and he had a knoife. I saw him in my dream, and thou were there with him. It wath London. I know it wath; as sure as I know the sun will rise tomorrow."* He fairly whispered this last bit as if he was remembering something he'd seen and not dreamt.

I was beginning to feel a great sense of dread, but I suggested lightly, *"Perhaps it was just a dream, Horatio. They're silly things. I never take much notice of them."*

Horatio answered me in a low but firm voice. *"No, Shales. They aren't alwayths silly. Thou shouldst take notice of them. Sometimes they are glimpthes into the future. I saw thee ath clear as I can see thee now, but I think it ith a few years away before it happens. Thou seemed to be older than thou art now."*

He was insistent. *"Thou muth heed my warning, and always be verwy careful, and especially at night. Beware of people wielding knoives!"*

All I could do was promise Horatio that I would be careful and always be on the lookout for danger. What more could I say? I wasn't sure what to think, but I did realise he thought it important enough to look me up when he didn't know if I was still in the area, or if I had found my way to London.

Then, Horatio looked at me with a far-off gaze to his enormous, green eyes that were the size of saucers, and then he leaned forward as if to inspect the hairs on my muzzle. He peered into my face as if he saw something hiding there. I wondered if perhaps a lop was scurrying about through my hair, though I didn't feel the least bit itchy.

Horatio, a fey cat, warns Shales of danger.

I had the sudden urge to lick him right between his eyes, as my heart felt a sudden burst of emotion for him.

Before I could do so, he gently asked, *"Shales, dost thou know what a funeral ith?"*

Without thinking, I flippantly answered, *"No. Never heard of one before."* I cocked my head. *"Why?"*

He replied with downcast eyes, *"Oh, noffink in particular."* He then peered at the grass beneath his feet and pretended to inspect it closely. *"You'll find owt sometime."*

Wanting to change the subject to something I did know about, I decided to tell him about the cook. I told him about the time she emptied my food all over the cobbles. There had been another incident when she had swung at me with a rather large and heavy frying pan. Luckily, she had missed me. I explained that if I was in the kitchen when she was chopping food with that great knife of hers, she would become angry, and the chopping would become louder and louder, and she would then scowl and mumble, all the while looking out of the corner of her eye at me. She frightened me to the point where I hoped she wouldn't be coming with us to London. I asked him if she was the one with the knife.

"No, Shales. It ith definitely a man, and he ith well-dressed and educated. I think he is a gentleman, but one who has evil in his heart."

I wanted to change the subject again, not liking its feeling of dread and impending doom, so I suggested we find something for him to eat and let him rest his weary body. I smuggled him into the house without anyone noticing his presence, and conveniently enough, the door to the kitchen was wedged open, allowing us entry. We dashed inside before the dragon-of-a-cook, who at that moment happened to be occupied with kneading bread (her brow was furrowed in concentration) could see us, and we ran silently upstairs to the landing where my bowls were. Someone had thoughtfully put out some tasty morsels of cooked meat, and I offered it all to Horatio. He ate all of it, though he chewed the large bits with some difficulty, they being too large for his dainty feline mouth.

Eventually, he licked his greasy lips, burped quietly, and then asked, *"Any chanthe of finding a cosy plathe to sleep?"* He cast a glance over his shoulder before commenting, *"Thou hast done well for thyself. Thy new master is obviously well-to-do. Well done, Shales, my lad."*

Of course, he would be tired after his long trek. Being hospitable, I took him into Jessie's bedroom, as her door was open, and he stealthily slipped under her bed for a nap. I told him to keep his head low, as I didn't know how any of them would react to finding a cat in the house. He assured me he wouldn't move until the next morning. I crept upstairs several times and watched him as he slept, curled up in a ball upon the bare floorboards, with a blue and white chamber-pot sitting just inches away from him. I just wanted to make sure he was safe and his presence hadn't been discovered. The next morning, after eating a substantial breakfast, which was intended for myself, he left.

His final words to me, as he started to walk away towards Ten Acre Wood, were spoken clearer than normal, and were spoken with such great emotion. *"I'm so sorwy. I hope it doesn't happen."* He looked over his shoulder, saying, *"I'm jes an old cat. Wot do I know?"* Then he hung his head low.

I watched him stroll away with that purposeful feline stride of his. Only a true friend would do what he did – walk for days to find and warn me of something dark, looming in my future. All I could do in return was go with him part way home, as I couldn't stay away from the farm for too long in case the family thought I had run away and done some sort of a flit. I bounded after him, and told him I wouldn't let him go all the way on his own. I guided him through the woods and pastures, which were now becoming familiar to me, until we came to St Margaret's Church, and from there it was familiar territory for him, where, from that place, he knew his way home. I had travelled with him for nearly one day at his pace, it taking us that long with his slow and careful steps, and then I quickly returned to the farm with all haste. All I could think of was that he, Horatio, would make it home safe and sound, and nothing harmful would befall him, there being a genuine danger from lurking foxes, badgers, and vicious dogs. As we travelled, he never mentioned my dark future again, but instead wished me happiness in my new venture. I knew I would miss him tremendously. And you know what? I did. Who would have thought that a dog and a cat could share a special bond between themselves? Some of you readers will understand this, but others, I'm sad to say – you won't.

* * *

I HAD BECOME ACCUSTOMED TO THE USUAL HABIT of Thomas returning to the farm at the week's end, with his father and brothers, if not sometimes mid-week, in the early evening hours, when then he would always rush to his bedchamber to change into his boots and breeches. The weather would be clement on these mid-week visits, and, so therefore, we would always go off on adventures throughout the countryside, just Thomas, Jasper, and me. I didn't at all question it when he sometimes left on a Sunday evening to go to the city, whereas his father and brothers would remain until early Monday morning. So, on one particular week's end, near the end of May, when Thomas did not return on the Saturday afternoon with his father and brothers, I clung to the rest of the family for comfort and attention, with the hope he would drop by during the following week.

It was during that Sunday afternoon, when everyone was letting their dinner go down as we relaxed in the front sitting-room, that Thomas became the main topic of discussion. They were mostly engaged in reading either newspapers or books, and they were still dressed in their Sunday church attire. The sisters all enquired as to his whereabouts; they were picking and pulling apart Thomas's excuse for being away the entire week's end, and his father, in a state of henpecked unrest, impatiently stated, "He has told me he is staying over at the Foster residence in Stoke Newington. He has done it often, of late, though not in the last fortnight. So, what of it?"

Thinking that his firm tone would put an end to his daughters' incessant wittering, he shoved his pipe between his lips and drew hard upon it, then reached downwards and pulled a newspaper from the spent pile that lay upon the floor at Edmund's feet, whilst emitting several puffs of fragrant smoke. He removed his pipe for a brief moment.

"I'm reading," he said, as he opened his paper. It was his way of preventing his being interrupted. He crossed his legs, and as he did so, glanced over at Edmund, who had been on the quiet side for the most part of the day.

Edmund smirked and pulled his face, as if he was going to speak up and say something of dire importance, or, just perhaps, something of a trivial nature, but he seemed to change his mind, and he cast his eyes back to his own paper. His father, in happening to notice this, prompted Edmund to reveal what he knew about his younger brother's sudden and mysterious preoccupation (with that Newington parish) outside office hours.

"Edmund, can you enlighten me? Is Stoke Newington really that busy that he needs to work extra hard, or is he off on a lark?"

"Dad, all I know is that Thomas says he is visiting with the Foster family and working a bit extra at the office for something or another, and there isn't any reason not to believe him. He has drummed up some extra trade over there: money is coming in. However, seeing that David works for us, I don't think it is right that Thomas spends so much time with him, nor lodges with his family. It doesn't seem right. Granddad wouldn't like it; well, it isn't proper. It's too familiar; they're not our sort." He added quietly, "It just isn't done."

"Ah. I see. But, besides that, you don't believe him, do you?"

Augustus was not in the least interested in reading his newspaper. Slowly, as if the flame of a burning candle had become brighter, it became evident to those who watched him intently that he suspected something underhanded about Thomas. He cast his eyes about the room, they falling upon each of his grown children. Lastly, he stared at Edmund, who was appearing to concentrate on *The Times*. With his very own newspaper now forgotten, Augustus slowly folded the pages and set it aside in an unconscious manner.

"You think he is up to something. It's nothing to do with his being too familiar with David Foster and his family." This came out as a statement and not as a question. "There is something the matter. What is it?"

Augustus watched Edmund intently; his son rudely ignored him. This ill manner was completely out of character for Edmund – it appeared he was more interested in reading a newspaper than answering his father's questions.

I looked at Edmund, such as a dog is wont to do with a bird or a rabbit. Something was bothering him, and I could sense his unease. I wriggled about on the carpet in a silly fashion, to draw attention away from him, but I was ignored.

I was not going to be the star of the hour.

Augustus had been smoking, but his tobacco was spent. He tapped out the ashes, and then carefully set his pipe down on a tray that rested upon a small table at his side. Then, he stood up and hooked his thumbs into the armpits of his grey waistcoat, exclaiming with annoyance as he faced his second son, "I can tell just by looking at your face that you've got something to hide. You never could tell a good lie!"

He leaned towards Edmund, and said matter-of-factly, "You always got caught out when you were a child."

Edmund looked away, as if remembering a guilty deed from long ago, then smiled. "It's been a lot of years since then."

My master then stood up straight, and then ordered in a demanding tone, "What is your brother up to?"

Edmund closed his eyes as if remembering something from the far-off past, but I think he was just trying to choose his words carefully, and he slowly replied, "I think there may be a woman involved, but I'm not entirely sure. I do know that on the night of the census – remember, it was a Sunday night and that he was in Stoke Newington, but later, when I asked young David about it, he said Thomas hadn't been to their house at all that Sunday. Thomas came in to work at our Hackney warehouse later that Monday morning, after the census, as innocent as ever. I'm not sure I believed him. I don't know where he was on the night of the census. He hasn't told me." His eyes opened, and he turned another page of the newspaper he'd been reading, obviously hoping the subject would be changed.

He was being bothered by something and it regarded Thomas. That was evident, even to me. But why not tell the family? Was it so awful?

Charles and the sisters all stopped what they were doing. They were all reading to themselves; well, they were pretending to read – the books and magazines lay open, but their eyes were now more intent upon their father and brother than the matter they were reading. They looked at their father, to see what his reaction would be to this bit of shocking news regarding his third son.

I was very aware that the air in the room seemed to have somewhat changed, and that a storm was about to brew; the fox was in the henhouse. I wondered whether to scarper for safety or to remain and hear what Thomas had been up to. There was a choice spot behind the settee where I could listen without being noticed, and to there I quietly slithered and waited for Edmund's interrogation to continue.

"What is this about a woman? What woman could he possibly be involved with?"

The room went deathly silent, except for the tick-tocking of the mantel clock.

"You just said you thought it was a woman whom he had visited! Tell me what is going on!" demanded my master as he sat back down in his chair. He pulled at his collar as if he needed air, and gasped loudly, "He's *only* twenty years old!"

I became alarmed and I cringed inwardly, tucking my tail between my legs, as there was rage in my master's voice.

Edmund, wearing his Sunday best and seated across from his father, uncrossed his perfectly creased trouser legs, tossed his newspaper to the floor, shook his head slowly from side to side, and confessed, "He hasn't said *anything* to me, but I have smelt perfume on his coat from time to time, and that has been fairly recently. He has been going out the occasional evening from Cassland Road, and hasn't been returning home until very late. Armstrong complained to me, because she had to get up in the early hours of the morning and let him in, disturbing her sleep. When I mentioned to him his smelling of ladies' perfume, and this just recently, he replied, 'Oh, do I smell of ladies' perfume? I didn't know. Fancy that!' As if he were ignorant of the fact. Dad, I warned him that he ought to be careful in his activities and that word could get back to you. Why, just this Friday morning I told him to sort himself out. He told me nothing would come of it and that he was just having a bit of fun. I warned him to be careful if there was a woman involved. I also told him that I'd tell you; that is, if it continued."

"Did you not think to tell me before now? Such as last week, or even a fortnight ago?" Augustus raised his voice, "You, of all people, should have said something!"

The finger of responsibility was pointed at Edmund. His father harshly criticised him. "You're his older brother by nearly twelve years, and you are responsible for him, just as the two of you are responsible for young Charles."

Edmund moaned loudly and leaned back in his chair. He rubbed his chin with his right hand, as if nervous. In a low and quiet voice, he apologised.

"Sorry, Dad. I'm *really* sorry. I should have said something to you by now, but I thought I'd wait until I saw him this week. I was going to give him a hard time over it. I hoped to get to the bottom of it without bothering you at all."

"Coming from you, son, I accept that. Wayward brothers can be difficult to deal with. I know all about it. I myself was a bit of a handful." He then said lightly, "You being here, in Stanford Rivers, doesn't in any way seem to be preventing your brother from getting into any bother, if that's what he's up to." He suggested, "If you had gone over there today you might have sorted the entire affair out without my even knowing about it. *Now* that I do know there is something peculiar going on with your brother, I'll have to see about it myself... no, the two of us shall see to it – together."

My master looked angry as he got up out of his chair and went and stood in front of the window and looked out into the direction of the road. The stagecoach was passing by, and the sound of the horses' hoofs could be heard through the opened windows. From where I lay, I could see his back was straight and his shoulders were tensed. Charles and his sisters were deathly still and quiet. They appeared to be uncomfortable, but they did not excuse themselves and leave the room.

"If he is seeing a woman then he should have informed me, as *her* parents would not want *her* seeing Thomas without their knowledge; after all, he is not yet of age. Things like this have to be done properly and not in subterfuge." He turned and faced the room, just as one of the sisters, Lucy, spoke up in Thomas's defence.

"Thomas wouldn't do anything like that. I am sure he is busy right now, taking charge of the Newington office."

The other sisters nodded in agreement. Emily protested to her father, "He wouldn't lie to us, or deceive us. Not Thomas."

Julia suggested, "We would have heard rumours by now, if he *has* been behaving indiscreetly."

"Rumours?" snorted Edmund rudely. "I would think any indiscretions would reach the front page of *The Times* before they get to Stanford Rivers. We are so isolated living here that you can't hear the beat of the local drums!"

Jessie quietly said, "Sadly, Edmund is correct. What news of family do we get out here unless someone thinks to write us a letter?"

Impatiently, my new master cried, "Stop! Enough of this friction; I'll get to the bottom of it soon enough." More civilly, he said, "If none of you know anything of your brother's whereabouts, then there is nothing more to be said on the matter."

The sisters had tried to defend their brother, but I noticed that Charles didn't say anything in Thomas's defence. His youthful face looked uncomfortable, and I wondered what he knew about his older brother's mysterious actions.

I clearly understood Thomas to be in some sort of trouble, and I, too, wondered who this woman was, as I had to confess that I had smelt the strange scent of someone who was not of this family upon his clothes from time to time. I hadn't understood it was the scent of a female and (or) that it had meant anything. Now, I was beginning to wonder. I remembered the letters he would read in private – they carried the same scent. I thought of all the mad dashes to the post office we had made, in order to post letters he had written in secret, and some of them composed in the solitude of Ten Acre Wood.

The discussion, or should I say row, ended. Thomas was going to be confronted by his father when he next returned home to the Cassland Road house.

Then, about a half-hour later, Augustus suddenly changed his mind and announced he had decided to catch the train and travel to Stoke Newington, to pay a surprise visit to the Foster family. He wasn't going to wait for Thomas Rowland's return. The Foster's son, David, worked for Augustus as a clerk in the Newington office, and it was thought he might have knowledge of Thomas's strange behaviour – unless, after all, Thomas was found to be telling the truth.

From this point on, all I know is what I heard by listening to the family discussions regarding the affair. I'll try to tell it to you, the reader, as accurately as possible, and, by heck, it's good!

Both Edmund and his father caught the next train from Ongar. They travelled to Stoke Newington, where, upon their arrival, they hired themselves a cab. The entire story was later revealed, and this is what took place: upon arriving unannounced at the Foster residence, it was disclosed that Thomas was not staying the night with them, that he never had stayed over, and that they had not even seen him recently. David King Foster, the elder, was completely taken aback at the suggestion that Thomas Rowland had been visiting with them. Young David had then been questioned by his own father, and had confessed that he, in fact, did have knowledge of Thomas spending time with a young woman. One who, in his opinion, was a bit older than Thomas. An address at Shelly Terrace was given as a possible place to find them.

With the hour then being late, Edmund and my master travelled as quickly as their carriage would take them, to the house in question, which happened to be a boarding house owned by Mary Ann Moore, who, as it happened, was a widow. The gentlemen were admitted entry to the large terraced house by the widow Moore herself. Immediately, young Thomas was called for. It was a most embarrassing situation for all involved. He was both shocked and angry, as well as obviously taken by surprise, when confronted by his father *and* his brother in the private sitting-room of Mrs Moore. Both of them quietly and politely had asked him to immediately return home with them, to Hackney, in order that the matter could be discussed and sorted out in a proper manner, and in the privacy of their own home. Edmund and his father let it be known there were no ifs, ands, or buts. Thomas was to be escorted away from Shelly Terrace – he had been found out, and was in a state of disgrace.

* * *

THE THREE OF THEM SILENTLY CONDUCTED their way back to Cassland Road, where they lived at number sixty-four, arriving late when most Londoners were taking to their beds. Once in the sanctuary of their home, and out of earshot of the servants who had been ordered not to leave the nether regions of the house, the affair that Thomas had been conducting was finally aired. From what I now know, Thomas had been indignant, and had told his father he would choose his own woman, and if she didn't suit the family's standards then that was their bitter pill to swallow. This is what happened; I'll tell it the best I can:

With a rising voice, young Thomas Rowland bravely stated, "Dad, I'm nearly twenty-one, so I think I can see whichever woman I like, and your opinion of her isn't going to change things."

To emphasize his point, he angrily flung himself into a large, overstuffed chair, then sat and scowled at the floor. He was still fuming from being tracked down by his father and brother. The result: his being humiliated in front of Mrs Moore, and most important of all, knowing that she would have informed Maud that he had been marched off, as if he were a naughty child. His face still felt red from it all.

His father angrily shouted back from where he sat upon a straight-back chair, just a few feet away from his son, "Nearly twenty-one? You, sir, are not anywhere near that age! You still have nearly six months to go before your twenty-first birthday, and until that time you are *my* responsibility, and I will not let *you* ruin your reputation *and* foil your chances of making a good marriage!" His thinning grey hair looked uncombed and untidy as his head moved up and down in anger and frustration.

"I don't want to make a good marriage!" shouted back a red-faced young man as he stared his father in the eye. Leaning forward with his elbows on his knees, he cried passionately, "I want to fall in love, and I *am* in love. I'm in love with Maud!"

He desperately hoped that Edmund and his father would see and understand the passion he had for this woman. He hadn't told them about her because he'd known they'd react this way.

Completely taken aback by his son's uncharacteristic outburst, Augustus shook his head as he sat across from his wayward son. "No, lad," he pleaded, "you only think you are in love. If she is the first woman you have had intimacies with, then I speak from the heart. You are not in love; you only *think* yourself so."

Young Thomas was exasperated, and he knew that he would have to fight long and hard to win over his father. He pleaded, "Dad, she is a wonderful woman and she is very lovely to look at. She's beautiful and she outshines any titled lady I've ever met. If you would just meet her, then you would see for yourself."

Edmund had kept quiet as he stood leaning against the mantelpiece, but now turned on his brother and spoke his bit harshly. "You silly, childish, little boy! Don't you think any of us men have not had our way with young women who were willing, when we were your age? Thomas, it's these willing young women you want to stay away from. *They* are the ones who get young men into trouble. They pay attention to you and make you feel good – as if you are on top of the world – hoping that the least you shall do is lavish them with gifts."

Thomas showed no signs of relenting.

Edmund's balled up fist thrummed against the mantelpiece as if to drive the point home. "They make you feel like you're the cock o' the walk, and they bat their eyelashes at you, and *all* the while they are weighing you up for what they can get out of you. They all want to be married to a rich gentleman."

Now Thomas got really angry, and he flew out of his chair and stood in front of his brother. His hands were clenched into tight fists as he faced his older brother. "You take that back! You have just about called the woman I love nothing less than a dirty prostitute, a whore! She isn't like that!"

He was furious. As for money, he was only well off, not rich.

Edmund didn't flinch or move an inch, but sighed deeply before saying wisely, in a patient voice, "I'm sorry, but I happen to be correct. However, unless you forced her to do something she didn't want to do, then she was *willing,* and the point I am trying to make to you is that you don't see or marry *willing* women. They are undesirable and not our sort. Understood?"

Then, as Thomas turned to take his seat again, Edmund continued with his brotherly advice, in a rising voice. "She'll get in the family way; she'll be carrying your child if you do not stop this now."

Thomas took his seat again and dared a glance at his father. The old man's face was grim.

Edmund confessed to his father, "I had no idea this was what he was up to, otherwise I would have sorted it out myself. You have to believe me that I would never have allowed him to get himself this far into trouble with a woman, especially if she was common and with no background."

The room went quiet. The subtle sound of the gas flames coming from the overhead gasolier was clearly audible.

Augustus had thought that Edmund was doing a good job. Thomas was squirming – he left them to it.

Thomas glowered at his older brother. Maud wasn't the sort of woman they thought her to be. She was beautiful, canny, and gay. Her background wasn't so bad when she could claim a connection to Lillie Langtry.

"Say something, Dad. Just tell him what he has to do." Edmund wanted his father to lay down the law – the law that was governed by society and kept people in their rightful places.

Now his father spoke. "Thomas, you are going to have to stop seeing her. Edmund is correct. You might not understand this now, but you will in a few years, perhaps even in just a few months, and you'll look back on this episode as a learning experience, a part of growing up and maturing."

He then firmly instructed his son, "Send her a letter, if you have to, but you can't ever see her again. You must sever your connection with her, immediately. You simply cannot see her again, except to inform her, but I would rather myself or Edmund confront her on this matter – not you. Afterwards, once she's been informed, you cannot get in touch with her again, not even by letter; not as long as you live under my roof, or you'll have to leave." This latter part was said as if it pained him, such as a bullet wound straight through the heart.

Edmund was aghast, "Dad! Don't give him an ultimatum! At his age he'll choose *her* over any comfortable home and inheritance. He's a young whip and he isn't using his noggin, nor will he if you threaten him with eviction."

Looking panicky, he pleaded with his brother, "Thomas, don't listen to Dad; he doesn't mean it. Just stop seeing the woman, and we'll put it down to youthful inexperience. You'll get over her and you'll find a more worthy woman to love."

"Is that why you are still a bachelor at the age of thirty-two, and all our sisters are spinsters?"

It was cruel, the way it came out – but it had to be said. He was sometimes ashamed that he had an elder brother and four sisters, all unwed and living at home. Well, of late he had been.

Edmund smiled knowingly. "It's better to be a bachelor than to be married to someone whom you'll end up despising. But that's my affair."

"And this is mine."

"No. It's *my* affair. I'm your father," interrupted the old man.

Augustus was now pacing about the room as if he were a caged animal. With a wild look upon his face he spread his arms out in exasperation and asked of Edmund, "What do you want me to do? Give him my blessing? Give him a medal? The whole situation is scandalous, I say, scandalous! It could affect the business! My brothers' too! We could lose money over this! Contracts could be cancelled!" He remembered, "Look what happened to your Uncle Charles's firm of solicitors!" Then he blamed his own brother. "I know where you picked this behaviour up from – my brother Charles who was having it on with his servant, right under my mother's nose."

"No, I didn't! Don't be silly." Thomas laughed at the preposterous suggestion. He still didn't know the truth about his Uncle Charlie.

"What is it with this family, then?" said his father. "Why is there a long line of us who either don't marry, or consorts with the wrong kind?"

"I don't have an answer for that, Dad. I love her and I want to be with her." His words were calm and quiet.

Thomas proved himself to be stubborn. He had known it would not go well, and had already prepared himself mentally for this eventual confrontation with his father, which had come sooner, rather than later.

"Well, I shall have to leave, then, and take up permanent lodgings at the boarding house. I'll start packing right away. I'll leave tonight."

He made a move to leave the room.

His father turned upon him in a fury and faced down his wayward son. "You shall do no such thing! Sit back down! I said... sit... down!"

"Yes, Dad, I shall, I... why, I shall leave," said a red-faced son who had tears welling up at the corners of his eyes.

Reluctantly, he took his seat. Admittedly, he was terrified. Defying his father's wishes was proving harder than he'd imagined. He was trying to be brave, but his words sounded feeble. "I shall have to leave. I'm sorry, but I feel as if I don't have any other choice. I'm not a child any more."

He quickly glanced at his father and his brother – he was nearly broken. "I have to go. I really have to leave. It's the proper thing to do."

The fear that had been building up inside him all through the last two days was ready to burst forth. He was going to be up against his entire family, his *entire* family, and that meant his cousins and all his other close relations.

In one silent motion he wiped away a tear with the back of his hand.

His older brother had raised his eyebrows, but then slowly lowered them, then narrowed his eyes as he peered at his sibling, searching for the truth, but knowing it before he asked, "How long have you been sleeping with her?"

Augustus had been surprised at the audacity of this question, and he stared at Edmund with his mouth partly open. It was a personal question of the sort that one doesn't ask of another, perhaps not even a brother, but he waited for young Thomas to give his answer – he wanted him to answer. Oh, yes. He wanted to hear the answer.

"Come on, Thomas, answer me," stubbornly demanded Edmund.

This was no time to hide behind social graces. There was no response from his younger brother, so he deftly pulled up a straight-backed chair and sat down. His knees touched Thomas's as he grasped his brother by the arms.

"Tell us!"

In a weakened and deflated voice, the young man replied, "Since the end of March."

He laid his head back against the chair's antimacassar and closed his eyes, wishing for it all to be over. The hour was late; he was mentally exhausted, and he longed for his bed. The mantel clock chimed midnight.

His brother and father both moaned out loud.

"You stupid, stupid boy," cried Edmund.

It was clear to them that Thomas had landed himself in a potentially explosive situation.

The family's reputation was at stake.

Edmund roughly enquired where his father was too polite to do so, "Did you use any sort of protection? What about her? Women know how to keep from getting pregnant; well, that sort usually does, unless –" Insistently, he asked again, "Protection! Did you use any sheaths?"

A bewildered Thomas shook his head in the negative. He leaned forward in his chair, hugged himself, and then hung his head low. He felt numb, frightened, and defeated, all at the same time. He thought to himself, "If I could only turn back the clock a few weeks, I wouldn't be here this minute, and this wouldn't be happening to me now. Oh, God, please help me."

"I want to know where it took place. Whose house did you use?" My master knew what the answer would be. Where else could they have gone?

"It was at Shelly Terrace."

"Do you mean to tell me that Mrs Moore allows this sort of thing to go on, while she has honest people sleeping in the rooms next door?" He was shocked. He cried angrily, "I could have her shut down and out on the street before this Tuesday! In fact, I shall go to the police and inform them of her situation."

"No, Dad. I was lodging there and we did it in secret. I have to lodge every now and then, as you may well know, when I'm working long hours. Actually, Mrs Moore was quite angry when she found out, and she was going to ask Maud to leave; the situation affects her own reputation. I spoke to her and said I would tell you that I'd be marrying Maud. It was only then that she didn't send Maud out onto the street – and Maud works for her as a dressmaker. She would have been out of work as well as destitute."

It was true. Mrs Moore had not encouraged them. He had paid for a separate room, thinking it all above board and that he would not get caught – except for this.

His father then gently asked him, though he dreaded the answer, "Is there anything else you want to tell us? Can this situation get any worse this night?"

Nodding his head, Thomas replied, "She's with child." The words were barely audible, but they were heard and understood. It was out.

There was no turning back the clock now.

Their father got up from where he was again seated, and paced the room with heavy feet. His face looked haggard.

"With child?"

He bent his head forward towards Thomas, and then hissed, "Did you not think of the consequences? Lord God! I hope you understood what you were doing and that you know where babies come from? Please tell me I haven't raised my son in total ignorance? Tell me that isn't so."

He stood in front of Edmund and asked of him, "Before this, did he know about babies and the trouble he could get into? Did *you* know, when you were his age?"

"Well, I should certainly hope so. He was told by me on his sixteenth birthday, and precisely so this wouldn't happen to him. Dad, you asked me to talk to him, and to make sure he understood what goes on between the bed

143

sheets. I also told Charlie before he turned sixteen." Edmund was not going to take the blame for his brother's situation.

"As if it's done any good!"

Then, as if to remove himself as far away as he could from any of the blame, Edmund said to his brother, "I warned you. You told me to mind my own business, but now look what you have done to yourself. You should have heeded my warning."

Thomas gave in, as if he had surrendered to the enemy. He leaned back in his chair as if exhausted from a long and arduous battle.

He felt ignorant – of the most stupid kind.

"Dad. Edmund explained it all to me, but I didn't think it would happen so quickly. I didn't know women could... you know, get with child so quickly. Besides, I wasn't thinking about the possibility of siring a baby. I was thinking about... you know... romance and all that."

"What you mean is you weren't thinking," said his father. He sounded disgusted. "You weren't thinking at all!"

It was true; he hadn't given babies a thought, and if Maud had, she hadn't spoken of her fears. If someone had only warned him, reminded him – about babies – and the consequences, he'd have stopped to think about his romantic interludes with Maud. He'd have done it all differently. He'd have done it all properly, and would have behaved in a more gentlemanly way.

A shocked Augustus asked, "How long have you known she was going to have a baby?"

Before Thomas answered, he sniffed, and then cleared his throat. "Em... she told me last week. She informed me by letter, and that is why I went to see her yesterday. We've been planning our future."

"God," responded his older brother. "You must be mad to continue a relationship with a woman who you know to be with child!"

"That is because I want to marry her," said Thomas. Then, in a petulant voice, he continued, "I was going to break the news to you this week. I've only just found out myself, and we needed to discuss it together first, and I have discussed it with her... and she is willing to get married as –"

His father had a lightning-quick verbal response to this, as he leaned back in an armchair as if physically exhausted. "Well, of course she is willing

144

to marry you, the son of a good family, a well-known name, and plenty of guineas in the bank. You're worth more than a few bob; what more could she want? She's landed herself on her feet. She'll be a lady of leisure and she'll never have to work for a living, ever again."

"She's carrying my child, *your grandchild,* so there is no other choice but to marry her."

He felt fiercely protective of his unborn child.

His father bellowed, as if with years of pent-up rage, and he suddenly thumped the padded arm of his chair with his balled-up fist, "I am so angry with you! I want to pick you up and shake you! You have behaved like an ignorant little shit! If I only say it once, I shall say it now: she is a common trollop and you have been trapped! You mark my words, she's got you where she wants you! You don't even know if it is your child!" Then he continued to rant, "Her family will surely be ashamed of her, because I know I would. If you don't marry her, they'll probably threaten to disown her, even if they don't have a shilling to their name, because *that* is the way of things. I don't know what I would do if this happened to one of your sisters – well I do know. The accepted thing to save face is to send the defiled daughter packing, out into the street, with nothing but what she stands up in. That's the way it is; like it or not!"

Both Edmund and Thomas stared at their father, but they both knew the ways of society and the attitude of all its levels towards fallen women and their bastards. The workhouses were full of these women, and some of them claimed to have excellent parentage, and others, they ignorantly repeated their parents' mistakes down through the generations, like mother, like daughter. It was the stuff of a Dickens novel, but so true.

Thomas stood up quickly.

With newfound strength he confronted his father face to face. "It *is* my child; I *am* sure of that. She isn't seeing anyone else. I'm sure of that, Dad. I *am* going to marry her and you shall have a grandchild, hopefully a grandson, whether you like it or not. There's nothing you can do to stop me."

Augustus demanded to know who she was and how Thomas had met her.

Thomas wondered if perhaps his father was coming round to the idea of his getting married. For a fleeting moment there was a glint of hope.

"Her name is Maud May Allen Diggins, and she is a dressmaker by trade. Her father is a draper, and they come from Norfolk. She has connections with Jersey, and she is supposed to be related to Lillie Langtry. I met her through Mary Ann Moore. It was the day of that snowstorm, in February, and the trains were running late. We were waiting for the coal to be delivered from Dalston – I enquired about a room for the night. Mrs Moore introduced us, as she had invited me to stay for dinner that particular day, and Maud was there as well. I also met Maud again, on another occasion, outside the church where Mr Foster is sexton."

"Dressmaker!" Augustus sounded disgusted. He nearly spat the word out onto the carpet. "You must've realised I wouldn't have *ever* considered your marrying her? As for being related to that Lillie Langtry; well, that doesn't make her look any more suitable. Everyone knows that *she* had an affair with the Prince of Wales whilst married to Mr Langtry. That's become common knowledge all over the country." He went on without stopping, "And even if you did stay for dinner at Mrs Moore's, you knew better than to become acquainted with any woman staying there for any reason other than to hold polite conversation." He wagged his finger at Thomas. "Polite conversation in a gentlemanly manner! Your behaviour has been disgraceful!"

"Dad, I saw a lovely woman and we had lots to talk about, and I wasn't expecting to fall in love with her. I wasn't thinking of you; I was thinking of her." With some afterthought, he confessed, "Besides, she was very well dressed, and at first I didn't know she had a trade. I thought she was better off than she actually is."

He had, in fact, been deceived by her appearance, until she started to speak, but by then he was intrigued by her, and being a polite young gentleman, had continued to converse with her until they had agreed to meet up again.

Edmund had more to say, even though it was too late to do any good. "Then you should not have pursued the matter. You have been brought up to know better. You are a gentleman, so don't say you didn't understand your own situation versus hers. Dear brother, you have behaved badly. I say, you will put your uncle Charles to shame with *this* folly."

Thomas spoke defiantly, "Well, I'm getting married, and that's that!"

He looked his father in the eye, "We shall need a place to live, and if Maud isn't welcome here then I'll have to get a house of my own."

If there was one thing he was absolutely sure of, it was that Maud would not be able to get on and live with his family. They would be better off on their own.

His father spoke the words Thomas dreaded to hear. "Yes, son. If you go against my wishes, then you'll *have* to live on your own. This woman you speak of is not welcome in any of my homes. I do not appreciate the way she has behaved. She should not have let you bed her. I simply cannot accept her."

Augustus peered at the pattern in the colourful carpet beneath his feet. In a businesslike manner he said, "You'll have to find a place that will be near the railway, so you can get back and forth to work. You still have your position in the coal trade – keep your place in the Newington office. I shan't turn you out on your ear, but you'll need a proper house. There are some new ones built up at Bush Hill Park, and I hear they have just run a branch line out there to a new housing estate, so I suggest you look there for something suitable. I won't have you living any place that isn't respectable, whether you are to be married or not." And then, in a voice tainted with shame, "But you can't live here with us. It wouldn't be proper. Also, you cannot live under the same roof with her until you are married, so you'll have to find elsewhere to live. If you do marry her, you know you will have shamed us. You know that, don't you?"

Thomas silently nodded. It was the first time he had ever gone against his father's wishes. He *had* been expecting to be cut off, disinherited, and so on. At least he was able to remain in the family business, and he was grateful for that.

"I take it, then, that I am to be shunned. I'm damned if I marry her as well as being damned if I don't. My own family will turn against me." Tears rained down his face and dripped onto his patterned silk waistcoat.

Augustus wailed, "Oh, it is bad enough with my brother Charles and his mistress! Eh, Dad, what would you say to all of this?"

Edmund then said, "Tom, you know our grandfather will be rolling about in his grave. If he were here, he would send you away." And then he asked, "So, why not just walk away?"

"I'm in love with her, so, therefore, that would be the wrong thing to do," stressed Thomas impolitely, "so get used to it." In complete exasperation, he reminded them, "I'm marrying her, and we're going to have a child."

It was perfectly clear to him that his decision was the correct one.

A fed up Edmund asked when the wedding would be, and Thomas answered, "As soon as possible. We'll have to have the banns read out in church, starting next Sunday. That's what we were discussing this afternoon when you arrived. We were actually planning the wedding."

He wiped away his tears, but held onto his handkerchief, folding it and re-folding it.

His father reluctantly asked, "Which parish will you have the wedding in, if you go through with this?"

"I think it will be better for everyone if the wedding takes place in Stoke Newington, in the same church where Mr Foster is sexton. It is where the bride resides." He looked at his dad. "That is the proper way, isn't it? To marry in the church the bride attends?"

Edmund nodded in assent, then pointed out, "It's the bride's family who pay for and arrange the wedding."

"It's traditional, only a small affair; just the immediate family. There won't be much expense; it's a... rush job."

"You're not of legal age. I shall have to give you my permission to marry," said his father. Then, as an afterthought, he asked, "She isn't Catholic, is she? I can't have you marrying a bloody Catholic! It just isn't done on our side of the family. That's well enough for the other side; they changed back to Catholicism, but not for us. Don't forget, you're Church of England, and so your children shall be."

"I don't know." Thomas shook his head – it felt numb. He squeezed his eyes shut. "No, I don't think so, or she wouldn't attend that church."

Thomas was white-faced as he asked of his father, "You won't refuse, will you? To give me your consent to marry her?" Then he spat out angrily, "The baby needs my name. I shouldn't think you would want an illegitimate grandchild... a bastard in the family."

He needed his father's permission, but thankfully, Maud was of age and could marry him without her own family's consent.

"If I refuse, you will be able to marry her in December when you become of age, but I doubt if any church will marry you with her in such an advanced condition of pregnancy. As long as you are sure, absolutely sure the baby is yours, then, yes, I shall permit you to get married, but then... my God, son! You are on your own. You can have your mother's money, and of course, there are your wages, but you'll get nothing else from me."

The room fell silent; the three men were contemplative and sullen. Thomas shook hands with his brother, who was reluctant to do so, but did. But his father turned his head, and refused to accept the gesture of goodwill.

The young groom-to-be left the drawing-room, and in closing the heavy door, leant against it and gasped for air. What he thought to be the hardest and most difficult day in his life, except for when his mother had died, was over with.

Still, he felt frightened out of his wits and dreaded what was to come.

That was it! The final words had been spoken, and the following morning Thomas quickly packed a bag and caught the train to Stoke Newington, and wasn't seen again until that dreadful day of the wedding.

* * *

THE MORNING OF THE WEDDING LEFT ME ALONE and in full charge of the farm. Early that morning the family disappeared to the Ongar railway station and travelled to Stoke Newington. The banns had been read in the parish church as was required, and Thomas married Maud on the third Sunday in June. Apparently, it was a very small affair, with not much celebration even for the times; large weddings were not yet popular. My master had refused to sign himself as a witness, so Mr David Foster had agreed to do so, he not being related, as no one in the family was agreeable to put their signatures to paper for an unwanted ceremony, not even cousins or uncles. As my family felt they had nothing at all to celebrate, immediately after the ceremony Augustus's children – Thomas's siblings (except for William) – and Augustus himself vacated the premises.

* * *

THOMAS *HAD* NEEDED HIS FATHER'S HELP to acquire one of the brand-new houses in Bush Hill Park, and help. had been given. Luckily for him there was one still available on Fifth Avenue, and from there he caught the train and arrived at work each morning, and worked as either a travelling agent or did car man work or warehouse work for his father, travelling between Stoke Newington, Dalston coal yard, and Hackney, depending upon where he was needed. Thomas could not avoid bumping into his father or brothers, as occasionally happened from week to week. Relations between them were strained, but they spoke; to his relief he was not completely shunned, merely a huge disappointment, if that wasn't enough. At the end of the workday, Augustus, Edmund, and Charles Clement went home to Cassland Road, and Thomas caught the train to Bush Hill.

* * *

HE SUDDENLY APPEARED AT WAYLETTS LATER THAT SUMMER. As it happened, it was a Saturday afternoon. I'd been thinking about him, as I had been missing him terribly, just as his sisters had also been missing his companionship. I'd been panging for him at the exact moment he arrived. I pricked up my ears when I heard a horse's unfamiliar hoof beats coming up the drive, and in wondering who it could be I ran barking to the lowest window in the sitting-room. He just strode in, after being dropped off in the yard by a carriage he'd hired at the station in Ongar. I was elated at the sight of him, well dressed in his town clothes: linen-coloured trousers and a long, soft brown coat, with a grey hat and a pair of matching grey gloves. At first his visit was slightly strained, and the air was tense, but then everyone warmed up to him. His sisters fussed over him, and his father and brothers spoke kindly to him, though, I could tell, could sense, the marriage to Maud was still not accepted. It was clear he'd been sorely missed at home and they were glad to have him back in their fold, if only for a few precious hours. As it happened, he stayed overnight, as his wife was visiting with her family and he'd taken the opportunity to seek out his own.

After an early dinner he changed into his riding clothes; his country wardrobe yet remained at the farm. He had Jasper saddled up by one of the farm boys, and the three of us went for a ride throughout the countryside. The air was hot and there was still plenty of daylight left in the day, and we travelled many miles in a roundabout sort of way. Our thirsts were quenched in Ongar, at the Kings Head, and we then travelled down the London road at a leisurely pace, stopping again at the White Bear, before arriving home at dusk. The saddle leather creaked, and Jasper was all-a-lather from the heat, as flecks of white foam thickly speckled his chestnut coat. My tongue nearly dragged in the dust as we walked home with lagging feet. My own feet proved to be tender from the romp. They pained me, thus causing me to limp along, but even so, I would do it over again. I can remember to this day the strong, sweaty odour of Jasper, the cricking sound of grasshoppers, and the happy and satisfied look on Thomas's face. I was immensely happy, and so was Jasper, who snorted contentedly many times.

We had missed him – and he us.

Sadly, I didn't see him again until after that autumn, when we had packed up and left Wayletts, and moved to the large house in Cassland Road where we were to reside for the winter months.

* * *

THE TIME CAME TO LEAVE STANFORD RIVERS, yet I was both excited and saddened at the same time. I wanted to see this mysterious place called Hackney, but I knew I would be restricted in my movements and would not have the same freedom as on the farm. Also, I hoped that our cook would remain behind, but sadly, to my great disappointment, she did not. Edmund drove me by way of horse and carriage, and, as well, we had several small and valuable articles stowed in the carriage, under our care and protection, and they would reside at the winter residence until the move to the new house was done, later the following year. There were also two trunks filled with documents and some heavy odds and ends (sovereigns). Edmund was perfectly happy to drive the carriage himself. No servants were required, as Paddy (the horse) and the carriage would remain in Hackney over the winter. I had not seen Horatio in order to wish him goodbye, but I knew I would return the following year, and I hoped I would see him then.

My new home was a large, grand house in Hackney. It didn't resemble a farmhouse in any way, shape or form. The front led out onto a small crescent set back from the main road, Cassland Road, and was filled with similar large houses on either side of us, and the streets and roads went on for as far as the eye could see. I thought I would easily get lost, as it all looked alike to me. I certainly wasn't used to living in a road as busy as that one was, though, I must admit, the road to London in front of our farm was a busy one at certain times of the day. There was a garden at the back of number sixty-four, though it didn't compare in size to the fields at Wayletts. There was no Ten Acre Wood to romp about in. I was to become a 'town dog'. My territory would consist of cobbled streets, cobbled streets, and more cobbled streets, and I only got out for walks when being taken by one of the family, and then, tied to a lead, not free to run about as I pleased. I knew I could accept this new life as long as I continued to live with my family and see Thomas from time to time, and could have the occasional visit to the farm, where a good romp through Ten Acre Wood and a visit with Horatio would set the world to rights.

* * *

THERE WAS HARDLY A DAY THAT WENT BY when my thoughts didn't stray to Thomas; I longed to see him. The very next time I did see him, it came as another surprise, when on one particular day the men had come home from the coal yard earlier than usual, and Thomas was with them. I was so happy to see him that, as he sat down, I crawled into his lap, even though I was too big to do so, but instead of admonishing me he rubbed my rib cage and gave me a generous hug, and he kissed the top of my head. I hadn't really understood at the time why we didn't see much of him any more, but now, as I tell you this, one comes to understand certain things as one gets older. We all get a little wiser as we grow older, but at the young age of two, I was quite unaware of how ignorant I was about life in general. I still had an awful lot to learn.

As I sniffed his clothes – he was full of strange scents – he spoke in a friendly manner. "Shales! You are the world's best dog, but I must point out to everyone here that you are getting fat." He laughed pleasantly.

Fat? What did that mean? I gazed about the room and then inspected the carpet, looking for some sort of a clue.

Jessie giggled, but spoke in my defence. "One of us takes him out twice a day, and we walk miles, or so it seems. Don't say he's fat! He's just not the thin dog we found last spring."

He stroked my sides but remained critical. "He's a bit too fat for my liking. He needs a good run. Take him out on the heath. There's lots of room there."

Julia interrupted. "He doesn't come when we call him! He runs off too far. We keep him on the lead."

Her brother smiled back at her. "You'll just have to learn how to whistle."

Giving me a vigorous rub, down both sides of my ribcage, his tone was conciliatory. "You always come to me when I whistle for you."

I knew what he meant. He did whistle for me, long and sharp, and I knew he meant for me to come to him. As for the sisters – well, I liked a good romp, and as long as I was within earshot, I didn't worry too much about returning to them.

As tea was served, Thomas's sisters doted on him with much sisterly affection. They had missed him terribly since he had married Maud. Polite enquiries were made about their new sister-in-law as biscuits and cream cakes were devoured in a mannerly fashion. An invitation for Thomas and Maud to spend Christmas Day with the family was offered by my master, surprisingly enough, due to the strained situation of his son's marriage to Maud. Thomas eagerly accepted.

Christmas? I wondered what this Christmas event could be? It had to be wonderful if it was able to reunite families. I eagerly anticipated the event, as I knew Thomas would be coming to visit again. Also, I would get to meet his wife who had caused so much scandal within the large family, the reverberations reaching as far as Broadwas-on-Teme and Ware.

Before he left he took me out for a long run. It was just the two of us again, and for a short while I felt as if everything was back to normal. In the dark of night we crossed Cassland Road, and on entering the house he stuck his head in the drawing-room. The mood was quiet.

153

"Well then," he said, "I'll say my goodbyes. I had better be getting home. I think I shall end up being a bit later than I said I'd be. Maud will be a trifle worried, I should think."

His family all stopped what they were doing and left their seats. They shook hands or hugged him close.

"Careful on the platform," said my master. "Stand well back. You don't want to slip and end up under the wheels."

"I know, I know," came the reply. "Cheerio, then. Bye."

I followed him to the door, and upon its closing didn't see him again until Christmas.

* * *

I SIMPLY HAVE TO TELL YOU about that first Christmas with my new family. It was so exciting! Actually, it was to be my third Christmas, but the first one celebrated as a member of a family, *and* inside a house. My first two Christmases were spent inside the kennels, with no idea that there was really anything special about that time of the year. Toothless George gave Toby and me a lovely meal, and said, "'Ere, it's yer Christmas dinner. Doan't choke on it." The battered bowl contained scraps of roasted goose, along with potatoes, barley, and gravy, and didn't seem to be much different from the other meals we ate. I wondered if this Christmas dinner would be as good, or possibly better?

Before Thomas and Maud arrived, a tree was acquired. I simply couldn't wait to see this. What would they do with a tree when there were plenty growing about outside? Young Charles Clement had chosen it, and had had it delivered to the house a couple of days before the festive event. I had wondered what they were going to do with it, but I soon found out. Would you believe they had it fetched into the house! Oh, my! It was planted in a large, decorated pail, and the evergreen tree was placed in the drawing-room, in a corner away from the fireplace. Its green, pointy branches poked out into the room in all directions. It was quite tall, about the height of any member of the family, except for me. They referred to it as the "Christmas Tree", and it became an honoured, new addition to the household. It was even gazed upon

154

with awe. To keep the tree from falling over, the pail was given additional weight for ballast by the placement of lumps of coal around its narrow trunk. I did wonder if the choice of coal, and not some other stone, was a family tradition or not. After all, they were in the business of acquiring and selling coal.

I watched with fascination the activity that went into the decorating of that Christmas tree. All the sisters had their turn at it. With happy merriment it was decorated with brightly coloured ribbons, and some glass and crystal baubles that resembled 'witches' balls' were dangled from its prickly boughs. The ribbons twined about its delicate fronds in a snake of coloured silk, and on the very top resided an angel. She was all white, and had large wings made from frothy lace. Whatever could the purpose of this tree be? What on earth had I missed on my previous two Christmases?

Even the servants gazed upon the tree in awe.

"Oh. It's simply beautiful," said Armstrong, the housemaid.

"Brings tears to moy eyes." This was spoken emotionally, from the cook, as she lifted her apron up to dab her face. I didn't think she had it in her: the ability to shed a compassionate tear for anything, or anyone.

I wondered what other surprises lay waiting for me. I couldn't imagine what people would think of next. The urge to lift my leg and water the tree nearly got me thrown out of the house on more than one occasion. But how could I resist? At first I didn't know any better, so ignorant was I. However, I did learn quickly to not do that on the tree, and now, when I look back upon that, I am ashamed to think I would have done *that* inside the house when I should have known better. I was always let outside to do my business, or as I learnt to think, "*Go to the loo*", whenever I asked. I shall simply put it down to being confused, and in absolute ignorance of the occasion.

When I eventually met Maud, I couldn't make up my mind whether I liked her or not. She did have a very peculiar way of speaking, and even Thomas didn't always understand her accent, a combination of London and broad Norfolk. Silly me, I was probably just confused. She also had a rather unusual shape to her, but now I know that it was her baby that was making her fat and roundish beneath her frock, as well as making her a trifle ungainly, like a duck with four feet.

It was my first Christmas with a family, so I didn't know what to expect, and worse still, I didn't even know what was normal. This time my dinner consisted of roasted beef and parsnips, as well as other vegetables and gravy, and to finish it off, I had pudding with rum sauce. I didn't even know what a present was, but that morning I did receive one from Father Christmas. He gave me a large, soft, stuffed ball to play with, which I found waiting for me beneath the tree. I loved *Ball*, and I carried it everywhere with me, all throughout the house, and Charles Clement and Edmund played catch with me until the ball threatened to come apart at the seams, and had to be hastily repaired with needle and thread. Sometimes I ended up being piggy-in-the-middle, my ball always tossed overhead and out of reach. Christmas carols were sung round the piano, in the large drawing-room, and the strange combination of singing and piano music set me off, howling like a wolf. I was laughed at and made a fuss of. It was a merry time, though there was a slight bit of tension in the air, which I put down to Maud's presence. It was good to see Thomas, but it was obvious, even to me, that he doted on his new wife. Still, I only saw him on rare occasions, they not being as often as I would have liked. I missed him dearly.

* * *

THAT FOLLOWING SPRING WE MOVED BACK TO THE FARM, and the usual routine of my master, Edmund, and Charles, flitting between Hackney and Stanford Rivers, was once again established as normal routine. Then, the hot month of August arrived, and so did Thomas, Maud, and their baby of nearly seven months. Her name was Mary Matilda, and Thomas doted on her. At times there was still a coldness regarding the relationship between Maud and the family. It seemed as if sometimes conversations did not flow smoothly, and a great effort to please from both sides was evident. I'm sure that at times the air could have been cut with a knife, as it was as thick as a slice of parkin. Thank goodness that I'm a dog, and such trivial matters did not affect my loyalty to others. I treated Maud with the same joviality as I treated everyone else. Her skirts became covered with my loose hair, saliva, and muddy paw prints, just the same as the sisters. I did not treat her differently, but welcomed her as one of the family, even though she shooed me away and cringed whenever I came in from the rain, and shook myself all over her before I could be dried off, sending drops of water and muck out in all directions. It took a whole fortnight before she started to warm up to me, and would stroke my head or speak to me with any sort of affection.

In the mornings, Thomas would whistle for me and I would find him already mounted, astride Jasper, waiting for me by the gate to the back pasture, and we would set off in any direction that took us away from the farm, as if the previous winter's separation had never existed. The odd time, we searched for our missing bees, which had travelled far and wide looking for pollen, and had been slow to return to their hives. As with the previous year, we travelled for miles, and always ended up slaking our thirsts in a local pub. After a good rest, we would return home weary. I would be limping but contented, and in the evenings the local news and gossip Thomas had acquired that day would be discussed with the family, and quite often he knew more than the locals themselves knew. I could always be found stretched out on the carpet or beneath a table, with one ear cocked and ready, and the rest of me half asleep in a sort of exhausted semi-slumber.

On a damp night the fire would be lit in the sitting-room fireplace, and it would crackle quietly, emitting a comforting warmth as the smoky aroma from the apple wood burnt away in an inviting red glow, something that I did not have when living in the kennel in Broadwas. If there were just one thing I would truly miss, if I ever found myself living rough again, it would certainly be a fireplace, and a soft Brussels carpet to lie upon in front of it. I think I could go without food again, but not without my fire.

Once again, I had a visit from Horatio. Somehow he had known I was there, and, incredibly, I had known *he* was in the wood. The day was cold and wet; it rained non-stop. I had suddenly thought of him, and had had the urge to go into Ten Acre Wood, which I did do, following my hunch, and there we met up on the northern path. He was full of news and interesting stories, and I listened, intently, as he related them to me as we took shelter beneath a large oak tree in the wood. As usual, his visit was an overnighter, and this time he slept in the stable, watched over by Jasper.

This time his parting words of wisdom were, *"No matter how bad loife becomes, it always gets a little better ath time goes on, and the bad becomes a dithtant memory of the past. Cheerio mate."* And with that he strode away silently, and as usual, I wondered if I would ever see him again.

The middle of August drew near, and it was time for Thomas and Maud to return to Bush Hill Park, to their own home, as Thomas's summer holiday was over with. We, too, were preparing to leave the farm and to move back to Hackney, but this time it would be to a different house. Whilst I had spent the summer at the farm, some of the servants had been busy and had helped see to the removal of the furnishings from Cassland Road to the newly acquired house in Darnley Road, which was closer to the railway and the warehouse, becoming a more convenient location for the family to reside.

When we returned to Hackney, it would be to an entirely different residence.

X

THE TELLING OF THE BEES

"The tempest has returned."

AUGUST, 1882

I TRAVELLED TO LONDON, to my new home, by way of horse and carriage. Jasper was tied to the back end, and trotted along behind us amiably enough, and I sat upon the comfortable padded seat next to Edmund, gently swaying to and fro as we travelled at a good pace along the muddy highway. Edmund was the only one from the family with me, as the others had gone by way of train, from the station in Ongar. We also had one of our men from Wayletts with us, who drove the carriage, and he was to return to Stanford Rivers by train, while the horse Paddy, and the carriage, would remain in Hackney.

We had with us some articles from the house that were quite valuable, though not so small, but heavy. Augustus didn't want them to go on the train or in the removal van, along with the rest of the baggage. They were placed within the carriage with care, and lay packed in a wooden box, beneath our seat, where they would be more likely to survive the journey to Hackney. A removal van had been hired for the furniture, as well as for the large and bulky straw-filled crates packed with ornaments, books, and china. It was all packed inside the van, but the farmhouse wasn't emptied of all its furnishings, merely the most valuable ones. I didn't understand the ins and outs of it all; it was just the way it was.

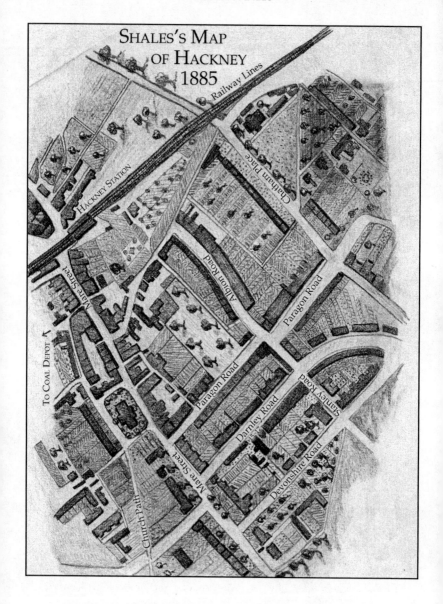

SHALES'S MAP
OF HACKNEY
1885

Our carriage was to lead the way along the London road, in front of the van, so I took the opportunity to brush up on my guard dog duties. I kept my eyes open, and I never napped at all during the seventeen or so miles to Darnley Road, even though I was quite tempted at times to give in to the feeling of sleepiness I experienced, when it should have been my nap time. I still don't know exactly how many miles it is, to this day, but I think I should be forgiven for not knowing – after all, I am a dog. It took us nearly the entire day to get there, but I thoroughly enjoyed the journey. We passed through some very pretty countryside of pastures, fields, and orchards, as well as some interesting towns and villages, and the day was a rare one, sunny and hot, and completely without any threat or any sort of danger to us. Amazingly, we were not held up and robbed by masked highwaymen brandishing knives or guns. Every once in a while Jasper would snort loudly, the way horses like to do, reminding us of his lonely presence bringing up the rear.

We arrived later that day, in a somewhat mud-spattered carriage, at 15 Darnley Road. I gazed at the old place, which was set a bit further back from the road than the newer, terraced dwellings, called villas, which lay close to the road. It looked to be quite large, though the narrow end fronted the road, and the actual front of the house was set a short distance back, somewhat behind the terraced villas. Edmund attached my lead to my collar. We went along the path and up the steps, and there he lifted the heavy knocker – tap-tap... tap-tap. The front door opened almost immediately.

"Oh, Master Edmund! Welcome home. Your father is waiting for you in his study," said an excited Armstrong. The housemaid then stooped to fondle my face, and she greeted me thus: "Shales, you lovely dog. Aren't you handsome... the handsomest dog in Hackney? And Darnley Road, as well as Cassland Road!"

I jumped on her, and nearly head-butted her on the nose. I was excited and could hardly contain myself. After wiping her face with the hem of her apron she unhooked my lead, which she carefully hung next to Edmund's hat, and without a backward glance I trotted off to explore the new residence. I discovered it had lots of rooms, but best of all, the furniture was familiar, as well as all the ornaments and carpets. It had obviously been fetched from the Cassland Road residence. A short time later, the men who'd driven the removal van began to empty it of its contents and carried the entire lot into the house. Jessie gave orders as to where each large item was to be placed, and Armstrong dashed about with a duster and a pot of polish. The other sisters peered into the straw-filled crates and removed the packed items. There were a lot of silver-framed photos as well as piles of loose ones, stacks of books, boxes of music sheets, and a lot of china, silver, and glass.

The house was in a happy mood, and so was I.

* * *

I'D ONLY BEEN LIVING IN DARNLEY ROAD A COUPLE OF DAYS, and hadn't even had the opportunity to leave the confines of the garden and have a proper walk along any of the nearby streets and roads, when news came about Thomas. I've already told you that Thomas, Maud, and their baby had returned to their home in Bush Hill Park about a fortnight previously. A telegram of the utmost importance arrived at our new residence concerning him. It was early evening, and the family had just finished their dinner, and we had all withdrawn to retire and let our meal settle. Silly me, I'd had my hopes up that Thomas was summoning me to go and visit with him, seeing that we had moved away from Wayletts. Why I had ever thought that, I do not know. It is what I had hoped the telegram would reveal. Augustus waited for Armstrong, our housemaid, to leave the room and close the door behind her. The telegram was held lightly in his hand. When he opened it, which he did with great solemnity in front of the family, he first read it quietly to himself, and then handed it over to Edmund to read aloud.

"Oh, dear!" Edmund moaned, angling the paper to get the best light from the ceiling lamp. "It's from Maud, and she says here that Thomas has been taken ill and that a doctor has been summoned."

He looked at his father, and appearing to be uncomfortable, rubbed the back of his neck. From the tone of his voice, I knew my own disappointment, so I flopped down rather heavily upon a familiar carpet that had resided at the Cassland Road residence, wondering what was to happen next. I feared that Thomas was once again in trouble, and I looked about for someplace to hide.

Augustus sternly looked at Edmund as if he were in any way responsible for his own brother's ailment. "Thomas has been working this week while we have been removing ourselves from Stanford Rivers, but you went over to the office today in Stoke Newington to see how things were. Was he not there?"

He sounded angry, and I cringed inwardly at the harsh tone of his voice. I wondered if I ought to slither away to the next room, or to blend in with the pattern of the carpet and listen to Thomas's fate.

Edmund looked guilty as he replied, "No, Father. Well, I mean yes, he had been there up until today, but I understood he was coming in later. I had no idea he was so ill, and I'm as surprised as you are."

All eyes, including my own, were upon Edmund, whose handsome face looked rather worried. Poor Edmund had wanted to keep Thomas in his father's good books, and had found that all was well at the coal yard, and young Foster had been managing at the Newington office along with their man, Armitage. He hadn't told his father that Thomas had not shown up for work that morning. Armitage had kept things running smoothly throughout the summer when Augustus, Edmund, Thomas, and young Charles Clement had taken time away from the coal yard to spend it in Stanford Rivers. With his father concerned about the move, he hadn't wanted to get his brother into any trouble, as well as give his father a reason to worry about what Thomas was up to next.

Edmund sounded thoughtful. "Dad, I don't think Maud would have sent this telegram if Thomas has a summer cold, or just a cut finger." Before his father could respond, he further said, "She could have informed us by letter post, but perhaps she thought a telegram would arrive in quicker time." He suggested, "Perhaps Thomas told her to inform us by telegram, and she was just obeying his wishes." He was looking at his father as if no harm was done, as well as wanting to keep his brother out of trouble, but he sensed something was wrong.

At this point, one of the sisters, Julia, thought to ask if Thomas could have received some sort of injury whilst at the large and busy Dalston coal depot.

Edmund explained carefully, "No, Armitage would have mentioned if anything like that had happened. It's always dangerous working around the coal wagons. There's always the danger of a collision by another horse-drawn vehicle carrying a heavy load, and he would have said so."

My master added, "If it were an injury it would say so in the telegram, and not that he is ill."

As if the stress of being seated was too much for him, Edmund got up and strolled about the room, and he confessed, "All I was told was that Thomas had gone home the evening before with a rotten headache, and I had wondered if it was caused by him having too much to drink."

He faced his father who was in the process of lighting a pipe. "I didn't think it important enough to mention, not with you seeing to the house and farm."

The pipe was successfully lit. Great puffs of aromatic smoke began to waft about the interior of the still strange drawing-room. Augustus did not look well, and I deemed from his countenance that it was dreadful news. I went over to him, and I rested my chin on his knee to give him comfort.

With his free hand he absently stroked my ears as his eyes followed the bit of paper around the room.

Young Charles and his sisters made various comments regarding the telegram, and all had their turn in reading it.

My master distrusted the telegram – either the news wasn't as bad as it revealed, or it was much worse. "I shall go over there and see for myself." He sucked deeply on his pipe. Now he sounded obstinate. "I still don't like that Maud and the influence she has over him."

He paused a moment to think, while the others in the room offered their opinions. I didn't think he paid them any attention as he seemed to me to be more concerned with his smoking. I was wrong, because he next said, "However, I do *not* wish to find him in a serious condition, either. Having a headache isn't the end of the world, but it could be serious, as it is summer. At this time of the year people in London can drop like flies. They have done so in the past. There's always a plague or two around in the summer time, a result of unsanitary conditions. She has probably forgotten to remind her cook to filter and boil their water, and now they are paying for it with an illness."

Edmund sent alarm bells ringing when he said, "Didn't someone just die a couple of days ago, over Newington way? It was in the paper – some sort of illness." He continued, "And there's been deaths over in Whitechapel – lack of proper sanitation, or so they say."

My master paused in his pipe-smoking to comment, "It's the heat. Everything becomes contaminated. We've had a miserable, wet summer, and now that we've had some hot weather, diseases will begin to plague us. He may even have diptheria, or perhaps smallpox, though I doubt it is the latter."

His children were not pleased with his assumptions, but they all seemed to agree that something was amiss with their brother.

Looking at Charles Clement, his youngest son, he then said, "Charlie, please see if you can hail me a cab." And then, "I'll go shortly. I can take the train to Bush Hill, and also, I shall go alone." He went on, "First thing tomorrow, I shall send word and let you know of his situation. I, as with all of us, am hoping that Maud has reacted foolishly by sending this telegram, and we are worrying over nothing. However, it says here that Thomas requests my presence, but to come alone. Mysterious as it sounds, I shall respect his wishes, and alone I shall go."

He pointed the stem of his pipe at them as if to finalise the decision. Obviously, no "buts" were allowed.

He looked up at the ceiling with a very worried look on his face. "If it happens to be cholera or something else which is equally infectious, then you must be patient and await my return."

He got to his feet and started to walk out of the room, but then paused. "I'll send a letter in the morning post, letting you know of his condition."

Charles Clement looked anxious. "I mightn't find a cab. You may have to walk to the station." Then hesitantly, "I... I won't let you walk alone. If I can't find a cab, then I'll walk with you." He got up to leave the room in a hurry. There was a frightened expression on his young face.

Edmund's eyes followed his brother. He calmly suggested, "Charlie, if you can't find a cab then I'll take Dad in the carriage. I'll harness Paddy myself."

I knew it wasn't good news, and that a dark cloak had descended upon everyone. I looked about me. All the corners of the room had become dark shadows. I thought to myself, *"The tempest has returned."* We had only just moved into this strange house, and now there was the atmosphere of something dreadful lingering over us. Looking at all their faces, I sensed they were worried, each and every one of them. I didn't want to stay behind with them. Instead, I hoped to go along with my master. I wanted to see Thomas again, though everyone was unhappy with him. I wasn't, though – we would always be friends.

A short while later the doorbell rang. It was Charles who had returned. As Armstrong closed the door behind him I greeted him happily as if he'd been gone for hours and not minutes, and he proudly revealed to the family he had indeed been lucky enough to hail a cab coming down Mare Street. It waited outside in the diminishing evening light.

Moments later my master descended the staircase. He was ready to depart. A portmanteau had been packed for him by Armstrong – he had no manservant. He would not be returning that night. When the housemaid opened the door for him to leave I tried to dash out, but Edmund grabbed me by my collar and sharply said, "No, Shales! Stay put. You cannot go." He yanked me back into the house, but I strained and pulled away.

"Let him come, Edmund," said Augustus as he settled his tall hat upon his head. "He shall keep me company, and hopefully, Thomas shall be cheered up by him. Whatever ails Thomas, I assure you, it won't be passed onto the dog."

I understood him, and was elated that I could go with him to Thomas's.

Edmund bent down, and taking the black leather lead used for walking me, attached it to my collar whilst I obediently sat still for him, and then, after standing, he handed it over to his father. Charles carried out the small bag for his father and placed it inside the Hackney cab. The evening air was still warm, and on it I could smell the pungent sweat coming from the horse, as well as from the cabbie, as I tugged my master down the low front steps and lightly bounded down the path, through the gate, and into the waiting cab.

It was such a lovely evening to have it overshadowed by such an awful feeling of dread. I was concerned that my master was disappointed in his son and daughter-in-law, but more than that, I sensed it would not blow over.

The cabbie was scornful. "I'll 'ave to charge you a bit extra on top, because o' the dog. 'Airs and that, you know. Gets awl over efferyone's cloves. Peep'l compline, they do."

My master politely replied, "Certainly, I wouldn't expect anything less." Then he loudly tapped the ceiling of the cab with his walking stick. "Now, to the station, and quickly!"

We jogged along at a very quick pace, and I hung my head out of the opened window. I felt a breeze upon my face and the cobblestones became a blur. It was a thrilling experience.

So that was how I accompanied my master to the house in Bush Hill Park. It was still daylight when we left Darnley Road, but it was well into the night when we arrived at the door of Thomas's house. The cab didn't have to take us very far when we left Darnley Road, as the station was quite close by, just at the top end of Mare Street where the railway tracks are. Still, it was all so new to me, as I'd only moved there from Wayletts a few days prior. I had no inkling as to what lay ahead of us that night, or in the least, as to where we were going.

Disappointingly, my thrilling ride came to a quick end. The cab stopped outside a large structure, and after paying the cabbie and tipping him handsomely, because of the dog hairs and saliva stains I'd left behind, Augustus led me inside and purchased something called a ticket. It was just a bit of paper, but it said First Class, and I hoped that included me.

* * *

OF ALL THINGS THAT COULD HAVE HAPPENED THAT NIGHT, we were to catch a train. That's what the ticket was for! I momentarily forgot the sense of dread that pervaded the air around Augustus, clinging to him like a winter cloak, as I witnessed a train come barrelling into the station, steaming and billowing smoke, and sounding for all things like some ancient dragon of lore. It was a most frightening experience and, I tell you, I was absolutely terrified out of my wits. The noise that came from that black monster went right through me, and nearly drove me to insanity. Huge clouds of white steam erupted noisily from the wheels, and the hissing sounds it made seemed to strike every nerve in my body. I nearly ran away, but I had been put on a lead and I was held tight, though I tried to pull free. But, Augustus had a good hold on the lead and he did not let go. All I could think about was the night of that terrible storm when I had been struck by lightning. The sounds coming from the train reminded me of that dreadful night, but I told myself it wasn't the same, and this was no thunder and lightning storm. Still, I trembled and I wanted to run, just run away and return to the house in Darnley Road, or to Cassland Road, or to any other place that was safe. I wanted to be back at the farm in Stanford Rivers – anywhere but this horrific place. I was in a state of utmost panic and I strained once again at the lead, and globs of saliva spewed out of my mouth and dribbled down my front, but Augustus still held on tight. The gigantic front part of the train, called a locomotive, had slowly passed us by, and then it came to a hissing, screeching stop, and sat still like some ancient, ferocious beast that had wearied and needed rest.

So terrified I had been, that I was completely unaware that Augustus had been speaking to me until I looked up at him, and I found him leaning over me with his lips moving in absolute silence. I was in such a state of panic that I had been completely unaware of anything, other than my fear of the train, and had not heard him speak, nor had I been aware of the small group of strangers who had gathered round us and stopped to gawp. Only then, when the train had become silent, did I realise he had been speaking to me, and had been stroking my body in a desperate attempt to calm me down. I started to get a grip on myself, and I pulled myself together enough to stop straining on the lead. I was panting heavily, but I was beginning to feel less panicky. I coughed and hacked, trying to catch my breath, as I felt as if I'd been strangled. My throat felt bruised. My toes felt sore, probably from my desperate attempt to drag myself away, across the wooden planking of the station's platform.

I dared a quick glance at the wheels, which were huge, and I could see through them to the track below. It was a dizzying experience. I felt groggy.

The gawpers, obviously with better things to do, departed just as a porter came along and opened a door to a carriage for us. "This way, sir. Please watch your step, sir."

"Come on, Shales. Come on," said Augustus in a pleading voice. Exasperated, he admitted, "Damn silly idea of mine to bring you with me! I should've listened to Edmund!"

The porter was taken by surprise with my reluctance to board the train. "Sir! Would like some assistance with your dog?"

"Yes. Thank you." Relief was evident in my master's voice.

A terrified Shales panics on the station platform.

I jumped up onto my hind legs and hugged my master's arm with my front paws, hanging onto him for dear life. I didn't care if I ruined his suit! He patiently pushed me off and started to board the train, pulling me in tow. My collar threatened to come off over my head, but I did not want to be left behind. I nearly expected him to drop my lead in disgust. I had a vision of him leaving me behind, waving back at me from the train, as I remained glued to the platform and he retreating off into the distance. My body hugged the wooden boards and my tail was all but gone, as it was tucked tightly between my hind legs. I didn't want the train to eat my tail. Augustus stepped backwards, up a step, and disappeared into the interior of the train. The porter, deftly stepping behind me, quickly picked me up and bodily threw me upon the monster before I realised what was happening. I shut my eyes in fear of the unknown, and I held onto my bladder tightly.

The door thudded shut behind me with resounding finality.

Once I was on the train, and dared open my eyes slightly, I almost immediately gave a sigh of relief, as the interior was very nice, like a small, furnished room, and I felt safer being closed in amidst four walls. Silly me! This wasn't so horrible after all. We seated ourselves next to a window, on some lovely, red plush seats with high, padded backs. I began to feel more safe seated there, gazing out of the window from within, and watching the to-ings and fro-ings of the various people as they came and went along the platform. It was a busy spot even for that time of the evening. There were people departing as well as getting onto the train. Most were men, but I did see a few women, as well, but alas, there were no other dogs. I was the only one.

Augustus rubbed my head and ears, and then said, as if to himself, "Let's hope that Thomas will be all right and that there's nothing to worry about. There is also little Mary Matilda to think about. I have always expected to hear that he has fallen from a horse, but never for him to come down with any sort of an illness."

I thought this wonderful man needed a kiss, so I leant over and licked the side of his face, a deed which I knew him to despise. For once, I did not get scolded for it. He continued to stroke and caress the back of my neck in his attempt to calm me, as I was still slightly frightened and I panted heavily. Saliva spattered the window-pane, and it fogged up from my breath.

I heard a loud tooting sound amid shouts of "All clear!" and then I felt the train begin to move with a slight jolting motion, causing me to dig my toenails into the seat. I could hear the deep chug-chug sound the locomotive made as we slowly left the station behind. Curiosity got the better of me. I had my nose pressed up tight against the window-pane, in an attempt to continue to see the receding station, but it was soon gone, replaced with fields, then tidy rows of houses. Shortly later, the warehouses and other outbuildings that lined the tracks at the Dalston coal depot slowly receded into the distance, and into the ever-diminishing evening light.

We had gradually picked up speed, and with it I came to the realisation that it really wasn't much different from the motion one felt from within a horse-drawn carriage, except it went clickety-clack instead of clip-clop. With interest, I watched the buildings and countryside as they all passed us by, and I started to relax, and then thought it an enjoyable and interesting experience after all, thus coming to the conclusion that I had behaved like an arse back there at the station, and one does not like to make a spectacle of oneself in full view of the public. Does one?

It would not happen again.

As we barrelled along at great speed, the fastest I'd ever experienced, I longed for Augustus to open the window. It would be a thrill to hang my head out of a moving train at such speed! The window remained up, shut in its closed position.

During the journey a polite young man came along with the tea trolley. It had nice-looking scones and other delicacies, set out on what appeared to be very good china.

I thought to myself, "*Goody-goody-gumdrops.*"

My master had a cup of tea, and not feeling like eating, he gave me his buttered scone. Ooh, the good life! How, when all those days I went without food, I never would have dreamt I would be travelling first-class and eating a scone from a bone china plate. There had been many days when my belly had thought my throat had been cut, it had ached so much from want of nourishment.

We soon arrived at Bush Hill, and then alighted at the newly built station. I was still a bit nervous, but I managed to do it without embarrassment to myself or to my master. Like I said, it would never happen again.

Augustus made enquiries regarding hailing a cab. We were directed to a platform at the station, where we found a four-wheeler carriage and driver for hire. Once again, we were travelling to the sounds of horses' hoofs, the chug-chug of the train now a distant echo inside my head.

* * *

SOME TIME LATER, WE DREW UP OUTSIDE THOMAS'S HOUSE, 18 Fifth Avenue. It was a lovely, small place. When I say small, I mean that it wasn't a huge, rambling family place like Wayletts, or Cotheridge Court. It was smaller than the house in Darnley Road, but it was very neat and tidy, with three storeys, and had what they now call 'tiles' on the roof, instead of slates. I might as well tell you that it was a house newly built, as were all the neighbours' houses. The railway station was also new, allowing the occupants of these new houses easy access to all areas of London, where they commuted back and forth to wherever it was they worked.

The housemaid opened the door just as we approached the house. She had obviously been expecting us, and had been kept up past her usual bedtime hour.

"Oh, sir!" she said as she curtsied. "I've been on the lookout for you. Please, do come inside." And then, "Mrs Berkeley is waiting for you in the sitting-room. She wasn't at all sure if you would be coming tonight, though she told me to stay by the window – turned me into a right curtain-twitcher, she did."

Then she saw me and looked doubtful, saying, "Oh, dear! Is the dog to come inside as well?"

I wondered what I would do if I couldn't go inside. The young woman, looking to be not much older than a girl, wore a horrified expression on her face as she looked me up and down.

"Yes, the dog is coming in. I happen to know that your master wouldn't at all mind. Shales *is* partly his dog."

Remembering that her master's father was also a respectable gentle-man, the housemaid bobbed another quick curtsey, and then she said politely, "Please, sir, let me take your 'at and things."

Augustus handed over his hat, gloves, cane, and portmanteau, as well as my leather lead. With her arms full, she disappeared through a door to our left. A moment later, she emerged empty-handed, then carefully knocked on a door to a room which was at the end of the front hall, stuck her head inside, and said quietly, "Mrs Berkeley, your fa'ver-in-law has arrived, just this minute. Shall I show 'im in?"

A voice from inside the room, which I recognised to be Maud's, answered, "Yez, send him right in."

"This way, sir," said the smiling maid, who eyed me warily.

I ran ahead of Augustus, pushing past the maid to greet Maud, and, in doing so, the door was roughly thrust wide open. Its doorknob hit the wall behind with a cringing thud. I wasn't sure of how she would receive me, because she never showed me much in the way of attention. She was a pretty, buxomly thing, with dark hair and a lovely shape, and no longer fat and ungainly. The deep blue of her long skirt and the magenta blouse complemented her already lovely features.

She bent forward to greet me. Her gold locket dangled against the tip of my nose, and she gently grabbed me by the head, and said, "My Tommy is ollis pleased ter see yew, Shales."

She examined her skirts for dog hairs, found some, and brushed them away with her hand. Then, on a serious note, she looked at Augustus as she straightened her posture, and said, "He 'as not been at all well these last few days. He 'as been complaining of a very severe headache, which is so unlike 'im. This morning he cud not even get out of his bed. It was sum tyme afore the doctor cud come, and today he 'as been vomiting. This ent influenza, or cholera. I fear it is serious, and I reckun 'twas better ter send a telegram instead ov a letter."

"Then I must see him right away, this very minute." Augustus spoke to Maud with an air of authority. He stepped up to her and kissed her lightly on her proffered cheek. "My dear, are you all right? Do you feel unwell?"

"Yer'll find me in good health. 'Tis just Thomas who has fallen ill."

Wondering where his son was at that moment, he asked hesitantly, "Is... he in bed?"

She nodded in reply. "This way. He's in the first room at the top of the stairs. When I last saw him he wuz sleeping, but that is more frum exhaustion than anything else. At times he have an ill dent!"

I could see she was upset as she turned her head to leave the room, leading the way, and at the bottom of the lovely, ornate staircase she gathered up her long skirts and began to ascend the stairs.

Maud led the way, and I bounded alongside but reached the top step first, in my eagerness to see Thomas. I was excited with anticipation, and I woofed loudly, announcing my arrival. She opened a door leading to a room off the landing, and I rushed inside the unfamiliar room. It was a very large bedchamber, and there he was, in bed, as if asleep. The gas lamp was turned low, providing just enough light to see our way.

I jumped up onto the bed and carefully lay down next to him. I licked his face. He lay on his back, and was so very pale, and his eyes were closed as if he were sleeping. I sniffed the air about him, as well as his bedclothes. I didn't like the smell of him. Illness was a new experience for me, and the smells that came with it were foreign and were overpowering to my senses. These alien smells made me feel aware that there was something not quite right with him, and he did not stir with my fussing over him. Still, I was so happy to see him that I gently licked his face again, with the hope of waking him up.

I heard Augustus pull out a comfortable easy chair that was nearby, and he carefully pushed it next to the bed and settled himself into it. He leaned forward and touched Thomas's hand, just ever so gently. As he did so, I wagged my tail, and I heard it "thwump-thwump" as it hit the side of Thomas's leg, which, with the rest of him, lay beneath the bedclothes. His eyes slowly opened, focused, and eventually rested upon his father's worried expression.

With what appeared to be a great effort, he spoke. "Father? Dad, is that you? Seems like forever since Maud sent word."

"Yes, Tommy." Then, my master spoke very gently. "I've just come; just this minute. I came as soon as I got the news."

He looked at Thomas intently, as if reading a book. "What is this I find? You, all tucked up in bed and feeling poorly, and it still summertime. You should be out riding Jasper."

This was said with such fatherly gentleness that I lay my head down upon Thomas's chest, and sighed loudly. There was no anger in his voice so Thomas was not misbehaving; my master was not annoyed with him.

"Shales. Oh... Shales, my boy. What are you doing here?" asked Thomas, in a weak and rasping voice. I wriggled about and wagged my tail in response. It was very warm and I panted deeply, causing the mattress to vibrate. I was so pleased that he'd noticed me that I basked in the attention. He stroked my chin with an upward lift of his fingers, but a moment later his hand fell back to the bed.

"I have brought him along to keep me company, but I also knew you would be pleased to see him." My master looked at me with tenderness. "It seemed important to bring him along. I don't know why; it just did. He went berserk at the station when he saw the train coming in, but then he settled down."

Augustus now laughed, as if he saw the funny side of my embarrassing moment. "He had to be picked up like a piece of baggage, and tossed bodily onto the train. People actually stood around and stared at us! The incident was... very embarrassing for me. He's all right now. He soon settled down when the tea trolley came round and I gave him a scone."

"I'm sorry, Shales. Poor... boy. I can't... lift my hand to stroke you again... I've missed you." Then, "I wish we were at the farm; you, and me... and Jasper."

He hadn't expected to see me. He was astonished to think his father had actually fetched me, and on the train! He was pleased beyond words.

A tear ran down Thomas's face and he started to cry.

"Father, I am so ill. I can hardly think... because of the head pain. My neck hurts, and I can't move my head. I've never had a headache like this before. Not even from that time I fell off my pony and hit my head against the ground. Do you remember when that happened? Never like this... I'm sorry, but I didn't go into the office today... or even over to the warehouse. I looked after everything whilst you were away, until today; there's nothing to worry about. Everything got sorted, and all the... coal deliveries were... made." He struggled to say, "There's... a... very large delivery to... Worcester... tomorrow at ten... I think." He paused even longer between his words. "It'll... be... about twenty... train wagons –"

The immense guilt he felt at letting his father down again made him inconsolable. Last year's row was still raw. He hadn't been shunned completely, but his relationship with his father was still strained.

"Don't worry about that, son. Armitage will help. I know you did a good job; you always do. I wouldn't expect you to go to work feeling as poorly as you do. What of the doctor?" asked Augustus. "Has he been yet?"

Barely audible to our ears, Thomas managed to say, "Tomorrow. I think he will come again... early tomorrow... morning." His father had to lean forward to catch the last few words.

Maud sat on the far side of the bed, clenching Thomas's left hand. She looked upset. Tears flooded her eyes. Slowly, she got up to leave the room, but paused in the doorway. Looking back at Augustus, she said quietly, "I knew it wuz serious."

My master responded kindly, "I'm staying with you tonight, if you can put me up, and I shall speak with this doctor tomorrow. I hope he's reputable and knows what he's doing."

Looking at Thomas with an intent gaze, he said, "Perhaps we can move you to a hospital." His tone was hopeful. "Has the doctor said what it is that ails you?"

In a tired voice Thomas replied, "No, he has not. He has said it may be contagious... and to keep little Mary away from me. I am not to see her at all." He could barely be heard, as his voice was very low and weak. I lay there on the bed next to him and I wished for him to get better. Up to that point in my life, I hadn't known that people could become ill, nor what illness meant. I didn't like it one jot, and wished for all to be normal again.

The two large windows in the room were open, and a weak draught of air wafted in, but it hardly cooled the place down. It was terribly warm in there, as a result of the lingering summer heat. Truthfully, it was stifling. The windows were opened from the bottom and not the top, the latter being normal for a sickroom, to allow the movement of more fresh air to come inside the room without causing a direct draught around the bed, but the night air was too warm and heavy to make much of a difference, and I felt little, if any, relief from the heat.

Maud came back into the room carrying a pitcher of iced water, which she then carefully poured into the enamelled basin of the washstand, situated to the right of the windows. I could see her bodice was damp from sweat, but even in this heat, in the upstairs of the house, her sleeves to her blouse were full-length, that being the norm for a lady, and especially one self-conscious in her father-in-law's presence. Sitting on the side of the bed furthest away from her father-in-law, she dipped a lace-edged white cloth into the water, and wiped down Thomas's face and hands in a feeble attempt to make him comfortable.

Augustus removed his summer-weight coat in the sweltering heat, and then, as an afterthought, loosened his collar and removed his tie. His silk waistcoat, a shade of grey with carved ivory buttons, remained buttoned, as did his shirt cuffs. The gold cufflinks glinted dully in the dim light. He was sweating profusely, and his odour mingled with those of the sickroom.

"What of my granddaughter? Who is looking after her?" His tone was not entirely pleasant.

Maud didn't look at Augustus, as she replied slowly with her strange accent, "I've sent her and Charlotte, her nurse, over ter my friend's place. She's a widow. 'Tis Mary Ann Moore, living over in Stoke Newington. Yew will remember her. She attended our wedding. 'Tis the boarding house where I used to live, and Thomas visited me there. 'Tis where we met – when yew found out about Thomas and me."

Augustus grunted and said, "Yes, I'm well aware of the result from that 'visit' as you like to call it. Two months later you were both getting wed in a hurry; a matter which I have not yet come to terms with."

Ignoring his snide comment, she said, "The baby will be well cared fur, and out of harm's way from all this sickness." Then she looked at Augustus, and said crossly, "I did not send her ter yew, because I did not think you wuz yet settled frum your return frum Stanford Rivers."

Anger was reflected in his tone. "We could still have had her come to us. We wouldn't have been put out, but would have welcomed her. Did you not think that you should have told us about Thomas sooner? What of the post? You could have sent a letter last evening, and I would have received it early this morning."

Augustus glared at his daughter-in-law.

I knew he was not happy with the situation, but above all that, I knew that they did not like each other, but merely tolerated each other's company. I had once heard Augustus say to the walls, in an angry tone, that, "A gentleman does not marry a common dressmaker, but neither does he leave her pregnant and on the streets or in the workhouse." You, the readers of my story, will well understand this, but it took me years to comprehend the meaning of those words.

Maud's explanation came in quiet, carefully chosen words. "Thomas, he went ter work on Monday, as usual, and he only complained of feeling ill sometime that night." She tried to keep her voice calm, but I could see she was ready to flare up at any moment. "He still went into work yesterday morning, but returned at midday. He could barely walk. 'Twas then I summoned the doctor, who came and attended him. He came at about seven o'clock and stayed with Thomas fur over an hour. We all hoped 'twas something that would soon pass, though we did wonder if it wuz typhoid, or *something* like that. The doctor came again at eight o'clock this morning, and again at four o'clock. 'Twas then he said that Thomas's illness is very serious, and that he 'asn't no cure for it. There's nowt he can dew."

Maud angrily wrung the excess water out of the cloth she had been soaking, and then roughly said, "It was then I sent the telegram ter yew. I wanted yew to find out this evening, and I had missed the afternoon post. As for Mary Matilda, I sent her away before I sent for the doctor. I wasn't sure if it was cholera, or a rum case of diptheria. Thomas wondered if he wuz infectious, and he wuz concerned about our daughter."

Her husband writhed about weakly, in a feeble attempt to push down the bedclothes. "Are you satisfied? She did as I instructed."

My master nodded his head, as if to agree. In a resigned tone he admitted, "I can find no fault in that."

He looked her in the eye. "You did what any of us would have done." Then, "What of this doctor? Is he reputable?"

Maud nodded. "The fogger comes frum the hospital. It's a new hospital. It's in Enfield, which ent that far away." She absentmindedly nodded her head in the direction in which Enfield lay.

She continued to wipe the sweat from Thomas's brow. His eyes were now closed. My master instructed Maud to go to bed, and he himself would stay up and tend to his son, due to the seriousness of the illness. Only the young housemaid remained, and the cook didn't live in – she had a husband to see to in Enfield. The maid was told to get a good night's sleep, because she would be up at the crack of dawn.

The room was very nice, and it even had a large, dark blue patterned carpet that filled the centre of the spacious room. The dark, reddish-brown furniture, which I now know to be mahogany, was new and fashionable, as was the Arabian-style bed that both Thomas and myself shared. The blue bed curtains with the gold cord and tassels had been pulled back and tied in place to allow for better circulation of air, though there wasn't any movement, it being too oppressive for that. Panting heavily in order to cool myself down, because I was mafted, I settled down for my vigil, not fully understanding the seriousness of the situation, but aware of something in our lives going dreadfully wrong, and sometime in the night I fell asleep despite the tropical heat of the room. I had tried very hard to not drift off, but I simply couldn't help it, and, as usual, it happened without my knowing.

* * *

WHEN I AWOKE IN THE MORNING, it was to find Augustus still seated in his chair, slumped over with his chin on his chest, but asleep. It was a wonder he hadn't fallen forward out of his chair, as if a ghostly hand kept him at bay. In the dim light of the late summer dawn, I looked at Thomas and examined his face. I could see he didn't look well. He was all white-looking, though he was sweating, and his lips had a bluish tinge to them. His breathing was shallow and irregular. Suddenly, everything all felt wrong, as if time had slowed down. I felt alarmed, so I jumped off the bed and nudged Augustus, and then licked his hands in order to wake him. I had to nudge him again before he stirred.

Alarmed at my insistence, he looked at Thomas, and became agitated.

"Oh, my lovely son," he said. "Oh, God, please don't take him away from me. I'm so sorry!"

He held onto Thomas's wrist, felt his neck, and then gave a sigh of relief.

"It's all right, Shales; he's still with us."

Immense relief was written all over my master's face. It was too soon. His son was only twenty-one years of age – still just a child. The clock upon the tall set of drawers chimed out five bells, and even I knew it was five o'clock in the morning, and cheery birds, unaware of our worrisome state, happily twittered outside to let us know it was dawn.

Hastily, he made to leave the room. I danced about at the door, which was shut, and I got underfoot. I desperately had to go outside to relieve myself. We both struggled to exit the room first.

Augustus followed me down the stairs at a refined pace. I shot down like a bullet.

He impatiently rang for the housemaid, who appeared rather quickly, but she looked as though she'd only just risen. He asked her to take me outside and said not to let me loose, but to keep me on the lead. She obeyed, willingly, but between you and me and the gatepost, I was the first dog she had ever met up close. She was frightened of me biting her, thus she held onto my lead as if it were on fire. Luckily for her, I held no compulsion to run away. Augustus then shouted for Maud to get up out of bed. All of this behaviour being completely out of character for him.

We breakfasted; the mood was glum, and afterwards, the doctor arrived. It was still very early in the morning and the street outside was quiet – the sounds of morning traffic were yet absent. He had a conversation with Augustus, which I was not privy to. The door to Maud's sitting-room was shut on me before I could enter, but I just knew at the time that it was not good news. It was like knowing that Horatio was in Ten Acre Wood, and then meeting him on the path there. I just knew, but I didn't understand what it all meant. Still, I lay on the floor, pressed up against the door, and heard a flurry of words spoken that were beyond my ignorant boundaries of comprehension.

When the door next opened, I took the opportunity to whip inside the room. I found my master, heavy of body and mind, seated in an easy chair. His countenance was one of fear. I leaned against his knee and wondered how I could help. The doctor had gone upstairs to attend to Thomas alone, but shortly afterwards came back down. He once again conferred with my master, but this time I heard all that was discussed, word for word, making it easier for me to understand.

It was obvious that it wasn't an easy thing for the doctor to relate bad news of the worst kind to the family of the patient. He pinched his brow betwixt thumb and forefinger, as if to relieve pain – but it was courage he sought.

"Your son has a malady known as meningitis. I'm now sure this is what ails him. The arthritis of the neck is a sure sign, and now I have no more doubts. I am sorry, sir, but I cannot do anything for him. I have no medical cure, and I can assure you, no other doctor will have, either. One has to wait out this disease; there is no other way."

He politely watched for a bad reaction from my master.

There was a long moment of quiet before Augustus spoke. "Is there hope then? He can get better?"

The doctor indicated towards the sideboard where a crystal decanter and several glasses were sitting idly. He asked, "May I? I believe you, too, should have a drink, for strength."

My master nodded. "Yes... Please do."

Two brandies were poured. I could tell by their smell. The doctor handed a snifter to my master, who had remained in his chair, but not out of rudeness. He had merely been frozen there. Fright and old age bound him to it.

As the two men gulped back their brandies, I braced myself for the news. The doctor bowed his head and spoke with gentleness. "Those who survive are almost always damaged for life." He turned his glass about in his hands, and chose his words carefully. "Most survivors are damaged in the area of the brain, or suffer paralysis – for life. I would hope for a full recovery, but I have not seen, nor heard of one, yet."

Then, he looked directly at Augustus, and said, "I am sorry, sir, but I think you should prepare yourself for the worst. What I mean is this: that your son should get his affairs in order while he is still conscious. He may lose consciousness any hour now, and after that it could just be a matter of hours, or perhaps a few days, before the end."

As an afterthought, he added carefully, "It will be better for him if he... dies, than survives and be brain-damaged and completely paralysed; that is something that no person should want to live through, nor should anyone want to witness."

Augustus looked ill. His shoulders were slumped and his face was ashen. He then asked the doctor, in an uncertain voice, "Would it be better if he was in the hospital?"

The doctor reached for my master's glass, and then poured two more measures of brandy, one for himself and one for Augustus. "There is nothing we can do for him there that cannot be done here. Besides, we don't want it spreading, and it may spread to others. There is always that possibility. We usually find that with this disease, someone else known to the patient catches it, though it doesn't run rampant. It seems to choose who it wants."

He went on to give advice. "I suggest you remain here and don't go out in public. Don't go home until it is over, and don't let anyone else into the house unless they know how to nurse. Chances are that no one else will become ill, but precautions should be made. We simply don't know enough about this disease except to say that most never recover at all, and those that do... well, I have told you my thoughts on that."

As if to make sure my master understood him, his final words were, "He is dying. There isn't much time, a few hours or perhaps a few days. I'm sorry."

So, the doctor left, and we had no hope of Thomas ever getting better. With my limited knowledge on death and dying, I wondered if it meant he would remain in the bed upstairs, forever. I thought that wouldn't be so bad, because I could visit with him, regular like. Cheer him up and all that. I just didn't understand the enormity of the situation at the time. I thought about Jasper. He would miss him, if Thomas couldn't go to the stables at the coal depot and visit him. Would Edmund take to riding Jasper, if Thomas was unable to?

What would happen to us?

A letter had already been sent to Darnley Road, informing the other family members that they should not come to Bush Hill Park. A second letter, which followed the doctor's visit, told them of the direness of the situation and to prepare for the worst news. A reply came later that same day. Written by Edmund, he asked if perhaps Julia or one of the sisters could be of any help in nursing Thomas. Augustus acquiesced, and even though he feared for her safety, allowed Jessie, the eldest sister, to come. She had had experience, having nursed her mother in 1872, as well as the younger children with their occasional childhood illnesses.

I was ever so glad to be seeing Jessie, and I hoped all would be well again with her arrival. Augustus was also relieved, as she would take over the burden of staying with Thomas throughout the long, night hours. When I didn't sleep, I listened to her as she read from a book. It was called The Bible. She read prayers from it in a quiet voice, whether Thomas was awake or not. When Jessie slept, either Maud or my master stayed in the sickroom. Unusual as it was for him to be there and not have a hired nurse, Augustus was insistent that he spend the time, what few remaining hours Thomas had left, in the sickroom with his son. He wanted to treasure the precious time he had left with his handsome lad, who was barely a man, but most of all, to forgive him for that terrible row they had had over his affair with Maud. It was a raw wound that needed to heal over, before they could part and Thomas could go his way.

Maud was beyond herself and had difficulty coping with the strain. Her broad Norfolk accented her words. "He'll niver moize agin!" she cried loudly with tears running down her face. The knowledge of her soon becoming a widow was too much for her to bear.

The deathwatch was an agony; it was as if the actual house listened and waited.

The remainder of Thomas's illness was horrid, and I won't tell you the frightening and depressing details. Quickly, before he got worse, he made his peace with his father, and instructions were given regarding the future of Maud and little Mary Matilda. He was feverish and incoherent most of the time, but there were moments when he seemed to be completely aware of his circumstance. At these times he would ask his father questions, or they would reminisce over the past, and at others he would express his concern for the rest of his family. It seemed he was worried that his unmarried sisters would remain thus so. What of his horse, Jasper? What would become of Maud and Mary Matilda? He had not written a will, so Maud was entitled to one third of his estate, and Mary Matilda would receive the remaining two-thirds. Sadly, there was no insurance policy. After the wedding, a generous endowment had been given to him by his father, money that had been Thomas's mother's, his

183

inheritance from the Owen side of the family. This money would keep Maud living comfortably.

Augustus promised his son that Maud and the baby would be well looked after. He would raise Mary Matilda as one of his own, and she would want for nothing. Knowing this eased Thomas's mind. He was aware of what was happening to him, completely aware that his young wife would be widowed at such an innocent age. Not being able to say goodbye to his other siblings was most difficult for him; leaving words unsaid was tragic and painful.

Just hours later, on the first Saturday of September, my beloved Thomas passed away. He had been unconscious for several hours that Friday evening, and then slipped into death at the time of night when most choose to go, silently and without anyone knowing.

Sleepily, I woke up, aware he wasn't breathing, and I sensed he was still. I could hear Jessie's light breathing, and the sound of the gaslight popped lightly, but I couldn't hear Thomas's breathing, at all. It had stopped; his last breath taken as we slept.

I jumped up onto the bed, whimpered and nudged him, but he wouldn't wake up.

I longed for him to wake up as if out from a deep sleep.

He did not move.

Jessie had fallen asleep in her chair during her deathwatch, too exhausted to stay awake for the duration of the night. I had been asleep on the floor, not far from Thomas's bed. I barked, but she didn't move. Then, I let out a cry and nudged her awake with a violent push. Almost immediately, I heard heavy footsteps on the stairs. Augustus hadn't been far. He had not been in bed where he should have been, so he must have heard me cry out and bark.

My master hesitantly came into the room, saw fierce tears running down Jessie's face, took one look at his son, slowly sat down on the side of the bed, and wept.

* * *

DOCTOR JAMES HAD ARRANGED TO CALL BY, later on in the day. Maud and my master looked visibly shattered, and each took to a quiet part of the house and

184

sat in solitude. Jessie was in tears and sobbed her heart out; she could not bear to lose her brother. The window blinds had been drawn within minutes of Augustus announcing that his son had passed away. The bed sheet had been pulled over Thomas's face, and he lay there like a lump – stiff and unmoving. I watched intently for any sort of movement from him, but there was none. I was beginning to understand, but couldn't get my head around not ever seeing this man, whom I loved, walk with me and throw a stick for me to fetch, ever again. He would never whistle for me again, ever.

How was it so?

How could this happen?

What of his horse, Jasper, who would never ride to the hounds with his master, ever again? This was death and dying. It had nearly happened to me, but I had woken up in the farmhouse kitchen, and Master Rowland had been so happy to see me open my eyes. I was beginning to realise that Thomas would never wake up and open his eyes again, but it was difficult for me to understand, though I sensed his departure as if a large piece of furniture was suddenly missing, leaving an empty place within a room. He had gone the way of the ewes – never to return.

Not knowing about death and its customs, I worried about what would happen next. I went over to my master and pawed at his knee. Augustus looked greatly stricken by the death of his son, sitting without moving, still as a mountain, and did not respond to my pestering. He was an old man with greying hair, and even I knew it would be hard on him. I could see he'd had a great shock. I would do my best to help the family, though I didn't know where to begin. Aimlessly, I wandered back upstairs, and jumped upon the bed to lie next to him – to keep him... no... to keep myself in his company, as his scent was still there – it lingered, though it was somewhat tainted.

The good doctor arrived earlier than expected. He gave us his condolences and also a certificate of death, which was promptly filled out by him. It contained all the pertinent information that Augustus needed, in order that Thomas could be buried and his death legally registered. Maud had no say in the matter of the funeral. Ah. Here we come to that word.

Funeral.

Then, I remembered what Horatio had asked me. *"Dost thou know what a funeral ith?"* Then, *"I'm so sorwy."*

I felt nithered as I remembered our conversation, and I then realised that Horatio was fey. There was no other explanation for his previous knowledge of the tragic event.

Thomas was born in Stanford Rivers, and that was where the family vault lay, in the churchyard of St Margaret's, a very ancient church with a wooden bell tower, which lay not very far from Wayletts. Augustus explained it was his duty to bury his son. Maud needn't make any decisions on the matter, and she should not remain in the house any longer than necessary, but should remove herself to Darnley Road, along with Mary Matilda and the nurse, Charlotte.

Hours later, after the doctor had left, my master was freshly bathed and shaved, though he looked like he'd been ill. Seated in a comfortable chair, by the window, with a half-empty snifter of brandy in his hand, he spoke to Maud with his usual air of authority.

"A lead coffin is required for the vault, but I can't register Thomas's death today because the Registry Office is closed and will not open again until Monday morning."

She sat nearby and sobbed. She managed to say, "Thank yew for not making me go threw this all alone."

Jessie came over to her, and said tearfully, "We couldn't do that. We wouldn't; we just wouldn't. Edmund will help Dad with all the arrangements; you don't have to think about anything."

Augustus took a large sip of brandy, as if for encouragement. "I shall go ahead and procure the coffin before registering the death. The certificate of death will be all the undertakers will require."

That must have been the paper he held in his hand. I saw him fold it up and secrete it in his breast pocket.

He continued, "The fact that Thomas has died from an infectious disease means he should be placed in a coffin, a sealed one, as soon as possible, and his body not left exposed in the stifling heat of this house to send out contagious fumes. He'll soon... You know, he'll begin to smell in this heat. But, anyway, in order to be buried in the vault, a lead-lined coffin is required.

It's the law. His death will have to be registered sometime during the week... I'll get Edmund to go with me."

Jessie had asked the maid for the use of pen, ink, and paper. "I shall make a list of all who have to be informed." Tears streamed down her cheeks and she genteelly dabbed them away with her hanky.

"A notification for the newspapers will be needed. Let Edmund deal with that," suggested Augustus.

He took another large sip of brandy, but then patted his knee, an invitation for me to sit by him. I sat with my chin on his knobby knee, and he stroked my face and ears, all the while gazing into my eyes.

"Poor dog," he said quietly. "Poor, poor dog. You'll miss him, too. Oh, Shales... what are we going to do?"

Just then, he swapped his brandy for his pipe, lit it with vigour, and gazed out the window as he puffed silent clouds of thick smoke into the air. His left hand lingered about my head; I was not forgotten.

* * *

A TELEGRAM HAD BEEN SENT TO A FIRM OF UNDERTAKERS who always had a large stock of finished coffins on hand, despite the high demand for lead-lined ones, and the following day two men with a lead-lined coffin arrived, and Thomas was sealed up inside it. The exterior was highly polished and decorated with shiny brass handles. He then was removed to Darnley Road, and his heavy coffin of five and a half pounds of lead to the foot was placed upon sturdy trestles, and he remained in the darkened front sitting-room (the one to the left of the front hall), until the time came for him to depart for the churchyard.

When I finally arrived back at Darnley Road with Augustus, Maud, Charlotte, and little Mary, we were quietly greeted by a family dressed in full mourning. Maud had already changed to black, and being the widow she was in deepest mourning, but I wasn't prepared for the other women, the sisters, to be dressed in the colour black as well. The house seemed to be unwelcoming, dark and brooding, as if it too had died.

Maud had been a dressmaker, and that week she spent her hours sewing as well as weeping, or as Toothless George would have said, "greeting". She required new clothes for the funeral and also for the twelve months she would remain in deepest mourning. During that week she sewed and sewed, thus keeping herself busy. She tearfully turned out a bonnet, a veil, several collars and matching cuffs, as well as many black-edged handker-chiefs. A seamstress was brought into the household to provide the others with funeral clothes and accessories, and what couldn't be provided in time was purchased from the city. There could be no funeral until everyone had either a new black suit of clothes, a black dress, or the proper attire such as veils, cuffs, hatbands, and so on. The funeral furnishers provided the smaller items such as kid gloves and hatbands. All this was achieved in quietness as the household solemnly went about its everyday duties. A wreath of black adorned our front door. The knocker was wrapped in black crepe, and the friendly stream of callers we were used to seeing had ceased to exist, and the house became as a prison. I never thought I would ever get used to seeing so much clothing in the colour black. Even the writing paper and envelopes they used were black-edged.

Jessie, Emily, Lucy, and Julia were missing their dead brother's exuber-ance for life, and they cried pitifully on and off throughout the daylight hours and into the night. Poor young Charles did not know how to cope. He had already had to mourn his own mother when she had died, when he was only five.

I tried to get him to take me out for a nice long walk, but he said tearfully, "Can't do it, Shales. It isn't proper to be seen out until after the funeral. Sorry!"

I felt so overwhelmed with emotion. It was as if the entire house – walls, windows, and all – were grieving, and I carried it about as if it were a large lump within my chest. It rolled about like a loose cannon-ball. I didn't know what to do with myself, and I mourned inwardly, keeping out of everyone's way.

In those next few days before the funeral, the only callers who came to the house were close members of the family, as the house was in interment. They, too, were dressed in black, being closely related to Thomas. One of these happened to be a son of the family, the eldest brother to Thomas. I didn't remember William, but he greeted me as "the other Shales", and I later realised he, too, had been at the gathering at Cotheridge Court, two summers before. I had incorrectly believed I had never met him. His wife, Mary, remained in Yarmouth with their children. She was looking after the hotel that they owned, unable to leave to attend the funeral. In fact, on the day of the funeral, I didn't know what at all to expect. I, too, was grieving, but I assumed I would have to stay behind with the servants. Jessie had tied a black crepe hatband around my neck, and my leather lead had been procured, and, so, I was called upon to join the family as they departed the house.

* * *

THE HEARSE HAD ARRIVED. I must tell you that as my gaze fell upon it when the front door opened, it was splendid in appearance, as it shone brilliantly and reflected the daylight off its glass and its highly polished wood. It was as black as the horses that pulled it. Nothing had prepared me for the beautiful glass sides that showed off the interior, filled with flowers after the coffin had been placed within. It gleamed with silver and gold. On top were masses of black ostrich feathers that gently wafted about in the early morning breeze. In front stood six enormous black horses. These were the genuine Black Brigade, as the coal horses were also known as the Black Brigade, but the funeral horses were the genuine article. These horses were absolutely magnificent, and came from across the English Channel, never being foaled in this country, but from a country called Belgium. Their coats shone black, with a gloss that was enviable. I knew Thomas would be proud to be carried away by such lovely horseflesh, as I knew he would have approved of them. Their huge heads were crested with several black ostrich feather plumes, which bobbed about gracefully with the slightest movement from the horses' heads.

The other carriages that were to transport the remaining mourners to Stanford Rivers, as part of the funeral parade, were in place behind the hearse. They, too, were black with shiny fittings that glinted in the bright light, and the horses were also glossy black with black ostrich plumes fitted to the tops of their bridles, in a spot between their ears. There were two of these carriages that we occupied, we being the chief mourners. There were six more, which carried many of Thomas's uncles, aunts, and cousins. I understood there would be others. Friends and more family would be arriving by train at the Ongar station.

We set off. The funeral parade slowly moved down Darnley Road and turned into Mare Street. We headed northerly. The hearse moved like a glass boat upon still waters, and to the sound of horses' hoofs it glided away in all its black glory. We must have made a magnificent sight, even though it was one of sadness and not joy. It was almost odd, in a way, being that we had only just moved into the house a fortnight previously, though I'm sure the neighbours were well aware of who lay inside the hearse. This might not have been Thomas's home, but it was where his family now lived, and so where the funeral parade would begin. I had noticed that as we were getting into the carriage the street was unusually quiet, as out of respect for our loss the traffic stood still, and people did not gawp at us, but instead, respectfully bowed their heads. Several of the neighbours and their servants came out and also stood with bowed heads. I was awed; it was my first funeral parade.

The window blinds of the enclosed carriage were drawn, so on our journey into Essex I could not look outside, but had to lie down on the floor. It seemed like a very long journey, and there was a definite lack of conversation in my carriage. Augustus sat with his eyes closed, as if in deep concentration, and Edmund, William, and Charles Clement said very little. Charles was on the verge of crying. All the men's eyes were red-rimmed and puffy. The air was tense, and I sensed they all could not wait for the funeral to be over with. I felt miserable and sick, and I didn't know what to do with myself. I was jolted about, and felt every cobblestone and rut in the road through the floor of the carriage.

After that day, I could always recognise a funeral carriage: distinctly black and pulled by at least one black horse, if not a pair of black horses, also decked out in black, and wearing those distinctive black ostrich plumes on their heads. Never mind seeing the hearse, once you've seen an entire funeral parade led by the Black Brigade, you will never forget it.

It was just about twenty miles, in my estimation, to the churchyard in Stanford Rivers. I had seen it before, the churchyard I mean, with Horatio, but the family had also attended church regularly on Sundays, and on those times I had waited patiently outside in the graveyard. As I walked up the pathway to the ancient church, still on a lead held by Augustus, we passed the vault, which lay directly to our left. Surrounded by detailed ironwork it merely resembled a sturdy, square, fenced area. It made me ponder what it was like down there, below ground, where Thomas would reside in perpetuity. It was just curiosity getting the better of me. Aren't you, the reader, at all curious about what it is like inside a burial vault? Have you ever been inside one? I'm still curious to this very day. Above ground, the large, square ironwork with its intricate designs was painted black, and carved into the stone at the base, facing all those who entered the churchyard, were the words *The Family Vault Of Augustus Berkeley*, and there, on the grass, lay a square, flat stone, declaring itself as the vault's entrance.

My presence drew a lot of attention. Dogs don't attend funerals. It seems to be some sort of law that has been about since the beginning of time.

It was explained that Thomas had requested that I attend the funeral as one of the family. The vicar would not allow me inside the church, and I was all right about that. I was placed in the care of a boy, a young cousin from Ware, and we stayed outside, near the open door, and from that spot we could hear the service.

There was an enormous attendance of people. Many were local, as well as those being family who had travelled several hours to get there. I recognised Thomas's cousin, Algernon Cecil, as he stood next to young Charles Clement, deep in conversation. The ones who had arrived at Ongar station had been fetched to the churchyard in style, and it was a sight to see: an enormous, snaking parade of mourners. I was reunited with my previous master, Rowland, who seemed very pleased to see me despite the sadness of the day. He stood next to his brothers, William, Herbert, and Edmund Robert (who looked splendid in his military uniform). I heard Edmund

Robert comment that if Thomas had been a soldier Jasper would be there, and he said quietly, "It is indeed the saddest thing to see – a horse at his master's funeral."

I wondered if anyone had told Jasper.

It was awkward for me to see my old master, as I felt a bit like a traitor, but the attentions of Rowland soon put me at ease. He was just relieved that I had not come to any harm, and was pleased that I was behaving myself and adjusting to living in a house. He did stress that it was indeed very odd that I had ended up at his uncle's house and not at some stranger's.

Though I was made to stay outside, the church door was not closed but stood wide open and I could listen to all that was being said. The vicar's voice was loud and far-reaching. The congregation was quiet. The little church had been filled to overflowing, and even more mourners spread out into the churchyard behind us in the late summer's heat. I settled down with my chin on my paws and listened to the muffled sounds as prayers were said and hymns were sung.

Sometime later, the church emptied itself of its black-robed occupants, and everyone respectfully departed and went their way, except for Augustus and the male mourners, namely those who had been closely related to Thomas. They stood around the vault in their black top hats, black coats, and black kid gloves, as if it were a cold winter's day. More prayers were said, and eventually the heavy coffin was interred in the below-ground crypt.

After the service, Augustus and his family, the other close mourners and I, went to Wayletts, where, at the farmhouse, we had refreshments. Brandy, sherry, tea, coffee, and sandwiches were served. Conversation was forced, and the air was glum. Shortly after the last of the close mourners left, they being Auntie Emily, Charles Clement the elder, Herbert, and Rowland, we performed an ancient ritual, and then afterwards we all returned to Hackney.

Shales attends Thomas's funeral.

I have to tell you about the ritual; it has to do with the bees. You know we kept some bees for the honey they made, and that wasn't unusual, as many farms have beehives. Well, I'll tell you what we did. Augustus put me on my lead, and Edmund, young Charles Clement, and all the sisters, including Maud, followed the master through the yard and out to where the beehive was kept. It was a large, funny-shaped thing that hummed with activity. I'd seen it many a time with Thomas, but this time it was different. The hive had been wrapped in black crepe, which I correctly assumed was for mourning.

But they were only bees, weren't they?

Augustus held a heavy, ancient key in his hand, which was for the front door of Wayletts, and as he stood in front of the rounded hive he rapped the key against it thrice, and then said, "Your master's son, Thomas Rowland, is dead."

This he said two more times, as if to make sure the bees had heard him. The bees became silent and still. I cocked my head in order to hear them better, but they were calm and silent; they now slept, or were awake, but definitely were inactive. Then we all solemnly trooped back to the farmhouse, and prepared to leave for Hackney. What a curious custom, I thought, as I followed my master back to the house. I wondered what Horatio would make of it.

I was not given the opportunity to roam. I was kept on a lead so, sadly, I did not get to romp about Ten Acre Wood, a place that would have given me comfort in my time of need. There had been no opportunity for me to seek out Horatio's consoling friendship, but it wouldn't have surprised me if he'd been there, all along, watching me from afar.

This time, on our return journey to Hackney, the blinds were raised and I could see out of the carriage window. When numerous people along the road saw us they stopped what they were doing and removed their caps and bowed their heads as we passed them by. I was awed at so many strangers showing an act of respect. It made a deep impression upon me. I would never forget Thomas, but he had had a fitting funeral, which would stay with me forever.

I had missed the farm terribly in the past fortnight, but I knew I had to go back to Hackney, so I silently said "goodbye" to the place, not knowing when I'd next return. I wished Horatio had been with me, to witness that day; his companionship would have been comforting. He would have approved of the style in which Thomas had been sent off, especially since he knew how much I had loved him.

XI

IT WAS BLEAK, BLACK, AND SO VICTORIAN

"...and I was sixpence, a tanner, richer."

LATE AUTUMN, 1882

THE WEEKS PASSED BY SLOWLY, the late heat of the summer having long since ended, and now the nights were once again gloomy and chilly. The fireplaces in our house all had fires blazing in them at some point of the day, giving the house a cosy warmth, though the ones in the bedrooms usually weren't lit until the evening hours. Often the weather outside was cold and drizzly, and on many of these days the London sky became a thick and brownish grey and the outside air smelt awful. They called it smoggy fog. It settled upon us in Hackney like a dirty veil. With most houses in the London area having several if not many fireplaces within their walls it was no wonder, even to me, a dog, that the air would become polluted. The chimneys chugged out smoke from the fires lit below, but on foggy days the smutty smoke struggled to become one with the sky, and a tell-tale coating of sooty smuts would be dusted about the rooftops, and just about everywhere else as well.

As winter beckoned, there were times when it rained and everything outside seemed to have a grimy coating of oily soot, which would not come off one's clothes, or white paws, so easily. To my own astonishment, the rain was actually dirty, something I'd never before encountered. Even the lush, green grass would become dark and grimy, and the trees and flowers were dark and depressed-looking from the coating of the filthy rain. Other times it became foggy, and at these times it was so thick you couldn't see across the street, the lamps appearing to be but a dim, disembodied glow, and the air would smell foul and repugnant. These strange fogs were commonly known as pea-soupers. Jessie referred to them as Purgatory. During a pea-souper, ordinary sounds such as hoof beats upon cobbles, or my own voice emitted as a bark, sounded eerily distorted, so they were an excuse for all Londoners to remain within the cosy confines of their homes and to cancel their evening's plans.

Everyone burnt coal, and I mean everyone. London town and its area thrived on coal. Every house had either a coal shed or a coal cellar, and the housemaids carried the coal throughout the houses in shiny coal-scuttles, and lit coal fires out of those black and dusty lumps and nubbles. We could not survive without it, and I marvelled at the amount our house burnt on a weekly basis, never mind the endless trips our maid-of-all did, carrying the heavy scuttle from room to room, to ensure there was always a plentiful supply of coal on hand.

* * *

Now, I've already told you the family was in deep mourning, and to my surprise they would be so for six months to a year, the duration being dicatated by the mourner's relationship to Thomas. I now wore a wide, shiny, black leather collar with a brass name-plate attached to it, inscribed with my own name, *Shales*. Seriously, it's true and not a fib – being a well-to-do dog I had to dress according to my station. On one particular day, I happened to see my reflection in a mirror, and I noticed how pretty the collar was, because its brass name-plate and buckle stood out nice and shiny against the black of the leather. It reminded me of all the shiny fittings on Thomas's coffin. At the time, I was stood on his bed, in the room he would have used if he had not married Maud and moved to a house of his own. Being on Thomas's bed was a no-no, and so was being in his room. The door to the room was usually firmly closed, but on this particular day, Armstrong, our housemaid, had gone in to light a fire to keep out the damp, and when she left she didn't close the door properly. All I had had to do was push it open; you know, give it a good nudge with my nose.

I entered out of curiosity, as Maud didn't use this room at all. Her bedchamber was further along, at the back of the house. I had a good look about, sniffing the carpets and such, recognising his furnishings as those from both Cassland Road and Stanford Rivers. I found the room had warmed up nicely from the fire and had become cosy, so I jumped up onto his old four-poster bed to have a lie-down, and that was when I saw my reflection in the mirror. I got a good look at myself, as I always only ever got to see myself from the shoulders downwards, whenever I turned my head, and usually, I only ever noticed my legs and paws, or the end of my tail. I confess I did admire my reflection, thinking myself the handsomest of my species. I *was* the handsomest dog in Hackney. I admired my shiny black coat, along with my white chest, legs and black and white face, and my soft, brown eyes. So this is what I look like! Satisfied with my appearance, I then decided to have that nap, on the bed, which actually turned into one of those really long, deep sleeps where one seems to descend into a weightless land of the imaginary.

Sometime later, I was found out and rudely awakened by Armstrong, who shooed me off the bed and hastily sent me out of the room, firmly shutting the door behind me.

"Shales! Don't let me catch you in here again!"

I scarpered out of her way, but I'd now developed a desire for sleeping in that room – his room. The bed gave me a comfortable feeling as if Thomas were not so very far away. Once, every week, she would return to this particular bedchamber to dust it and air it out, and I would follow closely behind her, but she always managed to shut the door in my face before I could slip inside. I would anticipate her movements, and she would find me patiently sitting in front of the door, waiting for her to open it and let me in. But she never let me inside as she dusted the furniture and lit the fire. Dejectedly, I'd lie there in a heap and listen to her through the closed door, while she made near-silent sounds as she dusted the furniture and cleaned the windows. The occasional squeak could be heard as she cleaned the window-panes, or, if I were lucky, she'd sing or hum a tune – for her own entertainment, not mine.

* * *

THE COOK had also removed from Stanford Rivers to Darnley Road. I was so, so disappointed. I had hoped we would have another cook, as she and I did not get on, not at all. During the previous winter, which I had spent at Cassland Road, I had tried my best to get on with her, but she did not like my friendly advances. We did not see eye to eye, and she seemed to despise me for some unknown reason. I didn't have any necessity to go into the kitchen except to eat and drink, and even that seemed to be too much for her to cope with. Augustus insisted that my bowls reside in the kitchen, in the cook's domain. Jessie put out my meals for me as well as deciding what I was to eat each day, which was a relief to me, but I would eat quickly then scarper away out of that den-called-a-kitchen. I think the reason I didn't like the kitchen at all was because of her; Cook had made it an unwelcome place to be. Sometimes, when I ventured into her domain, she angrily threw bits of food at me, such as carrots or potatoes. I'd try to escape, or even outwit her, but I wasn't always successful. They hurt, especially when they bounced off my head!

* * *

THE SISTERS RARELY LEFT THE HOUSE, and that went for their widowed sister-in-law, Maud, as well. The five of them would partake of different household duties every morning, to ensure the house was kept clean *and* in order. Jessie was the eldest, so she was the housekeeper, and she took her role seriously. She always told the cook what to prepare for their meals and teas, as well as keeping an eye on the cook's expenses. Also, she would inspect the linens and clothing, and anything else that needed mending would be set aside and would later be attended to by Armstrong. Sometimes the ladies would occupy themselves by embroidering decorative edges on pillow covers and bed sheets. These embroideries were finely done and were very intricate in their designs, but could only be done in good light, and the best light that came in through the sitting-room windows was in the mornings. I marvelled that they didn't go half-blind from all the embroidering they did.

Cheerfulness and laughter had disappeared out of this family. It was as if the earth had been shaken from beneath their feet and they'd never regained their balance; my master never mentioned Thomas's name after the funeral, for weeks. The entertaining conversations the family had engaged in at meal times and afterwards had ceased to exist. An uncomfortable mood dominated, as they instead read, or played board games in gloomy silence, and the piano slept undisturbed.

I happened across Edmund, one morning, as he was putting on his shoes. Tears were dripping from his eyes, which left little spatters on top of the polished surfaces. He was in the privacy of his bedroom, getting dressed before descending for breakfast, when I nudged his door open.

When he noticed me staring at him he said, "Come here; I know you miss him," and he gave me a hug, but it should have been the other way round, as it was he who needed the hug. Instead, I let him squeeze me to him, and in return I gave him a gentle lick to the face. He was understandably quiet during breakfast, and he ignored Maud's presence. I knew he was in deep turmoil.

The only happy person was baby Mary Matilda, who was too young to understand any of it. She wore dresses in normal colours, and happily babbled along in her own unintelligible language. She could crawl about at top speed, and I'd play with her, running circles around her and barking as she tried to grab my tail, and occasionally she was successful. "*Ouch!*" She'd squeal with glee as she held up handfuls of my crinkly tail hairs.

The gentlemen, and that included young Charles Clement – he was the youngest of all of Augustus's children – went out of the house every day, whereas the ladies remained behind. The men went to work at the coal depot, the warehouse, and the offices, just as before, as nothing had changed except for the week they took off prior to the funeral. They left the house wearing dark suits and tall, dark hats, and dark gloves, and Augustus always carried a handsome walking-stick that had a silver knob in the shape of a bear's head. Unless one looked closely, it wouldn't have been immediately apparent that *they* were in mourning. The men had invariably worn dark colours on working days, and blacks and dark greys seemed to be their favourite shades for working clothes. I think it was so the coal dust, which permeated the air in and around the warehouses and depot, didn't show up as smudges upon their coats and trousers. Now that they were in mourning, they didn't seem to dress much differently, except for their hatbands of black crepe, the width thereof which denoted their status of mourning, whether it be for a parent, child, or a sibling.

On Saturdays and Sundays Charles Clement had always preferred to wear shades of brown, and he favoured tweeds such as those from Norfolk, whereas Edmund preferred blacks and shades of grey, with the occasional colourful waistcoat, and *he* always avoided tweeds, being an immaculate, sophisticated dresser. But now they were in a state of mourning, and those tweedy and slightly colourful clothes remained locked away in their wardrobes.

Charles was employed as a clerk in his father's coal trade – a temporary situation only. Thomas had started off at that level before moving up to being a car man and a sales traveller. Edmund was an agent, but he also managed the office when his father was in the city, kept an eye on the warehouse, kept tabs on the Stoke Newington branch, managed the men, *and* saw to it that all the coal and carriage horses were looked after by the stable boys. He would take over the family enterprise in the future, but only when his father was ready to retire full-time. Edmund was very handsome. I think I've already said so, he resembling an older version of Thomas, and he sometimes smoked cigars in an evening as he read the papers or discussed the day's events with his father. He was also making up for the loss of Thomas Rowland at work, as no replacement had yet been hired, and he went over to the office in Stoke Newington regularly to keep an eye on things there. He was angry, and I could sense it, and it had to do with both my master and Maud.

Augustus didn't work as many hours in a day as Charles and Edmund. Being an older man approaching retirement age he came home in the after-noons around teatime. Actually, he did not have to work at all, but like most sensible men he kept control of his business, instead of leaving the running of it to his sons. At about four o'clock in the afternoon there would be the familiar clip-clop of Paddy's hoofs coming down our road, and I'd listen for the doorbell to ring, and would then hurry (woofing) alongside Armstrong, whose job it was to open the door and greet the master of the house. I, too, would greet him, with wagging tail – quite often I would jump up – and he would catch my front paws before they came in contact with his clothes.

Every day I would jump on him, and every day he would tell me "no!", but I still did it anyway – I couldn't help it. The housemaid would then hand over my lead, the black one, and after hooking it to my collar he would take me out for a walk along Darnley Road and onto Mare Street, or one of the other roads such as Paragon, Stanley, or Devonshire. We usually went for about a quarter of an hour, so we didn't go far before we turned around, and when we returned to the house the tea would be ready for us, set out on a table in the back sitting-room, unless we had callers, and then the parlour was used.

Sometimes Augustus would ask Armstrong if I'd got myself into any trouble at all during the day. Her usual answer was, "He's been a right jolly dog today, sir. No trouble at all. Not our Shales. He's what we call well-be'aved."

Then Augustus may have replied to this, "What? No teeth marks on any of my walking-sticks, or no new holes chewed into any of the carpets?"

Standing there in her uniform, she would smile at this, and say, "No, sir. He really is a well-be'aved dog. He doesn't chew carpets or shoes like Mr Hennessey's dog. That one'll put 'em in the poorhouse! You've be'aved yourself, 'aven't you, Shales?" She'd nod her head in the affirmative.

Then I would be given my cup of tea, in my own china tea bowl (a cup was too small), and also a biscuit from the table.

Jessie would break the biscuit into pieces, and then say, "One, two, three, four. There you are Shales; four pieces of biscuit."

Fondling my ears, she would often lovingly say, "Who's a good boy?"

This was how I learnt to count in order, from one to four. I often wondered what came after four, not realising it was five, though I knew five bells was the signal for some people to rise out of bed, and later on in life I managed to make sense of more numbers, all the way up to ten.

Sometimes we would receive *callers*. These were almost always ladies, ranging from the young to the aged, and possibly relations to the sisters, or simply just friends or acquaintances, or even just neighbours. Since Thomas's death the visits had at first stopped, then, as the weeks went by, the callers started to trickle in, venturing hesitantly, until they began to gain more confidence that their presence was once again welcomed. These visiting ladies were always immaculately dressed and highly scented for the occasion, and they were always received on either a Wednesday or a Thursday afternoon. It seemed these were the days of the week the sisters accepted visitors and were known to be quite often *at home*. The callers were oft-times the same ladies who had visited us at the Cassland Road residence. They were shown into the parlour, and tea was always served: a variety of sandwiches and cream-filled cakes, as well as plates of Cook's homemade biscuits, filled the round table. I believe it helped the gossip go down a little easier when one could sink one's canines into a cream cake. My goodness! Those women could talk. They knew everything about everyone!

My canine presence was slowly becoming to be accepted by these female callers, but I did have to be on my best behaviour to win some of them over. What I mean is this: I had to try my best to never drool on them, or wipe my mucky face on their lovely skirts, or jump up and shower them with my dog hair, or cause them to spill their tea, and yes, to not break noisy and foul-smelling wind in their presence. Eventually, they warmed up to me and began to greet me with a smile, and I'd wag my tail in reply, wondering how many bits of cream cakes or eclairs would be passed to me on the sly. My favourite trick to win them over was when I would sit, bow my head, and then whimper as I lifted a paw, pretending to be a poor little waif. They loved this and would clap their hands and cackle politely, and as a reward they would give me a biscuit from the table, or if the sisters weren't paying attention, a whole cream cake, held low beneath the table cloth. The thick cream was inclined to ooze out of the pastry and attach itself to my face; eyebrows and paws did not escape the attack of the oozing cream. In delectable satisfaction I would lick my paws *and* the carpet clean, with a thoroughness that impressed the maids.

One day, my master arrived just as the ladies were leaving. Armstrong said to him, "Shales has done a right good job of cleaning up all the crumbs from the ladies' tea. He's even licked the carpet clean!"

"Did anyone save me a cream cake?" He enquired hopefully, as she took his coat, hat and stick from him.

"No, sir... that'd be the one Mrs Hennessey smuggled to Shales, when your daughters weren't looking!" Seeing the huge disappointment on his face, she quickly offered, "I'll go and see the cook. She always makes plenty more. I'll fetch you a fresh one."

*   *   *

"**WHAT A LOVELY DOG,**" said the elderly Mrs Hennessey one Thursday after-noon. "His coat is so soft and silky. He's so clean, and he doesn't smell foul like most dogs do! How do you ladies do it? Come now, you must share with me."

One of the sisters, Emily, replied, "Oh. But we do our best to brush him and take him outside for fresh air. We walk him in the mornings, and our father takes him out for a walk every afternoon, without fail."

It was funny to see the visiting ladies, seated prim and proper and with their hands in their laps, then raise their eyebrows in apparent disapproval.

White-haired Mrs Hennessey dared to ask, "Do you mean to say that your *father* takes the dog out for a walk? I thought I had been mistaken, and I'd said to Arthur, 'It must be young Charles walking the dog.' It never is your father!"

Jessie graciously responded, in defence of her father, "Naturally, it was our father, though Charles and Edmund take him for long walks, too. He loves Shales, and doesn't like to leave him in the servants' care. Father needs his exercise, too."

When confronted with hostile stares, she went on to explain politely, "When he arrives home he takes Shales out for a walk, and meanwhile, our afternoon tea is being prepared. When he steps back through the door, our tea is ready. It's a routine he's got into, and I believe he looks fitter for it."

Jessie nodded her head as the last word rolled out of her mouth. Maud lifted an eye, and the other sisters sat frozen. They gazed intently upon the countenance of Mrs Hennessey, as did I. The room became silent.

The visitors straightened their shoulders and raised their chins; their sharp eyes darted from me and back to Jessie.

Mrs Hennessey said quite bravely, "I see. Perhaps I should be a little more diligent with the looking after of my own dog. You do know I have a most beautiful, little white dog named Frosty, and sometimes I do wonder if she has been receiving quite the amount of care she should get."

Mrs Hennessey then regaled us with a list of Frosty's house-demolishing habits. "She chews constantly! Carpets, curtains, chair legs! She's even gone for the hems of my dresses! The damages are amounting up to hundreds of guineas, and my Mr Hennessey is quite upset by it all, indeed he is."

Swallowing her pride, as best as she could, she continued in front of the other guests, "However, we are living in changing times, and I believe it is no longer frowned upon to be seen out walking one's own dog. One must have exercise for oneself. The doctors are recommending it. Am I not correct? Perhaps Frosty could benefit from a daily regimen, such as Shales."

She reached onto the table and took a ginger biscuit. Breaking it in half, she generously offered a piece of it to me whilst she nibbled on the other.

Everyone quietly nodded in agreement to the outburst, but secretly, they were peering into each other's faces to see who did not wholeheartedly agree with this shocking observation.

To settle unusual matters such as this, someone would invariably ask, "What do you suppose Her Majesty would do?" This time it was Maud who spoke up and asked about our Queen.

Mrs Purvis was obviously glad to be discussing the Queen. After swallowing a small mouthful of cake, which she washed down with a tiny sip of tea, she gushed, "Oh, Her Majesty doesn't walk her dogs. She has servants to do that!"

She then promptly dabbed at her lips with her table napkin, as if to say, "There! Let's see you better that!"

Mrs Hennessey lowered her teacup to its saucer, and tritely responded, "That is because she is unable to do so, now in her late years. She used to ride and amble through the highlands in her younger days. She would have walked her own dogs. I'm sure of it. In fact, I know it, and so shall I."

Mrs Purvis, a rather nervous sort of lady, rebounded with, "You wouldn't dare! Mrs Hennessey, I don't want to know if you are going to be seen walking the streets like a commoner. Please, do keep it to yourself! This is too much!"

To cut short a rather long topic of discussion, it became well known that Mrs Hennessey, in the company of her husband, started strolling about the streets of Hackney with little Frosty straining against the lead, as if walking into a gale-force wind. Dog walking by dogs' masters and mistesses began to be a common sight, but let's not forget where it began: started at my house – by my family – with me.

Many times, the topic of conversation was about the weather, or the latest clothing fashions, which were *safe* subjects for the ladies to discuss, and I would soon become bored to tears and would fall asleep. It almost seemed as if those teas had rules regarding what subjects could *not* be discussed, and what others fell into the category of *discussable subjects*. I regret that I was never invited along to call upon those ladies when the sisters returned their visits. I was nearly dying of curiosity as to what the interiors of their homes were like, or if they had a civilised cook, and I really wanted to know if Frosty could speak intelligently or not. Secretly, I had hoped that a friendship could be formed between Frosty and myself. I was missing the companionship of other dogs, there not even being an intelligent cat nearby, and upon hearing about this dog, my mind turned to thinking about Horatio. Oh, how I missed his companionship.

Now, let me tell you this: during this time, the sisters and Maud could not attend any music concerts, plays, balls, or in general go out and have a grand time, or be seen to be having a grand time, at all. If so, then they would have been deemed to be *not conforming to the rules for interment*. To the public, they were to *appear* to be bearing the weight of a family member's death, beneath the mask of demureness and piety, which they were, but I don't see, and never did understand, why they couldn't relax a bit in public. It didn't seem fair. They suffered enough from Thomas's death, but every day that they couldn't go out to visit anyone, or go to a museum etc., they suffered even more. They could and did go to church, to worship at the parish church of St John's, Hackney. I, however, could not go, which was unfair, as I think I would have enjoyed it, especially since I like music. Actually, I love music. It livens things up and makes me want to howl.

After three months of mourning, Maud was beginning to make the occasional comment about her state of semi-imprisonment. She was like a pent-up animal wanting to escape out of its cage. She was restless and yearned to live again, and frequently mentioned leaving and moving back into the boarding house. Secretly, I think we drove her mad with our own peculiar habits. At times like these she was always admonished, and reminded that her period of mourning would end, and would not go on forever.

Mary Matilda was still too young to be learning letters of the alphabet and such, but Maud had taken to reading to her from children's books, and I simply loved those occasions. I would listen to all the stories, trying to make sense of them. My understanding of English started to improve a little, even with Maud's Norfolk way of speaking, and so did my ability to count, as I *was* able to count past four. As a gift from her godfather, little Mary received a large box-load of books; their pages were filled with nursery rhymes and colourful pictures. I thought they were an awesome sight, and wondered what excitement lay hiding between the pages. These books were placed in the nursery, and I was allowed in there during story time and I could nap there if I wanted to, as Charlotte, her nurse, liked me, and we enjoyed each other's company. Other times, I played with the baby as she rolled about the floor or practised her crawling, and then later, her walking. I have to tell you that human babies are so *strange,* in that they must first learn to crawl, and then learn to walk, which is unlike any other baby animal I have ever encountered!

The men, now they were different. They did get to go out of an evening, once in a while, especially Edmund, who rarely stayed home on a Saturday night. He would get spruced up in his best evening clothes, and with top hat and walking-stick he'd go out on the town. Sometimes he went his own way, but usually he went with his father. They went to their club, somewhere in Westminster. I don't know which one it was or what drew them there, but Edmund and Augustus would go regularly, about once a week, and on those occasions would not dine at home; they met up with family – uncles and cousins. They would return late, smelling thickly of cigar and pipe smoke, and would be in a right merry mood. Apparently, this club they went to was a gentlemen's place, where females could not follow, and sadly, that went for dogs as well. Charles Clement remained at home with the women, and seemed content to do so, though he would be lightly teased about it. The sisters doted on him and knew that it wouldn't be long before he, too, would venture out for excitement in London, and try his hand at gaming or engage in some other form of entertainment that gentlemen did.

On the nights the men were at home they played chess, or occasionally backgammon, which was a favourite of the sisters, or simply read from a book or newspaper, such as the *Illustrated London News*, or *The Times*. There were several newspapers delivered to our door each and every morning, and even in the evenings as well. As we neared the end of the year it was a friendly atmosphere in this new house, when everyone forgot for a moment to be sad, as they all got on rather well together, apart from Maud, when she was in a mood and nothing would suit her. Edmund still had his quiet moments, but they had become less frequent.

I felt quite content on most evenings to lie in front of the fire and gnaw away at the latest bone I had been given, my thoughts always on the past.

* * *

ON ONE DECEMBER EVENING, the subject of Christmas was mentioned. I'd been happily playing with my ball. Edmund and Charles Clement tossed it between them and I tried to catch it from them.

Lucy spoke up. "Father, what are we to do for Christmas this year?" Before he could answer she then stated, "We cannot decide to not celebrate it at all. That wouldn't be right, would it?"

Augustus, after folding it up neatly, put down his copy of *The Times*, then removed his reading spectacles and carefully wiped them clean with a small cloth he used for that purpose, before answering. "I don't know, Lucy, my dear. We all miss Thomas, and it won't be the same without him, but we could all benefit from the distractions of Christmas. We can have a quiet dinner on Christmas Day, but perhaps we shan't dine alone. I know what. Shall I see if your Aunt Emily would like to come and stay with us for a few days? Perhaps for Christmas?"

He looked relieved that the subject had been mentioned. He'd obviously been dreading it, not knowing how they should celebrate the normally festive season.

All the ladies looked vibrant at the thought of Auntie Emily coming to stay with us. My ball was forgotten, as I was more interested in their conversation, especially when I heard the name Auntie Emily.

"Oh, yes, please do ask her," begged Lucy.

The sisters, their attention now upon their father, all mumbled in agreement.

"It might be too much for her," warned Edmund. "You know how she dotes on all her nieces and nephews, and now with Thomas gone she might find it too sad to be around us at Christmas. Perhaps it is too soon for her."

Edmund also came alive at the thought of celebrating Christmas. I think he knew it would be difficult, and he'd avoid it if he possibly could. I had sensed he felt guilty, was plagued with thoughts about Thomas's disgrace, but perhaps Christmas would be a marvellous distraction and he'd feel less responsible for his brother's death.

"I would love to see her, and it would give us something to look forward to," volunteered Charles Clement. Then he said, "Boys o' boys, mmn, mmn, mmn." He had a hopeful look on his face, which made him look younger than his seventeen years.

Before his father could respond, Jessie flew into him, as swift as a cannon-ball. "Charles Clement! Do not say that common, senseless string of words, ever again!"

"Sorry, sis, it's just that it is so catchy, and the men at work say it when they're happy."

My master interrupted Jessie and Charles. "She can always refuse to come, or your Auntie Emily might come and then make a quick departure, if you, Charlie, repeat that in front of her once too often," said Augustus with a smile. "She may have made other arrangements, though she hasn't mentioned any to me. I did read she might be spending Christmas with my brother Charles, but I think if she is invited to come here, then she might accept and Charlie will have to do without her."

I remembered he was the other Charles Clement in the family, the one with the colourful marriage, who, also, was responsible for embarrassing the family, and in certain circles, was branded a Scandal.

"I'll write tomorrow, and I shall ask her if she would like to spend Christmas with us instead."

I was all *eyes* and *ears,* and I noticed everyone in the room looked pleased, and the atmosphere had become somewhat lighter. Perhaps Christmas would be a good thing to happen to us, after all.

I thought to myself, *"Boys o' boys, mmn, mmn, mmn."*

* * *

AS PROMISED, a letter was sent off and Auntie Emily replied, accepting the invitation and saying that she would arrive on the twenty-third of December. Before her arrival a tree was acquired, and once again, like the previous year, it was delivered to our house shortly before Christmas. All the sisters had insisted we have a tree, even though we were in mourning. It was planted in the same pail, and once again lumps of coal were placed about the trunk for ballast, which were naturally black in colour and suited the current décor of the house, and not blue or red, otherwise they would probably have been covered up with a black cloth.

I watched with fascination at the activity that went into the decorating of that particular Christmas tree. Decorum had dictated that it couldn't be brightly dressed, so the tree was also in mourning. The ribbons that twined around it in delicate waves were a mixture of white, black, or purple. The same clear glass balls were hung from its boughs, weighing them down slightly, and the angel was placed upon its top, singular pointy branch. That Christmas of 1882 there were no boughs of holly with bright red berries decorating the various mantelpieces; there were only the tree and a collection of Christmas cards on display, where they had been placed alongside a framed photograph of Thomas, which sat atop the mantelpiece in the parlour.

December twenty-third arrived, and so did Auntie Emily and her lady's maid. Her full name was Emily Comyns Berkeley, and she was Augustus's only surviving sister, whereas he had four surviving brothers. She was a lovely lady with greyish-brown hair. She was small and wiry, and very affectionate, and her nieces and nephews flocked about her as if they hadn't seen her in years, let alone months. She kindly remembered me from the summer party, and also from Thomas's funeral, letting me know she was very fond of dogs.

I couldn't wait to see her reaction to the tree. When she saw it she simply said, "Oh, it's nice, isn't it? I do like the way it is decorated, even though it isn't very merry." She smiled, "Still, we must celebrate Christmas in our own way. Next Christmas will be a brighter one and you won't have to put any black or purple on the tree. I'm pleased you *have* put up a tree, even though we *are* mourning the loss of our dear Thomas."

All these comments as if it were perfectly normal to do this to a tree. So, I supposed we weren't the only family that did this at Christmas time. I had wondered if the potted-tree-thing was a certain peculiar trait accorded to just my family, and that no one else in England did it. Happily, I was wrong.

It was nice to know we were normal.

The next day, on Christmas Eve, we had a large family dinner, which included an extra guest at our table, a friend of our Emily's. Apparently, our Emily had a beau. I didn't know what a beau was, but it came in the form of a handsome young man. I had not met him before, as Emily had, apparently, been communicating with him over the last few weeks whenever she went out for a stroll, as he lived nearby at 20 Chatham Place. Really, she hadn't been seeing him on the sly, not like Thomas had been with Maud; she'd just been having a quick chit-chat on occasion, or they'd been communicating by occasional letter. This was because their possible public romance was put off until her appropriate period of mourning had passed. Sadly, it was a complicated affair, but secretly, I was pleased for Emily.

When the family discovered the secret romance, they didn't chide Emily like they had done with Thomas, but instead strived to find out more about Thomas White, who had been sent for by my master for a private interview. The result being the young man was a suitable match for Emily. Augustus thought Christmas would be an excellent occasion for the entire family to meet Emily's beau, as she was the first of his daughters to be even close to be getting married, even though the young man was yet a stranger and the question of marriage had not even been broached, though, that not being necessary, as the exchange of love letters had deemed them promised to each other. I liked him a lot. His name was Thomas, which was so strange to our ears after losing our own Thomas. When his name was spoken, it reminded everyone of the other, my beloved Thomas. Even so, he was nice, well-dressed, and well-spoken, and he was a cutler, which meant that if he and Emily ever married, then he would be able to provide her with a good income and a nice house. As I watched everyone as they ate, drank, and chatted, I could quite clearly see that they were all hopeful that Thomas White would prove to be an acceptable choice for young Emily, and that there would be no regrets.

* * *

CHRISTMAS DAY ARRIVED, and I wondered how different this day would be from any other I'd experienced in the past. Early in the morning, Edmund and Charles took me out for a nice long walk, and afterwards we went by carriage to where the warehouse and stables were, so that the men who were employed there could be wished a Happy Christmas and be given their bonuses. They had shown up merely for this and not to work, though the stable lad had already fed and watered the horses. Mucking out could wait a day. Edmund and Charles inspected to ensure that all was in good order, and the financial bonuses were handed out to the men and boys, and received with appreciative grins and thanks. They were given the remainder of the day off, as Charles Clement would return later that night to see to all the horses. This way all the employees could have Christmas Day off and spend it with their families.

I was left to linger about the stables for a few, short moments. As I wandered down the dark, narrow, horse-scented and crowded interior I encountered a familiar sight. It was Jasper. His long head was hanging over his stall door, and he blew soft, warm air across my face through his large nostrils. I quickly spoke with him and expressed my concern for his lodgings, and I was relieved to hear that he didn't mind the coalie stables, as he'd been stabled there every winter since he'd known Thomas.

"Hello there, Shales, my little pet." He bobbed his massive head up and down in greeting.

"I was worried about thee." I was truthful. I had wondered how he was doing.

"I'm well, though a little down because my young master is gone. Edmund has taken me out every week, though we just ride about town. He isn't stingy with his time; we go for a lengthy ride, but it isn't the same. I miss the hunt as well as our rides around Wayletts."

"I didn't know that. I mean that Edmund was looking after you," I said.

"Surprise, surprise," I thought to myself.

Edmund was full of surprises. I was relieved to know that he'd taken over the care of Jasper, and I had wondered why Jasper hadn't been stabled at Darnley Road. It would have been nicer for him there, though, perhaps, we didn't have enough room for him. I simply didn't know the answer to that one.

Just then, there was a whistle and a shout – my signal to go. I turned on my heels and shouted back to Jasper, as I ran to the stable door, *"Fare thee well and Happy Christmas!"*

Edmund smiled at me. "Come on, you. Home before you start smelling of the stable."

We returned to Darnley Road by horse and carriage, but on our return there were two carriages. Young Charles took an extra one from the stables, and I sat in the one driven by Edmund. It was quite cold out and snowflakes drifted down slowly in the frosty air, making the cobbles slippery and treacherous for the horses to walk upon. The effect was lovely, though, and slowly everything became white and clean looking, as if a magic wand had been waved about and all the soot and grime had disappeared from the streets of Hackney.

The reason for the extra carriage soon became clear to me as the family set off to go to the parish church for Christmas Day service. With Maud and Mary Matilda, as well as the four sisters, plus Augustus, Edmund, Charles Clement, Auntie Emily, and *her* personal maid, it was a large party that filled three carriages! As I gazed out of the window at the end of the house, from the second floor, where I always had a good, high view of the back drive, I noticed two extra drivers, and supposed they were earning a much-needed Christmas bonus for a couple of hours' service to my master. I, of course, was not invited, and glumly remained at home with the servants and the Christmas tree.

When the family returned home from church it was time to open the Christmas presents. I had received two gifts from Father Christmas. One was a new ball that had a little bell sewn inside, which jingled loudly when tossed about. I loved it – it was better than my other ball. The other gift resembled a stuffed animal, and from the scent that still lingered, Jessie had made it with her own hands.

The much-anticipated Christmas dinner was served at midday, after we had opened our presents. Auntie Emily and the others were dressed in their finest mourning clothes. The ladies all wore jewellery: earrings and brooches and necklaces made out of black stones. I thought it was coal, but I might as well tell you now that I later learnt it was jet. That's a particular stone that comes from the north east of England and is carved and made into jewellery. Victorian ladies-in-mourning loved the stuff, and there wasn't a shortage of it in our house that Christmas.

The table was highly decorated and covered with various dishes of food, and the smells nearly drove me insane. My appetite was enormous, and all morning long I went about the house salivating. I sincerely hoped that I would receive a large portion for my dinner. I was not disappointed. A little bit of everything was put onto a plate for me, and it was placed upon the floor next to the empty chair set for Jesus. A place had been set for him by Armstrong when she had laid the table, and Maud, not understanding this, had asked who else there was to come. She was told by Lucy, "We always set a place for Jesus, out of love and respect. It is, after all, his birthday." There was, of course, goose, roast beef, vegetables, gravy, sage and onion stuffing, and let's not forget the Christmas pudding with rum sauce.

I bit into something quite hard when I got to the latter pudding, and it nearly broke one of my teeth. Painfully, I spat whatever it was out onto the carpet, wondering what the heck it could be, as it was harder than a bit of bone. Our Emily happened to notice, and curiously reached down from her chair and picked it up.

"Oh, my." She stuck her arm up into the air and waved it about excitedly. "Shales has a sixpence!"

Why this was funny, I do not know, but the entire family erupted with laughter. The incident took them so much by surprise, that they laughed and laughed until they all nearly fell out of their chairs.

Apparently, the placing of money into a pudding was a Christmas tradition everywhere, and *I* was sixpence, a tanner, richer. The previous Christmas, I had either swallowed a small silver sixpence without knowing it, or I hadn't received the lucky portion of pudding where one had secretly lain hidden.

Augustus laughed and said, "We'll put it in a post office account for you, Shales. It'll make you a tidy fortune at four percent interest."

This just got everyone laughing even more. I wagged my tail because I knew they were pleased with me, even though I didn't fully understand what was being said. Their gaiety was infectious. I did know that I had sixpence, and that I could purchase things with it. It had value; I understood that. I got so giddy that I started to howl, and that made everyone laugh even more, completely forgetting their own state of sadness, which I think was a good thing. Boys, 'o boys, mmn, mmn, mmn.

Once everyone had dried his or her tears from laughing so hard Auntie Emily took an opportunity to give little Mary Matilda a present. Too young of an age to be at the dining table, Mary Matilda was upstairs with Charlotte, her nurse, who herself would dine later below stairs, with the cook and Auntie Emily's lady's maid, and Armstrong.

"Of course, she's too young to realise its value and appreciate its beauty," said Auntie Emily, "but someday she'll appreciate this present."

Maud had the obligation of unwrapping the little present, which was done up in bright blue paper and tied with a white silk ribbon, and I could see from where I lay that it was a lovely brooch. I got up from my spot in front of the fire to go over and have a look. It sparkled blindingly as it captured the light from the overhead gas-lit chandelier when she held it out to show everyone.

"'Tis lovely," said Maud as she held it up to the light where it sparkled. "Thank yer, Emily. I'll put it away for her 'til she is old enough ter wear it."

"That brooch was handed down to me," said Augustus's sister. "It came to me through my mother's side, the Comyns side of the family. She was from Essex, though not from Ongar, but from Hylands, in Writtle."

"It's valuable," commented Augustus as he looked over at Maud. "Really, it should be put in the family safe until she is old enough to have it. Those are diamonds, not glass."

"Dorn't worry. I'll ollas look after it," said Maud, smiling.

Then Auntie Emily said, "Now, as to you other ladies, my nieces, I have a piece of jewellery for each of you. I don't wear a lot of these brooches and necklaces anymore. Consider them your inheritance from me."

And with that she gave Jessie, Lucy, Julia and Emily either a necklace or a brooch, with an explanation to each of its history. Afterwards, when we retired from the dining-room, the sisters all had their turn at the piano, and Christmas music was played and carols and hymns were sung.

It was Auntie Emily who brought down the house, when she expertly played pieces of music composed by Beethoven and Mozart. I loved it, I loved every minute of that Christmas, and I howled along to my heart's content.

* * *

THE NEXT DAY we ate Boxing Day food. It was food, all of which was left over from Christmas Eve and Christmas Day, and we ate it *warmed up.* Yes, we did eat off china plates and not out of cardboard boxes. The boxes were for the remains, and there was a lot of it, which was parcelled up and was to be given out to the needy. On Boxing Day morning Jessie led her sisters and Maud out of the house, and they trooped out of Darnley Road and returned some two hours later with rosy cheeks. They had found a needy family or two in the poorest part of Hackney, and had given them our leftover goose, beef, sausage rolls, mince pies, and pudding to feast upon.

Auntie Emily stayed until the New Year. The eve before was quiet, with no celebrations at all, although Edmund and Charles took themselves off into London. Amidst goodbyes, my own ta-ra, and a fare y'well from Maud, she departed on the first day of the New Year to visit with her brother Charles

215

Clement, taking with her all our love, as well as Jane, her lady's maid, and an enormous amount of baggage. So ended the Christmas season and the year 1882, and so began a new year, 1883.

THE FOOL

BOOK III

XII

MR PEPPERMINT AND A DOG
WITH A JOB

"Hell's Bells!"

WINTER, 1883

I HAVE A SECRET TO REVEAL. Secrets don't like to stay quiet – they threaten to either escape or eventually drive one mad – so I shall now reveal mine to you, before I lose my entire mind. I was getting fed up with being inside the house all the time, as the feeling of being constricted started to make me feel threadbare, and my highest point of the day, the part that I looked forward to, was when Augustus would take me for my afternoon stroll, which was only a short one up and down the streets and not a lengthy romp through exciting fields and meadows. I do admit that the sisters did take me out for walks, and Charles and Edmund also took me out along Church Path for long walks, but it wasn't the same as any sort of unchaperoned adventure. Dear Reader, I suppose that you can clearly see I was missing farm life, and that I ached to round up a flock of sheep or even an escaped pig, as well as run through the woods again and chase squirrels and rabbits. The same daily routine of following either Jessie or Julia, or even one of the others about the house, was becoming a trifle boring, to say the least. The festivities of the Christmas season were over and done with; the house had settled back into its normal routine. When they thought I was sleeping peacefully, well, I was really quite wide awake, but daydreaming about my past adventures and escapades with Thomas. I yearned to get out and have a good run and stretch my legs, and to let the wind blow through my hair again.

I wanted to be free! Hackney was waiting to be explored by me, and curiosity about what was out there was gnawing away at me like a donkey at a fresh turnip, until I began to plan some sort of escape.

I couldn't easily slip out of the front or side doors when anyone came or went, because Armstrong was very diligent, and she guarded them like a true soldier on sentry duty; she would have made the Romans look inefficient. The only possible ways off the property were through either of the gates, situated near to the front and back of the house. But the gate at the front led out quite close to the road, and it was always closed, except for when kitchen deliveries were made or visitors called, and besides, it was made of tall, spiked, iron railings. The gate at the back of the house, though arched and wide enough to allow a carriage and horses through, resembled a solid wooden door, and was set into the brick wall, which formed a square yard. In the yard were the small stable and carriage house, both of which formed part of the square yard. It was not paved but was covered in pea gravel, and had some grass around the edges which held long, narrow flowerbeds. Potted plants sat outside the main entrance, giving it a decorated but tidy appearance. On the inside of the brick wall was a clipped hedge, though it did not reach the height of the high wall.

I never gained entrance to the small paddock at the back of the house. I only ever saw it from the upstairs windows in either Jessie's or Julia's room, or from the next floor above. The activity I usually witnessed from their windows was that of the family carriage and horses, either just leaving the drive, or just returning, always empty except for the driver, Soames. He was also stableman at the coal yard, in charge of looking after all our horses and carriages. Whenever the carriage was needed Soames drove it round to the front entrance on Darnley Road, and from there he would depart with its occupants. They never used the rear gate and drive, and naturally so.

The discovery of the escape route was completely accidental, and it fell into my plans for escape rather well. Lucky me! I had found it when I hadn't even been looking for it, where at the very bottom of the garden there was a gap in the hedge, and some low-hanging branches had been broken away, and behind the same hedge there stood the solid brick wall. I noticed that some of the bricks lower down and near to the ground, at the base of the wall, were missing, revealing a hole large enough for me to crawl through. It required a bit of digging, until I found I could get out by crawling on my belly, with a bit of a struggle, and I came out onto the path at the back of the stable. I was free! Oh, what a jubilant feeling! All because it was in the morning, and all the ladies in the house were busy doing their needlepoint and other activities, and I had been allowed to spend some time alone in the garden because it was a sunny, dry day – an unusual sight for January. In other words, I had been forcefully booted outside to occupy myself unattended, whilst the household happily continued with its morning routine. I had found the scent of a cat and had curiously followed its trail across the pea gravel and the winter-yellowed grass and around the dead-looking flowerbeds, where it led me to the bottom of the small garden. The cat's scent was familiar, as I had smelt it oft-times on occasion, but polite interest caused me to follow its trail, which revealed both fresh and faint scents. It was then that I noticed the hole further down to the left, away from the gate, but close to the stable. I got down onto my chest, with my bottom poking up high in the air and my tail waving about like a sheet on a windy day, and sniffed about and had a good look at it, all the while realising it could be my way out. It was obvious – the cat had been coming to and going from my little garden paradise (though we had not yet met face to face), possibly hunting mice in and around the stable. I was surprised at myself. I hadn't noticed the hole beneath the hedge before, but then again, I hadn't bothered to sniff about the hedge at this particular spot, cat scents being as common as mice. At first, to my dismay, the hole was a little too small for me to squeeze through. Oops! I accidentally scratched and pawed at it, and a broken brick became dislodged. I pawed again until the brick rolled out beneath the hedge.

"*Oh,*" I thought. "*It isn't my fault the mortar is crumbling away.*"

Gradually, after a bit of hard work, the hole became large enough for me to wriggle through. I was so pleased with myself. This was *my* secret. No one would know that I could leave whenever I wanted to, and could go off for a stroll and explore Hackney all by myself. And that is what I did. With a little difficulty, but not too much, I popped out onto the other side, and found I had the path at the back all to myself. I looked along its length. It divided our property from the long gardens belonging to the houses on Mare Street, and

221

was empty, save for myself. Soames was not around, and if the horses saw me they could not tell on me. With the stable and carriage house giving me sufficient cover should anyone have been looking out of the upstairs windows, I set off for a short excursion, as I didn't think anyone in the house would miss my presence, their minds intent on doing the housekeeping as well as the little things that ladies did, and they not giving me a second thought. I soon found myself at Loddiges, on Mare Street, where I paused to glance back and saw my house was no longer visible. I hesitated at first, not knowing which direction to take, and I then headed south, and trotted off to admire some of the other ancient and noble houses in Hackney.

How nice it was to be out jogging down the road like nobody's business. The old houses were really nice. The odd one being timber-framed, such as ours, and many of them were larger than our house on Darnley Road, which was not small in size, but in fact had plenty of rooms, unlike the small villas next door to us.

There was lots to see as I ventured down Mare Street. I discovered several objects of some interest. One was a badly worn horseshoe that lay in the gutter. Several crooked lead nails protruded from it, and it had obviously been thrown there by a horse. I paused to sniff it, but it was boring. Its interesting scent was long gone. Another was a tanner (a sixpence) that I found lying on the pavement. The human scent upon the silver piece was fresh. I had to leave it there, as obviously I couldn't just pick it up and carry it home – I had neither fingers nor pockets. I was aware that it was a coin of some value, having found my own sixpence in the Christmas pudding, and the discovery of this one, by a human, would put a smile on their face. My third and final discovery was a single peppermint. It lay at the edge of the kerb, obviously dropped there by accident. Naturally, I popped it into my mouth and ate it. The sudden burst of hot mint as I ground it between my back teeth reminded me of home and my next meal to come. I realised I was feeling peckish, and just as I swallowed the remains of the sweet, church bells chimed in the distance. The frequent number of bells tolled warned it was a signal to return to whence I had come. However, I had the urge to go on and on without stopping. This urge was extremely great, such as when one becomes thirsty and must take a drink of water in order to quench the thirst, but I knew I could ill afford to get caught. With peppermint-bated breath I turned around and cannily returned home the way I had come, up Mare Street and onto Devonshire Road, up the drive and behind the stable, then through the hole and under the wall and hedge, with the secret knowledge that I would do it again. Oh, yes!

All was quiet outside the house. It was all a hush; there was no one calling my name. I found I had not been missed, and felt pleasingly refreshed after that little bit of exercise. I licked my front paws clean until they gleamed pure white, thus removing any traces of dirt and other evidence of my escapade. I gave myself a good shake in order to dislodge any signs of twigs or brick dust clinging to my back. I stared at the gaping hole where the leafy branches of the hedge had been broken and pushed aside, and I hoped it would not be noticed. I knew that in the future I would have to be careful to not get caught. I could not risk discovery. In other words, to prevent my being found missing from the garden, future excursions would have to be short ones, but besides that I would have to be careful when crossing the streets and roads. They, especially Mare Street, were busy and dangerous because of the many cabs and other traffic such as omnibuses and delivery wagons, many of which travelled up and down them non-stop. And besides, how would I ever explain coming into the house with a broken leg or a crushed foot, when I had simply been sent outside to do my looing?

The weekday mornings were the safest for me to go off in exploration, after the men had left for the coal yard and when Soames wasn't hanging around our stable. This seemed to be when I was sent outside to do my business, and I was usually forgotten about for an hour or so, unless it was raining, snowing, or was as 'foggy as a short trip to Purgatory'. I soon started to know all the local roads and streets as well as the parks and other green areas. To the north of us, off Paragon Road, there was a small apple orchard, and this was a wonderful place to go for a quick retreat. In that place I chased the odd cat. My philosophy was this: if they ran, I chased. I thought they deserved to be chased, as they were so unlike Horatio. I also sniffed out mice and rats, which would hide in the sodden, dead grass as they fed off the brown, mushy apples, which lay there rotting after dropping from the branches above. The wild scent of the vermin gave me genuine pleasure as

I chased and pounced about the thick tuffets. Before I could be missed I'd sneak back into the garden and find a place to lie down, pretending to be napping, but waiting for Jessie or someone else to call me to come inside. The dreary winter days soon evolved into weeks, the cold season started to pass quickly, and spring bulbs began to sprout in the abandoned flowerbeds and clay pots.

* * *

ONE SPRING NIGHT, when Edmund and Augustus had just returned from their gentlemen's club somewhat earlier than was usual, an announcement was made. Augustus took the centre of the room and told the female population to hush, pointed to me, and then told Charles, his daughters, and Maud, that I had become somewhat infamous. He related to us that a particular gentleman who lived on Mare Street, in one of those old mansions, was also a member of his club, and the gentleman had commented to him just that very night about the dog, which he knew to belong to Augustus, that had been seen to make regular journeys up and down his street, and usually in the morning hours. Augustus, not at first believing this gentleman, then had had to accept the man's word when the unmistakable black collar with the shiny brass name-plate was described to him, as well as the dog's amiable nature and white eyebrows.

When I heard this being revealed to the four walls of the house, I felt my cheeks begin to burn, and I am sure they had a scarlet glow to them. Even my ears felt hot! Oh, what shame! I had been caught. The dismay I felt was akin to the floor being snatched from beneath my feet. I had a good idea of who had told on me. He did! It was Mr Peppermint! The gentleman at the club must have been that nice elderly man I sometimes encountered, who called me by my name, and who usually gave me an innocent peppermint, pulled from a small paper bag and offered with an ageing, feeble, shaking hand. On more than one occasion the feeble Mr Peppermint had by accident dropped a sweet onto the pavement, which I quickly snatched up – giving me a tally of two mints. Thus, I always associated him with peppermints; hence his name.

Jessie, upon hearing of my escapades, departed her place upon the settee and strode over to the corner of the fireplace. Then, she looked down upon me in absolute horror. In a very stern voice she said, "Shales! How on earth have you been going out on your own and getting up to high jinks?"

My cheeks were definitely glowing red!

I cannot tell a lie. I felt my body cower, and I rolled over onto my back with my paws in the air, exposing my hairy belly to the room. I thumped my tail and it landed across the fire-rail, which was just a simple, low-lying brass rail, and unbeknownst to me my tail came dangerously close to the red coals in the grate. About my escapades, I was caught out. No point in denying it. I felt ashamed that I had been discovered, as if I were a rare and exotic animal from Africa. I wanted to slither away on my belly and hide beneath something. Any piece of furniture would have done. It hadn't occurred to me that some person, or persons, living elsewhere in Hackney, and on Mare Street of all places, would recognise me and tell on me. I certainly hadn't thought the peppermint man would tell, as he was such a kindly old gentleman. It was something I hadn't even considered happening. Hell's bells! I should have been more careful! I knew it was wrong of me to go off on my own, without permission, as well as to have kept it a big secret, but I didn't see why I couldn't wander about Hackney as long as I was careful. They seemed afraid I would become lost, but I knew I could never get lost, not ever. I was careful of the traffic, and I was quite used to dodging in and out of it. I was getting better at crossing the busy streets all the time.

"Do you smell something burning?" interrupted Emily, as Jessie was about to speak again. Following her nose, she screamed, "The dog's on fire!"

"What?"

"What's on fire?"

"Shales is!" shouted Emily.

Jessie reached down and deftly whipped my singeing tail away from the fire, and at the same time Edmund quickly leapt forward and grabbed a vase of flowers from the mantelpiece, and then doused the end of my thick tail with its tepid water. A noisy blast of steam erupted, and droplets about the hearth sizzled. He stood over me. In his left hand he grasped a fistful of sodden stems, and his right hand held the dripping crystal vase. He tipped up every last drop of vase water there was onto my singed tail. In the background there were shrieks of alarm by the women. They had imagined me running from pain and fear, my tail alight, to set parts of the house afire, and they to die a frightful death.

Realising I'd been on fire, I scarpered to the middle of the room, flopped down heavily, and then examined the sodden stump of my tail. No real damage was done to my tail. My flesh was not burnt; the hairs were merely shrivelled where the tail hairs had smouldered and melted. The air stank unpleasantly of burnt hair.

Augustus had taken a seat in his favourite chair, and eyed me with awe. "Well, well, I never." He spoke with authority. "He wouldn't be the first dog to have burnt the house down. I've read of such stories – didn't think they had any truth to them."

"I say, that *was* close," said Edmund, as he carefully shoved the flowers back into the empty vase. With a shrug of his shoulders, directed at his attempt at flower arranging, he placed the flower-filled vase back on the mantelpiece.

Jessie, her long, dark skirts rustling as she moved, started to pace about the room with a frightened expression upon her face. Standing with her back to the fireplace, she addressed everyone present, and her worried expression revealed her concern for me. "He could have been lost again, or even killed, and we wouldn't even have known it."

Her voice was strained, and I was sorry I had upset her. When she sat back down on the settee I flopped across her lap, and lay there with my back feet still upon the carpeted floor. I was relieved when she hugged me to her. She was frightened for me, but was not angry with me.

The other women all had opinions as well, but in general they agreed with Jessie. I had given them a shock – actually two shocks all in the space of a few minutes. They all expressed surprise, and wanted to know how I had been gaining access to the outside world, and when.

15 Darnley Road, Hackney.

Fair-haired Charles, who looked nothing at all like his late brother Thomas, or his older brother Edmund, laughed when he asked, "I say, how did he get *out*, and then *back inside* without anyone knowing about it?"

Edmund settled himself back in his chair, drew deeply on his cigar, and casually blew a smoky-blue ring before saying, "He's been going out and loafing about the garden and yard every day, so there, that place is where I would first look." With deep concentration, he tapped his ashes into a tray.

"He can't get out unless somebody opens a gate, and then leaves it open for him to get back inside." Jessie pointed out the obvious.

"Just a minute!" interrupted Emily. "He nearly just set himself and our house on fire! Let's talk about that first!"

Julia agreed with Emily. She very patiently stated, in an even voice, "I think that first we should address the issue of fire safety in our home. A larger fire-rail is required to keep him further back from the flames and hot coals!"

"Ladies! If you please!" My master took control of the situation. "We shall address the issue of... fire safety, as you call it, as well as getting to the bottom of Shales's runs, walks, or whatever we should refer to them as."

With narrowed eyes, Edmund questioned one of his sisters. "Jessie, don't you send him out into the garden every morning? At least somebody in this household does. No doubt he is guilty of jumping over the hedge and wall. I'm sure of it." So, Edmund had cottoned on as to how I had got out, though I had gone under the wall and not over it. He patted his knee and beckoned me over to him, where he then gently stroked my head. I dared look him in the eye, and he winked back at me, as if to say, "Well done."

Their father was now stood in front of the fire, warming his backside, with a snifter of brandy held in his left hand (to steady his nerves) and his pipe in his right. The aroma of my burnt tail still tainted the air, and a puddle of water pooled over the marble hearth, still waiting for someone to wipe it up.

"I actually think you may be correct, Edmund. Tomorrow morning we'll get Soames to inspect the garden and see if it has been breached at any place. Perhaps he simply jumped over the hedge, which isn't entirely impossible for a dog of his breeding, but he may have found another way out. Right behind that hedge is the wall, and the gate at the front is always closed, unless someone has left it open. If he got out through the back gate, then he wouldn't be able to get back inside unless *that* had been left wide open, and I'm sure that isn't the case – it would be seen from an upstairs window. It isn't just the one time he's been out; no, according to Driscoll, it's been many times, and all in the morning hours."

Jessie then came over to me, crouched down and stroked my head, running her fingers around my ears. She examined my tail. "But why? I thought he was happy."

"Hmph," snorted Augustus, "he needs more things to occupy his time. Remember, he would have been happy working on a farm. These dogs need to work each day, otherwise they turn silly. He's a sheepdog, not a housedog. I think he needs something to do each day to occupy his mind, and we need to give him more exercise. He had lots to do at Wayletts, but now he's living in the city and he spends most of his time inside. We'll have to do something about it, but I'm not sure what."

It was Edmund who first suggested that I go out to work, to the coal yard – the depot – and to the office every day. The idea did not catch on too well with his sisters, but Augustus and Charles readily agreed with him. The sisters were bothered that I would forever be in danger from the horses, the heavy wagons, and the overhead chutes filled with coal travelling at ferocious speeds. Augustus said I would be perfectly safe and would be kept on a *short rope*. He added heartily, "Besides, a lot of the time he'll be in the office with me."

Charles suggested in a kindly voice, "Just spending the day away from the house would be a distraction, as well as the walk to and from the warehouse, done on occasion when it's fine." Then he asked, "Will you be taking him to the Coal Exchange?"

"I haven't thought about that, Charles." Then my master laughed a low, deep laugh. He explained, "The Exchange is not a place for dogs; it is where serious men decide the price of coal. As a member of the Coal Factors' Society, I must say, it is no place for a dog to lark about in. But now that you mention it, I could be persuaded to take him along, just to see how he behaves in public, especially on the trains. Besides, I could use his companionship – there isn't always anyone worth talking to on the train. Perhaps I shall set a new mode and others will fetch their dogs with them."

Edmund started to laugh. "I would give anything to witness you taking Shales to the Exchange. Just to see the looks on the other men's faces when you enter that domed building with a four-footed friend." In a more negative tone he said, "He'll not like the Underground railway. If you ever seriously consider taking him there, you'll have a struggle on your hands."

In a patient voice, Augustus replied, "My dear Edmund, I disagree with you and I'm going to give him a chance." He set his glass upon the mantel and strode to where his pipe tray lay upon a small table. After knocking out his spent ashes, he merrily rubbed his hands together and said heartily, "Well, that's that. Don't worry girls; he'll be well looked after and he can walk home with me in the afternoons, instead of us travelling by carriage. I'll deliver him to you safely at every teatime." Evidently, his mind was made up on the matter.

Emily started to cry; she had tears in the corners of her eyes. "Just don't lose him. He's absolutely lovely and I don't want him to go missing. London's no place for a dog. That is how he came to be with us. Remember? He ran away from cousin Rowland's."

I didn't like to see her upset, but I didn't want to stay home with the sisters all day long, even though they took me out for walks. I felt I needed to be doing something important, and not just being a lazy so-and-so who went out for occasional walks on a short lead.

Jessie put her arms around her sister Emily, who was dabbing at her tear-stained face with a lace hanky. "Dad will make sure he doesn't run loose. When we come out of mourning, then we'll be able to take Shales with us on daytime excursions, and perhaps he won't need to go to the coal yard again. We'll plan special days out, just for him, and we'll all benefit from the fresh air and exercise."

I listened to all that was being said. I was in trouble, but it wasn't that terrible. I mean, I wasn't being sent away to a dogs' retreat in the country or anything like that. At least I hadn't caused the police to come knocking. Not yet. The truth is, I was absolutely thrilled to be going off with the men each morning. Perhaps it was a good thing that I had been seen and my master informed of my wayward habits. I could benefit from this. I was so happy that in my mind a singsong voice kept singing, "*I have a job, I have a job. Boys o' boys, mmn, mmn, mmn.*" I, Shales the sheepdog, was going to go off to work with the men each morning, instead of loafing about the house. Already, I was daydreaming and wondering if I could be a guard dog, as then I would patrol the streets around the warehouse and offices, and keep away all miscreants and vermin. There might be enormous rats and ferocious cats to chase, as well as the odd drunken geezer. I was so excited with the importance of it all that I didn't think I'd get any sleep as I looked forward to the next morning and my new job.

* * *

THAT NEXT MORNING, I consumed a large breakfast of scrambled eggs and toast, and a large bowl of tea. Whilst I was occupied with drinking my tea, Jessie trimmed off the end of my tail with a pair of scissors. All the burnt hair was gone, and it was shorter – squared-off at the end like a Hackney pony's. I set off out of the house on a full stomach, with the men, though I couldn't tell you if it rained, snowed, or was fine, as my mind was set on one thing, and that was starting my new job.

When we arrived, Augustus took me into his private office and quite firmly told me to stay. He didn't tie me up, but rather he left the lead attached to my collar, which trailed around my feet and along the floor whenever I moved about. I understood – I could not leave of my own accord unless I wanted to jeopardise my position within this family. It wasn't so bad. I lay down upon the carpet and looked about the room. It was very nice, like a drawing-room or a sitting-room, but more masculine than a sitting-room, as there was no evidence of any female presence on these premises. There were a couple of comfortable leather armchairs either side of a vast fireplace, that gave off a wonderful, warm glow, and also, there was a large, heavy desk set close to the windows, and along one wall were tall cabinets with drawers. On the walls were some framed pictures, oil paintings of various scenes, as well as some marvellous maps of the city and surrounding area. The floor was covered with a large red carpet patterned with colourful, intricate designs. There were some similar ones back at the house, and they were referred to as Brussels carpets. The large windows looked out onto the railway lines and they were filled with umpteen panes of glass, which allowed a lot of daylight into the room. It was very comfortable and genteel, and obviously belonging to a gentleman, as the feminine touches of potted plants and lace tablecloths were evidently missing, and obviously, not welcome. Augustus was already seated at his large desk, writing letters, as he had his grey head bowed and he held a pen to paper. I could hear the scratching of his pen as the tip moved up and down across the paper, and occasionally, there was a pause when he dipped his pen into the inkwell.

So, with nothing else to do, I got my head down and had a long nap in front of the cosy fire. There was no fire-guard for safety. The sisters would have had a fit if they knew, but as far as I could glean, none of them ever entered this room. At midday, I was collected by Soames and taken outside for a short walk and given the opportunity to relieve myself. Once that was done he quickly returned me, bade me stay in Augustus's office and guard it until my master and his sons returned from their dinner, shut the door on me, and left. I guarded the room until they returned at half past one, whereafter they went back to work, and I had another nap.

At half past three it was time for Augustus to leave, and so we walked home together. I knew that when I got home I would find the hole beneath the wall had been repaired. I had overheard Soames say to my master, "'E won't get out now. I've bricked up the 'ole." Edmund and Charles stayed behind, as they worked longer hours than their father and would knock off at five o'clock, and the remainder of the men at six – if *their* work was finished.

I was ready for my cup of tea, and I felt like I'd actually done something useful, even though I'd only spent the day at the office, and most of that I'd slept away. It was a long walk home and we were late for tea. That was the routine for the first couple of weeks, and I did not get to accompany Augustus to the Coal Exchange until some weeks later. At times I was allowed to keep Charles in company, as he welcomed my presence in his own office. A bone would be provided for my entertainment, and as young Charles Clement tallied the long rows of sums in his large ledger, I'd gnaw away at my bone and half listen to the various noises of the warehouse and distant coal yard, that were forever a din in the background.

* * *

EVENTUALLY, Edmund took me out with him whenever he drove a coal wagon around Hackney, or loaded up with coal from the railway depot. There were other men who did this job as well, but now, with Thomas gone, and another man recovering from a badly broken arm, they were short-handed, so Edmund had gone back to driving a wagon when needed. He believed that his father should have hired another man or two to fill the gap, as driving a coal wagon was shamefully beneath him.

"Pennies saved turn into guineas in the bank!" Edmund would mutter this between his gritted teeth. For the sons to start off at the bottom of the business and work their way up, gaining knowledge as they went, was one thing, but Edmund was years past that! Driving a coal wagon was not an occupation that a proper gentleman would ever do. It was scandalous! He wouldn't be surprised to have read about himself in the papers – a juicy bit of local gossip, printed for the sole purpose of selling more papers. He knew why his father was not hiring extra men. It was because he was *cutting corners,* trying to make up for the huge expense dished out for Thomas's funeral. The monthly cost of running a household with two sons, four unmarried daughters, a widowed daughter-in-law and a baby granddaughter, as well as the servants, was staggering. Top that off with a lavish funeral, and it was enough to make anyone look twice at their accounts. He wondered if his father was in financial trouble and the principal had been dipped into. He hoped not – the money was his and Charles's future, along with their sisters'. Financial security and the promise of retiring rich – that's what it was all about. He knew about his father and his uncle George. As young men they had borrowed heavily from their father in order to set themselves up in their own businesses. Only the first-born son inherited Cotheridge Court, along with the bulk of the manor's wealth, and that was William Comyns, and *his* first-born was Rowland, Edmund's cousin. The rest of the family had to make their own way.

I loved going out on the coal wagon. I felt like I was on top of the world as I sat on the seat next to Edmund, who was inclined to be moody on those trips. He'd be dressed in coarse, heavy work clothes, and not his usual well-cut suit, and it was only when he opened his mouth and spoke that it was obvious he was educated, his manner of speaking so unlike that of the other workers at the depot.

The wagon swayed and jolted as it bounced across the rounded, well-worn cobbles that paved Hackney's streets. Covered in black dust, right down to the wheels, it was enormous, and I imagined that it would weigh a fantastic weight when fully loaded, as coal, whatever the quality (all ours was the best), was heavy.

I came close to death on one occasion, when I nearly fell off when we pitched sideways at an alarming speed. It was my first day on the wagon.

"Hold tight, Shales!" shouted Edmund as he grabbed my collar, just in time. The seat was slippery, and my hairy front feet slithered about as I struggled to gain my balance, with my back feet hanging over the side, perilously close to the massive wheels. I squealed in alarm, such as a pig in distress, but to my relief my collar did not slip off, and I was dragged back up onto the seat by the neck. How Edmund ever managed the wagon expertly *and* saved my life, I'll never know. I soon learnt to keep my seat, not wanting to fall off and get caught up in the enormous wheels turning not so far beneath me.

Some of the horses were massive in size, and these Black Brigade horses were more muscular than the other Black Brigade of funeral horses. The coal horses were usually black, although some were dark bays or liver chestnuts. The largest ones were gentle giants, with enormous feet and long, hairy feathers that grew down their legs, and they worked very hard for their living. Two summers ago, in Stanford Rivers, Jasper had told me that my family looked after animals properly, so I assumed this included the coal horses as well. I hoped so, because I thought they were simply marvellous. Nothing ever happened later in life to change my opinion of them. Simply marvellous!

I am afraid I am going to turn into a lecturer like my cate, my cat-mate Horatio, but how can I tell you my life's story without filling in all the little details? They're important, and they help tell the story. You must bear with me, but what is to follow is very useful information, and it might do you, the reader, a bit of good to know it. This is what I have learnt from being in the coal trade all these years, and I shall pass it on to you: on an average day in London, every person burns the equivalent of a quarter pound of coal each hour, and that adds up to six pounds a day, or a ton of coal a year. London burnt five million tons of coal a year in the 1880s, and also burnt three million tons or more of gas. Most of the horses that shifted all this coal collected it from either a wharf (along the Thames) or a railway station. The gas and the coal entered the city by land or water. If the coal came by land, then it came by train; if by water, it came by ship or coal barge, and oft-times the barges were towed by horses. A strong horse, in the employ of a top-notch coal merchant, could shift up to thirty tons of coal each week. There were supposed to be about fifteen hundred good horses, owned by the best coal merchants, in the London area at about the time I went to work. A few merchants owned as many as one hundred horses, and had several stables and warehouses to their names scattered over different parts of London and its boroughs.

I don't know how many horses there were in our coal stable in Hackney, but I do know there were more than four horses. I counted four horses, then four more, and then another four and then Jasper. Silas and Bess, and sometimes Paddy, were the horses stabled at Darnley Road, and these were riding or carriage horses, and not coal horses. I don't know what we had over in Stoke Newington – I never went there. The horses were quite friendly and knowledgeable, and could communicate with me rather easily, thus telling me lots of interesting things, but I'll tell you what they said later. Right now, I want to get back to telling you about my rather exciting job of being a coal dog.

It was a wonderful distraction from the tedium of listening to the ladies' daily chatter and such. I have already mentioned the offices, where all the paperwork and records, such as bills of sale and the ledgers, were kept. When young Charles Clement wasn't at his desk, fair head bent over a ledger, there was another young man who took his place. His name was Pim, and he was rather tall and gangly, and he had reddish hair and a longish nose. The latter he was inclined to wipe at frequently with a rather large, white handkerchief. He was a local, and spoke the dialect known as cockney, and at times, with a dripping nose, he would educate young Charles in the rhyming way of speaking. He seemed friendly enough and always responded to my kind affections, giving me an occasional sweet. I could get up and walk about the offices at leisure, and choose which fire I wanted to lie in front of. The freedom to do so was nice. At other times, a man called Armitage would enter, handing over receipts and cheques given to him from businessmen who had purchased large orders, but he would soon leave again. I believe he also worked out of the other, Stoke Newington, office and warehouse. In Hackney, we did not sell the coal retail to all and sundry, as we usually sold to large retailers, and some of those were in other cities, and they in turn sold the coal again by way of delivery to people's doors. After saying that, some smaller deliveries were made, but they were full-wagon orders only, which is the reason why Edmund had to drive a wagon. Normally, we took in huge amounts and stored them in the enormous warehouse, where the full sacks were stacked from floor to ceiling. Retailers would arrive with their own wagons and buy directly from us, nearly emptying the warehouse before it could be filled again.

Occasionally, Augustus had visitors of a business nature, usually gentlemen in the same trade. At other times a family member, such as his nephew Algernon (who was to become a commissioned soldier after all), or a cousin, or even a brother such as Comyns Rowland or George Brackenbury, would visit Augustus quite frequently. At these times they would recline in comfortable chairs and sip brandy, whilst they smoked cigars or puffed on pipes, and discussed either their own businesses, or the ups and downs of the financial markets, or simply just their own various interests in life, most of which, to my greedy ears, always sounded like gossip. I would stretch out upon the carpet with my back to the fire, my tail safely tucked between my back legs, and the drone of their voices would send me off to sleep. Occasionally, their conversations were actually family gossip, whereby Charles Clement the elder, and uncle to our Charles Clement, was a most popular topic. I listened with thirsty ears and learnt lots about the family, though a lot of it I have forgotten over the years. Boys o' boys, mmn, mmn, mmn.

Edmund did not like to go to the coal bays where the coal was obtained and loaded onto the wagons. As well as it being beneath him, it was a noisy and dusty place, thick with black coal dust, and not to mention extremely active. The merchants rented bays. Some had many, and smaller merchants had just a few, or perhaps just the one. The brick bays were beneath the huge railway arches, and there, in the ceiling of the bays, were the coal chutes, whereby empty sacks were held up to the end of a chute, and from above, amidst a deafening din, hurtling lumps of coal would thus travel from the car sitting on the tracks above and down a chute to a coal merchant's bay below. A car man would release the coal by pulling a lever, and the exact quantity desired would hurtle from the platform above and down the chute. The dust would spew about, thickly clouding the air, and the men were forever being covered and blackened from all the coal dust. We would always stand back out of the way, in observation, until the coal dust had settled. The sack of coal was then loaded onto a handcart and trundled off to where the wagon stood waiting. The patient horse was usually standing calmly, half asleep and daydreaming, it being used to the noise and bustle of the bays, but the soot would get in its eyes and up its nostrils. I've actually heard the horses sneeze from all the coal dust in the air. These wagons, which I've already told you about, would then remove the coal to the warehouses for stockpiling, or to those larger retailers waiting for a full wagonload delivery. Edmund and I would return with the laden wagon to the warehouse, where the sacks would be unloaded and stacked in neat rows, from floor to ceiling. We did not do this alone; there were other men and wagons with us, and we formed a sort of *train* as we left the coal yard and made our way back to the warehouse or elsewhere for a delivery. There were some customers who would take just one full wagonload, and occasionally, Edmund made the delivery himself, directly after leaving the coal bays. Then the coal, each individual sack of it, would have to be weighed, some two tons of it; hence, a lengthy process at best. I sensed he was embarrassed on these occasions, even though I noticed he was always treated with the utmost respect.

It didn't take a genius to understand that people lived their lives according to their class, and that on these deliveries Edmund was well beneath his class. Later in life I came to realise that Augustus had had his sons work in order that they would have a deep appreciation for where their money came from, as the old money inherited down through the centuries was running out, it having been divided too frequently between too many children. Now were the times when many sons of noblemen worked to ensure they themselves could enjoy a comfortable retirement, proving to their fathers they were worthy of inheriting that ever-depleting inheritance, especially when they had unmarried sisters needing support in the style according to their class.

All this coal was what allowed me to live very comfortably – high and mighty – and I appreciated the difference between that and the lifestyle of the homeless dog I used to be, where for a few weeks I had been always hungry, homeless, and hadn't had a fireplace with which to keep me warm.

XIII

THE PRICE OF COAL

*"I pondered the complicated life of a
nubble."*

MARCH 1883

O NE DAY, AND IT WAS INDEED A WEDNESDAY, I was allowed to
accompany Augustus to the London Coal Exchange. Oh, what
a day! I was thrilled to bits to be seeing something different, as
I always wanted to learn new things. This is something I had learnt from
Horatio: that it is perfectly normal to want to expand one's knowledge of the
world. How right he was, when he taught me that life is interesting and there
are always new things to see and learn.

To get to the Coal Exchange, which is in the City of London, we
travelled by train, and you know how terrified I was of the train that night we
went to Thomas's house in Bush Hill Park. This time I braced myself, as I
knew what was coming. First, the appearance of a huge engine spewing forth
smoke from its chimney stack and the deep chug-chug sound as it slowed
down, then the screeching sound of the brakes, and then the eruption of steam
which would hiss loudly and envelop all that happened to be near the edge
of the platform in a white cloud. The coach doors would then be opened,
and a mass of people would emerge from within, and porters would give
assistance to anyone who asked for it. This time I jumped in my skin, but only
momentarily, and I did not embarrass myself, or my master, with unbecom-
ing behaviour of any sort. We boarded the train like any gentleman and a
gentleman's dog would do, and placed ourselves upon the thickly padded
horsehair seats with grace. A man, a conductor, shouted, "All aboard!" After

a very short time the train lurched forward and slowly left the station behind, and we watched as the suburban background merged into city as we slowly approached London. It was raining and the soot from the engine's smoke stack mingled with the raindrops on the exterior of the window, and rivulets of dirty water ran down the large panes of glass, blurring the landscape. The outside world appeared to be dismal and uninviting, and I wondered if we were going to experience a pea-souper, as the daylight seemed to diminish and it had a greenish tint to it.

Now, people sometimes refer to Hackney as London, but really it is only one of the city's outlying areas, or boroughs, and there are many others, but in reality London City is the old part, that area which lies along but north of the great river they call Thames. This is the very London I would have been looking for, had I not been befriended by my cate, Horatio. Without Horatio I could very well still be searching for this London, and living the life of an urchin, or worse, lying dead in some ditch with no one the wiser.

We ended our journey at a station, and there I saw signs that seemed to read Broad Street, Liverpool, and so on. So, where were we? Well, later I came to realise that we were in Broad Street Railway Station, but we weren't anywhere near the Coal Exchange. We had to do some walking, and then entered another station, where we then went underground via a steep flight of stairs. There, in that place, in the heated bowels of the earth, we waited for another train. The curved tunnel walls were lined with shiny white tiles, with no daylight, streets, or trees in sight. Beyond the glow of the oil lamps was an inky darkness, and out of its echoing depths a train noisily appeared, though it did not stop. It sped by so loudly that it was almost deafening to my ears. Minutes later we caught another train, and a short while later we stopped at Cannon Street Station. As we emerged from that station I couldn't help but look up. I noticed its lovely roof of glass, which stood high above us in a semi-circular fashion and enveloped all in light. It was colossal; I was awed.

There were omnibuses and ranks of cabs for hire, waiting outside the station for all those who needed to get to the central parts of London. Masses of people walked to and fro in a hurry, representing the different classes by their way of dress and manner of talk, and the street was busy with non-stop, horse-drawn traffic. From there we travelled a short distance by cab towards Lower Thames Street, and on that street I captured my first sight of the Coal Exchange. It was magnificent in a small way. The narrow stone building had a high dome, which sat upon eight piers, creating a rotunda. We left the cab and walked up the flight of steps, and entered through the doors at the front of the rounded exterior. There were men milling about everywhere, and most were too busy to even notice my presence, though some gave me an odd look or two. I sighed, as I had noticed the floor, which was highly polished and remarkable in its manufacture, as it had a large intricate design set into its surface. It was both fascinating and beautiful. A reminder to me that man creates buildings and things like trains, not animals such as dogs, horses and cats. I later learnt that the floor contained some forty thousand pieces of inlaid wood, which beautifully represented the face of a mariner's compass. The floor was too nice to walk upon, and yet it was being walked upon by hundreds of leather-soled feet. As Augustus stopped to converse with somebody he was acquainted with I tilted my head back and looked up at the ceiling. High up, it was a long way off, as there were three galleries encircling us, and there, above the last and highest gallery was the dome, some seventy-four feet above us. I started to feel dizzy from staring upwards at all that height, even though I had four legs to balance myself upon. I actually got so dizzy that I nearly fell over, but I was saved from that possible, embarrassing occasion when my master tugged on my lead, and I followed him, albeit a bit wobbly, as he went upstairs to where all the merchants, who were members of the Coal Factors' Society, were convened and waiting for the twelve o'clock bell.

What more can I say, other than we purchased coal. All of which would be later delivered to Stoke Newington and Hackney by rail. The Coal Exchange closed at two o'clock, and we left, returning to Hackney by train via the same route we had come. A thick fog had indeed settled over London, so I could see nothing of the outside world from the window of the train after we left Broad Street Station.

On the way home I pondered the complicated life of a nubble: a small, single lump of coal. I want you to know just how much I was learning about life, and a large part of our life in Darnley Road revolved around coal. Firstly, coal is useless to people as it lies hiding underground in its natural state.

Then, during my Victorian life, it was mined by miners (men and women and children), who risked their lives to dig it out by hand, and then it was transported out of the mine, to the mouth of the pit, by young boys and small pit ponies. I must mention that it was only after the Mines Act, in 1887, that the minimum age for children miners was twelve years; before then many were younger than that. From the moment the coal reaches the earth's surface there is a long series of events that the coal participates in, until it eventually reaches its final destination, which is the fireplace, or oven, in someone's home or place of business. During its journey it is transported by rail or ship to places such as London, and once there it is bid upon by coal merchants at the Coal Exchange, and once bought (by a coal merchant) it is again transported to the merchant's warehouse (wherever it may be), or the coal might be sold off directly, its destination another city and a retailer's warehouse. All these costs incurred (miners' wages, transportation fees, dues, whipping fees, merchants' and retailers' expenses, and any profit the mine owner, merchant and retailer wanted) were added onto the price of the coal.

This little piece of well-travelled black coal was an expensive luxury to those who could afford to buy it on a day-to-day basis. I was later to learn that many could not afford to buy coal as they needed it, and these people picked it out of the river mud at low tide, down by the London docks – fallings from the coal barges (even in the winter) – or they picked it up out of the street, whenever a sack of coal burst open from the constant, harsh treatment the cobbles gave to the wagons, dribbling its contents, nubble by nubble, onto the uneven cobbles as the coal wagon ignorantly trundled along. Poor children were taught at an early age to grab any nubble they should come upon, and to run home to mummy with it, right away, before it could be prised from their grubby little fist by another half-starved and equally grubby child. These rough children barely had enough clothes to cover themselves with, and usually went barefoot regardless of the weather, even in the winter, except for those lucky ones who wrapped their feet up in rags. Many of them didn't even have families. They lodged together, wherever they could find shelter. They were known as *urchins,* and whenever I saw them I was reminded of all the stray dogs I had encountered on my journey between Worcestershire and Essex, especially those that travelled in packs.

XIV
A Wedding and a Removal

"Loyalty is a trait I admire in people, as
well as in animals. Most have it – some do
not."

Spring, 1883

O NE EVENING, IN EARLY SPRING, we received an unexpected but
welcome caller at the house. The untimely knocking sound at the
front door had disturbed my contented state of drowsiness. The
brass knocker went tap... tap-tap... tap, and then tap-tap, thus repeating itself
a second time. I was in my usual spot, in front of the fire, what with it being
miserable and foggy outside, and I was so warm and cosy that I didn't want
to bother to get up and see who was at the door.

Augustus, head slightly bent to catch the light from the closest lamp,
had been quietly reading from a book. He volunteered thoughtfully, "I know
the sound of that knock, but I can't for the moment think whom it could be."

The rest of the family, their heads bowed in a similar fashion, also
wondered who was at the door on such a drab day.

Lucy moaned, "It had better not be sad news."

"Shush." Jessie was hopeful. "It could be family. Perhaps Rowland,
Herbert, or even Algernon. If it *is* a stranger at our door, they would have
knocked thrice and waited, then repeated it. No, this is someone whom we
know that is descending upon us this evening. It's about time we had a family
visitor."

However, I did respond to the sound of the knocker. I sleepily dragged
myself away from the warmth of the fire, yawned widely, and trotted off to

see who Annie Armstrong, our lovely housemaid, had let in, as I had vowed to protect the family, and a place by the warm fire had to come second place to guarding the front door. Well, well, to my surprise, it was Stanley. Do you remember me telling you about the man who had drawn my picture on that summer's day at Cotheridge Court? This was he, and he had come to call upon us. I was ever so happy to see him, and I wagged my tail so hard I thought I was going to spin about like a top.

Stanley petted me affectionately whilst Armstrong took his hat, gloves, coat and stick. He said to me in a voice as smooth as treacle, "Lovely dog. What a good boy. I remember you; yes, I do. Yes, I most certainly do. I have a painting of you, and I think I've captured you *rather* well."

He was ushered into the drawing-room by Armstrong and me, and was greeted affectionately by everyone, except for Edmund, who had gone out for the evening into the city, we knew not where. Edmund could be secretive at times, but perhaps he went to the club in Westminster. A glass of brandy was offered and accepted, and so, Stanley, after having made himself comfortable on the settee closest to where Augustus's chair was situated, revealed to us the reason for his unexpected visit.

"You are probably not going to believe this, but I am to be married." He was beaming from cheek to cheek, as if he could not contain the enormous smile.

Being taken by surprise, the ladies all spoke at once, and all I could hear was, "Married! Oh, Stanley, how wonderful for you! Do we know her?" Their questions were piled one atop another, and the women sounded for all like motherly hens cackling over their newly laid eggs.

Augustus was smiling and looked very pleased for Stanley. He stood and offered Stanley his hand, saying, "Well, lad, I *am* very pleased to hear your good news, and I'm sure you shall be very happy. It *has* come as a surprise. I thought I'd recognised your knock; it's been awhile since you last dropped by. We'd love to have you any time, and now that you are to be married, well, we hope you won't forget about us. Now, you must tell us all about her. But first let's have a toast."

As soon as everyone had a full glass of spirits in their hands they all raised their glasses and toasted Stanley and his soon-to-be-bride, and I found myself a cosy spot right at Stanley's feet. I did not intend to miss any of the evening's gossip, and I had a front row seat.

Stanley stroked my ears as he spoke enthusiastically, "Well, you may have heard of her late father, as he was a very good printer. Her father was Thomas Choate Savill. Edith herself is also an artist, and she hopes to make a career out of painting, and I'm encouraging her to do this. I met Edith at Lambeth Art School, and I think we'll make a very good team: husband and wife, and both of us painters. We may even become famous." He laughed when he said this last bit.

"But you are already doing rather well for yourself," said Jessie, who adored his work and always knew of his latest project. She clipped out any of his newspaper illustrations she would chance to come upon.

Stanley nodded in agreement. "It could be better, though – it takes just one well-known person to speak well of me in public, such as someone from the royal family, and then my career could soar... the sky being the limit. Just as long as we don't starve; that's what I keep saying to Edith."

Charles said he'd like to hear more about Edith and her family, with everyone else agreeing and wondering who she was. "Yes. Go on. Tell us," cried several voices at once.

The floor was cold and draughty, and so I moved away from Stanley's feet and once again got myself feeling comfortable in front of the fire, listening to the excited voices as the news was revealed. From that spot I could see their faces as well as watch their animated body movements – it was all language to me.

Stanley smiled, and he replied patiently, "Well, now. Let's see. Her mother's name is Eliza, and Edith lives with her in Brixton. That's in Surrey, but I'm sure you know that." He went on to say, "Also, she has a brother who is a doctor."

The women all chimed in at various times, asking Stanley questions about his own family. They were fine, he assured us. His mother had been managing the rather large household without his father for years now, as he had passed away when Stanley had been a boy.

"You'll see all of them at the wedding. I certainly hope so, as they had better all come. It's going to be a big day for me, and I must tell you, I'm as nervous as a chattering squirrel just thinking about it. I just turn into a cold sweat whenever I think about it all. Edith says I'll be fine, and I'm not to dwell on the wedding at all, not until the day itself arrives."

Emily got up from where she was sitting, and then walked over to Stanley and assured him, "Everything will be all right. You'll be fine, Stanley. I *am* looking forward to attending it, and I think I can speak for the rest of us here, that we are very pleased for you." She patted him on his arm, and then revealed her own news. "I, too, am to be married."

Stanley was happily surprised at this little bit of news. "What? Married? You, as well? I say, Emily, you are full of surprises. Who will be the lucky man? Do I know him?"

To this she answered, whilst bearing a smile like a Cheshire cat, "His name is Thomas White, and you don't know him. He lives not far from here, just around the corner. We haven't set a date, but I think it shall be in about two years from now."

Augustus cleared his throat, and in Emily's defence he patiently stated, "She doesn't want to hurry things along, and it is still very proper to have a long engagement. Two years used to be the accepted length of time for an engagement; there's no reason to hurry." He then puffed away on his pipe as he winked at Emily in good humour.

Earlier, Jessie had overheard what Stanley had said about having a painting he had done of me, so she broached the subject boldly. "Stanley, did I hear you correctly in saying that you have done a painting of Shales?"

And to this he answered, "Yes. I used him as a subject at Cotheridge Court. I had only done some sketches and a quick water-colour of him, but then, later on, I set to and painted a lovely oil painting of him. It isn't a large one –" and he gestured with his hands the size of the painting, and then continued, "but I'm very pleased with it. It was good practise. I rather enjoy painting dogs, and he has so much character in his face."

She leaned forward and eagerly asked, "Is it for sale?"

Looking surprised but pleased, and baring a large smile, Stanley said, "Why, yes, it is for sale." He folded his arms across his chest, and he cocked his head as he waited for what she would say next.

"You must name me a price."

To which he replied, "Ah. Let's see. A fair price... for family. Half a guinea will suffice, if that is agreeable to you, Jessie. For that, I'll see that it is nicely framed and ready for you to hang. I'm sure you shan't be disappointed, and I've already turned down some offers for it. I had wanted to wait and see if the family was interested in having it, before I sold it to a stranger."

"Sold." She got up to shake his hand and affirm the deal. "I shall pay you before you take your leave, and perhaps you could have it sent over, sometime soon?" She looked rather pleased with herself, and I thought she looked as if she was going to jump up and down and do a dance. I could hardly wait to see this portrait of myself. I wondered where Jessie would hang it.

* * *

THE PAINTING ARRIVED IN THE POST, mysteriously wrapped in brown paper and tied up with twine. I wagged my tail as I sniffed the parcel – Stanley had wrapped it up himself. Jessie set the parcel upon the library table, hastily withdrew her small sewing scissors from her secret pocket, snipped the twine, and unwrapped its several layers of thick, brown paper. Once it was free of its protective wrappings, she delightedly exclaimed, "Oh, it is splendid! Just look at it! The frame is beautiful. Stanley has outdone himself." She was beaming from ear to ear.

As she admired the painting at arm's length, she said, "Now, Shales, we must hang you where you shall be seen and adored all the time. I think over there, in the front hall between the archway and the staircase. Whoever enters this house shall see it, as well as anyone who goes up the stairs." Whereupon she immediately removed a small, framed picture of no apparent value, depicting a simple country scene, and placed Stanley's oil in its stead.

Dear Reader, how self-important I felt as I gazed upon my own portrait, and there I was, in all my glory, painted in dark oils for everyone to see. A dog with a glossy black and white coat stared back at me. He had painted me lying down upon the earthy ground, in front of a doorway to a shed, with the interior filled with rakes and buckets, and the shed floor scattered with wisps of yellow straw. It was well done, and was framed in a lovely gilt frame.

246

When the rest of the family saw it, they too were generous with their praise of Stanley's ability to paint dogs. I, too, was pleased, and as I gazed upon my portrait I felt as if I belonged to this family, as well as being loved. The excitement of it all got to me, and I raced up and down the long hall like a maniac, causing the rugs to skid up against the skirting-boards.

Jessie admonished me. "Shales! Slow down and behave yourself! Just look at the mess you've made!"

* * *

STANLEY'S WEDDING WAS TO BE IN MAY, the third day to be exact, and it took place in Brixton, Surrey at the county church of St John's. I had hoped to go, but in the end I had to stay behind with Maud, who had decided not to accept the invitation, as she felt she didn't know Stanley well enough to attend. At least *she* had been invited, as, I hadn't, and my disappointment was great.

The eventful day soon arrived. It was a Thursday, and the family left for the wedding very early in the morning; they went by train and met up with other family and friends en route. I just hoped it all went well and everyone had a wonderful time, though I didn't know what a wedding was. I did know it was something to do with a church ceremony, but about the living and not the dead, such as a funeral. Speaking of the dead, the four sisters, Jessie, Julia, Lucy and Emily, had come out of mourning to attend the wedding, as the appropriate six months duration for mourning a sibling had passed. They did look lovely in various shades of colour, although they weren't too brightly dressed, and I was very pleased for them that they could go out into public and not be afraid to enjoy themselves just a little bit. I knew, deep in my heart, that they had not forgotten nor ever would forget Thomas. For the happy occasion Augustus and his sons had donned suits that did not resemble the dark office clothes they wore to work each day, or those in mourning. Maud, however, still wore her ink black dresses commonly known as widows' weeds. She was in a rum mood as well, so I kept well out of her way.

Charlotte, the nurse, had taken Mary Matilda out somewhere for the day, and so, feeling a bit lonely, I went upstairs to find a place to sleep the day away, and to my surprise I found the door was open to Thomas's room. Of course I went in there. I wasn't going to walk past and go elsewhere. No, that isn't the way of dogs. I entered the room as reverently as if it were a church, tiptoeing along to keep Maud from hearing me. I very carefully jumped up onto his bed, turned three times, and then lay down to have a soothing nap. The atmosphere of the room, though Thomas had never slept there, was inviting, as if he'd just been in there. I sniffed the bedclothes deeply for any lingering scent, but to my great disappointment, any trace of Thomas had completely disappeared.

Have you ever found yourself in a deep sleep, that is so deep you cannot seem to wake up when you want to, and you continue to fall asleep ever the more deeply and dream the day away? This was the state I found myself in on that day, as I lay upon Thomas's bed. I seemed to dream I was running through fields around Stanford Rivers, and then I was jogging down the High Street in Ongar, and then I suddenly found myself inside the King's Head. In my dream there were men stood at the bar, supping glasses of beer, and they all looked at me as if they knew me, and I heard someone shout, "Shales is here," as if to announce my arrival to the entire inn. But I then found myself walking past them and around the bar towards the back, and then I suddenly turned to the right and left through the side door, which was propped open as it always is in fine weather, and found myself outside in the yard. I looked to my right, where the archway was, where carriages and wagons passed through from the High Street to gain access to the back of the inn, and then I looked to my left, which led down to the stables and then on to a paved area, and then, eventually, to a garden. There were faint sounds in the background, those usual of horses, as I trotted past the inn's stables. I felt drawn to the garden, and in my dream I went there, willingly. Still, I was drawn further along, beyond the garden, to where the boundary lay, which was, in fact, a small river. There, on the riverbank was a huge tree, which was in full leaf and shaded the area with an inviting blanket of comfort. I recognised it all, having been there before with Thomas. I felt drawn to walk further along the embankment. I took a few eager steps, and then a voice stopped me.

"Well, Shales, I'm so glad to see you again. Have you been behaving yourself? Come here and let me hug you."

I felt arms go around me, and I smelt a familiar smell – a man's smell of horse mingled with sweat and cigar, but I didn't look up to see who it was. I was busy noting the fawn-coloured trews – no – they were breeches, which disappeared into the tops of familiar, tall brown boots. Disbelievingly, I knew I recognised the voice as well as the individual's scent, and I was about to look up in anticipation of seeing his face, when it all completely disappeared in an instant.

"Git off that bed!" screamed Maud. At the top of her voice, she shouted, "Yew dirty dog, git off the bed."

I was stunned, as I was groggy from sleep and not yet fully awake. I felt myself being grabbed roughly by my collar and then physically dragged off the bed. I was confused. I didn't like it at all, and I became very scared and anxious. I was still half asleep and had a job waking up. I growled – I don't like anybody to grab me roughly by the collar. Maud slapped me on the top of my head, and I reacted to this by turning and staring at her with my lips curled up and my teeth bared. Then, I snarled as viciously as I could, sending her a dire warning. I certainly did not feel like being nice to her, and I don't know if I could ever forgive her for what she had done: awakened me at just the moment I was about to see who the person was in my dream. I know who it was, but I so wanted to see him with my own eyes, and she had taken that away from me. I had felt his presence as real as that slap that Maud had given me. It had been more than a dream, as it reminded me of the night when the god-cat entered my dream, when I had been banished to the harness room after frightening the horses. I felt like something precious had been stolen from me.

Her face was white, and her eyes were hateful as she leaned towards me. She picked up one of his riding crops that lingered close by in a porcelain stand, and holding it by its ivory stock, she poked me with it, forcing me to walk backwards. She jabbed at me again, the tip painfully digging into my left shoulder. I was shocked at her behaviour, and decided to leave the room before I got myself into more trouble. Turning on my heels, I ran down the stairs and then downstairs again to the kitchen below, where I lay upon the cold stone floor beneath the massive table that Cook prepared the meals upon. Ignoring the cook, who was not pleased to see me, I stayed there until the family came home from the wedding. In my mind, I repeated the dream over again and again, in an attempt to ignite the spark of life, of him – he whom I knew had been there in flesh and blood, as if he were immortal.

* * *

IT WAS TEATIME WHEN THEY ARRIVED. I eagerly greeted them, though more with relief than happiness, as they paraded through the front door, their merry moods obvious, having had a wonderful day. I was relieved to have the house full of voices and cheer again. I waited to see if Maud would tell on me, because if she *had* done, that would have meant I was in trouble again. She did not tell. Nor was *I* able to tell on her, me being a dog. I tried to think images of what had happened, but nobody picked them up, and they assumed I had had an uneventful day. I had seen a side of Maud that I believe no one had previously seen, and I hoped I wouldn't see it again. What admirable qualities had Thomas seen in her, other than that she was very pretty to look at? I vowed to stay clear of her whenever I was to be left alone in her presence, and I didn't think I could ever forgive her – she had robbed me of a precious moment. I went to bed that night with a heavy heart, but hopeful for the future that the magic of the bed, the dream, whether it was a just a dream or reality, would be repeated.

* * *

AFTER STANLEY'S WEDDING we lived our lives as usual, but the sisters had come out of mourning and wore half-mourning colours of greys and lilacs. Maud was struggling against decorum and she was threatening to come out of deep mourning before the full twelve months was ended; she still wore black from head to toe. I am positive that if she had not been living with us, she would have come out of mourning months ago – a shocking thing to do. The sisters bade her wait just a few more weeks, until we all went off to Worcestershire for a summer visit. Meanwhile, I went to the coal yard and the offices each day with the men, and sometimes I went to the Coal Exchange. I had taken so many trains into London and back those last few weeks that I was sure I could do it all by myself, blindfolded of course, and I harboured a secret plan for the future, which included myself, a train, and a tour of London on foot.

* * *

SUMMER, 1883

AFTER MUCH ANTICIPATION, THE MONTH OF AUGUST ARRIVED, and we set off for Worcestershire. This year, we were to spend our holiday at Cotheridge Court with my master's brother, and all of us, except for Edmund, went there, including Maud and little baby Mary Matilda, who wasn't so much a small baby any more, and of course, me. We travelled there by train, as to have gone by coach and horses would have taken several days. Oh, what an exciting journey it was. I went from London to Cotheridge by train, and by first-class coach as well. How many times had I imagined, in my mind, the way from Cotheridge to London, and vice versa? Many times. The journey was incredible, and I was so used to travelling on trains that I now thoroughly enjoyed the leisurely time spent on them. I saw countless churches with their villages, and fully realised what a distance it was I had travelled (the two years previous), when I had spent several weeks searching for London on my own. Usually, as you well know, I enjoy gazing out of the windows at the countryside beyond, with the clickety-clack sound and the gentle swaying motion of the train rocking me into an eventual slumber.

There was no station in Cotheridge. We travelled the last couple of miles by carriage and horses from Henwick Station, they being sent from Cotheridge Court to meet us, and it took three carriages to transport all of us to the house. There was the luggage still to follow, piled onto a separate wagon and travelling at a much slower rate of speed than the carriages. When we approached the great house, the ancestral home, even though Augustus and his siblings had all been born in Essex, it was with a sense of awe. Augustus commented on the many times he had changed residences in his life, and then said, "This is the one place that is always here for the family, and I hope it will be in Mary Matilda's future as well."

I just knew I was going to have a grand holiday. I eagerly jumped out of the carriage and ran about the grounds, sniffing all the new and interesting scents; my human companions were momentarily forgotten, their voices just a dim drone in the background.

My holiday soon had a damper put on it when Augustus's brother, William Comyns, informed us that I could not enter the house. According to his brother, I, being a sheepdog, had a place in the kennels. Auntie Emily, who lived there with her brother, tried to intervene on my behalf, but William put his foot down. My master disagreed with his own brother, but, in the end, met him halfway. Augustus permitted me to remain outside, free to roam, and not locked up in either the hounds' kennels or the stable. Well, no matter. It was all the more opportunity for me to run loose and explore the countryside, and perhaps wander off, whenever I felt the urge. After being confined to the garden in Hackney, I wanted to be free to run about at will, and not be confined to the kennels, which happened to be occupied by hunting dogs, and no doubt they would have mistaken me for a fox and had evil thoughts of tearing me apart.

For the next fortnight I spent my time loafing about the wonderful gardens where ancient yews, enormous in their old age, provided ample shade, or I swam in the large fish pond that resembled a small lake and had an island in its middle. There were carp in there that were nearly as large as me, and they would nibble at my toes as I swam about. Graceful swans sailed about as if they ruled the place, and I think they did, and I was ever aware of their cantankerous nature, having to observe them from a hiding place amidst the bulrushes and tall grasses. Frogs leapt about the muddy shallows, giving me many hours of entertainment-with-friendly-chase, and birds sang their songs as I dried off, panting and basking in the warm sunshine. At night Jessie, or Charles Clement, smuggled me inside the house when all the servants willingly looked the other way, pretending not to see me. I would sleep on the bottom of Jessie's bed until daybreak, when one of the maids would whisper for me, and then she would sneak me down to the kitchen. In that place I would hobnob with the servants and receive a marvellous breakfast – all to the ignorance of the master of the house. Boys o' boys, mmn, mmn, mmn.

I was not allowed inside the dairy, which was situated in a building some distance to the rear of the house, as it was a place of pristine cleanliness, let alone mystery to me, but oft-times, if I dallied about outside the door, the dairy maid would toss me slivers of cheese she had pared from a wheel. Into the dairy went the milk, carried in, in large urns, and later on out came the butter and ripened cheeses, all the delicious smells of which made my mouth water. The fresh-made cheeses were wrapped in cloths and remained in the dairy, maturing until ripened. If I were waiting outside when the door opened I would catch a glimpse of those cheese wheels and blocks of butter. Even now, the smell of cheese always takes me back to those simple summer days in the country, when colourful butterflies danced about, and warm, gentle breezes ruffled my hair and gently tickled my skin.

One day, I decided to go back to Rowland's farm and reacquaint myself with Toothless George and Toby. I ran through the orchards and fields at full speed, as I was so excited to be returning to my old home. Breathless, I ran into the courtyard and skidded to a stop, and then barked as loud as I could, announcing my arrival, so excited was I.

Shales spends the day at Butts Bank Farm.

At first nobody appeared and I wondered what to do, but then I saw George in the distance. Familiar Toothless George, in his baggy trews and shirt. He was walking towards me, so I ran up to him and greeted him like an old friend. I stood upon my two back feet as he held onto my front paws, and my body vibrated in joy at our reunion.

"Why, 'tis the maister's dog, returned to us," said George, patting my sides with vigour. "Yer do lewk to be in good health. Champion, you are." Then he said, "Come un' see our Toby; 'e'll be ever so gladdened t' see thee."

I trotted over to the kennels, and there was Toby, in the darkened interior of our old kennel, lying on his side and panting from the heat. I greeted him warmly by licking his face. It was a very hot day, and I was doing a lot of panting myself.

"Shales. I am so pleased to see thee 'ere. I did wonder if I was ever to see thee again. It's been a hard winter for us 'ere, and it seems to have taken its toll out of me, and I can't see owt at all. It's just dark all day lang, as well as in t' night. I'll tell thee summat: it's all the same to me these days."

I felt so sorry for him – this was no way for a dog to be. I wanted to lift his spirits, so I laid myself down next to him and spent the rest of that day telling him my story, from the very last time he had seen me, to arriving back at Cotheridge Court a few days prior. I made him laugh, and I made him cry. He said he'd never been so entertained before, not ever, and he said I had a knack for telling stories. He thought my story incredible, but he did believe me, because he said it was too complicated to have ever been invented. I promised to see him every day I was at Cotheridge Court, and I'd inform him of my leaving before I returned to London.

On my way out I met up with the new dog, the replacement – he who had taken my place. His name was Bala, and he was a kindly chap. I didn't dawdle about – it was his farm now, but I knew I would always come back to visit.

Edmund had come from Hackney, for a short visit; just for a day and one night. It was all the time he would allow himself away from the business, even though they were no longer short-handed. To his relief, he would never have to drive a coal wagon again, and better than that, the office duties had been reorganised between himself, Charles Clement, and his father. Charles would not be spending all his days being a clerk; instead, he would be schooled by Edmund to do Thomas's old job. Pim would do all the clerking at the Hackney office, instead of hopping over to Stoke Newington when needed; David Foster now had enough experience to take on all the office work at that location.

It was a busy spot, was this house in Cotheridge. Once again, family members from different counties came to gather. Even William and his family came from Yarmouth, though they put themselves up in an hotel in Worcester, the house being filled by us from Hackney and from Ware, and no more room left for any of the other relations who had come to visit. If you don't remember, William is the other brother of Edmund, Charles Clement, and the sisters.

There was even some scandal, which was discussed in hushed tones, but I still heard everything that was said, as I lay close by in the shade of a leafy bush. I already knew about Augustus's brother, but you, the reader, shall need an explanation. Apparently, as you already know, one of his brothers was named Charles Clement, and not to get him confused with my Charles Clement. Shush now! He had committed the appalling shame of marrying one of his servants! Oh, how scandalous it was! According to the women, the subject was too shameful to be discussed. However, it *was* discussed in private amongst the men, and I can attest to that. People had a tendency to forget that I was always listening, and with greedy ears I heard the entire story. Some of them even doubted that the two had legally married at all, but were instead living *sinfully* in the eyes of the Lord and just about everyone else: a crime that deserved tarring and feathering.

"I still don't know what possessed him to marry her," said Comyns Rowland.

"I do." This was his brother George Brackenbury speaking. "Have you *seen* her? What a looker she is. Handsome woman, with a lovely, curved figure. I say that there is no man here today who would not have looked twice at her." George wagged the forefinger from his right hand at the small crowd of men who had gathered. He dared them to disagree. "He simply could not resist her."

"What's this, George? Do you fancy her yourself?" Male voices guffawed at this accusation, and even George himself laughed at the idea of it.

"But to have children by her and have them living in the same house, and they still be unwed, is such a repugnant crime." This was William Comyns speaking his mind, and he was a clergyman, ministering to the locals at St Leonard's Church, which stood close by. "It is such a shameful act to be committed by anyone, let alone a member of *our* family. One does not dally with servants, nor get any woman *with child* before they are wed. But our brother has done worse than that – he has sired even more children by her." He shook his head, his white and hairy jowls fluffing in the breeze.

I was watching their faces intently, and it was clear to me that the men held differing opinions regarding the older Charles Clement.

Augustus then added, in a timely way, "At least he did marry her, even though it was on the quiet, and in the end made an honest woman out of her. It would have been more shameful to have allowed the situation to continue as it was. It was going on for years, so we were to find out sooner or later."

I wondered if he was thinking about his own son's situation. When Thomas had created a scandal with Maud.

William Comyns was the eldest of all the brothers, and so he had inherited the ancestral home. He was an old man in his seventies, as well as being a widower. He spoke harshly, "I disagree with you. I don't believe they are married, even though they wear rings on their fingers. He has not yet shown me a certificate for marriage. I say to you that he has not married that woman! If he married her now, and made an honest woman out of her, I still would not welcome him back into the folds of the family. I've told him he's not welcome here! I know I'm being harsh with my own brother. You will all think me unforgiving, and me being the Reverend Berkeley, but it was a sinful act he committed, and it goes on to this very day. I cannot forgive him! It's simply scandalous!"

William's longish sideburns disappeared into a neatly trimmed beard. It was his eyes, as well as his tone, that betrayed his disappointment in his brother Charles.

"What has *happened* to this family? We all seem to be scattering across this great country. And what of our grandchildren? They shall grow up and never know their cousins' names. This house, this Cotheridge Court, is what binds us all together and defines us as a family. What of our great-grand-children? Will they come here when they are grown?" Then, as if deeply saddened, he asked the sky, "Will my son Rowland and his children keep this place going, or will it be sold after three hundred years of occupation? How will our future children know where they have come from? Will they be told that those living in Spetchley and Berkeley are their distant cousins, just different branches of the same family?"

There was a pregnant silence, as everyone gathered there seemed to ponder William's words deeply, then the uncomfortable silence was broken.

George Brackenbury's son, also called George, laughed and loudly blurted, "I have so many children that even I don't know them all. How many do I have? Has anyone here counted them?" He then pointed out, "Even I wonder how they will live in this changing world. Everything costs us more, each and every day; even the price of coal is not what it used to be. I simply will not have enough money to pass on to all my children. The eldest male will inherit the bulk of it, and the others... well, one is becoming a doctor, and so on. They shall have to make their own fortunes. I wonder how even *we* shall manage in twenty years from now; I'm worried about it all."

The crowd of gentlemen did not take offence at George's outburst. They too saw the funny side of it and had a good laugh, as in the truth of the matter, George did have a lot of children. The more serious side of the conversation was then acknowledged by all the men, when they bowed their heads and nodded in silent agreement, worried about their futures.

"When our Queen eventually passes on there will be a great change come to everyone's way of life. It has already begun. Times are changing quickly as we approach the next century with alarming speed. We are becom-ing more modern as each year passes by." My master spoke with sadness, and everyone agreed with him and nodded their heads.

The three present brothers of William Comyns, George Brackenbury, Comyns Rowland, and my master, all agreed that their brother Charles Clement and *his* family were welcome in *their* homes. But then, they lived in London, and perhaps Londoners were more modern and also less strict in their ways than country gentlemen. Yes, it was scandalous, but they would not turn their backs on their own brother. That led to a discussion of the dress code that London women had to yet obey, which included the covering of hands, but also the peculiar and uncomfortable fashions of dress women put up with, that were forever a puzzle to the male species.

Life was so different on the farms compared to living in a bustling town or city. William Comyns retained a coachman, a stable full of horses, and several carriages, but many Londoners had no such need, as cabs could be hired when required. Many times they would walk to where they were going, unheard of in the country (except by the young and healthy). Yes, many Londoners still retained horses and carriages, but the stabling of them and having a coachman and groom on hand was an additional, if not extravagant, expense. When not in use, oft-times these handsome teams of horses were rented out to others for additional income. Fortunately for my family we had a stable man and a boy already in our employ looking after the coalies. Tending to our carriage horses in Darnley Road took little effort, something done merely twice a day. London had lured the men with the offer of good money to be made. There were balls, gentlemen's clubs, restaurants, the theatre, art galleries and many other places that offered a full social life. The city was a necessary evil when one was not the first-born and one needed to create a future, whereby a comfortable retirement would be there waiting, and also something to pass on to one's children, however small the divided portions would be.

I don't suppose my opinion on the subject would matter to anyone but me, but I shall tell you that I loved the city, but I also loved the country. To be able to enjoy both the farm and the city, each year, was a blessing. I wished our stay in Cotheridge would last all summer long, but it was nigh drawing to an end, and the next day our little branch of the family left; the train journey was done in reverse, and we arrived back in Hackney with fond memories as well as quite a large supply of butter and cheeses, all made in the Cotheridge dairy. Sadly, we would not return to Cotheridge again until the following year.

* * *

THE ONE FABULOUS THING about going away on holiday to Cotheridge Court was that the cook didn't come with us. What a letdown to come home knowing *she* was in the house. Was it just me? Did any of the others have any feelings of intense dislike for her? Well, I know that Thomas hadn't liked her, and I also sensed that Edmund didn't like her either. If Jessie ever had to broach the subject of our cook, he was disinterested, but I could tell from the look on his face that it was more than that. As for the others, well, they didn't have to speak to her or acknowledge her presence, except for Jessie. Not like Armstrong, who was all about the house, keeping it in order, and answering the door and setting and siding away the table, or serving tea in the afternoon. I knew that everyone liked our housemaid, because I have heard it said so, many a time. Don't forget, dogs have ears, and we are listening all the time, *especially* when you think we are sleeping. We just listen with our eyes closed.

* * *

THANK GOODNESS COOK had her dungeon to hide away in, but after saying that, I encountered her many times throughout each week. In Hackney my food bowls were in the kitchen and not upstairs like they had been in Stanford Rivers. Jessie had told her, in no uncertain terms, that I was a member of the family, and that even though she didn't like dogs, Eliza was to treat me according to the respect I deserved. Whenever Jessie was around and she was in my presence Cook would pretend to cosset me, giving Jessie a false feeling of an improved camaraderie. Remember, I told you (when at Wayletts), Thomas had laid down the law, so to speak, and had threatened her with dismissal? She hadn't changed at all.

So, what has got me on my high horse again? Well, this is what happened. One day, after we had returned from Cotheridge, I met the dreaded cook face to face, on the stairs that led down to the kitchen, as I was on my way down there for a drink of water. I paused in mid-step, wondering if she was in a sour mood, or not. I could see her face was stern and set, and she had that look about her that said, "Run for it, Shales!"

"Get owt of m' way, you horrid mongrel!" She dared say this out loud, because the men were at their place of work, and the women had all ventured out of the house for one reason or another. I was home simply because when the men set off for work the rain was siling down so hard, in a torrential downpour, that it was decided that it was better that I stayed home. Augustus didn't want a 'drowned rat' stinking up the offices, because he had some important men (to do with the business of coal) stopping by that day. Cook was in the process of sweeping the stairs that descended to the kitchen when she pointed the bristly end of the broom at me, and roughly thrust it in my face!

"Get back!" she said sternly, "Back! Back! Back!"

I retreated in fear, and my bottom bumped up against the door; it swung open freely as I backed into it. My eyes had nearly been poked out, and my bowl of cool, fresh water was left untouched, and I with a thirst that wouldn't be slaked until teatime. I couldn't understand why she hadn't warmed up to me. I can truthfully say that I had not attempted to bite her or frighten her in any way. Perhaps my appearance offended her? Perhaps I smelt overly pungent? Well, I hadn't done anything to her on purpose, not up until now. That was it! I was fed up with tiptoeing around her whenever I needed to go into the kitchen. After all, this was my house and she was merely a servant. I vowed to myself that the next time I saw her unawares I would get her; meaning that when next I saw her ample backside exposed for attack, I wouldn't hesitate to bite it.

I waited patiently. Weeks went by, and on one particular afternoon when Jessie and the rest of the ladies were out calling upon friends, and Charlotte was out pushing Mary Matilda about in the perambulator, I finally had the long-awaited opportunity for revenge. Of all places it was in the kitchen, or the *dungeon,* as I not so fondly thought of the place. Eliza, the cook, was bent forward from the waist down, and was sweeping up some spilt flour off the floor. She was using a hand brush and, in bending over, her ample bottom of gigantic proportions was on display. It bulged enticingly. I hesitated for only the briefest moment, and then grabbed courage with all my might, and I ran at the bottom end of her and I bit her good and proper, sinking my teeth in as deeply as I could, thus drawing forth an ample supply of warm, red blood.

Her loud shout must have hit the roof rafters. "Ah! Oh! My God! Ughhh."

She dropped the brush and dustpan, thus spilling the flour back onto the stone floor, and then dropped to her knees with her right hand tightly clapped to her backside. I turned and ran like a hare back up the stairs, and charged at the door with my head down, thus butting it, causing it to violently swing open, and I ran across the hall and hid in the sitting-room, beneath a small, lace-covered table that held a lovely, large Staffordshire horse ornament. I had thought that if she came in there after me there was a second door leading into the dining-room that I could escape through. I waited, with my heart pounding, and scarcely able to breathe, but she didn't come after me. Later, that same day, she told on me, informing Augustus that I had savagely bitten her but, incredibly, nobody believed her!

Eliza exposes her ample bottom for attack.

Armstrong laughed outright at her. "Not Shales," she said. "He wouldn't 'urt a mouse!" Then she taunted her, "Eliza, you've sat down on one of your large kitchen forks. Come on, Liza, tell us the truth! Don't blame it on the dog!"

So, you see, I had had my revenge, but I realised it didn't help matters any. I then wondered what else she would do to me. I knew I would have to be careful, and never, ever trust her.

Less than a week later, she struck back at me. I'd kept out of her way as much as possible, but I had noticed she walked with a stiff gait, and looked uncomfortable, as if in a great deal of pain. It was a Saturday afternoon, and once again I found myself alone in the house with her. The housemaid had nipped out, sent by the cook to purchase some particular spice needed for the evening meal. Now that I think back on it, I think she sent Armstrong off on a wild goose chase, in order to have the house to herself. Edmund, Charles Clement, and Augustus had left, presumably on their way to Westminster to visit their club, and they would not be returning until very late. The sisters and Maud had gone out to view a painting of Stanley's, on display in an art gallery in London, and Charlotte had taken Mary Matilda out for the day – lessons for a toddler in learning how to behave in public places.

I'd gone up to the nursery for a nap. I had thought it would be a safe place to be, should I ever need to *retreat*, as the nursery was no place for the cook to be found. It was simply out of bounds to her. There was no ample reason for her to ever be in there. I had been asleep in an overstuffed chair, which I had claimed for myself months before, when I sensed movement, an unwelcome presence, but by then it was too late. I felt a strange, sharp, stabbing pain in my left side, where my ribs are. I jumped up with a loud yelp; I felt my side searing with pain. I saw her leave the room quickly, and she was holding something in her right hand. I saw it was a small knife from the kitchen, the sort used for peeling potatoes and carrots.

She'd stabbed me!

I licked the wound, which turned out to be not very deep, as the blade had glanced off one of my ribs. It did bleed profusely, at first, but after quite a long time of my licking it, it began to slow down and stop. It hurt, and it wasn't long before Julia noticed there was something wrong with me. That evening she had leaned over to stroke me, and I had flinched and growled as her fingers came near the wound. She bravely parted the hair there, and gasped, "Jessie! Come and look at this! There's a wound in his side. It looks like Shales has been stabbed, or poked with something sharp."

Maud quickly snarled, "I niver done anything to the dog."

Julia replied in a shocked tone, "Why would we think you've done anything to Shales?"

"Northing," was Maud's Norfolk reply.

We must all of us have given Maud a strange look, as a result of her statement. Maud blushed and insisted, "I would niver hurt Shales, but it looks as if somebody has."

The women all had their turns examining my side, and they all seemed to agree that something unnatural had befallen me. It was decided that the men should be informed at breakfast, as they would return late into the night, after being out in London, long after the ladies had retired to bed.

* * *

EDMUND HAD A LOOK. "It seems he has tried to push his way through the hedge at the back of the garden; he's merely been poked by a sharp branch, that's all. We'll have to make sure he isn't trying to escape again."

Augustus and Charles Clement didn't know what to think of my wound. They wondered if it had happened on the Friday, when I'd been at work.

Julia didn't believe this. "No. Look at the wound. It looks as though he has been stabbed with a knife!"

"Nobody's stabbed him," said an exasperated Edmund as he ran his fingers around his starched collar, which appeared to be too tight for comfort. But then he looked across the room at me, "You don't suppose the cook did anything to him, do you?"

Augustus had to ask, "Why would she do that?" He rarely saw the cook, so he wasn't aware of her moods, and had never witnessed her hateful behaviour towards me.

Julia answered, "Because she says Shales bit her. He is supposed to have bitten her... you know... where she sits... on her... *bottom*."

263

Augustus said three words. "Good boy, Shales."

Jessie was furious. "Dad, that isn't good! Shales mustn't bite, no matter what. If he did bite her, then there is something the matter between them, and that should stop. That would give her reason to stab him, because she doesn't care for dogs. In fact, she despises dogs more than anyone else I know. I wouldn't put it past her to have struck out at him with a knife."

"Who believes our cook stabbed Shales with a knife?" demanded Augustus. Nobody answered. They all seemed to be intent in looking at the variations in the pattern of the Brussels carpet, and the subject was changed. I don't think any of them wanted to see Eliza dismissed without more proof, but I was pleased to know they were on to her. Boys o' boys, mmn, mmn, mmn.

* * *

LOYALTY IS A TRAIT I ADMIRE IN PEOPLE, as well as in animals. Most have it – some do not, which brings me around to the subject of Maud. I could sense unrest within her, and something else almost secretive there, lying just below the surface of conversation. Before the summer was over with Maud had moved herself, along with all her belongings, Charlotte, and Mary Matilda, back to Stoke Newington, to a house just a few streets away from the boarding house. Apparently, she had taken it upon herself to rent this house before informing Augustus and the rest of the family of her intentions of moving out.

The deed was done. The papers were signed. And in her very own words, "There is no going back."

Perhaps she did it this way because she thought the family would talk her out of moving to a residence of her own. I think they would not have done so; in fact, I think they would have encouraged her, and in doing so, the atmosphere in the household would have been lighter than the heavy pall of disappointment and disloyalty that pervaded the air as the removal men came to shift her belongings. She wanted Thomas's furniture from his bedchamber, but after a family row that made me cringe and hide under the table in the library she relented from her demand and, of his things, she took with her just

264

one of his riding crops, though later we found out that she had also taken the family Christening gown. I did wonder what had happened to all his personal belongings and furniture from the house in Bush Hill Park, as I hadn't seen any of it appear at Darnley Road.

In the end it was agreed upon that because she was not removing herself very far from us, just living a short train's journey away, she would be visiting us regularly and dining with us every so often on a Sunday, and she would bring Mary Matilda with her. She would also continue to take her holidays with us, and that also included going to Cotheridge Court with us on family visits. It was important for little Mary Matilda to grow up knowing who her cousins, aunts, and uncles were, otherwise she would become cut off from them, and that was not a good thing, since her father was dead. My family, after all, was Mary Matilda's family, and on her mother's side there were relations as well, but she didn't see much of them, if at all.

The house they took was a good, middle-class residence, but on the small side, as nothing impressive was required. A maid-of-all was hired, and also a housemaid who also did the cooking; a difficult task at best, to find someone clean and amiable who could cook and also be willing to clean *and* answer the door when required. Maud set herself up in the dressmaking trade (one that she was qualified to do), and she set her sights on making garments for the middle-class women, or better, of Stoke Newington; but she still remained friends with Mary Ann Moore. The larger house on Fifth Avenue, in Bush Hill Park, returned to her a generous income. I found out it was rented, along with all the furnishings.

XV
THE SEASIDE

*"How does a dog explain things to
people?"*

1884

ONE SUMMER'S EVENING, as we were all gathered in the dining-room, and as knives and forks gently clinked when they touched the delicate surfaces of the china plates, and as glasses of red wine were lifted up from their places and were slowly emptied, the conversation took a turn, causing all, except for Augustus, to exclaim with delight, "Wonderful!"

Edmund asked, "All of us?"

My master simply nodded, and continued to chew his food.

"When are we to go?" Many voices rang out in unison.

You see, it was Augustus who had said the most trivial of words, when he thought no one had been listening, they all intently discussing a man called Julius Caesar. "If you fetch your buckets and little spades, you'll be able to go to the seaside for your holidays. Anyone up for it?"

It was something that would normally be said to a child, but he knew everyone would be keen to go, as this summer we were not going to Cotheridge Court for our entire summer's holiday; to visit, yes, but not to stay for a fortnight. He had caught their attention, though they had at first been unsure of his intent. The seaside; I had absolutely no knowledge of what 'seaside' meant. I was excited, and hoped I would be able to go along as well, and so I went up to the dining table and sat nice and smartly next to the master, and then whined. I looked at him expectantly, and then wagged my tail. He looked at me, and I looked at him, sending him mental pictures of myself being included in the family outing. Thank goodness he understood!

"Of course, Shales can come along as well. William said to fetch him with us. It won't be any difficulty on their part to have him stay in the hotel. We shall set off on Sunday next, if everyone agrees."

I had picked up on the excitement that filled the room, and as usual when this happened, I was filled with the urge to tear about and fly from chair to chair. This I was not allowed to do, but instead, I was encouraged to fetch my bunny. Oops! I wasn't supposed to tell you about my bunny! Too late now! As they say: "The cat has been let out of the bag." Just don't tell anyone I had one of those floppy-eared things. So, I tossed my large, fat, soft, grey bunny with the long ears about the room and, as everyone retired to the drawing-room, Charles participated in a game of tug, whereby one of Bunny's ears came off in his hand. Oh, dear!

Jessie to the rescue: "Oh, Shales, I'll sew it back on again. I'll put its eyes and nose back as well..." (I had nibbled them off) "...but it'll have to wait until tomorrow morning." She ruffled my ears and kissed me on my nose.

I wasn't really bothered if Bunny only had one ear and that he had gone blind, as well as not being able to smell anything, but oft-times he ended up in the pile of mending along with the shirts and hankies. After my saying this, you, the reader, are supposed to *smile*. Now, where was I? Oh, yes. The summer holiday was the main topic of conversation over tea and coffee, and later in celebration they overindulged in their sherry, brandy and cigars. Later that evening they all went to bed in a merry mood, laughing and tripping up on the stairs as they retired for the night. I couldn't stop thinking about the holiday. It meant going on a train again, and I now *loved* trains.

I thought to myself, *"Boys o' boys, mmn, mmn, mmn."*

* * *

I WAS SO DISTRACTED BY THE UPCOMING HOLIDAY that I let my guard down, and I narrowly avoided another incident with the cook. You see, she didn't have to sharpen her kitchen knives herself. She could have had one of those knife-sharpening contraptions, but she always insisted, "They don't work as well as an experienced 'and an' a whetstone." Being a servant to a wealthy family, a man stopped by once a week, and with his whetstone he would sharpen all her knives to a soldier's *envied perfection*. Usually, the kettle went on the hob, and as he sharpened he would relay to Cook and Armstrong the latest gossip, picked up second-hand and third-hand from the kitchens of Hackney's mansions and houses. He would drink two cups of tea and demolish several biscuits before he would be finished. It was a thirsty job, was gossiping. They called him Mr Finchey.

"Mr Finchey," she would say, as she let him in by the tradesman's entrance, "we'll 'ave a nice cup'a tea, an' thou canst fill us in on wot's new."

Mr Finchey was quite tall, and a bit dirty-looking, if you know what I mean. A bit like old Toothless George, though Finchey's clothes were in better shape. He had an annoying habit of smacking his lips after every sip of tea, and he always dipped his biscuits into his tea first, before taking a bite. I think it was because he didn't have any teeth at all, but just a large, gaping hole surrounded by loose, wet, flabby lips.

On this particular knife-sharpening day she had requested that a certain few knives be extra sharp, as she had a "job to do". When Finchey was all done he said, "'E're you are, Eliza, moy luv. These 'ere noives are sharp enuff to butcha' your very o'n cow. 'Ere, you ain't finn'ink of doin' som'ink dodgy, are ya?"

I didn't pay much attention to what was being said. I didn't really understand much of it, and I didn't take the time to think about what had been said, nor to make sense of it. Besides, it was difficult deciphering Finchey's words. He was a right cockney! Sometimes I had to think really long and hard to understand just one sentence when people were speaking, let alone a whole slew of sentences, and him speaking cockney made it even more difficult.

Finchey left, not wasting an extra minute as he had other houses to visit, and shortly later, when it all was quiet downstairs, I tiptoed below to get a drink. Thinking Cook had gone into the pantry, I thought that if I nipped down to the kitchen I'd be back up the stairs before she could see me, but instead of silence I heard her footsteps coming quickly across the stone floor. Before I could escape, she was there, large knife in hand. She waved her favourite knife in the air, the one she used, two-handed, whenever she chopped up large vegetables or joints of meat on the table. After the incident when she had stabbed me, in the side of the ribcage, I became more aware of the fact that I could easily go missing for an entire day, and then appear as the main course, served from our best Minton, in the form of, say, a giblet pie with gravy and vegetables, or a beef curry with rice. Did I have an overactive imagination, or was this an actual possibility? I could just imagine her gloating. A secretive, gleeful expression on her face as Armstrong served up the pie or curry, and someone in the family asking, in an enquiring voice, "What of Shales? Any news of him? We hear he's gone over the hedge again. Wonder when he'll be back?" All the while, Eliza, the cook, would be below in the kitchen, sipping a cup of tea, and out of my bones planning soup for the next day. There wouldn't be anything at all left of me – not one jot of my existence. Nobody would know what had happened to me, or that they had eaten me! My innocent bones to be carted off by the dustman.

She slowly crept towards me as water dripped from my lips and plopped back into the bowl. Ploppety plop... plop.

"I'll cook you, I will. I'll cut you up in li'l pieces o' meat, and nobody'll know. I'll serve you up fow dinner!"

Her face told me she meant it and she wasn't larking about. She came towards me, blocking off my escape route to the stairs. I was terrified and I felt my hackles bristle, and I went into my defensive stance: feet squared evenly on the floor and head slightly lowered, with a slow, deep growl coming from between my bared teeth. I now knew without a shadow of a doubt that I had to get away from her. I turned quickly and ran to the back of the kitchen, where the door to the tradesman's entrance was, and then came around in a tight circle and jumped completely over the work table. My toes didn't even touch it. As she brought the knife down onto me, I was already past her and up the stairs, as fast as an English cannon-ball shot at a French ship. I ran so fast that I skidded on the turn at the front end of the hall, and the floor mat was flung up against the skirting-board. I ran all the way up the large flight of stairs, and continued up the next flight to the second floor, and ran down the corridor and into the nursery, having no other place to go. I cowered down

269

in the far corner behind my comfy chair, listening for her footsteps on the servants' stairs, which were nearby.

I waited there a long time. She didn't come after me. But what would she do when I came back from being on holiday?

What was I to do?

Oh, dear me! I did worry about it.

The very next day I was awakened from my late afternoon nap by the tantalizing aroma of roasting meat. I'd already been to work and had had my tea and biscuits, and, as usual, I had settled down to let the late afternoon pass by before dinnertime arrived. The smells of the sizzling joint gnawed at my appetite, and though I tried to ignore the delicious smell all I could think of was what I'd be having for dinner. I got up from where I had been lying in front of the sitting-room fire. It was a miserable day. A pea-souper had cast its cloak over us, with its damp and evil smells chasing everyone inside for the day. I knew I couldn't patter down to the kitchen and find a friendly cook who would be kind to me. I sighed deeply at that thought. I well remembered the days I had spent feeling starved and lost, and now, though I was not *hungry,* I was still tempted to follow the drifting smells of that night's dinner. I thought that I might find some carrots on the chopping table, and if Eliza's back was turned I could pinch one without her knowing it. Yes, I know a carrot is a poor substitute for a slice of succulent meat, but what can a dog do when it's feeling peckish? I couldn't open the biscuit tin and help myself to a couple of ginger snaps, because I don't have fingers.

The door at the top of the stairs, which led down to the kitchen, pushed open easily with a gentle nudge of my nose. I was always thankful that it was the sort that never had a knob to open with: it was free-swinging, and would open in either direction, thus allowing me free access to come and go as I pleased. I bravely tiptoed down, a few steps at a time. The carpet cushioned the sound of my footsteps, and there she was, slicing vegetables, and the newly-hired maid-of-all was doing the washing up, and *she* had her back turned to me. I spied the small joint. It was not spectacular in size. It was sitting on top of the chopping table, and its delicious, dark liquid was oozing onto a plate beneath it. At that point, I dithered. I didn't know what to do, because the cook was stood there wiping her hands on her apron, saying, in a huff, "I'm just off to the loo. You'd better still be stood at that sink when I get back!"

The young maid-of-all glanced over her shoulder at the retreating cook. "Yes, Eloiza. Oi'm not goin' anywhere soon." As if she wasn't in the least bothered by the cook's dominance.

"An' keep your 'ands off that roast beef!" shouted the cook, as she quickly trotted down the passageway to the servants' loo.

This was my opportunity, my opening for success. I knew what I was going to do. I ran up to the maid and did my "*need to go outside and use the garden loo*" dance. This new girl was always good to me. "Awright, Shales. Le' me ge' to the door."

She left the tradesman's door open, a normal practice when I was only going outside for a quick wee or something. I did that, quickly. Then, I deftly crept back inside, and very quietly jumped up onto the top of the solid work table, where the roasted joint and the uncooked vegetables lay. The maid-of-all was intent on scrubbing a large pan, humming away to herself, so I casually grabbed the roast beef between my jaws, and then silently jumped back down onto the stone floor. It was heavy, and I didn't think I'd be able to manage what I had to do. I had not been noticed, so I ran for it – outside and up the steps – dropping the roast because it was hot and too large for my mouth, whereby I dragged it into the garden, where, with my right paw, I then rolled the roast, which was still very hot, underneath the holly bush at the side of the house. As quickly as I had done this, I turned about and casually walked down into the kitchen, cooled my burning gums with a drink of water, and gave the maid a friendly, wet nudge, letting her know that I was now back inside the house. I then went up the stairs and lay in front of the sitting-room fire. The room was deserted, there being distant voices coming from the library, and the rich scent of pipe tobacco coming from the drawing-room. I licked my chops and cleaned up my paws and wrists. I knew Cook would soon be looking for me, and I didn't want to look mucky. I would portray innocence of any wrongdoing.

It wasn't long before she came charging up the stairs like a mad bull, and burst into the sitting-room, flinging open the door with excessive force so that it noisily bounced back off the wall, her rage all apparent by the red colour of her face. I thought she must have forgotten that the house was not abandoned and we were not alone. Armstrong was about somewhere, possibly upstairs, and I wondered if she'd heard the banging of the door. Cook found me relaxing in front of the fire. She stormed forward and stood in front of me, sniffing the air, and her fat, mad eyes searched all about.

The maid-of-all came in behind her, with a frightened expression on her young face, and whispered loudly, "We shouldn't be in 'ere! If the roast was in 'ere, 'twould smell of it, and it doesn't."

"Then, where is it, you silly girl?" hissed the cook.

"P'raps someone came in be'ind me and nicked it. You were in the loo, and the door was open 'cause Shales was outside. The roast was there then, 'cause I noticed it." Evidently nervous of being caught up to no good, she stuck her head out through the doorway and listened for footsteps.

"The master will be very, very angry. What am I goin' to say? 'Ow do I explain where 'is roast beef 'as gone to?" The cook huffed and puffed these words out as if in mortal fear of the consequences.

I was really enjoying this. Unfortunately, nobody came to investigate the noise made by the banging door but, still, she couldn't do anything to me because the house wasn't empty. I knew that eventually she would have to stand in front of either Jessie or the master and explain herself. The frightened young maid tugged on the sleeve of Cook's blouse. The two departed for the kitchen in all haste, and I wondered what would appear on our dining table in place of the missing roast. Eliza would have to work some powerful magic in order to get away with not serving roast beef to the family. Especially when it was roast beef, Yorkshire pudding and so on that was what was expected to appear on the table. Jessie had requested it. Boys o' boys, mmn, mmn, mmn.

She pulled it off! I could hardly believe it, but she did manage to get away with it. She had made a beef curry out of stewing meat, after the young maid had been sent out to the butcher's, in all haste, and had explained to Jessie that the roast had been so gristly, she'd had to make a curry out of it in order for it to be eaten. I'm not quite sure what Eliza, the cook, said to Armstrong, our housemaid, but I think she told her the truth. Everyone, meaning my family, was satisfied with the explanation about the beef being too gristly to carve, but the butcher would have to watch himself, as he came under harsh criticism from Jessie. Cook would have to cover the cost of the extra expense for the stewing meat in some way, if not out of her own pocket. Still, it had felt good to do that to her, and I enjoyed seeing her squirm, but I worried about what she would do to me, in return, when I returned from my holidays.

* * *

I HAD NEITHER SEEN THE SEA BEFORE, nor a sandy beach. I had no idea, no actual thoughts, as to what to expect. As we travelled, comfortably seated in a first-class coach near the back of the train, with my nose pressed against the window, making little smeary, smudgy marks upon the glass, I tried to imagine what I was to expect. I simply couldn't. Because I knew neither what the sea was, nor a beach, I didn't have the ability to imagine the 'seaside'. Curiosity was getting the better of me, because I knew we were going to a good place, otherwise the family wouldn't have been so happily animated about going. It was the hottest part of the summer, so the coal trade lagged a bit. Actually, it lagged enough to allow both Edmund and Charles to accompany us to Gorleston-on-Sea, near Yarmouth. The men in Augustus's employ had already had their short summer breaks, so it was left to them to ensure that it all ran efficiently, in the absence of their employer. Even the horses benefited from the slower trade, which gave them extra time off in the sweltering heat, and an opportunity to pasture on green grasses, instead of being stabled and fed on hay and oats at all times. I was relieved to be away from Hackney. I didn't know what to do about the cook, so I decided to stop thinking about her, and I concentrated on enjoying my holiday. I was sure she would be there when I got back, but for a short while I could be free of her, and I planned to enjoy myself.

The train slowed down, tooted its whistle a few times, and we approached the station, coming to a stop amidst the sound of screeching brakes and loud hisses of steam. When I alighted at the station platform I sniffed the air, noticing its strange, bitter saltiness, so foreign to my senses. It smelt brisk and clean, despite the thick, black smoke chugging from the locomotive's stack; the aroma was unusually delicious. Why didn't the air around London smell like this? This was good enough to bottle and sell, and make some silly nit a large fortune. Also, you wouldn't *believe* the amount of baggage we had brought along with us! The ladies each had a large travelling trunk as well as a small trunk and a hatbox. The men had managed with a large trunk for each of themselves, and I had one small, leather case, which contained my Royal Doulton food bowls, comb, hairbrush, spare lead, spare collar, and my Nubian Liquid Waterproof Blacking, which was used on my collar and lead to keep them shiny black and immaculate. Bunny was in there somewhere, used as ballast, as well as Ball. For this amount of baggage we needed the help of a porter, and he carefully stacked the mountain of trunks and hatboxes onto a very large wagon, which he trundled along, with some effort, by pulling on a long handle. The wagon noisily rolled along the platform on its cast-iron wheels, and then out of the station. William's hotel was very near, and definitely within walking distance. Really, it was right there, across the road, a hop, a skip and a jump away, and it felt good to stretch my legs as we walked over to it.

The station was a busy spot, as most railway stations are. People milled about, from the poorer ones whose Sunday dress didn't quite fit them properly, to the wealthy, where ladies twirled expensive silk parasols, and with one glance the cut of the men's clothes and their confident posture denoted them as gentlemen. Regardless of their station in life, the many faces glowed, and showed they had either enjoyed their stay in Southtown, or Gorleston, which was now over with and they were returning home, or that they were anticipating having a grand time, as they had yet to begin their holidays.

The baggage was being taken care of, as William had sent one of his men to see to the transference of it, from the station to the hotel. Augustus was up for walking the short distance to the hotel, after being seated all morning long on our journey. He tugged on my lead and led the way, with Edmund and young Charles bringing up the rear. The ladies grumbled under their breath, as they would have preferred the luxury of a carriage, even though the distance to walk was embarrassingly short.

We walked out of the station, and a few moments later we were at William's hotel. It was called The Bear. It looked quite imposing with its stone-fronted facade partially covered in ivy, and the top edge of the rooftop finely decorated with a wall of stone fretwork. Up above me, atop the fretwork of the parapet, were two large stone ornaments, set apart with the word Hotel in-between them. They looked odd and out of place. They were of an animal I had never before seen, and I wondered if these seated beasts were bears. Then I remembered that my master's walking-stick had a bear on the end – the part where he held onto it – and I thought, "*Yes, those are bears.*" I could only see two floors, but the rooms were well lit, as the windows were large and plentiful.

We entered the hotel through a semi-circular porch, where then we milled about in a large group, which included all the sisters, Edmund, Charles, Augustus, Maud, and the nurse Charlotte, and of course, Mary Matilda and me. William and his wife greeted us with open arms. What a happy family reunion we had standing there. William's wife was called Mary, and they had a daughter named Marie Matilda Isabelle, who went by Isabelle, or Belle, and was eight years old. Then there was Shales Augustus, who was nearly six years of age, and I was named after him, and last of all there was little Philip, who was about three or so.

The hotel was very nice on the outside, and the inside of The Bear passed muster as well. Not that I was fussy; it was a treat to be staying in an hotel, and not a slew of dog kennels. I was living the *good life,* and didn't I know it. The children came up to me and gawped, mouths agape, as if they'd never seen a dog before. Admittedly, I had been worried that I would have a week of being a victim of these children's cruel acts. I swallowed deeply, wondering how they were going to treat me. Stepping forward, they then gave me lots of friendly attention. They seemed honest enough and were gentle with me, so I licked their faces for them and rubbed my nose all over the fronts of their clothes, thus covering them with dog slobber. It was the very least I could do to let them know I liked them. William reached down and patted me on the head. I was not to be banished outside, after all, but could live with the family in the rooms of the hotel.

The Bear Hotel in Gorleston-on-Sea.

That evening the family went out to a restaurant in Yarmouth instead of dining at the hotel. A rare treat for William and Mary to be away from The Bear, but I had to stay behind with Charlotte and the children. It was a lovely evening; the temperature was very mild, so Charlotte gathered us all together with instructions to not wander away, and to hold hands, and we set off for a walk down the road, crossing Southtown Bridge, from where we stopped to gaze at the flowing river, which is called the Yare. At that spot we were not far from the hotel, with it being just about a hundred yards behind us. There was something new I learnt that evening about Mary Matilda's nurse, Charlotte: she loved walking the legs off children. I didn't think we'd go very far, it being our first outing, but we walked and walked for what seemed like hours, until little Mary Matilda complained, and pestered to stop and rest.

We had followed the river for quite a distance, and then had turned into some of the side streets, which had plenty of shops. They were closed at that late hour. Mary Matilda kept asking to stop and rest, and eventually Charlotte gave in but wouldn't allow her to sit down on the kerb, as that behaviour was common, and curious people were stood watching us.

Behind us there was a shop window, typical in its bay shape, and inside, beyond the glass panes, was an array of summer articles on display. Charlotte, in an effort to appease Mary Matilda, bent down and pointed to something.

"There. See that bright red bucket with the yellow spade? Tomorrow, when the shop opens up, I shall come here and purchase it, and we'll all go onto the beach, and then I'll show you how to build sandcastles. We didn't have a bucket and spade to bring with us, and you simply cannot play in the sand without a set."

Mary Matilda smiled and repeated, "Sandcastles! I'd like that." Then, "Charlotte, will I be so tired tomorrow?" The poor child was bone-weary.

"I promise you, we shan't do as much walking tomorrow. I believe you'll do more sitting and playing," answered her nurse.

Shales and Isabelle asked if they could also come. Charlotte said, "I believe *everyone* is going, even Shales the dog. It is to be an all-day event, as long as the weather cooperates."

Charlotte was so nice. I started to wag my tail, and she stroked me gently. I was eager to go and experience a sandy beach and watch the waves roll in, even though I didn't know what *waves* were. So far, all I had been able to conjure up in my mind was the fish pond at Cotheridge Court, with its grassy banks and bulrushes, populated with twittering birds and delicate butterflies, as well as charging swans. Liking the pond at the Court, I thought I would be very satisfied with a week of something like that, with fields of tall grasses to run through and explore.

William and his wife managed to take the following day off, away from the demands of the hotel, leaving it in the capable hands of their staff. They accompanied us out onto the sands, which was a rare occasion for them, the summertime being their busiest season.

277

Shales digs in the sand, whilst Augustus roasts his shanks.

* * *

TWO LARGE HAMPERS OF FOOD HAD BEEN PREPARED, filled with all sorts of food delicacies such as cucumber sandwiches, slices of toasted bread, jars of potted meat, and plenty of water, lemonade, ginger beer, as well as cold tea with lemon. Napkins, tablecloths, beakers, and china plates, along with a plentiful amount of cutlery, were also packed in a hamper. From the onset I knew we were definitely not going to go short of food for the day. We couldn't walk to the beach, as it was too far away, especially since we had heavy hampers and large umbrellas, as well as folding chairs and blankets. Several large four-wheeler cabs were hired for the short journey, and off we went. The day was beautiful, and it was only going to get hotter than it already was. Our cab set off at a fast trot, and I hung my head out over the side, enjoying the swift, salty breeze as it blew through my hair and stung my eyes.

Suddenly, I was pulled backwards by my collar.

A horrified Jessie cried, "NO, Shales! You'll be decapitated if you're not careful!" With her hand clasped over her mouth, she said, "Oh, God! Shales, sit back down!

A dray wagon had passed quite close to us – actually, within inches. It was loaded down with tuns; you know, large barrels, and I could very well have banged my head on them, resulting in a headache! I'm sure decapitation isn't as bad as a thumping headache, whatever it is.

We continued down Regent Road, and a short while later pulled up at a cabstand, and at that place we all alighted. The sun was bright on the eyes, making me squint, and the air smelt so wonderfully fresh. Strange-sounding birds floated about in the air. They were noisy and plentiful. What was that I could see? It was nothing but the sky, a brilliant, cobalt blue with white, fluffy clouds, and some unusual, flat ground in a bright sandy colour, that stretched for what seemed like miles either side of me. In the cobalt blue was water, which was a bluish-green, and lots of it, too. More water than I had ever before seen, in my entire life! It went on forever, just like the sands and the sky! This was the beach! Of course, I couldn't imagine what it was, not without first seeing it. Who could? How can one imagine a star, if one has never before seen the night?

Jessie removed my lead, insisting I not run away but stay close. As the grown-ups started to carry the baskets and other paraphernalia onto the sands I took absolutely no notice of what Jessie had said to me, and ran off with my four feet flying. It was strange running across that sandy stuff. It was soft and hot, and it gave way under my feet with a strange sliding sensation. I directed my course straight for the waves, which were still a good distance away, and I didn't stop. Eventually, as I met up with the sea, I leapt into the air, meeting a little wave at about chest height. The impact from the incoming wave pushed me upwards, and then rolled me over onto my back, and water went down my throat as well as up my nose. I gagged and coughed at the saltiness of it, but gained my feet and took off down the beach as fast as a horse. Oh, what joy! I was as happy as a grunting pig. I heard a whistle and my name being called, so I returned to my family, who were in the process of laying out blankets and setting up umbrellas near the chairs, to provide ample shade. I gleefully skidded to a stop, spraying sand over everyone, and then gave myself a right good shake, which resulted in protesting moans and groans.

"Shales! No!"

"He's getting sand everywhere!"

"You horrid dog!"

"Go away!"

Even though I was shouted at, they all had smiles on their faces. This little area was to be our *camp* for the day. I thought it was marvellous! I wasn't going to be kept on a lead, so I was experiencing a freedom I hadn't felt in a long while. The children were already enjoying themselves, as they had been given brightly coloured buckets and spades by Charlotte, and already she was helping them near the water's edge in getting the dampest of sands, and they were eagerly shovelling it into their buckets. After my burst of energy and romp around the beach I couldn't wait for elevenses because I was starving, and I wanted some of that potted meat and a slice of watery cucumber. There were absolutely no signs that an early lunch was about to be served, so, feeling disappointed, I waited patiently.

I stood there in the hot sun with my four feet sinking into the baking, dry sand, and surveyed the sea, a vast expanse of rolling, bluish-green waves, which came towards the beach and collapsed into flat, foam-specked wavelets that after a certain point quickly receded, drawn back again into the sea, and all to a new sound, the thunderous sound of crashing ocean waves. It was marvellous! These were the *waves* and I was standing on *sand*.

It was so captivating, to the point that I didn't at first notice my feet were cooking – and cook they did.

Ouch!

The sand was hot, and I didn't know what to do about it. My feet burnt, and I lifted them in the air one by one, keeping myself balanced on just three legs at a time.

Charles started to laugh at me, so I hobbled up to him, whereupon he pulled me into the shade where he sat, and then gave me a generous hug. "Come here, you silly dog." He got up from the blanket. "Come on and cool your feet off."

His trousers were rolled up to his knees and his feet were bare. I followed him, and we ran down to the water's edge. A wave rushed up around my legs, feeling deliciously cool and soothing on my pads. My toes craved to dig into the soft, wet sandiness beneath my feet. There was an unusual sucking sensation as the water receded, tugging at my feet and wanting to sweep me along with it. Charles encouraged me to swim when he threw a small stick into the sea, which then was carried along by a wave. I swam after it, feeling extremely buoyant, and after grabbing it with my mouth allowed the waves to roll me into shore, whereby I got up and had a good run about, sending clods of wet sand flying until I was exhausted. I enjoyed the sea tremendously, running away from the attacking waves, and then chasing them as they receded, only to be consumed by a *number seven*, one of those large waves with an enormous amount of pent-up force, which rolled along higher and further than the all others.

Apparently, I made quite the spectacle, and the family roared with laughter as they watched my antics from beneath the large umbrellas. After some length of time I shook myself, and then made a beeline for the camp in anticipation of receiving some sustenance, as well as water that was fit to drink. My mouth was gritty, and sand had got into my eyes and up my nose and between my toes, but most of all, I was tired, as well as feeing hungry enough to eat a horse with a scabby head. Finally, after what seemed like hours, but was really only a short time, the picnic baskets were opened and lunch was served. Jessie, who was always good to me, sorted me out with some fresh water and some of that lovely potted meat I'd been hungering after, along with some toast, and yes, slices of cucumber, as well as some cold tea and a ginger biscuit.

If a dog could laugh out loud like people do when they are greatly amused, then I would have done so. However, I couldn't laugh, but had to be content with merely wagging my tail. Dear Reader, what could have appeared to have been so hilariously funny? Well, the sight of Augustus's bared legs, from just below the knee and down to his toes. He had a pair of hairy, sinewy sticks, which were catching the sun, and were being slowly roasted to a porky pink. He sat in his reclining chair, in his usual gentlemanly position of having a straightened back with a slightly forward tilt to his torso, and his two hands gripped the knob of his walking-stick, which was thrust into the sand between his knees and supported his weight. His trousers of summer-weight linen, procured especially for his seaside sojourn, were rolled up to the knee, displaying a casual side of my master that I had never before seen. From his knees upwards he had done a marvellous job of remaining in the shade, but I think he forgot about the rest of himself. He looked so completely happy and relaxed as he gazed out to sea that it would have been a shame to have disturbed him in any way at all.

My very first day on South Beach would not have been complete without the building and destruction of sandcastles. Sandcastles! Except for Augustus and William, the rest of the family had a hand at building those sandy fortresses, which, after no amount of moats and outer walls, could not keep out the advancing sea. They had momentarily shirked off the shackles of Victorian life, and got down into the wet sand and forgot about manners and decorum, regardless of the fact that others might have been watching and judging. It was good to see Edmund smile as he scraped slightly wet sand into a bucket, turned it over and positioned it, giving it a good tap on its overturned end before removing it. I had a lovely time jumping onto their fortresses' walls and digging them out as fast as I could, sending damp sand flying out from between my back legs. Mary Matilda thought I was being funny, so I worked even harder at the destruction. Isabelle and Shales made a frantic effort to fortify their work, telling me I was being "naughty", and they playfully slapped me with their little, colourful spades.

As the day wore on, the waves came in increasingly higher, washing away the elaborate castles. I crawled about in the wet sand and rolled over into the foam at the water's high mark. The foam was smelly and dank. I probably didn't smell like a flower, either, which was probably why late in the afternoon Jessie procured a bar of soap, and came across and offered it to Charles Clement, wearing a big, sisterly smile upon her face.

"You're already wet, Charlie." She then suggested, "Why don't you give Shales a good wash, and get a lot of that sand out of his fur?" As an afterthought she said, "And put him on his lead so he doesn't run away, and please *do* try to keep him from rolling in the sand again."

Charles looked at me, and I looked back at him. I wasn't too fond of baths, so I jumped to my right in an attempt to escape, but he had outwitted me, and before I knew it, I was once again a dog on a lead. I received a good soaping as the waves rolled in, as Charles made sure he lathered me up rather well, then he rinsed the rose-scented soap out of my hair, leaving me smelling like a flower.

Emily said, "Shales will sleep well tonight. He'll probably get his head down and won't wake up until the morning." She yawned as she swatted at a rogue fly.

Charlie replied, "I think that goes for both Shaleses." He too gave a lengthy yawn, "I agree with you Emily, but I think we'll *all* sleep well tonight."

Early evening had arrived, and it was time to pack up and go. I wearily dragged my feet along. All of my pads were sore and tired, and they stung somewhat from the sea salt, which seemed to have invaded their every crack and pore. Not being able to walk all the way to the cabstand, I collapsed upon the sand in pain, so Edmund and Charles took turns carrying me. They moaned and groaned, complaining I was too large to be carried over such a long distance. I didn't care, just as long as I didn't have to walk across that sand any more. I was actually in a lot of pain, and Augustus said he sympathised with my plight, as the soles of his own feet had been sunburnt. He hobbled along upon his roasted shanks, but fell behind as his gait grew slower and slower. Emily and Lucy urged him along as the rest of the family wearily carried the deconstructed remains of the camp, and all were eager to get back to the hotel. Once there, I limped from the kerbside into The Bear, and up the staircase to the landing, where I found a door open to a room. I know not whose it was, and at the time I did not care; thus, I collapsed upon a bed too tired to think about my dinner or my supper, and I did not stir until the following morning.

Apparently, I had slept with an elderly widow from Huddersfield, who had been unable to waken me, and though confused at my sudden appearance in her room, later said, "He wor smelling so pretty like, that I thought he mun stay and ger a good night's kip. I told 'im t' shift oover, and we shared bed t'gether."

* * *

DON'T THINK THAT MAUD WAS FORGOTTEN in all this gaiety. Oh, no. *She* was enjoying her holiday as much as everyone else – a bit too much, I'm afraid. She was eager to walk up and down the sands, unaccompanied, twirling her parasol about in her hands with a sauciness that vied for competition with her swaying skirts; she always had an audience wherever she went. At these times she was keen to be seen without her daughter, although her wedding ring betrayed her status. Remember, she was neither of single status nor married, spinster nor wife, but a widow, and a mother – yes. As I watched her behaviour, I realised she was yearning to escape the confines of motherhood. Being a widow and a daughter-in-law, as well as a sister-in-law, and living with a family she had hardly known three years previously restricted her. I wondered how long it would be before she upped sticks and left us for good. I'm sure that if I could notice her poor behaviour, then the others did as well, although nothing was ever said.

The sisters Jessie, Julia, Emily and Lucy dressed in bright summer colours, but were ever so careful not to bake their skin in the sun. If they wore short-sleeved dresses, then they held a parasol over their shoulders. They wore summer hats woven from delicate straw, which were decorated with colourful ribbons and dried flowers. Many times the ribbons and hatbands matched the colour of their skirts. These skirts remained long, hanging down past their ankles, and some of them trailed out behind them in fashionable design. They did discuss the possibility of bathing in the sea, but none of them were brave enough to be the first and don a ladies' bathing costume, which would have been quite revealing, and rather a bit shocking. They did, however, enjoy lounging in the chairs on the beach, in the shade of a parasol or large umbrella. They nattered non-stop. I hadn't realised the four of them could be so chatty. They observed other holiday goers from afar, with casual but curious glances cast their way.

One afternoon, and Maud included herself in this excursion, they changed into 'bloomers' before departing the hotel. They had managed to rent for themselves those strange bicycle contraptions, and in order to pedal about without restriction from their long skirts and petticoats they put on shorter skirts with long trousers underneath, which billowed out, but were drawn in and tied about the ankles. They were very self-conscious in these garments, as they weren't used to wearing them. They were funny looking, and I think *they* thought so as well. After a severe attack of the giggles, they staggered out of the hotel like a flock of cackling hens that had got into the beer barrel and had drunk their fill. Hours later, they returned with their faces slightly sunburnt; their large sunhats not quite large enough to keep them in the shade as they pedalled about the countryside. They were all very pretty, not ugly in any way, shape, or form, but out of these beauties, Emily was the only daughter with the promise of a marriage to come.

The men went for long walks, and also explored inland for miles on foot. Augustus was too old to ride any more, but his sons hired horses and went off for long rides in the countryside. The sisters could ride as well, but Maud had never been on a horse before and refused lessons. Even Thomas hadn't been able to get her to ride. Maud and Mary's preferred method of transportation was by gig. They two had something in common, for they were both born and raised in Norfolk, but the difference between them was like chalk and cheese. Mary, her Norfolk was not as broad as Maud's, and as well, Maud was – well, let's say Maud was Maud.

What was there for us to see in Gorleston? What brought people there and coerced them to spend their money? Why did people become *Day Trippers?* Well, there were the sands, the beaches, and there were miles and miles of that golden strip, which disappeared into the distant horizon. There were the shops on Bell's Road, a racecourse, colourful fishing boats, lighthouses, piers, hotels, pubs, more shops, and at the bottom end of Gorleston, several miles from The Bear Hotel, were the famous cosies: part of an old wooden pier where people fished, or went there to court, or simply sat down in the cosies and took in the roiling waves and the bracing sea air.

One day, I went for a scenic tour around town in a gig with Charles Clement. It was a lovely day, and actually, we never saw a drop of rain the whole time we were there on holiday. From atop a great hill we looked out over the pier, where the cosies were, and then out across the River Yare to the sands far off in the distance. It has changed now, many years later. It has been built up, and now there are more hotels and bed and breakfasts than before, and there is talk of a railway station being built further to the south to accommodate the massive increase in holiday goers. When we went there in the '80s it was still unspoilt, with many of the shops and houses looking quaint.

Partway through our holiday little Mary Matilda started to show a preference for wanting to run off, which proved to be dangerous should she ever venture too close to the sea. After nearly giving everyone several heart attacks, it was agreed upon that she couldn't wander far if she was tied to me. So, she was tied to my collar by a length of twine, and thus I was tied to her. I didn't like it one jot, but I understood why it was done. She was quick on her two-year-old legs and gobbled up the beach in seconds. She could put any racehorse to shame with her flighty feet. When she did wander, dragging me along behind her, someone would call out to me, and I would go over to them, dragging the toddler, gently of course, behind me. It was a system that appeared to work, as it kept her from running into the sea. She did torment me, though, by throwing sand at me and pulling my hair, crossly, in her tight, little fists. Her hands got slapped for this, and nurse Charlotte insisted that she "learn how to behave."

* * *

IT WAS TO BE OUR LAST AND FINAL DAY ON SOUTH BEACH. Our holiday was nearly over, and the next morning we'd be returning to Hackney. I knew I was going to be sad when it came time to leave. William and his wife Mary accompanied us to the beach, along with their three children, for one last day in the sun. Augustus seemed to thrive off the sunshine and salty air, which gave him a wonderful, healthy glow to his face – in fact, they all glowed like I'd never seen them glow before. I thought it must be something in the sea air as well as the sun. I lay down in the shade of an umbrella, as I'd learnt my lesson about staying out on the burning hot sand with the sun beating down. The pads of my feet had recovered, but it had taken a few days. Apparently, my feet had had rough treatment during my journey from Worcestershire to Essex, and would never be the same again, resulting in them being tender and prone to injury. Mary Matilda was in safe hands, so I settled down for a nap, planning afterwards to go in the sea for a swim. Before I fell asleep, I had wondered if I ought to give serious thought to leaving Hackney, and my family in Darnley Road, behind. I had gone through a lot to find them, but having that evil cook, Eliza, around had changed things. I dreaded going back to Darnley Road, and the closer we came to ending our holiday, the more I dwelt upon it. Was it time for me to leave? Should I take advantage of being off a lead whilst we were here on the beach? I gave it serious thought. It would break my heart to leave, but I had done it once before. I could do it again.

I was terrified of going home.

Getting up from where I lay on a blanket, I casually walked away without looking back. I would miss them all; my heart felt heavy and inside I started to cry. I wept, silently and without tears, but it *was* time for me to leave. I could not go home and live in the same house with the cook. I just couldn't do it!

I started my new journey by walking along the water's edge. Waves lapped at my ankles but I hardly noticed – my mind was on my family, they whom I couldn't bear to leave behind. I hadn't gone very far when I heard an odd sound. It came from the sea, where a variety of bathers, all up to their necks, with arms outstretched sideways to balance themselves when the incoming waves pushed them along, bobbed about in costumes of different colours. That little one out there bobbing about was our Shales. I wondered how long he'd been in the sea? I could see that he was unaccompanied; I saw neither Edmund nor Charles out there with him. Should he have been so far out, up to his neck, with waves rushing in over his head?

I heard him cry out a watery, "Help!"

It was all so wrong. I knew he was in trouble. What could I do about it? I was supposed to be leaving, running away, but something wasn't quite right.

Oh, what to do?

OH, DEAR ME!

In a panic I turned around and quickly ran along the beach and up to his mother, and she kindly ruffled my ears and kissed my forehead as she chatted with the women. I went over to Charlotte, who was with the other children, but she didn't understand I was trying to tell her something. I looked out at Shales and saw a flailing hand disappear, his bright red costume no longer in sight. The other bathers hadn't seen his plight.

OH, DEAR!

I said a panicky "*Woof*", hoping to bring attention to myself. I pranced about and whined in front of the men.

I was ignored.

I gave up, and ran out into the waves. They uplifted me, making me buoyant, and I paddled my legs with all my might in order to catch up to the lad. My plans for leaving were forgotten for the moment. I tried barking as I swam, but that only caused me to swallow sea water, making me gag.

I swam past a female bather, floating off to my right, who suddenly noticed me with wide eyes. She must've then realised there was a drowning boy, because she shouted very loudly, "Help! Help! Somebody's drowning!" Then I heard her shout, "Over there, with the dog. I think it's a small boy!"

I was nearly there, to where I'd last seen Shales. I had just a few more feet to go, when a large wave lifted me up and backwards, threatening to sweep me back into shore. He must have seen me as he came up to the surface, and he flung his arm out in order to grab onto me. I swam harder against the swell, and I grabbed him by his sleeve with my teeth, and probably had some of his arm in my mouth as well. I didn't care. I turned about and swam back to shore, hoping the waves would propel me along, and swiftly. I found it difficult, as it felt like he was pulling me down and under, along with himself. I struggled with my weighty catch; my chest strained with the effort as I gasped for air. Salt water went up my nose, and I felt as if I was suffocating.

I could see masses of people had begun to approach the shore, with their hands pointing in my direction. Suddenly, strong arms swept Shales up out of the water and I let go of him. My feet hit bottom on the wet sand beneath, and I seemed to feel extremely heavy as the waves threatened to pull me backwards and out to sea. I wearily walked the last couple of steps, but then safely collapsed on the dry sand. I coughed up water, briny and bitter, and burning my throat as it came up. Unseen hands thudded against my ribs, forcing out any water that was left in my lungs.

A man's voice said, "Incredible! I saw it myself. The dog saved the boy's life!"

The lad was carried ashore by the capable hands of his father and Edmund. Charles ran to collect the blankets that had been laid out on the sand as part of our *camp*, and in retrieving them he shook off their accumulated sand, and with them hurried over to his nephew.

William said, "Wrap him up in order to keep him warm!" Then he looked at Edmund, "We need to get air into him. A tube! We need something to put into his mouth!"

Edmund looked at his brother with obvious confusion. "What do you propose to do?"

"I'm going to breath air into him. Give him some oxygen."

A lady, stood just back off to the side, could be heard saying, "Has anyone got a feather?"

And the strange voice of a man asked, "What do they want with a feather?"

She replied back, "Don't you know? You resuscitate a drowner by tickling their nose with a feather; better though, if it has smelling salts on it."

Another strange male voice shouted over to her, "That's what they used to do. Now, these days, they breathe air into them; that's what they do."

The lady spoke quietly, "Still say you should use a feather."

"Here you are. Use this." Charles handed over a piece of writing paper he'd procured from somewhere amongst our picnic articles. William snatched it out of his hand, tilted Shales's head back slightly, pinched his nose, and shoved the now rolled-up tube of paper down his little throat, and then blew his own breath into it. Breathing air into Shales must've worked, because after a minute he coughed, spluttered, and was then sick all over the front of himself, the blankets saving his bathing costume from being spattered. Everyone sighed with relief, and the voices in the gathered small crowd of spectators murmured, "Thank God," and "The Lord be praised." The women were all teary-eyed, especially Shales's mother.

Charles came over to me. "Oh, Shales. What would we do without you?" And then, "Nobody noticed the lad had gone into the water on his own."

Charles Clement hugged me tightly to himself, and as I glanced at the rest of the family from between his encircling arms, I saw nothing but shock on their faces. They were all white-faced and quiet. They didn't know what to say. Again, I coughed up some water, but I actually felt quite fine.

"What an incredible dog you are," said Charles, as he firmly patted my ribs to clear my lungs. Eventually, it was ascertained that the little boy Shales was going to live, even though he would have a right lovely toothy bruise on his arm as a souvenir. It was said that we'd had a near miss of a tragedy that day.

We packed up and started to leave, as nobody was in the mood to remain. The family were all in shock. Shales was quickly stretchered off the beach to a cab, and he, William and Mary started on their way back to The Bear. Before they left he was talking and was bouncing back to his usual self, and I think he was indulging in the extra attention he was receiving, such as the cat that got the cream. I hoped he didn't think drowning was a good way of getting lots of extra attention and sweets. Strange: we shared the same Christian name of Shales, but we had both died and had been given a second chance at life. I wondered what Horatio would say about it? Was this the danger he had foreseen? I had a dark feeling that there was more to come in my future. However, I simply couldn't leave now. Not now. Besides, he had mentioned something about knives, and a man.

A funny little man ran across to us and, after wiping his sweaty brow, asked if a photograph of the dog could be taken. He meant me. He pointed in my direction and eagerly asked, "Is that the dog that made the daring rescue?"

They all answered, "Yes."

He spoke quickly, "The story will be in the newspaper, tomorrow, as all near drownings or actual drownings are always reported in detail. People have the right to know; they have to be made aware of the dangers of going into the sea. We've never had a dog rescue anyone before, although there is a particular gentleman who makes daring rescues from time to time." He licked his lips and looked out to the water. "Swimmers get pulled out to sea. The currents are quite strong, you know."

So *that* was how I got my photo taken, and the story appeared in the *Daily Press*, a Norwich newspaper. The photo was framed, and it had a place of honour hanging on a wall in The Bear Hotel. I was a hero! Below you can read the actual newspaper article. Boys o' boys, mmn, mmn, mmn.

* * *

It seems that once again the sea has managed to lure one more possible victim into her briny depths. She (the sea) must view English holiday goers as voluntary sacrificial victims, as they cannot stay away, but flock towards her in ignorant droves. This time, the victim was but a child of nearly seven years: a boy, who without his parents' permission, and without informing any of his adult companions, went into the sea for a swim. The sea lay waiting, and she drew her currents and waves along, pulling the boy out to sea, whereby he started to drown. On the beach, happily ignorant holiday goers drank their beakers of lemonade, or bottles of ginger beer, as they built sandcastles. If it weren't for the superior intelligence of a dog, a trained sheepdog, the boy would now be drowned, and his family would now be preparing for his sad funeral. But no, the dog had the foresight to launch itself into the sea and swim out to the drowning boy, and after grabbing onto a sleeve, swam back to shore, dragging the boy through the briny water to safety, as if he were a drowning lamb. A young lady, Lucy Rye of Tottenham, noticed the swimming dog's efforts and shouted out for help. The family were greatly shaken, but praised the dog's actions, which resulted in a happy ending. This happened yesterday afternoon on South Beach, near Regent Road. Oddly, both dog and boy share the same name of Shales Berkeley.

* * *

THE RETURN TO DARNLEY ROAD was a bit of a letdown after such an exciting week. The weather had cooperated, as the fog had remained out at sea and the sun had shone hotly every day. We all said our goodbyes, and then had a quiet train journey home. The one hundred and twenty or so miles seemed to take forever, and as we approached the city the weather changed. The closer we came to the outskirts of the great city of London the drabber the weather became, as if the sun only showed itself along the seacoast. Admittedly, I was frightened to go home, because I knew the cook was waiting for me, and Edmund had to physically drag me off the train, because at the last moment I had decided I wasn't getting off. With my tail between my legs, I slinked off the platform, but was held tightly by Edmund, who showed surprise at my strange behaviour. Once we were off the train Hackney greeted us with a cold drizzle, and after the heat of the seaside we shivered as we made our way home.

Jessie ordered all the fires in the house to be lit, in order to chase away the damp, which had settled into the rooms in our absence. Our housemaid had the fires in the drawing-room and dining-room blazing away when we arrived, but the upper floors were as chilly as a tomb, and according to Jessie the furniture was damp to touch, and she even found mildew on some of the furniture. If Jessie said there was *damp* in the house, then there really was *damp* in the house.

She was quite miffed with our housemaid. "Armstrong! I didn't expect to come home to a damp house after only being away for a week. Didn't you notice the dampness creeping in?"

A wobbly-kneed maid replied, "But, oh, Mistress Jessie. It's the middle of the summer, an' the sun was out for a couple o' days. I gave everything a good cleaning after you left, an' I left all the doors open to let the air flow about. I didn't realise I still needed fires in all the rooms."

Jessie looked at her, not unkindly mind you, and said, "But in this house we are very prone to damp at this time of the year. The air is always moist, even when the sun is out, and to be gone from the house for a few days doesn't change that."

Armstrong bowed her pretty head. "I'll remember that, Miss. I won't do it again."

"I'm sure you won't," Jessie was curt, and then changed the subject as she slowly removed her gloves, finger by finger. "Did you decide upon what we are having for our dinner tonight, you and Cook?"

Now Armstrong was smiling. "Yes, Miss. We wondered if you would all like steak and kidney pie. It's something Cook hasn't made in a while. Also, there is fresh apricot tart, made just this afternoon."

Now, I knew that Jessie always decided upon what we ate; she was the housekeeper and she gave the final nod. It was unusual for her to leave the meal-making decision up to the cook, but as we were away on holiday, it seems Cook had made a good choice. Better a hearty meat pie and gravy than a cold, limp salad on a dismal day like today.

Jessie lightly smiled, then sighed and said, "Yes, tell Cook that we shall enjoy her steak and kidney pie."

It became foggy, and as evening fell the fog became thicker, causing it to fall dark earlier than usual. I trotted upstairs to the second floor to see if I could catch sight of the lamp lighting man as he came round to light the street lamps, to provide light at night up and down the streets of Hackney. There! He was working his way from the direction of Mare Street, just barely visible beyond the flat rooftops of the neighbouring terraced villas. I watched him from the window at the top of the stairs, my front paws against the sill and my nose pressed against the multi-paned window, momentarily entertained as the lamp lighter set his little ladder against a lamppost, and climbed it, reaching upwards with his wand of flame, igniting the gas in the lamppost and creating a sputtering halo of light. When I first came to Darnley Road I had been intrigued by gas, which gave us light instead of the use of candles. Inside the house the gas lighting sputtered and plopped, and I knew it could be dangerous, but we were never in the dark, and candles were unnecessary, except for the servants' quarters, unlike in the country where gas lighting wasn't always available and everyone used candles or awful-smelling oil lamps. We didn't have anything like this at Master Rowland's, or even at Wayletts in Stanford Rivers, but there we didn't have streets paved with cobbles and a raised path paved with flagstones for walking on, either. In Hackney, all the streets were lit up at night, but that was because it was a modern place to live, and all the streets were well paved and the houses had water piped in, so the servants only had to turn on a tap, leaving the hauling of numerous heavy pails of hot water from the kitchen to bathrooms an unnecessary task.

Once the lamp lighter was out of sight I had a job to do. I had to go outside into the back garden, so I searched for Jessie, finding her in her bedroom, and gave her my *silent stare*. When she asked, "Do you want to go outside?" I did my dance routine in acknowledgement. Willingly she followed me down the stairs to the main, front door, and let me out, and she left it to, just open by a little crack. I did what I had to do, my looing, and then I went over to the holly bush. I didn't have to sniff a lot to find what I was looking for, because it was quite rank in its smell. I was surprised that it was still there, but other dogs didn't have access to my garden, but then again, I wondered why the rats hadn't taken it away. Boys o' boys, mmn, mmn, mmn. I was overjoyed to find Cook's missing roast beef, still where I had tossed it. I picked up the rather ripe-smelling, maggoty joint of meat and entered the house by nudging the door open, and I then tiptoed across the hall with my weighty prize, and then ran up the staircase (past my handsome portrait), hoping no one had heard me, and I then headed straight for my master's bed. I carefully deposited the evil roast upon the middle of the bed, nudging it beneath his dressing gown where it might not be seen straight away. You are now wondering, why do this to your master? I was not intending on insulting Augustus, or wanting to offend him in any way, but was only bringing attention to the fact that a piece of old, cooked meat had never reached our dining-room table, and the very first person who should be questioned would be the cook.

A short while later, when everyone had retired to their beds, I heard, we all heard, Augustus shout in a most angry voice, "I say, look here! Sakes alive! What on earth is in my bed?"

I decided to keep my head low and out of sight, but the short and long of it is that it was questioned as to how the roast had found its way upstairs, and I was accused, and naturally so. But also it was questioned: where had I got the piece of meat from? The answer had to be supplied by the cook, Eliza. She was questioned immediately, and she had no intelligent answer. I was held blameless, as it was perceived that it was only natural, that I, being a dog, would find a smelly roast that had been loafing about the property, and would want to jump onto a bed with it. It's what dogs do. It had not been forgotten that just before we had left for our holidays, beef curry had been served in place of roast beef, vegetables, and gravy, oh, and let's not forget the Yorkshire puddings. Jessie had remembered the change in fare.

There was one bright side to our return to Hackney. Eliza the cook gave her notice later that next day. In other words, she was leaving us for a place closer to her family, someplace in Essex. With a sour look on her flabby face she said, "I've found a new position in Essex, close to home, I 'ave, an' I'll be close to moy mum. Now that she's not getting any younger, I thought I'd move back home an' look after her."

Jessie, surprised at the sudden idea of being left without a cook, said, "Oh. Do you really have to leave us? We're willing to let the roast beef incident go. You should have said at the time that it went missing, and not deceived us with the curry."

Bowing her head, Cook answered, "Yes, I do 'ave to leave. It'll be better this way. I seem to be getting a reaction of some sort from the dog. Makes me sneeze a lot." And with that she glanced in my direction as she shifted from foot to foot.

I didn't know whether to poke her eyes out with one of my sharp toenails, or to sit and gloat in front of her. Secretly, I gloated. I didn't have to leave my home; I could stay. I was so relieved that I had won! I had outwitted her. I thought to myself, "*The ol' bag'll be gone in a fortnight from now. Oh, what joy! Boys o' boys, mmn, mmn, mmn.*"

* * *

I HAD JUST A FORTNIGHT TO AVOID HER, though I hoped she hadn't planned on harming me just before she left. I worried about that a lot, and I made sure I was always with a family member, or Armstrong, or Charlotte. I took immense joy the day she left, by watching her leave from the window at the top of the landing, her bags placed in a cab and she climbing in, and then the cab departing. The only thing I regret was not having the opportunity to have a right good long wee, all over her bags.

Jessie advertised for a replacement, and interviews were conducted. Our new cook was called Holmes (not related to Holmes at Cotheridge Court). She was very young and very fair in colour, but Jessie thought she would do well, especially since she liked dogs and had no objection to my presence. She came from Lambeth, and had been taught to cook by her mother, who had been in service for a well-known London family. From the first moment we met, I knew we would get on. I was no longer banished from the kitchen, but instead, I was encouraged to keep Holmes company, whereby she fed me the most delicious meals. As she chopped and stirred, she would toss bits and pieces into the air for me to catch. I began to enjoy the kitchen, and no longer looked upon it as a dungeon. Once again, I felt safe, and I knew that if the family had known that the old cook had been bent on harming me, they wouldn't have hesitated in letting her go. How does a dog explain things to people?

XVI

OF WEDDINGS AND FUNERALS

"They rue the day, those who marry in
May."

1885

WE HAD A MARVELLOUS CHRISTMAS. Nobody close to us had died, and the festive season of yuletide filled our house in Darnley Road with joyous merriment. Bright, thorny sprigs of red-berried, green holly tied with colourful ribbons found their way behind picture frames and mantelpieces, and the annual Christmas tree was decorated with more colour than one could ever imagine. Millie Holmes was such a good cook that the mince pies and custard tarts, as well as the sausage rolls and slices of Christmas cake, were consumed faster than she could replace them. She frantically worked amidst a kitchen cluttered with scattered flour and jars of preserves. The maid-of-all scurried to keep pace, with the clutter and the washing up, as they both hummed Christmas carols in tune to their work. Once again I had received a helping of pudding generously covered in white sauce, laced with rum, and hidden inside its curranty depths was, yet again, another sixpence. I was now worth a whole shilling. Emily and Thomas White were going to be married in May, and the summer would bring another holiday for us at Cotheridge Court. I looked forward to the summer of 1885 with aching excitement and joy, as the thought of running free about the manor made the waiting for the months to pass difficult – I simply couldn't wait.

As the winter months slowly receded, time drew closer to Emily's wedding. Her intended, Thomas White, was a visitor to our house on every second Sunday afternoon, whereupon he would join us for Sunday dinner. On the alternative Sundays Emily went over to Thomas's house and had dinner with his family. It had been like this for over two years, and I wondered if it would ever change. I was happy with the way things were.

Their wedding was to take place at the parish church in Hackney, but some objections were raised as Edmund voiced his undesirable opinion. Apparently, the architecture of the relatively new church was not to everyone's liking in the parish of St John. Edmund merely gave us his point of view, when on one Sunday afternoon, after we had all withdrawn to the drawing-room after our dinner was over with, he sat down in his comfortable leather armchair and lit up a cigar, sending clouds of smoke across the room.

"It is the ugliest church I have ever laid eyes upon! I'm not the only one to comment on the church's lack of charm." He continued distastefully, "I don't know why you'd want to get married there, of all places. It has no character – I find it too modern. Little sister, can't you find another church?"

Emily, small and dark-haired, immediately threw down the book she had picked up to read. It bounced off the settee and hit the floor with a dull thud. She was in no small state of rage. "No, Edmund! I simply cannot and will not find another church!" She hissed between her teeth, "It is, after all, the parish church for this area of Hackney, which is where we live. Must I remind you, the bride gets married where she chooses to do so, and as we live in Hackney, the wedding shall be in Hackney!" By the time little Emily had finished this tirade against Edmund, she was nearly in tears. I had never seen her so upset before, but I knew she was being teased, and she had fallen for it, yet once again.

Edmund stretched out his dark grey-trousered legs, crossed his ankles, and then waved his fragrant cigar innocently about. "I was only thinking that the church near to where you were born is much lovelier. I just wondered whether you had given it any serious thought, that's all."

"How can I get married in St Margaret's when it only reminds me of death? As a bride, I don't want to have to walk past the family vault with dear Mama and Thomas perhaps lying there beneath my feet." Her eyes blazed as she faced Edmund down, which only added more fuel to the fire.

I saw Edmund then wink at Charles Clement, before he said, "You know, you don't have to get married this year." He said this casually, then brushed some of my hairs off the front of his trews, and said, "You could wait another year or two."

Charles looked at Edmund, and said wisely, "Edmund, I think you should seriously consider ending this discussion before she throws that book at you. At this close range, I'm sure she can't miss."

Edmund, so like our beloved Thomas Rowland, said, "All right, Emily. Now just gently put the book down." He spoke as if addressing a toddler who had picked up a valuable ornament.

She laughed through her tears. "I know the church isn't old and quaint, but I just want to get married, and I don't want anything to spoil it."

Thomas, her betrothed, finally spoke up, "Emily dear, if you want to get married elsewhere, then I'm all right with that. It is entirely up to you, but whatever you do decide, please don't postpone the wedding any longer. I fear it is the longest engagement in history."

Charles said, "I don't think there is anything that could happen that would spoil your wedding day. After all, you are our first sister to be getting married, and we, your brothers, and I am speaking for Edmund here, will do anything to prevent your wedding day from being ruined in any way. Isn't that so, Edmund?"

A smiling Edmund replied, "Of course we'll see to it that your special day will be remembered fondly." He examined the lighted tip of his cigar. "Nothing untoward will happen, and the sun shall shine and no rain shall fall upon your pretty little head. Isn't that so, Shales?" I wagged my tail at being included, and crawled out from beneath the table where I had been listening. I did the rounds and said hello to everyone, and they, each and everyone, fondly ruffled my ears and stroked my sides.

Augustus finally spoke up, after remaining quiet and studious through all of this banter. "Don't speak too quickly, boys. Anything can happen between now and May. She could fall down the stairs and break a leg, or she could come to find her dress might not fit. Better still, we could have a flood! We do get floods here, you know. Who knows what can happen to a bride-to-be, especially when they plan their wedding for the month of May?

You know what they say about May weddings: 'They rue the day, those who marry in May.'"

Emily pleaded, "Stop it!" She had clamped her hands over her ears and had squeezed her eyes shut. "Please, just stop teasing me," she begged. "We don't have floods here any more. It is also more accepted these days to marry in the month of May than when you were young. I'll be glad to move out so that I can get some peace from you lot."

Her father replied, "Move out! Ha! I say, you're only moving up the road and round the corner to Chatham Place. It's only about a ten-minute walk away. You'll be here every day. Won't she, girls?" And then, "Thomas, you'll forever be over here yourself. You won't know which house is your own home." Now Thomas was being goaded.

Jessie and the other women smiled and laughed, nodding their heads in agreement. Yes, Emily would be in and out of our house, just as if she hadn't left it. That pleased me, because I didn't really know what to expect from this wedding. Actually, I didn't even know what a wedding was, not really, and I was learning little bits here and little bits there, trying to piece it all together.

* * *

I LATER CAME TO REALISE that a wedding is somewhat like a funeral. You're going to say "pooh" to that, but the reason I say it is because both weddings and funerals bring distant family members and friends together. The afore-mentioned is a very happy occasion, and the latter is a sad occasion. However, for both events church services and hymns are sung, a vicar etc. is present, and also the church pews are filled with lots of family and friends. There are advantages to having a funeral, namely, that one doesn't have to plan it oneself if one doesn't want to: it just gets planned by somebody else, after you're gone. Unlike a wedding, which is planned well in advance, leaving the bride and her family, including the dog, in emotional turmoil for weeks and weeks prior to the happy occasion.

* * *

THE DAY OF THE WEDDING FINALLY ARRIVED, and there was no flood, nor any broken bones to mar the occasion. It was the twenty-third of May, and there we all were that Saturday morning at the parish church. The ladies were all beautifully dressed, with lovely new hats set upon delicate hairdos. Their long dresses swished as they moved about, and their genteel hands were enclosed within tight-fitting gloves. The men were handsome in their morning suits, with grey-tailed coats, gold chains adorning their waistcoats, their watches tucked into their fobs, and their heads crowned with top hats. They held handsome walking-sticks in their gloved hands, and their faces were either clean-shaven or with moustaches. Their trousers, or trews as I called them, were well pressed. The sharp creases descended downwards where they met with highly polished shoes.

William and Mary had arrived from Gorleston and were staying with us in Darnley Road. The children had also come; it was an opportunity for them to meet their widespread cousins. Thus, our house was filled to the rafters with family. My previous master, Rowland, and his wife Mildred were at the wedding, and so were Rowland's brother William Nichols, and his wife Jane, as well as another brother, Herbert, and Auntie Emily. Except for William Comyns, all of Augustus's brothers and their wives were there, including Charles Clement. He had not brought his wife-cum-lady friend, and a good thing too. Oh, what gossip! In this day and age one did not have any hanky-panky going on with one's servants, but everyone knew that Charles Clement did. Officially, the woman in question was his housekeeper, but what about the children? The long and short of it is this: it was so confusing, and there was so much gossip about Charles Clement and his situation that I don't think anyone knew the truth about them. My guess is that they weren't married, though I knew that others in our family actually thought them to be – that they had married on the quiet. Quite shocking, isn't it?

There were friends of the families in attendance. Many were strangers to me – I cannot name them all. Stanley and Edith had come. Some men were in uniform, either naval or army, and one of these was Algernon Cecil, cousin to us, and you may remember he rode off on a horse and Thomas Rowland was sent after him to fetch him back. Algernon looked resplendent in his officer's uniform, and he only recently receiving his commission. Another handsome soldier was Captain Edmund Robert, nephew to Augustus and brother to Herbert, William Nichols, and Rowland. Thomas White's mother, Emma, was there, and also his sister Elizabeth. There was also a vicar, a friend of Augustus's, and his name was George Campion Berkeley. He shared the same surname as the rest of us, but I don't know if he was friend or family.

Herbert snapped pictures; he had brought his camera with him. The church was filled with our family and the groom's family, as well as many close friends. We had a very large family, back then, and it is even larger these days, though many have spread their wings and have moved to distant lands. There was a lengthy service, and afterwards Herbert took lots of group photographs to record the event. A few very close friends and family members, from both sides, were invited to our house for the traditional celebratory drink and bite to eat.

I don't think the curate, Mr Leach, knew I was present in the church. Charles had smuggled me in, and we were seated at the end of the pew, me being at the very end of the outer aisle, perched upon the slippery, polished wood. Next to me sat Charles, and then Edmund and the sisters (minus the bride), then Auntie Emily, with Augustus seated at the end. I remained unseen, as I blended in with the congregation in the background. Directly behind me were seated Stanley and his wife, as well as Herbert, so they weren't going to make a fuss about my being there. I was quite intrigued with the goings on in the church, as it was the first time I'd been inside one. The interior had been filled with fresh flowers, and their gentle scents wafted about and mingled with the strong perfumes of the ladies. We stood up and sang hymns, sat down and listened to some sermons, and so on and so on. I did find it difficult to sit still for too long, but I tried my very best.

When the actual part came for them to be married, when it got all so serious, I got rather a bit itchy. I simply had to scratch myself, and in doing so, my hind leg beat against the back of the pew, sending banging sounds reverberating around the church. Once I stopped itching, I found I had to sneeze. It was quite loud, but someone in the back was sincere with his "Bless you!" When he heard this, Charles started to laugh. He tried to keep it low, but I'm sure that if I could hear him then the rest of the congregation could hear him as well.

Edmund gave his brother a nudge in his ribs, and said, "Shush!"

Herbert leaned forward and whispered, "We can hear you! Stop fidgeting."

I didn't want to ruin Emily's big day, so I held onto the fart that was dying to be let out – a result of the previous night's cabbage. It had been building up inside me, but I sensed it would not be a good time to let go. Too late! It sounded ever so loud! A few people laughed, but most groaned. Both Charles and Edmund's faces turned bright red, and their embarrassed blushes spread down their necks. Ignoring my rudeness, I was intent on watching the ceremony, and I could clearly see Emily's bright red face, with clenched jaw. If she'd turned her head to her left, she would have seen me seated, leaning outwards so that I could see past the torsos of Charles and the rest of the family. I was leaning so far forward that I nearly fell off! I hastily scrambled to retain my balance, with my toenails noisily gouging the wooden seat of the pew.

It was warm inside the church. I panted loudly, spraying saliva all over Charles's suit.

Oh, how lovely she looked. She was radiant in her white and cream silk dress, with her tiny, corseted waist, a string of pearls around her neck, and little flowers woven into her hair in the shape of a wreath. She had been adamant about being married in white and cream. The cream would set off her pearls, or so she said. The church had been filled with a variety of flowers, but it was the scent of the sweetpeas she held that pleasantly wafted across to me and smelt most delicious and, forever, from that day onward, reminding me of her wedding.

Later, standing outside our house after they had stepped down from the wedding carriage, she berated her brothers, assuming they were to blame for the rude noises, though they both objected and said it was my doing. She was indignant, "Do not blame Shales for those noises! Shame on you! The both of you! Edmund, you are a grown man and you ought to know better!" And she gave a final wail as she stamped her foot against the pavement, "You promised me you wouldn't ruin my wedding day, and you have. I didn't know Shales was attending the wedding. I was so embarrassed, and that sound couldn't have come at a worse time!"

So, now you have it. I thought the wedding was a success, and I had enjoyed it immensely. There was nothing wrong with the church; it's capacious interior accepted the entirety of our enormous flood of family and friends. I would have preferred returning to Stanford Rivers, whereby a reunion with Ten Acre Wood and Horatio would have exceeded witnessing Emily's wedding – but who was I to complain? I had actually been to church.

* * *

WE FINALLY WENT TO COTHERIDGE COURT for our summer holiday. I had been anticipating it all winter – I yearned to be reacquainted with Toby. Emily stayed in Hackney with Thomas, as they had a holiday of sorts planned for just them. I had the usual grand time in Cotheridge, and managed to get over to Broadwas to see my old companion Toby. He was now blind as a bat, but amazingly still managed to get around. Maud arrived a few days later with Mary Matilda, who had a grand time playing with her little cousins. What we hadn't known whilst we were visiting Augustus's brother was that it was the last time we would ever see him. Sadly, on the seventh day of August that summer, whilst we were visiting, William Comyns passed away. He was quite elderly, and according to Augustus, he was seventy-five years old when he died. Being the first-born he was, of course, the eldest in the large family of brothers and sisters.

* * *

I WAS HAVING A LIE-DOWN, OUTSIDE THE STABLES, when I saw the four brothers parade down to where the beehives were kept in Church Field, the pasture that was nearest to the avenue of lime trees. I knew what they were going to do, and out of respect I followed and watched. How would they perform the ritual here in Cotheridge, I wondered? The hives were not wrapped up in black crepe such as they had been at Wayletts.

Rowland held the large front door key to the house in his hand, and he rapped upon each hive thrice and said firmly, "The master of your house is dead." This he said to each hive, after he knocked upon them in turn. The bees became quiet, as if their internal activity had come to a stop. The four brothers, Rowland Comyns, William Comyns, Edmund Robert and Herbert Bowyer then took the black bands of crepe they had fetched with them, and between them they wrapped up the round-shaped hives. It would now be clear to everyone that the hives were in a state of mourning.

The ancient church of St Leonard's, in Cotheridge.

It was indeed a sad occasion, and the funeral took place in Cotheridge the following week, with William being interred at St Leonard's. Being a widower, William's wife Harriet Elizabeth was already interred there, outside, at the back of the church, where her stone coffin stands at the corner. People came from all around the county, as well as there being a lot of his relations and close family in attendance. It was sad, but the sadness seemed to be different than when Thomas had died. I think it was because it was expected with William at some point in his future because of his age, whereas Thomas had been young at twenty-one years, and his death had been unexpected and tragic. Still, I didn't quite know how it would affect us, the rest of the family. Meaning, my master and his brothers.

After the funeral I heard something being said about the new master with regard to the bees. I was still curious about this ritual, so when I saw the four brothers leave the house, with the front door key held in Rowland's hand once again, I simply had to follow. As before, we were standing in front of the hives, all of which were still unusually quiet, and yes, still wrapped in black.

Rowland rapped upon each hive thrice, and in turn said, "I, Rowland Comyns Berkeley, am your new master."

Then, the hives came alive and buzzed, as if the bees understood and were happy. The men removed the bands of crepe, and hordes of bees flew out and swarmed away from us, as if on an important mission.

* * *

OUR HOUSEHOLD IN HACKNEY, except for the servants of course, went into full mourning once again, but this time it was only for about six months. It seemed we were forever mourning a family member. Did it ever end?

XVII
TINKER, TAILOR...

"This was my family, this was my life, and this was me."

AUTUMN, 1885

OUR CHARLES CLEMENT WAS NOW A YOUNG GENTLEMAN, but with that came along the urge for him to set out on his own and make his own way in life. He did not any longer want to partake in the family business; he did not want to be a clerk for his father, even though he knew he could possibly, just possibly someday, inherit it all. He wanted to try his hand at something else. Augustus wasn't at all pleased when he heard of his youngest son's wishes. He did understand why Charles wanted to try his hand at some other form of work. After all, eventually, Edmund would be inheriting the business, with Charles merely working for Edmund; always an employee, and never a full partner, unless Edmund died. It seemed fair enough to Edmund, but, then again, it always does to those who are next in line to inherit.

The eldest son, William, had his hotel in Gorleston, and the holiday trade could only increase in the upcoming years, so *he* wouldn't be inheriting the coal business, or any part of it, even though he was the heir. William was set for life, as an hotelier, and Edmund was a coal agent – it was he who would inherit the business. Charles could hardly set himself up in a rival coal trade, competing against Edmund, and besides, he had made it clear he wasn't interested in coal, except for when it came to having a warm fire. There was already enough competition in the area around Hackney and the other London boroughs; coal merchants were plentiful. So, in the end,

Augustus gave Charles his blessing to try something new, such as his own father had done. Poor Charles, he didn't want to work for any of his uncles. They were either solicitors or wine merchants, and his cousins ranged from being officers in either the navy or the army, or were working their way up through their own family businesses. He definitely wasn't the sort to be a gentleman farmer, otherwise his father would have offered him a lease on a farm – he could have had Wayletts. His future definitely wouldn't be related to agriculture. So, what do you suppose Charles proposed to us? He had made enquiries, and was able to take a position in a tailor's shop. A tailor's shop! At first, nobody knew what to say in response to Charles's announcement. Tailoring, that was a new occupation for the family, and a lowly one, as well! Crikey! Cor blimey! Augustus informed his youngest son that he would not ever get rich off making gentlemen's suits, especially when that shop was owned by someone else.

Charles responded emphatically, "But after a few years I could set myself up in business and have my own shop, with workers of my own. Don't you see? It would be mine, and I would have done it on my own. I'll do well once I have earned a good reputation."

We were in the library, which was a large room and was seldom used by all the members of the family at the same time. Usually, one of them would saunter in to look for a particular book and would take it elsewhere to read, but Edmund liked to entertain his visiting cousins and other gentlemen in there. The armchairs were large and soft, and upon the polished floorboards was a very beautiful red and blue patterned carpet. I thought it a nice, comfortable room.

On this day my master was busy looking for a particular book that had become lost amidst the book-filled shelves. I stole one of the comfy chairs and settled myself in it for a nap. Charles had followed him in there to plead his case. Augustus turned to survey his youngest son who was stood only a few feet away, and looking anxious, and very, very young.

He spoke wisely, "You'll need money to do that, but sometime you'll be inheriting your share, and I suppose you could use that. I know Edmund is going to inherit the business, but you have a share coming to you – I'm not leaving you out in the cold." Augustus quickly glanced at Charles as he continued to search for his book. "I could give you your inheritance before I pass away, but first you'll have to be capable of handling the tailoring trade." Then he spoke seriously, "I'd rather you put your money to some good use, instead of wasting it and having nothing to show for your life when you reach old age. It'll take a few years before you'll be an expert in the tailoring trade. Yes, son, I'll stand behind you, if this is what you want." He then glanced over to his other son, who was intent upon looking at an old map, which lay weighted down upon the large reading table, a candlestick at each corner of the map. "Edmund, what is your opinion of this? Do you think your brother should try his hand at something else?"

I glanced over at Edmund, who didn't look very happy about it all. He sighed quietly; actually, he looked a bit depressed. I wasn't sure if it had to do with the map he was looking at, or if it was because of his brother. "If it's what you want, Charlie, but I'd rather have you working for me than employ someone else in your stead. As far as I'm concerned, that would be a waste of good money."

Charlie, with a flush to his fair cheeks, said, "Well, if Thomas was still here with us, then I suppose he'd take on the coal business with you, but he isn't, and I'm not going to take his place. I'm sorry, but no!"

A disappointed Edmund said, "All right then. It'll have to do. I'll find someone to replace you, but the firm seems to be getting smaller instead of increasing in size. If it's really what you want, then I'll side with you and Dad."

Smiling, Augustus wisely said, "Edmund, when I'm gone you can do what you want with the firm. You can expand if you want to, or perhaps sell it off and retire on the proceeds. It isn't as if it is the family estate." Then he waved a rather small book about and happily proclaimed, "Found it! Dad gave me this when we were living at Coopersale Hall."

Oh, no! I didn't want to hear any talk of Augustus leaving us. I didn't want him to die! Please, don't do that to me. I knew he was getting old, but I couldn't bear thinking about him dying. That's what an inheritance is: you only get it because someone dies and it is left to you. Feeling a bit low myself, I evacuated the chair, and went up to him where he was now seated across from me in another of those comfortable chairs. I put my two front feet in his lap and leaned across him, reaching up and giving his face a little lick. He put his arms around me and stroked me. Looking at him you wouldn't think he was really a big softie, but he *was* good to his family. I loved Augustus, and he had provided me with a safe and loving home.

Edmund said he'd remain in the coal business, as it was financially rewarding. He didn't want for anything except for a family of his own, but he knew that probably wouldn't happen, not now that he was getting older, nearing forty, and no intelligent women about, so to speak of, except for his own sisters, and three of them were spinsters with no future husbands in sight. The sisters were 'thinkers' and they firmly refused to be married off to an old man, which is what would have been done in the olden days. Oh, what a family. It took a lot of thinking on my part to understand the ins and outs of this household. I suppose most families didn't have five grown children still living at home, but then again, there were plenty of others who had never married. There was Auntie Emily, for one. She had never married, and she had lived with the family all her life, and she still did. Actually, bringing up the subject of Auntie Emily leads to her and Augustus's brother, Charles Clement. She used to reside with him when he was a bachelor, but had moved back to Cotheridge Court, probably at William Comyns's insistence, he then being a lonely widower.

I decided to do the rounds. In other words, I went from chair to chair, doling out my wagging tail and doggy kisses, and receiving pets and cuddles and kisses from all the men. I couldn't read the expression on young Charles Clement's face; either he was pleased that he could now plan his own future, or he was regretting having brought the subject up and was having second thoughts.

Now for Jessie, Lucy and Julia; they still hoped to meet some fine, handsome gentleman, who could support them in the style according to their status at birth. There just didn't seem to be enough of these available men; sort of like a shortage, especially in the right area of age. Then there was a problem of how to meet these men? There were invitations to balls and concerts, and many of these were gleaned through their father's and uncles' connections, but the girls simply did not find their future husbands anywhere. Jessie was determined to remain a spinster if she could not find the right man.

I heard her once say to Emily, "Men. They steal your mind so that there's nothing left of what was you. They sap all your strength, until you've no longer your own opinions or ideas; only what goes for the man."

An incredulous Emily responded, "Oh, no, Jessie. It won't be like that. I'll always have my own opinions, and I shall always speak my *own* mind."

Jessie had said, "When I see you starting to change, I shall let you know. Emily, be ever watchful. After a couple of years of marriage with your Thomas, you'll be just like him. Your opinions will change, because they won't be *yours* any more."

Actually, Jessie was correct in her assumptions about Emily. Even I noticed that after a few years of marriage to Thomas she would no longer say, "I don't like the taste of that particular sort of cheese." Instead she would say, "*We* don't like that particular cheese; *we* don't have it in the house." Whatever had been *her* opinions on simple, everyday things had now become *their* opinions, both hers and Thomas's, as if individuality no longer existed. On one occasion, Jessie did point it out to her, but Emily nearly lost her wig over it, and she quickly left the house in tears!

Jessie was more outgoing, and she would leave the house on her own and go to the London Hospital to visit with the sick and do charity work there. She was inspired by Florence Nightingale, and also by her cousin George Harold Arthur Comyns Berkeley, who was on his way to becoming a doctor, and not just an ordinary doctor, but one who would specialise in a certain field of medicine.

The sisters, though, were well provided for, and according to Augustus would be set for the rest of their lives, and would never have to rely upon having a husband to provide a comfortable roof over their heads.

Besides Edmund and Charles being bachelors, there was Algernon Cecil. Yes, he was still wet behind the ears – one has a tendency to forget how young he was – but also there was Captain Edmund Robert, who was still unattached, and *he* was in his late thirties. Let's not forget handsome Herbert Bowyer, the photographer – he was still unmarried. Not all of their many cousins were married, male or female, and from what I gleaned, none of them suffered greatly from the state of bachelorhood or spinsterhood.

And what of me? I too was unattached. I had no dog friends, except for Toby who lived halfway across England. I spent many hours during the week relaxing at the office, or if I was exceptionally lucky and someone left the door wide open, I would trot off down to the stables and visit with Jasper and the other horses. I was canny enough to never wander any further than the stables, knowing full well that I would be shouted for before long. The constitutional walk to and from work with the men, in fine weather, kept me trim and healthy, and at the end of each work day I was worn out, and by nine at night I was ready for my bed. This was my family, this was my life, and this was me.

XVIII
A HEAVY HEART

"...no churchyard for dogs, cats, and
horses. Sadly, I wondered why?"

1886 -1887

IN THE SUMMER OF **1886** we went back to Cotheridge Court for a whole
fortnight's holiday. This time neither young Charles Clement nor Emily
accompanied us. Instead, Charles was now apprenticed to a tailor's shop,
and wasn't able to take his holidays when he wanted, and Emily was now
married, and she and Thomas had made their own plans and were going to
Bath, a place made popular by Jane Austen. Maud came along with us for the
holiday as she was still a widow, and Mary Matilda was now four years old.

Augustus's brother William Comyns had now been gone for nearly an
entire year. Rowland, my first master, was now lord of the manor, which
meant there had been a few changes made in the past year. For one thing, I
was not barred from the house and banned from the kennels. To my surprise, I
was now allowed in the house, which I appreciated, especially at night, when
I could freely sleep on the bottom of any bed I chose. Many times I chose to
sleep with Jessie, because she liked my companionship at night. As for the
servants, well, they still seemed to like me, and they proved it by keeping me
very well fed whenever I visited the kitchen or dairy.

You are probably wondering about Toby, my dear old friend. I, too, had
been thinking about him, so one afternoon I trotted off over to the old farm
to see him. I knew the way well: through the pastures, orchards, and fields
of hops and beans, until I came to the first gate. Then there was the highway
to cross, another gate and a narrow strip of land, another gate, and finally

the little road, and there I was, trotting through the courtyard like nobody's business. I was in a state of high anticipation, as I couldn't wait to have a right good natter with Toby. I had missed him a lot. Actually, as you now know, I had greatly missed the companionship of another dog. The farm had after all been my first home, and I felt I had a right to visit whenever I wanted, and besides, Toby was there.

I found George kitted out in the same baggy trews and tired-looking shirt that he had worn when I had been a small puppy. One would think he didn't receive any wages! He used to say, "Am saving oop fer m'retirement." And there he was, leading a draught horse by its halter and coming through the gate at the end of the yard. I ran up to George, carefully mind, so as not to startle the horse – the coal horses and Jasper had taught me plenty about themselves.

"Well, I nivver... why it's Shales. Cum 'ere lad. Yer lookin' well fed. Tha allus wuz a bonnie dog." He didn't reached down to pat me, but he kept his distance – so typically Toothless George.

It was good to see him; more a stranger these days than a friend, but nevertheless, good to see him. I wondered about Toby, and knew he would be glad to see me. Before I could run off to the kennels, George said roughly, "If you're lookin' fer Toby, he's lang gone. Dead 'e is. Died in 'is sleep 'e did, a few weeks ago."

Then, George, remembering his business with the horse, turned his back on me, and led it out of the yard and into the stable. The animal's heavy hoofs clipped and clopped across the smooth stone of the cobbles until they became silent, as they then treaded upon the soft straw scattered within. I hardly noticed this, as my mind felt numb. I stood there, solid as a statue, not knowing what to think. I could only feel a deep emptiness, as all emotion seemed to have left me. Toby gone! Oh... no! I was so shocked, in that my surprise visit had instead revealed to me his absence, when I had been so excited about seeing him. It was a most awful feeling of despair that began to invade my mind, and I now understood that I probably would not ever return to this farm again. I understood death, and I knew I wouldn't ever be seeing my mate Toby again. I felt miserable, and with there being no point in lingering at the farm, I slowly journeyed back to Cotheridge Court, with my tail tucked between my legs, and feeling appallingly glum.

People don't seem to know when a dog has lost a friend. People are peculiar that way. Nobody in my family knew that my friend Toby had died. I tried to tell them, I sent them thoughts and pictures, but still they just didn't seem to understand. It seems communication is a one-way road – dogs have to learn English, and lots of rules, and even laws, but people never learn to understand us, no matter how much you think you do. We love you, and speaking for myself, I forgive you for that, but it would really be nice if someday I could talk to a person who could understand me, word for word and thought for thought. That would be nice. Wouldn't it?

After the sad news about Toby, I tried to enjoy my time left in Cotheridge. Yes, I moped about quite a bit, but at times I did swim in the great pond and chase frogs about the bulrushes, which grew along its banks, and I also played about in the garden with the children. The cousins Edmund and Rowland rode together each day, and like I did with Thomas I followed them about the countryside as they inspected the fields of wheat and the other crops famous to the area. It wasn't the same without Thomas and Jasper. Edmund and Rowland weren't so adventurous and daring as Thomas had been, but we did travel a lot of miles and see the insides of quite a few pubs.

One of my favourite pastimes when in Cotheridge was to linger about outside the dairy, which was situated near to the rear of the house where it took full advantage of the shade, there being many a time the door would open and a bowl of milk, whey, or a plate covered with slivers of homemade cheese would be placed in front of me. Sometimes I'd even get a glimpse of the interior: white walls, immaculately clean, with wooden blocks being filled with butter, smelly cheeses hanging from hooks, and the dairy maid busy at her task beyond the thick, stone walls, which kept the building cool in the summer and warm in the winter. It seemed that these days I never went hungry for more than a few hours, though those days of near starvation when I was searching for London were not forgotten. I vowed I would never forget that experience.

Sometimes Jessie and her sisters Julia and Lucy would ride with Mildred, the new Mistress of Cotheridge, but Maud never did. No one had been successful in getting her to mount a horse, not even a pony. Maud spent her time in the lovely garden with her daughter, and sometimes wandered off on her own for long, unaccompanied walks about the orchards and country lanes. Rowland's children were also growing, and they played games with Mary Matilda as well as with William Nichols's children.

The day we were to leave Cotheridge was a Sunday, and the family went to the Sunday service at the little church of St Leonard's, which was just a short distance away from the house. I had once overheard a conversation between Augustus and Rowland, in that the church had been part of the family's property for a few hundred years, and that generation upon generation of the family were interred either beneath the church or in the churchyard. Whilst the family was at church I occupied myself by having a look about the graveyard, something I had never before thought to do. I wasn't a very good reader, but I could read a bit these days, after all those hours spent in the nursery with Jessie trying to teach four-year-old Mary Matilda how to read. Sometimes the child came to our house, while Maud sewed for her clients and Charlotte had her day off. Jessie taught her words and counting, to keep her occupied. That year we were both still learning the alphabet, but I could read quite a few words, and I could spell everyone's names. Shortly, the lessons would end, as Mary Matilda would be attending school, a place where I was forbidden to go.

I found plenty of gravestones, and some were so old they were difficult to read. I had never before thought that reading the writing on gravestones was good mental exercise, and also excellent reading practice. Round I walked, through the lush, green grass. Somebody came here regularly and cut the grass to keep it neat and in order, exposing the older gravestones, leaving them tilting in odd directions. The place was well cared for; that was obvious to anyone who wasn't blind.

I came across some graves at the back of the church that were recognisable. In the background I could hear hymns being sung and even parts of the sermon from time to time, as a gentle breeze blew the sounds from the church in my direction. Some of the graves seemed to be fairly new. It took me ages to decipher the writing, but eventually I made sense of it. One solid stone coffin revealed it belonged to Harriet Elizabeth Bowyer Nichols, wife of the Revd William Comyns Berkeley of Cotheridge Court. She had died before I was born, September 16th 1875. I'd never had the opportunity to meet her – I'd wondered where she'd been. Out of curiosity I sauntered inside the church, the huge, oak-studded door being left wide open because of the summer's heat. As the small congregation sang hymns, I quietly wandered about the small church and admired its beautiful stained-glass windows. Neither the rector nor the congregation batted an eye as I quietly padded past them to get to the east end of the church, where a smaller room, beyond a stone Norman arch, awaited me. There were more pews in there, small ones, and there were plaques on the walls. High on the wall to my left there was William Comyns Berkeley's plaque: Graduate of Cambridge, died August 7th 1885. That was just last summer. There was another William, the father to all of the brothers and Auntie Emily. He had died on the 13th November 1869, in his eighty-sixth year.

An ancient window in St Leonard's Church.

I was just reading the plaque of a Thomas who had died in some foreign place called Turkye [sic], in 1669, when, the service being over with, the parishioners began to leave the church. I quickly nipped between them and out the door, criss-crossed my way through the graveyard, weaving around the leaning headstones, and jumped the fence, not bothering to follow the path and use the gate. There, I waited for my family outside the churchyard, as they had stopped to linger and speak with some of the parishioners before walking back to the house. I was greeted with friendly smiles and pats and, as usual, was made a big fuss of. Rowland's brother, William Nichols, was the Rector of Cotheridge, and he and his wife Jane said their goodbyes outside the church, as we were now going to leave; our holiday in Worcestershire was now over, and our bags and trunks were already packed and on the way to Henwick station.

Once aboard the train I sat upon the coarse, padded horsehair seat, and gazed out of the window at the lovely countryside. Lush green pastures and quaint villages came and went. I thought about Toby. There was no headstone to mark his grave, no churchyard for dogs, cats and horses. Sadly, I wondered why.

* * *

WE HAD ONLY BEEN BACK IN HACKNEY FOR LESS THAN A WEEK when we packed up again and caught the train to Ongar. Apparently, the lease was up on Wayletts and Augustus wasn't going to renew it. Charles Clement not wanting to become a farmer and the sisters not wanting to reside in Stanford Rivers during any of the winter months was reason enough to say "goodbye, ta-ra, and fare-thee-well" to the place. I had two things I had to do when I got there. The first thing was to run over to the churchyard and visit the family vault. I desperately wanted to go, feeling some sort of a pull to go there and lie down next to the wrought iron railings for a few hours. Thomas was in that place, entombed underground, and just being near him would make me feel somewhat closer to him. I sensed this was to be my last visit there, and not knowing for sure, I wanted to make my own goodbyes whilst I had the chance. The second thing I had to do was to go and visit with Horatio, my old friend.

When we arrived in the farmyard I jumped out of the carriage and ran off without first going inside the house. I simply ran away, out of the yard and across the fields, taking the shortest route to St Margaret's. Panicked voices shouted my name, for me to come back, but I ignored them – I knew what I was doing. Once at the church I flopped down upon the grass in front of the vault. It was a beautiful day, hot and sunny, but I was well shaded from the heat by the large trees behind me. Grasshoppers disruptively hopped about, landing on my head, and pretty butterflies fluttered about silently as they danced from grave to grave. I lay there quietly with closed eyes, in a glum but meditative state, as I drew upon past memories of wild rides about the local countryside.

After some time had passed a small group of people came into the churchyard, obviously to visit the grave of a loved one. Walking past the vault, they saw me and spoke kind words. "Oh, that lovely dog. Isn't he ever so faithful to his master? I remember him being at the funeral. That's the dog everyone was talking about." And then, "I used to see this dog follow the young master all around, that summer before he died. Sad, isn't it, to see a dog lie upon a grave? Brings tears to my eyes."

The woman started to cry, and searched for her hanky, secreted in a pocket of her dress, but in doing so she lingered beside the vault. She stretched a hand down and hesitantly stroked my head. I responded with a gentle wag of my tail, but nothing more.

Then a deeper voice followed, a man's voice. "Come on, Meg, or we'll be here all day."

Meg replied, "I know, but I was just remarking on the dog lying at his young master's grave. You don't see it very often, but we do hear about it." She then blew her nose.

The man asked her, "What's that got to do with us?"

Exasperated, the woman said, "I didn't mean it had anything to do with us. Just that it is more sad for me to see that dog over there mourning his dead master, than it is for me to visit the grave of my own mother, and I loved her."

The man then said, in a kind voice, "Oh, I see. You are soft. Don't be daft – it's just a dog. It's having a nap; that's all."

Meg suggested tearfully, "When we leave, go and give the dog a peppermint. He'll like that. Dogs like sweets."

I sighed. I did remember those wonderful days when I followed Thomas about, very well. That was my first summer with the family, and then the following year the sudden illness and death of Thomas had changed everything. I lay there in the shade, remembering it all: the visits to the pubs, long rides with Jasper, and friendly evenings in the drawing-room whilst everyone chatted about their day. Oh, the family was changing. Emily was living in a different house and at times seemed to be far away, even though she was just around the corner from us, and Charles Clement went to a different place of work. Rowland was now Master of Cotheridge, since his father had died, and the old farm in Broadwas wasn't the same since Toby had died. Oh, so many changes, and I haven't even told you most of them – too many to mention – and now we no longer owned Wayletts, and I wouldn't be coming here again, which meant I wouldn't be able to see Horatio ever again.

Night came, and I could hear my name being called from a long way off, carried upon the breeze. It was Jessie – she must have been wandering about the woods and roads calling my name. I went home to the farm, and upon my arrival a very anxious family met me at the door. They had been worried about me, but once they could see I was obviously all right they calmed down, and after a bit of prompting, Jessie remembered to set out my dinner. I was very hungry and thirsty, and all I had had to eat since breakfast had been a single peppermint, kindly given to me by those two visitors at the churchyard. As I ate, I thought about the following day yet to come, as I was about to disappear again for more than an entire day. It couldn't be helped; I had to go, and I did try to tell them, though frustratingly enough, and as usual, they simply didn't understand me. Humans! Why do we always have to have this language barrier? Did God make a mistake, or did he do it on purpose?

The next day, right after breakfast, I set off for Harvest Farm, home of Horatio Harvest. The breakfast, a tasty one at that, had been a rather generous portion of porridge made with milk and cream and smothered with golden syrup. I knew it would stick to my ribs, thus keeping me feeling full for most of the day. The family was busy organising the vacating of the premises. Augustus was busy making sure that the repairs needed had indeed been done, over the past few months, in order to turn over the property in a state of good repair. The women sorted out the furniture that was to be sent on to Darnley Road and also to Emily's house, with the remainder being sold off; the reason being there was not enough room to put it all at our now one and only residence in Hackney.

As I travelled down the paths and lanes of the local countryside, with the delightful taste of golden syrup still lingering in my mouth, I knew that I would be missed, as I would not be returning to Wayletts that night. They would worry about me, thinking me lost, but it couldn't be helped. I had to see Horatio for one last time. Oh, Horatio! Please be there. I was so saddened by Toby's death, not ever having given in to the realisation that it was to definitely happen at some point of time in the future. I simply hadn't thought about him dying, even though I had known he had been old and blind, and now that he had died, I had opened my eyes and it had then dawned on me that it would soon be Horatio's time, as he was already elderly when I had first met him, whereas I was still very young back then. What of me, I thought? How long afore I die?

I ventured towards his farm with all haste, fearing the worst but hoping for the best. Once there, I cautiously surveyed the farm from a distance, not wanting to get shot by his unfriendly, musket-wielding master. It seemed that I waited for hours without any sign of him at all. I sniffed the air searching for a scent of him, and nothing! I crept closer and hid at the back of some farmyard junk, where I had full view of the back entrance to the old farmhouse. It was very hot; the sun beat down upon my head making me unbearably uncomfortable, and I panted and gasped for air in an effort to cool myself down. Still, there was no sign of Horatio or any other farm cat. I was beginning to get the uneasy feeling that he had died, just as Toby had. The sun started to set, and then I smelt a familiar scent upon the late evening breeze. I saw him come plodding along, ever so cautious in his stride. He stopped and looked about, and he, too, sniffed the air. He knew I was there, and he came striding across to me, and I was so happy to see him that my violently wagging tail dislodged some of the junk in the pile, and it all came crashing down, sounding like an isolated thunder storm. The farm came awake! Horses neighed and dogs barked from somewhere close by, and the farmhouse door opened and out shot Horatio's master with his ancient musket at the ready. He ran into the yard looking for all like a wild bushman, and then stopped to listen.

I crouched low and clamped my jaws shut.

"Who gows there?" he challenged the air with a mad glint to his eye. When nobody replied he ventured a bit further into the yard, and then noticed the rearrangement I had done to his pile of rubbish. Old pieces of twisted metal displayed their rusted coats amidst broken chairs, and there was even a half-door from a barn partially buried beneath rusted, empty tins. I kept myself hidden, but I could see him approaching closer and closer. The long musket was held low to his body as he crept forward ever so carefully. Horatio, seeing that disaster was going to strike in the form of his best dog mate being shot dead by his master, casually strolled out and rubbed himself around his master's legs. Then he darted, cat-like, into the rubbish, and came out with a mouse, its little body swinging its long tail in protest, and its arms and legs moving about within the toothy confines of Horatio's mouth. Very prompt thinking on Horatio's part!

His master gave a shrug. "Well, that's wot it's all about! Jes' thee catchin' mice. Thowt we was goin' to get moidered in our sleep!" And he suddenly turned about and stomped heavily towards the farmhouse, kicking up dust as he went, and then disappeared inside, to my obvious relief.

"That wath a clothe one, Shales," said Horatio as he let the little mouse go. *"Run frwee. Run away little one,"* urged Horatio. He, himself, was obviously relieved, as he blew out a puff of breath. *"Phew! I was afeared thee were done for! It wath only lasth week that he shot a dog; one from the willage. He kilt it dead, and now it's bewied somewhere in that field ower there."* He gestured to the field that lay beyond the dilapidated fence.

"I simply had to come an' see thee," I pleaded. *"We're leaving the farm, and I don't know if I'll ever 'ave a chance to come back 'ere an' see thee again."*

"Oh, Shales. Ith's so good to see thee, although I do admit I'm not in the leatht surproised. Actually, I'd been finkink about you on and off, awl week long, so I did wonder if thee were back at the farm. I had thowt of walking

ower there, jes' to see if I was corwect in that assumption, but I hadn't giffen any thowt as to when."

I looked at him. He always seemed to know where I was. I'm sure that if I hadn't made an effort to come to Harvest Farm that he would have showed up at Wayletts in a few days. However, I may have been back in Hackney by then, and I would never have known if he were still alive, or if he'd died from old age, or worse, been killed.

I noticed he looked very thin and his stomach hung low to the ground. I assumed he was very old, so out of curiosity I asked him his age. His reply was spoken with pride, *"I'm seffenteen years owd."* He smiled cat-like.

I sighed. Seventeen seemed to be a very old age to live. I had difficulty counting past four, although I could if I had to. Why, I was only just seven years old, and the reason I knew that was because someone had asked Jessie my age, and when she had replied, I realised I could remember and associate a major event in my life to each year; so, it was easy for me to understand that I was seven. Well, it was only easy as long as I didn't think about it too much.

Horatio.

It was so good to see the old chap that I gave him a good licking, right across his face. In return, he purred away and rubbed himself around my legs, like some cats do, and his tail then curled around my face. Jointly, we decided to go off for a walk and put some distance between his master and us, just in case he came back outside to patrol the farmyard, in the unlikely event of an attack from invading marauders.

It was a lovely summer's night, so neither one of us minded sleeping rough. We dossed down in the soft but damp grass beneath the branches of a great oak tree.

"*Shales, thou ith keeping well? I afear for thee at toimes.*"

Casually, I said, "*Oh, yes. Loife is busy dodging knoives and rescuing drowning children.*"

"*Yer don't thsay, old chap!*" he said. Then in typical Horatio form, he said in a serious voice, "*I did warn thee. There wath danger in thy future.*" He paused, and then said knowingly, "*There ith still danger looming afar into the distance. I don't know what it ith, but it will find thee, if thou don't find it firwst.*"

This was frightening news for me. I didn't want to hear it, and I wanted to clap my paws over my ears. I had hoped that my altercations with the cook had been the 'danger' that he had warned me about. Horatio was so fey, I should have realised he would know more than he had let on. He had, after all, hinted at Thomas's fate when he had asked if I had known what a funeral was. Now I remember him saying, "*You will know soon enough,*" or something similar to those words.

He changed the subject. "*Thou weally did find a luffing family, didn't thee?*"

"*Yes, I did,*" I answered with pride.

"*Goo'. But thou has had obsthacles?*"

Getting quite serious, I said, "*Horatio, thou warned me ov danger. It came from where I least expected it to cum from, but I survoived. Believe it or not, it was the cook, Eliza.*"

"*Thsay! That is quite shocking, ithn't it?*" he commented. Then he said, "*I did wonder about her, as I'd had a stwange dream where she was cooking*"

a dog, an' I did know at the time it meant danger for thee, but I didn't fink she
would actually kill thee."

I said, "*She didn't kill me, but she certainly tried it on. In the end she*
gave her notice and left."

Wise old Horatio said, "*Yeths, I knew she wouldn't kill thee, but the*
danger wath still there."

Now it was my turn to alter the subject of our conversation. Only Horatio
could help me with this. "*I was wondering. Do thee ken a better way with*
which t' communicate with people? I tried to warn them, mi family, about the
cook, but they simply did not understand me. Not one jot."

"*Oh, Shales. Don't awl animals ask that werry question sooner or later*
in loife? I have nao answer to that. It is so werry difficult to communicate
to people jes' the werry basic things, such as 'I'm hungrwy' or 'I'm cowld'.
They jes' don't seem to be able to learn our language. What am I talking
about? How many cats an' dogs hast thou come across who can't efen speak
cat or dog?"

"*Plenty of those,*" I answered honestly.

Horatio continued, "*Efen so, now I'm talking about people, and we can't*
help but luff 'em. 'Tis a special thing when a person not ownly opens their
door to us an' inwites us inside to liff wiff 'em, but also opens their hearts to
us, as well."

* * *

I SPENT PART OF THE NEXT MORNING WITH HIM, but I had to say "*ta-ra*", as
much as it broke my heart to do so. He understood that I had to go back to
the farm; I understood that I would never see him again. My chest felt heavy,
as if I were carrying around a cannon-ball in there. Feeling weighted down,
I slowly found my way home along the secluded paths and narrow roads,
until I crept into the farmyard, unnoticed, and lay down for a long sleep in
the vicinity of the stables. Sometime later I was discovered by my master,
and suddenly I saw him in a new light. He, too, was getting older, and then I
counted two cannon-balls rolling about my chest. He bent down to stroke my

head, and then offered a few loving words. I knew this would not be my last visit to Stanford Rivers; I just didn't know when I would return.

* * *

THAT WINTER THE WEATHER WAS COLD AND DREARY. It snowed on and off during the dark weeks that followed Christmas, and at times the fogs would freeze, leaving the trees' branches and the iron street railings dusted with frost, as if a magic wand had been busy at work. The pavement was slippery to walk upon, and there were many collisions reported in the newspapers: coal wagons and cabs sliding into each other, resulting in injured pedestrians and horses with broken legs. No such accident happened with our coal horses and wagons, but Edmund said it was just a matter of time, inevitable, with the streets and roads so icy.

On a day similar to what I have just mentioned, I had to be stretchered off the road. I lay there in the middle of Darnley Road, holding up traffic, whilst the maid-of-all from the house across the road sounded the alarm, ran over to my house, and fetched Armstrong. When our housemaid had responded to the frantic knocking at the door, the maid-of-all had blurted out, "Come quickly, miss! Your dog's been run over!"

Annie Armstrong ran out into the road to see for herself. She blurted out, "Shales! Oh, Shales!" And then ran back to the house to get help. The men were all at work, and so it was the sisters who were at home and had to deal with the emergency. White-faced, they came running towards me thinking the worst – that I was already dead. I lay there in agonizing pain, as a cab's wheel had run over my left hind leg, and it had got caught up in the spokes, and I had been twirled about like a Roman Candle, and then thrown through the air only to land at the feet of the nice little old lady who lived across from us. I howled because of the pain, and also the fright from being run over, and she nearly had a heart attack, so alarmed was she. But it hadn't been her cab that had run me down; hers had been parked, waiting for her to clamber in.

She sent her young maid to our house. "Run full haste and fetch their housemaid! Watch for the traffic! Silly girl! Oh, dear! She's almost just slipped on the cobbles herself!"

These were the last words I heard the old lady mutter as her cab slowly drove away, the driver careful to avoid me and not run over my prone body.

The sisters crowded about me in a state of panic. Doors opened up along the road, and mob-capped maids wandered out to see what the commotion was.

"Shales has been run down by a charging horse! Poor dog," I heard them say to one another before they disappeared back into their masters' houses. Needless to say, the cab that ran me down did not stop, but kept going. Another cab stopped and caused traffic to back up behind him, as it was mid-morning, and it was the busiest time of the day in our road. The driver shouted out, "Do ya noid a lif' to the vet'rinary?"

Jessie went over to him and acknowledged they did indeed need the services of a cab, but not before some sort of a stretcher could be found to first place me upon. I lay there panting and growling, as my leg, hip, shoulder, and ribs (the ones on my left side) all felt as if they had been mangled.

Well, they had, in a sort of trampled way.

Dear Reader, now you are wondering: "Shales, how on earth did you get yourself into this predicament?" What can I say? I was being nosy, and the kitchen door to the tradesman's entrance was propped wide open because we were taking some very large deliveries of goods, namely tuns of ale, sacks of flour and potatoes and such. I had ventured outside through the wide-open gate without Holmes noticing me, and I had gone for a short stroll. My intention had been to just have a quick sniff about, but I had thought I had seen something of interest across the road: some sort of a bird fluttering about in the frozen hedge. In my haste to get to it, I crossed without looking, and at the last moment when I had realised that a horse was nearly upon me, I had slipped on the frost-covered cobbles. The horse had done a sort of jump and dance routine, missing me with its hoofs, but the wheel had found its mark. It was my very own fault. I couldn't blame anyone, not even our cook. A blanket had been provided, which served as a stretcher, and I was placed inside the cab, whereby Jessie accompanied me to the closest veterinary. The cab made all haste to get there, and after depositing us outside the premises the man charged my mistress sixpence extra. "For the dog 'airs and blood," he said. "It'll 'ave to be cleaned up afore I can go back to work."

Reader, can you believe it?

The kindly doctor gave me ether, making me unconscious before he set my leg. I left, later that day, feeling both femmered and nithered, with my back leg bound in a splint. I couldn't bend it at all to walk, and so I had to sort of roll a bit and swing it out in order to move forwards. I had stitches in my left shoulder where the flesh had been torn. I also had a rotten, thumping headache, as well as an upset stomach, and I wanted to go home so badly that when I did get home, with the help of Jessie, I rolled and hobbled in extreme pain across to the fireplace in the sitting-room, and there I passed out in a heap, in the warm glow of the coal fire.

This was definitely worse than decapitation.

The sisters, Armstrong and the cook were all so relieved that I hadn't been more seriously injured, or even killed. I was awake when Augustus came home at teatime, but I didn't even attempt to get up and meet him at the door. The day's events had not yet been revealed to him, and he had asked Armstrong why I wasn't at the door to greet him.

"He's in front of the fire, sir," she replied quietly. He strolled up to the fire to warm his hands and found me there at his feet, in a sorry heap.

"Good God! What on earth have you done to yourself?"

I mournfully looked up at him and tried to thump my tail. It wasn't working too well, and I wondered if that, too, had been broken. I whimpered and sighed, and my eyes felt moist.

The sisters came in for their tea, and tearfully told of the tragic and frightening event. Augustus said to me gently, "Would you like your cup of tea, Shales?" He poured it into a saucer and placed it under my chin. I lapped it up greedily. It tasted like nectar.

I wondered how I was going to get outside to the loo.

Jessie commented, "All this because we thought he should stay home today."

It was true. I had been kept from going to work because the weather was horrible, and it was easier for the men that day to work without having to think of my safety, and so on. I should say their safety as, truthfully, I'd nearly burnt down the office when on the previous day I'd tossed my ball too close to the fire, and it had become ignited by a rogue spark. I hadn't realised it was smouldering and I'd tossed it about, when it had landed upon Augustus's desk amidst a pile of paperwork. The result was a quick blaze, which was desperately doused with the liquid contents of a chamber-pot by my master's brother George Brackenbury, who had happened by for a visit at that crucial moment.

"Somebody's watching over you. I'm sure of it," Augustus said, as he gently stroked my head. "Somebody is watching over you – if not, then you'll be the death of us all." He chuckled to himself and then covered me with a blanket. Then, he thoughtfully placed a cushion beneath my head, and tucked my stuffed bunny close to my chest. I whimpered, as I was in an extreme amount of pain. I don't remember anything else until I awoke the next day.

XIX
Horse Tales

"...they tell the most wonderful stories."

1886

DEAR **R**EADER, please don't think I had stopped going to work every day with Augustus and Edmund. No, I still went there on a regular basis, although not necessarily every working day. Also, I still escaped from the back garden at various times, but I'll tell you about those little excursions later. Now, back to the job. Sometimes I was allowed in the stables, but not very often, because when I'd been in there with the horses the stable odour clung to my coat, which was rather long-lasting, not to say exceedingly pungent. I was a housedog so, therefore, I had to remain fresh-smelling and clean, and in no way carry an offensive, rammy odour about the house. To put it bluntly, the stables were out of bounds to me.

On any of the rare occasions I happened to secretly gain access to the stables I would have a really good natter with the horses that were there on that particular day, and weren't working at pulling their wagonloads of coal. Eventually, we all became close friends, as most horses are quite intelligent, but best of all, they tell the most wonderful stories.

The stables were relatively dark, but were always kept as clean as possible by the *coalies,* the men who worked for my master. The horses told me lots, and I learnt to respect them, as I didn't know of anyone, human or animal, who worked as hard as they did. First of all, they hadn't always worked six days in a week. They said that a new, youngish horse would be made to work perhaps two or three days each week, and he'd be about five years old at this point, and not London-born, but brought in from farms located in various counties of England. When he could pull his load without difficulty, and not get upset from the frightening sounds and scenes on the busy Hackney and London streets, he would then gradually work an extra day or so until he was pulling his loads for six full days out of seven. Sundays were always the day of rest, and that went for humans as well. A good horse would work like this for three, four, or possibly eight years, or even longer, depending on the coal merchant and how he treated his horses. Many of the horses worked an incredibly long day, from sunup until sundown, and moved about thirty tons of coal each week. For those hard-working horses, breakfast was usually served at around four in the morning, and after about two hours given to eating and digestion he went to work at about six o'clock. When he left, the wagon driver took along a nosebag and a sack of bait so that later in the day he could give his horse something to eat. He wouldn't return to the stables until the work was completed, which could have been as late as six o'clock, or even later, sometimes making it a twelve-hour day. Their feet, those enormous things that were three times larger than my head, had to be kept in good order. Their shoes had to fit properly, and their hoofs had to be kept from being packed with manure and straw, to prevent rotting and lameness. It was essential they ate a good diet. They could not thrive off musty hay and oats, which would give them breathing ailments. No, good quality hay, oats, and straw was brought in from the countryside, and proper grooming was conducted every day, leaving them looking healthy, robust and very proud-looking. They were either blacks or dark bays (and never piebalds, chestnuts or greys), and were casually known as the Black Brigade, but everyone, and even the coal horses, knew that the real Black Brigade were those massive, black Belgian giants, which were the funeral horses. Boys o' boys, mmn, mmn, mmn.

I found the stable smells soothing, and I loved to be around the horses when they were munching their hay. The combination of sweet smells and equine sounds would make me sleepy enough to kip down and have a right good sleep.

I learnt a lot from those horses. They all knew the streets and roads of Hackney, memorised from their frequent passages along the cobbled routes. They filled my head with stories of wagon collisions and horrible accidents at the coal yard, or the worst fog that happened on such and such a day in such and such a year.

Jasper was there, living in the same stable as the coal horses. Now, *he* wasn't a coalie, but as you already know he was a hunter, and his colouring was of the brightest chestnut. He was quite a valuable horse. In other words, he was worth a few bob. He missed Thomas terribly, and although Edmund and Charles both took him out for long rides, and sometimes Edmund, during the season, even hunted with Jasper, he said it wasn't the same. He preferred the countryside, where he could pasture at leisure when he wasn't being ridden. He didn't like the town, with all its smells and sounds. He missed the hunts, as Edmund didn't hunt as often as Thomas had done, and Charles had never hunted. Charles simply couldn't take a five-foot jump, whether it be a hedge or rail, and especially not knowing what was on the other side of it, but Thomas had been reckless in the way that he trusted his horse to sense impending danger. I know what Jasper meant, as I had witnessed, nay, followed Thomas and Jasper on their wild rides about Essex, although I had never witnessed them hunt.

Apparently, Edmund had taken a bad fall off his horse many years ago and had broken his leg, which had taken weeks and weeks to heal: a serious thing to happen to anyone. I now understood why sometimes he favoured his left leg, although he didn't actually have a limp. It had never put him off riding; he was just more cautious as he got older. According to Jasper, there had been a woman involved, and because of the seriousness of Edmund's injury, she had taken herself off and had married another man. Oh, poor Edmund!

Jasper told me a little about Thomas and Maud. Now, after hearing this, I understood why there seemed to be some tension at times between Maud and Augustus. Apparently, Thomas had been working over in Stoke Newington, and there had met up with Maud at the boarding house of Mary Ann Moore. Maud had had lodgings with the lady there, and both were dressmakers. David King Foster worked for Thomas and his father, but David's father, also by the same name of David, was a church sexton at the parish church where Thomas and Maud had been married. One Sunday, when Thomas was visiting the Fosters, he met Maud again outside the church, after the service was over. They were introduced to each other again, and according to Jasper, "She set her cap at him. Poor chap didn't know what hit him!"

It seems they had a secret romance, and even the Fosters didn't know about it. Well, perhaps the younger David did know something, but didn't tell. I remembered hearing all about it before, but this time it was coming directly from the horse's mouth, meaning Jasper. Their secret romance resulted in the 'bun in the oven', that even I knew about. I asked Jasper how he knew all this, and his reply was:

"A little dicky-bird told me."

Oh, how interesting.

I now could see it all a bit clearer than when it had happened. Augustus had been extremely unhappy about it all: less than a month to prepare for the wedding. Hey up! It took Emily nearly three years before she finally wed Thomas White. Oh, what scandal! Of course, it was all falling into place. To avoid a scandal they had a rushed wedding, but it was all done properly. Banns were read in church and afterwards the baby was said to be born early. Oh, now I see how Jasper thought about it all: my master thought his son could've done better, and perhaps if he'd never married Maud he wouldn't have been living in Bush Hill Park, and then wouldn't have succumbed to that fateful disease, and in that case, would still be here with us today. Poor Jasper; I could see he was still bitter over losing his master. But I wasn't bitter, just very sad over the whole affair.

XX
WILLIAM

*"I sensed their emotions within my every
pore."*

1887

I T SEEMS TO ME THAT THE LIVES OF PEOPLE are extremely complicated
with the forever announcements of deaths, births, and marriages. I
have mentioned deaths before the other two, because death seems to
be a state that my family always had to cope with. It never gave us pause to
breathe, there being the gloom of mourning about the house as if it had been
painted with an artist's brush, dipped in the dreaded expectancy of, yet again,
another funeral.

When Armstrong, our housemaid, entered the dining-room with a little
envelope on a silver tray, carrying it as if it were an invitation from Her
Majesty herself, and said to the master, "Sir, this just come; not a moment
ago," my master reached for it slowly, without excited anticipation but
instead trepidation, and very carefully sliced it open with a letter knife (that
the housemaid had offered to him for that very action). The others at the table
held their breaths, and no comments were offered until after they had seen
their father slowly lower the bit of paper to the table, and reach up to his brow
and rub it with his weary hand. I remember seeing him do this, and knowing
full well that bad news of the worst kind was to be delivered to this family
yet again. He slowly raised the telegram, and read its contents out loud, with
a tremble to his voice, having no other way of breaking the devastating news
to his children.

"'It saddens me to inform you of your son's death. He was recently ill and has succumbed to pneumonia this very day. Please contact us. Arrangements must be made regarding his burial.'"

This time I could barely understand why. Once again it was a sudden announcement: 'Please come quickly', such as it had been when Maud had telegrammed us about Thomas Rowland. However, this time when Augustus opened the telegram, I had seen immediately that he was severely wounded by what he had read. It was his firstborn son, Augustus William, who had died that very same day, Monday, the eighteenth of April, of pneumonia. We hadn't even known he had been ill! The news of his illness and death was shocking, coming to us with no forewarning. Now he was dead. Another son to mourn, another brother to mourn, and yet again, another funeral to attend.

As I lay upon the carpet and saw the faces of the grief-stricken, I felt utterly helpless. I'd had enough experience with death to know what to expect. Tears burst forth from all, and Julia ran out of the room. Lucy was inconsolable, and Jessie sat there with her unfinished plate of curry before her and just stared off into the distance, as if there were no solid walls to the house. Augustus, ever so pragmatic, spoke quietly; nevertheless, his words were important, even though his voice shook.

"I should send them a telegram asking about the funeral arrangements. I have a feeling that she will want him to be buried close to her, and he won't be coming home to us, to Stanford Rivers."

Jessie was shocked. "What? Dad, you don't think he'll be buried in Gorleston, do you?"

"Yes, I do. It was something he mentioned in passing, at Thomas's funeral, that her family have an area set aside and that she, I mean Mary, wants to be buried with her children *and* her husband."

Edmund looked as white as a sheet as he said, "So, we had better prepare for the funeral to be near Yarmouth. I just can't understand it. Pneumonia! He must have become ill, because you don't just wake up with pneumonia one morning and then die of it the same day!"

My grieving master put his hand up and said, "Settle down, Edmund. Perhaps it came on quickly. They may have sent a telegram informing us of his illness and we just didn't receive it. It does happen now and again."

Jessie, though grief-stricken, spoke up. "Dad, everyone knows that telegrams are important. They are delivered quickly, and they aren't lost. They may not have realised he was so ill until it was too late."

"Aye, I suppose you are correct. I'm just making excuses, because I don't understand any of this." He continued with a shaking voice, "It seems that Mary's brother-in-law, Henry Lane, sent the telegram. I suppose he will be helping with the arrangements."

I got up from where I lay, and put my front paws on my master's lap, and then leaned forward to lick his face. Although he was seated at the dining table he did not push me off, but instead placed his arms around me, solidly, and held onto me, burying his face in my neck. It was the only way I knew of how to console a person in need.

"Edmund, will you please see to the telegram? First thing tomorrow?" My master looked ill, and I could see he wasn't up to coping with his first-born son's death and whatever arrangements were required. Edmund simply nodded; he couldn't speak.

The weight of knowing that William had died was difficult for me to bear. The whole mood of the house had changed within an instant of that telegram being opened and read. I sensed their emotions within my every pore, and I became weighted down with their sadness, and could only mope about.

Charles wasn't home that evening. He had gone out with a small group of friends, and they were at a Beethoven concert being performed at Alexandra Palace. That night I envied Charles his couple of remaining hours of ignorance, but he had to be told as soon as he came through the door, which would be late into the night. I knew he would see from Armstrong's face, as she let him in, that something was amiss, and I would be there to console him.

Lucy and Jessie consoled their father, whilst Julia sought sanctuary in her bedchamber. Edmund had the task of walking over to Chatham Place to give the dreadful news to Emily and Thomas. He whistled for me, needing my companionship that evening. We set off down the road just as the lamp man was lighting the lamps. I'm sure Edmund counted every step between our house in Darnley Road and Emily's house in Chatham Place. As we neared their house our steps slowed down, and we lingered outside, momentarily, whilst he found the courage to speak his words of sadness. I won't talk any more about that night, except to say that it was dreadful, and it only brought forth horrible memories from a similar night that had happened nearly five years before.

*　*　*

THE FUNERAL WAS TO BE ON THE FOLLOWING SATURDAY, and I was very surprised when on Friday my own personal belongings were packed in my little bag, as I had expected that I would remain behind with the servants. A black crepe band was tied around my neck. A blubbering Charles Clement, with shaking hands, had insisted I wear it. He had not taken the news of his brother's death well. I was going to Gorleston to entertain William's children and help take their minds off the dreadful day. Those poor children, growing up without their father; it would be difficult for them. At least they had their mother's family nearby. We left on Friday, all of us, including Maud and her daughter, as well as Emily and Thomas. William's body would be interred in Stanford Rivers, though the funeral was to be held in Gorleston, where he had become well known and respected.

When we arrived in Gorleston, we found he wasn't laid out in his hotel. Instead, his coffin was at his parents-in-laws' house, set upon trestles in a darkened room. He had passed away *there,* and not at the Bear, and the reason for that I know not why to this very day.

I went from person to person and child to child, to give them a bit of loving. Mostly they pushed me away, but some of them responded to my attentions. I watched for the hearse, that black, shiny vehicle with the glass sides, in which the coffin was to be placed amidst an abundance of flowers. The magnificent horses, black as coal, pulled the hearse effortlessly, the black ostrich plumes looking as if they grew out of the top of the horses' heads. All the leather trappings shone with professional care, and all the brass buckles glowed as if made of gold. The house emptied as the chief mourners climbed into their appointed carriages, part of the funeral parade, and set off for the church where the service was to be held. I was pleasantly surprised as I watched. There were a lot of people on foot who were a part of

336

funeral parade, from well-respected businessmen down to ordinary punters. They followed in turn behind the carriages in a long, black, moving mass. The streets became blocked with those paying their respects as the funeral parade set off. I was pleased that a great many people showed their love and respect for him. It was as if all of Gorleston had come out that day to pay their respects. I remained behind and guarded the house belonging to Mary's parents, and awaited the family's return.

After the funeral service ended, the coffin was then transported by train to Ongar, and from there it went to the churchyard of St Margaret's, in compliance with Mary's wishes. My master and his sons went to the church for William's interment in the family vault, but I returned with the women to London. Because the funeral service had taken place in Gorleston, there wasn't another one at St Margaret's, just a simple interment. That is all I know. I wish I could have gone with the men, but I was told that my place was with the women. The family once again spent their time coping with the customs of mourning. It seemed they never came out of it for very long. Poor William's wife, Mary. She had four children and the youngest, Myra, was yet a baby. From listening to conversations about her, I heard she had been advised to leave the Bear Hotel, sell up and move on, or let a man manage it, all because she was a woman. Her kind father was going to let her manage the Angel. It was another hotel, situated on the opposite side of the River Yare. I would not see the Bear Hotel again.

THE FOOL

BOOK IV

XXI

I Became a Day Tripper

"Ee's just off on a lark."

1888

I PROMISED YOU THAT I WOULD TELL YOU MORE ABOUT MY ESCAPADES, mainly in the form of vacating the premises for a few hours at a time, in order to do some sightseeing around Hackney. I found it difficult to not give in to my curiosity, a trait which I must have been born with and not simply acquired along the way. I think that through the years my curiosity had been nurtured, and like a flower that needs water, it also needed nourishment, but in the form of adventure, resulting in a feeling of contentment once my curiosity had been fed. To put it plain and simple: I was a nosy dog. In fact, the plain truth of the matter is that I was and still am a very nosy dog, and I was forever wanting to see what was going on down the street, or I would listen in on people's private conversations, discreetly hidden beneath the table or pretending to be asleep on the floor at their feet. Sometimes it was just family conversing amongst themselves, or at other times it was visitors: gentlemen with a cigar in one hand and a brandy in the other, and comfortably seated in a leather chair in the drawing-room, or those ladies who came to *call,* with lots of gossip about the gentry of London and its surrounding areas. At other times it was to stop and rabbit to strangers, as I valiantly patrolled the streets and roads in my neighbourhood. I loved to *rabbit and pork*, which is cockney for talk. But I gleaned knowledge from all these experiences, and so my knowledge and understanding of the human race slowly expanded, and I became a little wiser.

This curious trait of mine enticed me to jump that hedge and wall in the back garden many more times. The original hole that I had previously used had been repaired, and so, with that exit bricked up, there was only one other way out if the gates were closed, and they usually were. All I simply had to do was jump high, and after several attempts I could grasp the top of the wall with my front paws, and then I was up there. Then I simply had to jump down. I got rather good at it, and once over the wall I would trot off on my merry way for a few hours of entertainment. On one of those particular Saturdays in 1888 nobody of importance was at home, so that morning, with the weather being fair, it had been decided that I should stay outside for the day in the garden. Both water and food were provided, until the eventual return of the family. The servants had been told to let me be, as I needed the fresh air. I wasn't really interested in where any of them were going, or if they were together as a group or not, as I was quite happy to stay at home on my own. It was a case of easy come, easy go. When I overheard that I would be staying outside the house all day long, with the weather being warm and dry, as it was early summer, I decided it would be a perfect opportunity for a day trip about London. Boys o' boys, mmn, mmn, mmn.

Once I was over and running free, and of course not feeling the least bit guilty about breaking one of the house rules, I pointed myself in the direction of Hackney Railway Station. I knew exactly how to catch a train. You probably won't believe me, but I even knew which train would take me from Hackney into Broad Street Station, and from there I knew how to get to the Underground platform. I had done it many times before, but never on my own, but that didn't matter. I only had to follow someone onto the train without the conductor or any of the station staff noticing.

I knew which side of the line to be on, as I was going to London, and I had done it many times with Augustus, to the point that I am sure I could have done it blindfolded. What I hadn't prepared myself for was the rather abundant amount of people, who nearly crowded me out as I attempted to board the train. I nearly got caught when a lady asked the conductor about me, just as I was about to step aboard. I realised at that time that I could have easily got caught; if I wasn't careful some honest gentleman or lady would turn me over to the authorities, and in that case I would end up in deep trouble. I quickly ran off and hid behind the spoked wheels of a parked wagon, the sort used for trundling trunks and large cases along the platform. After thinking about it for a long time, I decided to catch the next train and travel with the lower classes amidst crowds of people. Then nobody would notice if I wasn't wearing a lead, or that I was with no one person in particular. I heard the all too familiar "all aboard" and "Broad Street" shouted out, and so after dodging around the conductor I successfully boarded a coach amidst the lower classes of the Hackney population, and for the first time in my life literally rubbed shoulders with them. I much preferred to travel First Class, it being less crowded and much more comfortable, such as when we travelled to Gorleston and Worcester, but I wasn't in a situation to complain. I cowered down by the feet of a seated lady, her dark skirts billowing out and giving me a small amount of cover. Nobody took any notice of me; they didn't comment to the lady about her dog, too busy were they looking out of the windows or reading their semi-folded newspapers. A lot of them spoke cockney, making it difficult to understand what they meant, but after careful listening I managed to increase my knowledge of the local lingo. Eventually my stop came and it was the end of the line. The coach door opened, and I disembarked amidst a crowd of quick-moving legs, knowing full well where I was: on one of seven long platforms in a station at the edge of London City. I had to get to the Underground, and I casually walked along, following at the heels of the crowds as if I were with one of them.

Down in the white-tiled tunnel I waited for my train. A risky thing to do, but I did manage to get to the correct side of the line and catch the proper train, which let me off at The Monument, the station closest to the Coal Exchange.

Now that I was in London, on my own in the great city for the first time in my life (just like I had dreamt about, when I set off on that journey to find London and a new family), I had to decide what I was going to do. It was all there, just waiting for me to explore it: The Tower of London, St Paul's Cathedral, and lots, lots more. London was special to me, as if it were the centre of the world and all roads led to it.

I was closer to the Tower than any other place, so I decided that was to be my first destination. I trotted off towards Lower Thames Street, and after a short distance passed the Custom House, which was on my right (the

Thames side of me), and the Coal Exchange on my left. There it was, further up ahead. I approached the Tower from the end of Lower Thames Street, and from there I could see part of the square tower, famous for its white stones and four towers, a tower being at each of its four square corners. Surrounded by an enormous wall and other buildings, which made up the huge fortress, it looked powerful and overbearing. I couldn't gain entrance. I could hear the rough 'cawing' of ravens coming from the vicinity, from someplace beyond the walls. It was their right to be there, but not mine. There were people milling about at Spurr Gate, and I was shooed away and accused of being a mangy cur. I had seen myself in a mirror, and I knew the difference between my handsome visage and that of a cur: an ignorant dog, a scruffy dog, an ill-tempered dog, with neither home nor master, and I can tell you, Dear Reader, I am definitely not a cur.

Dismissing the Tower, I wondered what to do next. The river was just there, to my right, so I trotted over to the wall situated at the edge of the embankment, and paused to look about, up and down the great river, seeing the massive piers of the Tower Bridge sunk into the Thames, which was under construction and not yet close to being finished. It was very near to where I stood, though outside of the city, being in the East End. I then decided to skirt around the grounds of the Tower of London, and I set off in a direction that led me along Great Tower Street and then up King William Street, and I eventually found myself in Poultry Lane, where I nearly got my front right foot run over by the wheels of a passing wagon. The fright of it reminded me of my broken leg, so I vowed to myself to be more careful. I could see the dome of St Paul's Cathedral just up ahead but a little off to my left, so I continued along Cheapside, ignoring the large crowds of people and being more careful of the ever-increasing, busy traffic, until I came upon the cathedral proper.

The doors were propped open at the entrance, the one where there is a long flight of steps going up to it. Up the steps I went, and into the great church, and oh! What a strange feeling! I felt a sudden surge of emotion hit me. I glanced about – I was in a beautiful place where the ceiling lifted upwards in the same fashion as that at the Coal Exchange. There was even a walkway that I could see, high up, just at the base of the dome. I wasn't going up there, though! I tiptoed about, trying to prevent my longish nails from clacking against the marble floor and thus alerting the vicar of my presence. I wasn't alone; there were other people there, and I'd had a feeling that if I *were* noticed, I'd be evicted rather sharpish. I found a stairway that descended, and being of a curious nature I went down the stone steps, that strange feeling becoming even stronger, to the point that I felt as if a hand was pushing me downwards, into the floor. So strange!

I walked about in what appeared to be a cellar of sorts, but later I found out it was the crypt: a place where dead people are entombed, such as a vault. I came across some marble tombs that were enormous in size and very showy. At first I didn't know what they were, but after some time taken in reading the inscribed words upon them, I realised I had been standing in front of the tombs of two British heroes. One was the Duke of Wellington, who had, well, saved us from the French at Waterloo, and the other was Lord Horatio Nelson, another great man who had, yet again, saved us from the French. I then realised that this Nelson, this Horatio, was the man, the hero whom my Horatio Harvest had been named after. I remembered him saying he had been named after some naval hero. Here I was standing at his namesake's tomb. Horatio would love this! Oh, if I could only tell him.

I had started to become overwhelmed with emotion, and felt that I had to leave the cathedral, or else become eternally sad.

Once outside, the strange feelings began to leave, and I found myself trotting down Fleet Street, dodging pedestrians both left and right. Horse-drawn vehicles created a fair amount of background noise; it was a very busy street. I stopped outside the offices of the *Daily News* and looked about, giving my back leg a rest as it was starting to ache. There was a pub close by, and sounds of joviality poured out into the street, accompanied by the strong smell of ale. I wasn't at all sure of whether to continue, or to go back to the station and return another day, but I continued on, wondering what else there was to see in the vicinity. I neither knew where Westminster was, nor how to get there, so I decided to leave the Abbey, and Big Ben and the Parliament buildings for another day.

Out of nowhere the voice of a strange man spoke to me.

"'Ello," he said. "Wot've we got 'ere?"

I stopped in my tracks to look at this man, who seemed to be an honest person by way of his dress, neither shabby nor noble. He was of average size, and had the general look of friendliness about him. I wagged my tail, in the hope he would offer me a sweet as most strangers liked to do. I have already told you that I like to talk to strangers. He turned to another, larger man, who was nearby, and said, "Now, Fred, this 'ere is the perfec' example of wot I was tellin' ya abowt. Stry mongrels runnin' lewse in our city, when they should 'ave an 'ome to go to, and two squares a die."

I waited patiently for a sweet.

Fred looked at me, and said, "I fink you are wrong there, Bill. This 'ere dog doesn't look in the leas' bit starved. In fact, it looks like it knows where it's goin'. Ee's just off on a lark."

Looking ever so proud, 'Average Bill' then took out a small notebook from his trews pocket, as well as a stubby bit of pencil, which he gingerly dabbed at the tip of his tongue. I was disappointed that there was no peppermint or humbug forthcoming. Holding his little notebook in front of himself, with the dampened pencil poised in mid-air, he said, "Today, Fred, I 'ave been writin' an article for the *News* about such dogs. Ain't I lucky that this one 'ere has cum alon' just in toime. It can go into m' story and be printed in t'morrow's piper."

What on earth were they talking about? *"Piper? Newspaper? Me? Well, I nivver!"*

Bill came over and stroked my head, looking me over with a grim set to his jaw. He found my collar and read the inscription on the brass name-plate.

"Shales, my dog, I'm goin' a write about you. T'morrow all of London'll read about you."

He didn't let go of my collar. Instead, he tied a short piece of rope to it, one that had been given to him by Fred, who just happened to have had it in his coat pocket. Wasn't it just my luck? The next thing I knew, 'Average Bill' was leading me away down Fleet Street, and in the wrong direction. I heard words such as, "...drop 'im off on m' way 'ome," and then, "This'll keep 'im safe, he bein' a luffly dog, an' all."

Oh, bloody Hell! What had I created for myself now? Blast! Blast and more blast! I fully realised that once I was in the hands of a person, tied to

346

them with a bit of rope, I had to go where *they* went, and so on. We went further down Fleet Street, which was in the opposite direction from the The Monument or even Cannon Street Station. I started to worry. What could I do now? I thought to myself, *"Shales, yer a gormless idiot and daft as a brush. Thou canst only blame thissen."*

* * *

Shales sees St Paul's Cathedral.

As it turned out, I couldn't do anything but follow where I was led. We did take an Underground train to a station called Waterloo, but I had never heard of it before, so I had absolutely no idea, no reckoning, of where it was or where we were going to. I had the horrible sensation of being lost. There, at Waterloo, we changed to an above-ground train, where the outside view from the window was strange and alien. The day had become rather long. The sun was lowering itself in the sky, and my tummy was rumbling.

After we disembarked we did a fair bit of walking, then Bill led me into a building, and from behind closed doors I could hear the sounds of other dogs: barking dogs, dogs in the state of panic and upset. An explanation was given to a very nice lady about my appearance in London, and with that, I was marched off quick-like, through a doorway, and placed in a small inside area, similar to a kennel. A short time later someone quickly opened my door and shoved in two bowls, one filled with water and one with dinner, which was a type of meat stew. Being both hungry and thirsty, I tucked in, and when finished, I realised I would be spending the night in this place, and also that my family would be searching all of Hackney for me when they arrived home and discovered I was not in the garden at all. I hoped Armstrong and the cook would not get the blame for my disappearance.

Well, I have to tell you I was in that place for a few days, four days to be exact. Four whole days of thinking that I would never go home again. I was absolutely miserable. I wondered what would happen to me, and to the others as well. The nice people who cared for us in that place were wonderful, but none of us dogs understood why we were there. There were moggies there as well. Some of them were in a horrible state of being. Many were half-starved, but not from being in that place. They had been starving because they'd lived off the streets and food was scarce to find, they having to compete with the rats. A situation I was sympathetic to, having sampled its sparse cuisine and dangerous elements only a few years previously.

We were all kept in large wood-and-wire cages, with yesterday's newspapers spread out on the floor for us, to use for obvious reasons. There was a dog across from me who was a rather friendly sort. We got on, and had a few good hours spent in the art of conversation. He could speak rather well, and he was smaller than me and was browner in colour; not quite black, whereas I'm black with white. He called himself Nat, and he had lovely, sad, brown eyes. He had been in that place a long time, weeks he had said, and when I asked him what was to happen to him, he had replied:

"Oi'm whiting for a famlee to come by an' chewse me. Then I'll 'ave an 'ome; for the firwst toime in moy life I'll 'ave a proper 'ome, Shales."

I wondered if this would happen to me. What would I do if a strange family took me away? Would I stay with them or would I attempt to go home to Hackney? I decided that every possible attempt to get to my true home would be made, even if I had to perform some sort of daring escape.

In this place, this gaol, I had ample time to reflect upon the years Life had so far dealt me. After observing and conversing with some of the others there – I'd had it good. I knew that. The others had no idea of the luxurious life I had so far led, and I felt rather a bit guilty but there was nothing I could do for them. Whilst there, we were all in cages, and every one of us waited with the expectation of being rescued. Especially me.

On the fourth day I became aware that someone had come in from the street and was conversing with the lady who was in charge of this place. I strained my ears, mostly out of boredom, but also because I had hoped that I would be rescued, or perhaps that man Bill would come back and take me back to Fleet Street, letting me go so that I could find my own way home. I did have hopes that that would happen. It didn't. In straining my ears, I thought I recognised the voice. Snatches of the conversation filtered through the walls to me. I had definitely heard my name mentioned.

I heard "Shales...? That one... yes... four days now... a contribution... be appreciated." It was the voice of the lady in charge.

Then I heard "...fetch him now?"

It was Edmund's voice. I was sure of it! Edmund! Edmund was here!

I started to bark and to paw at the bars. I was terrified he would leave without me! My mind screamed out to him, *"Edmund, 'ere I am. Over 'ere!"* I thought to myself, *"Please, Edmund, don't go. Please don't leave me 'ere. Please tek me 'ome!"*

It seemed like ages passed, and the door to the room did not open, and Edmund did not walk through it. Deflated, I hung my head, whimpered and keened, fully believing he had left without me. I thought, *"That's it now; 'e's gone, and I'll 'ave to stay 'ere furever."*

Eventually, I fell asleep.

I was wakened when someone came into the room, and the other dogs all barked and whined as if they were going mad.

The sound was deafening.

It was Bedlam.

Every one of them was screaming, *"Hoy! Me, me."*

Edmund was standing there; always handsome, well-dressed Edmund, and I was never so relieved to see my lead held in his hand, either before or since that moment. My lead meant only one thing: I was going home; I was rescued. He opened the door to my cage and hugged me tightly, kissing me on my head before he attached the lead to my collar. Then he said, "Come on, you. Time to go home. Yes, Shales. You're going home now."

I was so relieved to leave that place, but at the same time I felt guilty, as I was going home to a lovely place with a lovely family, whereas some of the others back there would remain at the Battersea Home a very long time.

Over my shoulder I shouted out, *"Ta-ra, Nat. Good luck!"*

In reply, I heard, *"Huwwrah fowr Shales! E'es been rescued!"* Nat was cheering me on.

Lovely.

* * *

So, how did Edmund know where to find me? Why did it take him four whole days before he rescued me? Was I left there on purpose in order to teach me a lesson? Well, apparently, it is quite the story, and what I know of it I shall tell you now. It starts with Bill; remember, he said he was writing an article, a story, to appear in the next day's newspaper? It was for the *Illustrated London News*, and this is what was printed:

> *Complaints abound concerning the quantity of stray and homeless dogs about London. Genuine concern for these abandoned or lost creatures is the reason why*

*a movement is at hand to capture and round up these
creatures of God – many ending up in Battersea, where
there is a programme to rehabilitate these individuals,
and release them to homes that will provide a comfortable
and responsible atmosphere for them. This is not a new
idea, it being first started in 1860 by Mrs. Mary Tealby,
who strives to have the animals, cats included, re-housed;
and not one shall be destroyed, no matter how long it
takes to find it an eventual home.*

*I came upon one, myself, just yesterday, in Fleet
Street. The dog, a healthy specimen of a sheepdog, with
its characteristic black and white markings, was running
loose without any sign of its master or mistress in sight.
The intelligent chap was trotting down Fleet Street as if he
knew his way, and perhaps he did; but, as a responsible
citizen of London, I found I could not leave this dog to
roam about freely. I noticed he was wearing a collar, a
black one, made of good quality leather, and upon it a
brass plate with the dog's name clearly engraved upon it.
The name is Shales. This dog now resides at The Dogs'
Home in Battersea, and awaits his master to come and
free him. Perhaps his master's identity is known to any of
the readers of this paper, and who, I am sure, will inform
said person of the whereabouts of his lost dog.*

As it happened, that particular story was not read by any of my
family, though the rest of the newspaper had been read and passed along
from person to person, and when the last one to read it had finished, it was
placed in the pile normally set aside for burning. My fate had been literally
held within their hands! They had passed me over without even knowing I
was there. They, who were frantic about my whereabouts, and had gone in
search for me up and down the streets and roads of Hackney St John, South
Hackney, Hackney Proper, Homerton, Clapton, and Kingsland, as well as
West Hackney; all these places being parishes of Hackney. And, they even

went as far as Stoke Newington to look for me, where Maud and the Foster family resided. Edmund and Charles, both mounted, had spent hours in the saddle searching for me, whilst their sisters had ridden about in cabs, and asked other cabbies if they had seen a dog like me. They feared I had been stolen, and during those times it was popular for dogs to be held to ransom. After the second day of my disappearance, with no ransom note delivered, an advertisement had been placed in the lost column of all the city's newspapers, advertising an unnamed, handsome reward for my safe return, but no honest citizen had responded.

It is indeed curious how things happen. Our old friend and distant relation, Stanley, the one who was the painter, was also an illustrator for that same newspaper. In a roundabout way he had heard that I was missing. He had been looking through that publication, printed three days earlier, in search for one of his own published illustrations, when the article about the lost dogs in London caught his eye. He read the entire article from beginning to end, and he knew full well the identity of the dog *Shales*. Stanley was my saviour. He then caught the next train from where he lived, in Brixton, and went directly to the house in Darnley Road.

Armstrong took his hat, gloves, coat, etc., and ushered him into the drawing-room, where the family was letting their evening dinners go down. Once inside and comfortably seated in the same room, he then pulled out the copy of that paper from under his arm and said, "Did you get your dog back? I don't see Shales anywhere, and he usually greets me at the door."

When the sad response from everyone was a firm "no", and he was given an explanation about my being missing, he then said to Augustus, "Read this. You'll find it somewhat interesting."

By the time Augustus had reached the end of the story, he was excited and shouted out, "He's safe; he's in The Dogs' Home!"

There were sighs of relief, and the paper was passed about with exclamations of "Oh, I passed this story over" to "I didn't even notice that article on the dogs".

Stanley was their hero. He had been the reason for my being found. That next morning Edmund took time away from the coal business, and after catching several trains he eventually arrived in Battersea, with every intention of not leaving without me.

He had been shown about the premises of the Dogs' Home, and as he was obviously a gentleman, had been offered tea and a full explanation about the charitable work done there. In deepest gratitude my family provided a very handsome contribution, to add to the funds providing care for the dogs and moggies, along with promises of future contributions to come.

Upon my return home after a rather lengthy journey I was hugged and cried upon by all, even by the servants, and told to never leave the garden again. They still had no notion as to how I managed to get to Fleet Street! I didn't even begin to try to tell them, knowing it would be useless, but also that if they cottoned on to the fact that I could catch a train on my own I really would have been in trouble. So ends another rather exciting chapter of my life.

XXII
MY FLING WITH FLORRIE

"Boys o' boys, mmn, mmn, mmn."

1888

LOVE IS A PECULIAR THING, especially when it arrives in the form of a beautiful, four-legged variety, positively female and living just down the road at the local pub. She was brand-new to the vicinity, and I spotted her when Edmund had taken me along to the pub one Saturday. In all actuality, he had taken me out for a long walk, and we had found ourselves a long way down Darnley Road, and with Edmund feeling a savage thirst come upon himself, he had decided to enter the pub known as the Duke of Devonshire. It was one of those times when the men gathered at the bar, drink in hand amidst clouds of thick cigar smoke, and they hobnobbed over travel, finances and the newspapers. It was something I used to do with Thomas, in and around Ongar and Stanford Rivers, so I quite liked the atmosphere of the dark-timbered room with the low ceiling and horse brasses adorning the many black beams, with laughter, clinking glasses and the smell of stale ale and tobacco smoke in the background.

On this particular occasion I was stretched out at Edmund's feet, half asleep, when another dog strolled past me. Hey up! It was indeed a female dog, and she was *beautiful*. She was the colour of driven snow, and her size was about the same as mine or a bit shorter, but she was slim with very long legs. Her head was small and delicate. Her name was Florrie. I never found out much more about her, other than her name and that she had just recently moved into the Duke of Devonshire, her master being the publican. She was lacking in the art of conversation. Sadly, she was a thick as two short planks, as lush as a desert, as smart as a box of pencils, and as bright as an unlit match. However, after reviewing her mental capacity, or rather lack of it, I should say she was still lovely to look at. We had very few conversations due to the above-mentioned, but we did have one thing in common, that being the true feeling of *love*. Boys o' boys, mmn, mmn, mmn.

After just that one meeting I arranged with her to meet me on such and such a day at the back of my garden wall. In other words, we were to have a secret assignation, and as I had invited her on a foot tour of Hackney I was to be her personal guide. Florrie was the reason why I attempted to escape from the garden, yet again, after the Battersea incident. Yes, I was going over the wall like I usually did, and the fact that I had been mangled by the wheel of a passing cab, a year and a half previously, did not prevent me from getting a good launch at it. One good calculated leap and I sprang forth like a cannon-ball aimed at a French ship, and I landed tipsy-like on the very top, and I nearly fell off. I was up there, though, crouched low and catching my balance at about six feet up in the air. On this particular day I knew she was supposed to be there on the other side waiting for me, and yes, when I looked down, there she was, sitting like a pretty little Staffordshire ornament, looking up at me with her large brown eyes. Obviously, she had not got lost on the way, it being a reasonable distance between my house and number seventy-two (the pub). I told her to, "*Keep yer head down,*" as we crept along behind the stable and jumped through the railings of the fence, and then came out onto Devonshire Road.

No words were spoken. She didn't offer any, so I set off in the direction of Victoria Park, with her trotting closely behind me. It was a good day, as the sun was out and the streets were dry, and there was just enough of a breeze upon the air to cool us down. I did all the talking and she did all the listening. I just hoped she wasn't deaf as well as dumb. I told her all the local history as I had come to learn it. I took her to the park, it being a fair distance from our road, and named after our great Queen, Victoria. It was nearly three hundred acres in size, and it had a boating lake and a bathing lake in it. It was a quiet day, with there not being many people there, as it was mid-week. We paddled about the water, rested, and slaked our thirsts before setting off again. I purposely avoided taking her near to where our coal warehouse and stables were situated, in the event I would be spotted by one of the men and my delinquency reported, as I was well known to them. I also had to avoid the area on Mare Street where Mr Peppermint lived, as he would definitely tell on me again if he saw me running loose. I thought a look at the River Lea would be nice, but once there she wasn't taken with the cargo-laden boats. Some of them were nicely painted and fascinating to watch as they quietly floated upon the water, towed by draught horses. I took Florrie to Church Street and showed her the Town Hall and several other institutions in that street, as well as pointing out to her that the Knights Templar were supposed to have had a mansion there, as the land round about had belonged to them many centuries before.

Florrie just looked. She asked no questions, so thinking she wasn't impressed with the local sights, I had one last place to take her to. I then showed her the railway station, managing to get both of us onto the platform without being noticed. I pointed out the various interesting aspects of the steam locomotive, and attempted to describe what it was like to be onboard a train travelling along at vast speeds, but when one noisily pulled into the station she shot off like a hare, and I had to chase after her, through the station, dodging people left and right and out into the street. The sight and sounds of the smoke-spewing behemoth had sent her into a sudden state of panic, one that I did sympathise with. Once I got her calmed down – she had drooled excessively and had shivered like a terrified bird – I led her home, leaving her at the back door of the pub with the promise to never take her to the station again. She was exhausted – we had covered a lot of ground. I thought that overall it had been a successful day, and rather interesting, although a bit quiet, and I was still in love with her.

She finally spoke, saying, *"Fank you, Shiles."*

I thought to myself, *"Boys o' boys, mmn, mmn, mmn."* Then I trotted off home.

After that day we went off together quite often. There was more opportunity than before, because I went to work with the men less often, perhaps only one or two days a week – the women had promised to, and did, take me out places. I got rather cocky about my wanderings with Florrie. It was my secret. Nobody in the family knew what I had been up to. I only left the confines of the garden when I knew I wouldn't be missed, and I was so careful, that I practically felt free of guilt.

* * *

THE WEEKS OF ROMANTIC BLISS PASSED BY, but my family was important to me, as well as my having that nosy habit of wanting to always know what was going on, so I took notice whenever Charles started going out every Saturday and Sunday, smartly dressed with his hair plastered down with Macassar oil, and smelling nice and clean after his rather long baths. I wondered what he was up to. I didn't think he was going to his club, as when he went there he usually mentioned it beforehand as part of the general conversation over the evening meal. This seemed more like a secret assignation, and I knew all about those. We didn't have to wait long to find out about his recent activities. He broke the news over Sunday dinner. They were just starting to eat their roast beef, with all the usual trimmings, when he nervously blurted, "Em. I met a rather very lovely lady the other week."

When I heard him say this, I cocked my ears so that I could better hear from where I lay (beneath the large table amidst a clutter of chair legs, ankles and shoes, and the hems of ladies dresses). I then crawled out from beneath the table, and toddled over and sat just off to the side, from whence I had a good vantage point of the diners' faces.

I knew it was going to be good.

Charles had stopped eating. Knife and fork were poised mid-air, and he just looked at everyone, waiting for their responses. He looked rather frightened, as if he thought his family were going to pounce on him, or something like that. Smiles appeared on almost everyone's faces, and I could sense a teasing incident coming on.

"Why, Charlie!" A surprised Edmund was the first to speak. He leaned forward and gently punched his brother on the arm. "I say. You are full of surprises."

Jessie then had her say. "Edmund, isn't it about time that Charles found someone?" She continued intelligently, "We have been hoping it would happen sooner or later."

Charles pointed out, "I have only just met her, so don't you sisters of mine start planning any weddings just yet. I'll have to disappoint you there." His face was flushed and so was his neck, which was a shade short of beet red.

Both Julia and Lucy were pleased for their youngest brother, and wanted to know when his lady friend would be introduced to them. Charles was quite embarrassed from all the attention, and especially since, I think, it was because this was his first female companion.

"Please don't make anything of it," pleaded Charles, as he sputtered with cheeks glowing red. "I don't really know her yet." He looked like he was ready to bolt.

"So, *she* is the reason you have been preening yourself," said a smiling Jessie. " I knew you were up to something."

Augustus, ever so much the father of the family, finally managed to interrupt. "It's only natural you'll meet a lady friend. Just be careful, Charlie lad, and always remember you are a gentleman, even though you happen to be working in a tailor's shop and bringing home a wage." He warned his son with gentle words, evidently not wanting to be disappointed by his youngest son's behaviour.

A very serious Charles said, "I know. It's just that I want to be sure of her, before I introduce her to you."

His father then suggested, as he cut into his meat, "As a gentleman, you have your own reputation to protect. Let's not forget what Thomas did." He was reminding Charles of what had happened just a few years prior.

"I know, and Dad... I remember... and don't worry, I'll not do that."

Jessie offered, "Why don't you invite her along for tea on Saturday, if that isn't too soon. Make it clear to her, first, that it is just tea, and she doesn't have to feel that she is accepting any sort of a marriage proposal by accepting. All right, Dad?"

Augustus nodded. "Her family has to know she is coming, as she needs their permission."

Charlie said, "She might refuse. She could say 'no' and ask me never to speak to her again." He paused and looked around at his family, seated at the table, only half interested in their food. "There's just a little matter, of the fact that she is older than myself."

Everyone seemed to be in agreement that an age difference didn't matter, though, in most relationships, the man was generally older than the woman.

Maud was dining with us on that particular night – a rare occasion. Offering Charles some support she said, "Az long as yew dorn't tell her stories of how frightening we are, I reckun she'll come. After all, we are a respectable family." Then she smiled as she carefully said, "Please do tell us all about her, Charles." And then, "I think it's all rather exciting."

Augustus agreed with Maud. "We *are* respectable, and don't you forget that, lad."

He then asked Maud if she would be there for tea on Saturday, as well as Mary Matilda. It was an opportunity to see his granddaughter.

"I am gorn to be here. I wouldn't miss it for northing."

So there it was. Charles was in love! Boys o' boys, mmn, mmn, mmn.

* * *

SATURDAY ARRIVED, and in the morning our wonderful cook made heaps of fresh egg and cress sandwiches, and baked cakes and fruit pies, enough to feed a small army. The sitting-room, dining-room, library and drawing-room were cleaned, and the carpets were swept in an effort to rid them of my dog hair. The young maid-of-all we had taken on two years previously was crouched on her hands and knees, with wisps of dark hair escaping from her mob-cap as she scraped at the Brussels carpets with a brush and said, "Crikey! Cor blimey! I 'ope this 'ere young lady isn't frightened o' dogs, but most of awl, that she don't notice the dog 'air. Surely she is goin' to get some 'air on 'er skirts!"

My shedding of dog hairs was a passionate topic throughout the house. Everyone loved me; I know they did, but they hated my hairs! I admit the stuff got everywhere and it was hard to clean up. Jessie spent many a time trying out new inventions that promised to pick up dog and cat hairs. I think the best item she had close at hand was a sack full of rather large teazles, those prickly things used in cloth mills. These she would somehow sew together in a bunch, and scrape them down the front of her dress etc., thus removing any unwanted dog hair. She vowed they worked better than a clothes brush. Thing was, I had to keep my distance from those things – I once tossed the interesting-looking sack about and ended up being covered in clumps of teazles. Jessie was not pleased, and neither was I, when she grabbed her sewing scissors and cut them free, my tail and trews shorn considerably shorter than normal.

At half-past three in the afternoon the young Charles Clement arrived with his lady friend. Introductions were made, and she was very nice to me, obviously having been warned ahead by Charles that there was a family dog to be included at teatime. Her name was Amy Oswald, and she was quite pretty, with very dark hair, as well as being well spoken. Like Jessie and her sisters, Amy had received a good education, but *her* family wasn't wealthy, nor were they middle class. Her father, John, was employed at a foundry, and Amy was, in fact, a schoolteacher. She was also an older woman, not younger than our Charles but, in fact, about four or five years older – a bit too much older in Augustus's opinion. He'd had a change of mind.

When Charles escorted Amy home to another part of Hackney, the comments in our house were rife! Although they liked Amy, the general conclusion was that if Charles was in love, then he would still be in love with Amy a couple of years from now; if not, then the relationship would fizzle out and perhaps he would then find another young lady. Augustus did point out that because Charles had left the family business and was now employed in a tailor's shop, his chances of meeting a woman from a very respectable family, and with a dowry, were somewhat diminished, and that he would have to set his sights lower, or like Edmund and his sisters, remain happily unattached. I oft-times wondered about Edmund. I haven't mentioned it before, but he had a lady friend hidden away somewhere. I know, because there were times I could smell her on his clothes.

I am sure Maud had her own personal opinions, as I saw the look on her face when it was revealed that Amy was a schoolteacher. The look spoke volumes: mainly that she thought it funny, in a malicious sort of way, that Charles had brought home a schoolteacher, whereas Maud herself had, in fact, been a dressmaker, which has always been considered a lowly occupation.

I'm just reminding you of how things were back then. I had one thing to say about Charles: at least he had been open and honest with his family, and had introduced Amy to them properly; whereas Maud and Thomas had had secret liaisons, of sorts, in Stoke Newington, resulting in the quick preparations for their wedding, and Thomas coming very close to being disinherited.

So, how had Amy and Charles met? I know how they met, and I suppose you want *me* to tell *you* all about it. Well, let's see. I overheard enough to piece it all together, and it goes something like this: apparently, they passed each other in the street quite often as he went to work at the tailor's shop, and she went to the school where she taught. One day in particular, Charles had stopped at a sweet shop to purchase some humbugs, or mints, and in coming out of the shop had accidentally collided with Amy, sending sweets scattering across the pavement and school papers fluttering away on the breeze. Ample apologies were made amongst shy recognitions, resulting in the exchange of their forenames, or as we usually say, Christian names. The rest is, as we say, 'history', as after that event they always spoke and acknowledged each other whenever they crossed paths, and a slow-forming friendship was forged. In the proper fashion, Charles had already met Amy's family, and his meeting *their* approval resulted in Amy's invitation to tea at our house. It was Florrie and me all over again! "Boys o' boys! Mmn, mmn, mmn."

*　*　*

CHARLES WAS POSITIVELY IN LOVE WITH AMY, and I was in love with Florrie. Something happened though, and I didn't see her for quite a few weeks. I didn't even know if she was still living at the pub, or if something dreadful had befallen her – the roads could be very dangerous and horse-drawn wagons and carriages did not always stop for a dog, don't I know it, let alone a slow-moving lady. People and dogs got run over all the time; it was an everyday occurrence in certain areas of Hackney, as well as in the rest of England, and my left hind leg hurt just thinking about it. I ached to find out about her, but I had no way of knowing her whereabouts. I suspected she was still at the pub, but I couldn't find any sign of her there on the few times I was able to run down there, have a quick sniff around, and swiftly run back to the garden before being seen. I was afraid one of the maids would see me running down the road from any of our upstairs windows, as she washed the panes and straightened the curtains, or someone else should they happen to be peering out of a window, 'twitching' their curtains. It was as if Florrie had just disappeared.

One evening, the mystery regarding Florrie's whereabouts was revealed to us. Edmund had been in the Duke of Devonshire this particular evening, and when he came home he called for a family meeting to convene, immediately. He said there was something of the utmost importance to be said. He warned that he didn't think anyone would believe him.

Jessie couldn't wait, "Come on, Edmund, I can see you are dying to tell us something."

Edmund looked about the room. They were all there, including Augustus, who looked very comfortable in his slippers and smoking jacket. Edmund laughed, "You are simply not going to believe this!"

I was dying to hear what was so interesting. *"Oh, cum on, Edmund,"* I thought, *"tell us. 'Urry it up. I want to know, too."*

So, Edmund looked directly at me, and then said, "You're not going to believe this, but it seems that Shales here has sired a litter of puppies, with the dog from the pub, here, in Darnley Road. Once again, he's been in high jinks."

"Well! I nivver! Sired a litter of puppies? Me?" I had to think about that. Now, what had I done to deserve this accusation? I really didn't know. I honestly didn't think I had done anything wrong or out of the ordinary that I hadn't done before.

Mouths were agape. They all looked at me with various expressions on their faces, but mostly they thought it incredible.

Charles burst out laughing. "I'm sorry, Edmund, but it is so hilarious! When has Shales been able to do what he has been accused of doing? When he's been with you at the bar, in full view of everyone?"

Lucy slapped her younger brother on his arm, saying, "Charles! That is positively disgusting! Don't be vulgar."

Julia thought to ask, "How do you know it is Shales who is responsible? I mean, really, how do you know?"

Augustus chimed in, "Here, here. Julia is correct. How do you know for sure it is Shales before we go and accuse him of running free around Hackney again? He hasn't been truant at all."

Edmund smiled and said, "Well, because when I heard the publican's dog had had a litter of puppies, I politely enquired as to their breeding etc. I was told they didn't know the dog responsible, but that it must have had a lot of black in it, because all the puppies are black and white. So, I thought this was suspicious, thinking of Shales, and I asked if I could see the puppies. I was merely curious and wanted to see if they resembled Shales at all. They were delighted to show me all four of them, probably hoping I would take one home with me. They all four look like him!" And with that, Edmund pointed his finger at me, accusing me of the unwanted deed.

Lucy actually asked a good question, when she said, "But, Edmund, there are many black dogs in this neighbourhood. We see them every time we leave the house, and there are some running loose over Cassland Road way as well as in our own neighbourhood. Why accuse Shales, when you haven't even been aware he has escaped the confines of the garden again? Unless he has got away whilst he has been at the warehouse with you men, and has spent time wandering about Hackney, and *you* haven't known it. Or have you?"

"A very good point," replied Edmund, as he casually stood leaning against the mantelpiece. "No, he has not been a vagabond when he has been under *our* care." He continued talking as he seated himself in an easy chair, and proceeded to light up a cigar.

"The reason I know it is Shales who is responsible, is because all four puppies have the markings of a collie, like himself, but especially since one of them also has two little white dots for eyebrows. This puppy is the spitting image of our dog. Besides, the publican did mention that he had seen Shales sniffing about the pub, even though that was after his dog had had her litter of puppies."

I listened to all this banter going back and forth and wondered how it would affect me. Was I deep in trouble? Was I to be punished, and if so, how? I realised I had probably seen the last of Florrie for at least a long while, and perhaps that was not such a bad thing after all.

The conversation then led to how had I got away with it, without my presence being missed? They decided that I had *gone over the wall* again, and that it should be raised in height to prevent any further attempts of escape. They were concerned about my safety, and I did understand all of it, as I had been caught running loose along Fleet Street last year and had spent four days in the Dogs' Home in Battersea. That event had frightened me out of my wits, but this time it was different. This time I had been in my own neighbourhood, and I had always known where I was, at every moment. Hadn't I?

Augustus sighed, rubbed his tired eyes, and said, "He is as much trouble as Thomas ever was. We'll get the masons in this week and add a foot or so to the wall. That should keep him in." He sighed loudly, "He can start coming to work again, more frequently, if it will keep him out of trouble."

Charles said, "I wish I could see him when he jumps over, just to see how he does it. And, don't forget, he always manages to get back over and pretend he's never been gone. It's as if he plans it all out in his head and knows he has to return by a certain time, otherwise he will be missed. He must be the canniest dog in the country."

My elderly master was concerned about my safe-being. "I shouldn't think he could do it, what with him breaking his leg nearly two years ago. Gallivanting about Hackney will be the death of him one of these days."

Lucy quickly stepped in. "Perhaps he needs a companion here at home; one of his own pups? He might like that."

This question, or suggestion, nearly brought down the house.

"No! No!"

"No more dogs!"

"Why not?"

"One at a time is enough," spoke my master.

Edmund stuck up for me. "I've got so used to having him around, and he is such a gentle and happy creature that I'll miss him if he ever goes. Well, I think you know what I mean."

"Yes, I know what you mean by that," said his father. "It'll be a sad day when he is gone from us."

They all agreed to this, the atmosphere not exactly glum but thoughtful, as they all looked at me. I decided it was time to go to bed, so I very politely got up from my spot beneath the table where I had been lying, and I slowly walked out of the drawing-room, dragging my feet as I left, and plodded up the large staircase to bed. Tomorrow would be another day, and by then they would have forgotten all about Florrie and the puppies, as well as my future death.

* * *

THE PUPPIES, *MY* PUPPIES, WERE GIVEN AWAY. I never saw them, but I would have liked to have seen them, just the once. Florrie was kept at her home on a *short lead,* so I only ever saw her occasionally, when either Edmund or Charles took me to the pub with them. Motherhood had done nothing to increase her mental capacity, and months later I wondered why her presence had excited me so much. I think I fell out of love with her, pretty thing though she was.

At that point, I had thought I would always remember 1888 as the year that I had flirted with the dog from the pub and got caught. I would associate it with my age, as I was nearly nine years old.

XXIII

JACK

*Psalm 22-13. They gaped upon me with
their mouths, as a ravening and a roaring
lion.*

END SUMMER, 1888

I HAD ALREADY THOUGHT **1888** WAS AN EVENTFUL YEAR. It was not yet over, although my Battersea fright and my amorous liaisons with Florrie were over, well behind me, and far into the past, leaving the quiet months of late summer and early autumn to slip by unnoticed and uneventful. What happened next, from those hot and lazy summer days and into the following year, could never have been imagined either by me, or by the good and honest citizens of London in a thousand years. How could anyone have thought that human nature could create a rent in the fabric of time, where reality appeared to be suspended, and what should have remained unreal became actual reality, as if the entire city was turned topsy-turvy.

You have no idea, do you? Dear Reader, you don't know what I'm alluding to, but just stop and think for a moment, because you have all heard of those terrifying days of the latter part of 1888 and into 1889. Remember the murders? Even I knew all about it; in fact, too much. I couldn't help but know, as Augustus, Edmund, Charles Clement or one of the sisters would read out loud for all to hear the horrifying articles from the newspapers, as they appeared, going from one paper to the next and comparing them, all of us keeping track and wondering who the murderer could be. He was known as the Whitechapel Murderer because of the location of his murderous sites, but then he had sent letters to the police and had signed them *Jack the*

Ripper. He frightened the sisters (Maud included) as well as the servants, so that they only left the house in the daylight hours, and never alone, even though the murders had not taken place near Hackney, and had always been committed after dark. Maud expressed fear, in that she lived at the boarding house, which was at times vacant of a man's presence, leaving herself, Mary Matilda, Charlotte and Mary Ann Moore vulnerable to this sort of attack by mad, murderous criminals, and with no man close by to protect them.

The events unfolded this way. In early August the body of a woman was found. She had been stabbed to death with thirty-nine stab wounds in her body, near Whitechapel High Street. And then there was another one. Charles Clement read the article about this one from the *Daily News* as we were having afternoon tea. Whilst the sisters were delicately nibbling their biscuits and sipping their cups of tea, he read these unpleasant words: "'...the body of a woman lying in a pool of blood on the first floor landing.'" Then he said, "Well, I never!" He put down the paper and took a sip of his tea, and then said, "You don't suppose these two murders are in any way related, do you?"

Jessie answered, "How am I supposed to know that, Charles?" And then she eagerly asked, "What does it say about the police? Do they suspect anyone?"

He answered slowly as he searched about the paper, the pages needing to be folded in some sort of order. "No. It just says here... that they are working on the cases and are making enquiries."

Although we were having afternoon tea, and the grisly subject wasn't fit for discussion at that moment, the family soon found themselves caught up in the excitement of horrible murders and stories of horrible deeds, done long ago in the past, retold by Augustus, as he remembered such stories told to himself and his brothers by his father and his grandfather Rowland, and also of ones he had read about in various newspapers over the years.

On the first day of September Edmund held up a copy of the *Daily News*. He had picked it from the pile first before anyone else could read it, there being several other newspapers waiting to be read, and he read for all of us to hear in a matter-of-fact voice: "'Shortly before four o'clock, Police Constable Neil found a woman lying in Buck's Row, Thomas Street, with her throat cut from ear to ear.'" And then more emotionally, "'The body was fearfully mutilated.'"

"God protect us!" exclaimed Julia and Lucy, both at the same time. Julia then said, "There must be a maniac on the loose!" And then, "I fear we shall be murdered in our beds! I don't think I can take any more of this! I want to get away from here and go to Cotheridge!"

"Really?" said Edmund in an enquiring voice. "Why do you suppose this *maniac* will want to come to our house?" Then on a serious note he said, "After all, these women that have so far been murdered are of the lower sort, and not our kind at all. I think you ladies shall be safe here in Hackney. What do you say to this, Father?"

Up until this point Augustus had been quiet, but he soon caught the thread of conversation and eagerly added to it.

"I do think Edmund is correct. These murders are being committed in the poorer parts of London, not here about Hackney, but I do think... I do say that from now on you ladies do not go out of this house alone and unaccompanied, and I would rather Edmund or Charles go with you, if I am unable to do so, especially in the evenings."

Lucy spoke up, but I could tell that she was frightened. "I'm sure we'll be all right, but it would be a sensible idea for us women to stay together when we go out of the house, even in the daytime."

Jessie wanted to know where Thomas Street was, and her father replied, "You can find it on a map; Whitechapel, I think, but it isn't a place where you would ever need to go to."

"Do we have a map of London and all the surrounding boroughs?" She asked this of no one in particular.

Charles Clement replied, "Yes, it's in that rather large brown book, on the bottom shelf near the volumes on London history. I know, because I was only looking at it a few months ago. It's old, but the streets are the same. Also, in the drawer of the large table there is another old map, and I believe it is mixed in with the ones of Africa and Asia."

So with that the element of fear had been introduced, resulting in the frightened demeanour of the sisters, not to mention the female servants who also kept up with the latest on the Whitechapel murders. Curiosity as to the locations of the murders got to them as well; they were intrigued about Whitechapel, having never been there. They, too, were frightened, and I'm sure just as everyone else who lived in or about London.

* * *

THERE WAS YET AGAIN ANOTHER MURDER, at the end of the first week of September. Augustus read the article to himself from the *Star*, before passing it over to Edmund, who asked if the rest of them wanted him to read it out loud. They nodded their heads, answering in the affirmative.

"'London lies today under the spell of a great terror. A man half-beast, half-man is at large.'" Then he read, "'The Whitechapel Murderer, who has now four if not five victims to his knife, is one man, and that man a murderous maniac.'"

When Edmund had finished, the general opinion of the family was that this was a serious situation, and though we were far removed (by about five miles) from where those murders had been committed, we should act with the utmost diligence and care regarding strangers, and if anyone suspicious were to be seen after dark then they should be reported to the police. Need I say that the hairs bristled on the back of my neck more than once when I went out after dark, in the garden, to do my looing, a place which was as dark as a coal mine, as there weren't any street lamps back there, only a meagre glow cast by the closest lamp situated to us on Darnley Road. Although I could see in the dark, I still found it unnerving. I vowed to keep the family safe, and other than keeping a sharp eye on the front door when anyone called, I didn't know what I could do. Normally, our house was always locked, and the custom was that if any of the family went out and returned, they would knock or ring the bell, and Armstrong would answer the front door and let them inside, they never having to use their key to let themselves in, and naturally so. And, I should say, they all had a different knock. The door at the front of the house was locked, as well as the side door, which led out onto the road, and as well as the door leading down to the kitchen from the outside. This trade entrance was always locked; thus, anyone delivering had to ring a bell and wait for the door to be answered. Knowing this comforted me, and I slept better at night, although I did wonder what I would do if this man did break into our home. Would I have the courage to bite him, good and proper? Like I had done with Eliza? Or would I hide beneath the furniture? I hoped I would never have to find myself in such a situation, even though I had promised I would defend this family I loved so much.

* * *

ON THIS PARTICULAR DAY IT ALL WENT WRONG, but *had* I known when I first got up, or *had* I wondered how the day would end after the normally relaxing hours of a Sunday, I wouldn't have left the house, even if I'd been forced to do so against my will. No, definitely not! I would have stayed home within the safe confines of Number Fifteen, Darnley Road. It all started when the family returned from their church service at St John's, and after I greeted them I decided to go upstairs, to the first floor landing, and settle myself at my favourite window to see what was going on in the road; mainly, if there was anything of interest such as an extravagant carriage or a speeding cab passing by. My awful habit of being a nosy so-and-so caused me to see the apparition of a cat slinking away across the road. I was astounded! Why, it appeared to be Horatio! My brain went into 'mad gallop' and I looked again. My paws scratched against the window-sill as I leaned forward in anticipation. I pressed my wet nose against the immaculately clean pane. Yes! There was a cat that looked just like my friend Horatio Harvest, and knowing Horatio full well, it would be just like him to come all this way to Hackney to see me. As I watched the cat slink away and disappear out of sight, in the direction of Mare Street, I was convinced it was my best friend, and I knew that I had to fetch him and not let him wander away to get lost in this large and greatly populated area of Hackney. He would come after me if he saw me in Essex so, therefore, I would go after him. Oh, my cate, Horatio!

I bounded down the stairs, all two flights of them, and I ran to the kitchen door and did my best *must do my looing* dance in front of the cook. She was rather good at opening the door and letting me outside whenever I asked, so this time I must have done a good impression of being about to burst, as she nearly tripped over herself in her attempt to get to the door quickly enough.

Once it was opened I was out like a shot and turned the corner, running to the back of the garden where I had to breach the wall. At least it was daylight and I could see the top of the wall fair enough. It wouldn't be as easy to do at night. Jump, jump, and then I sprang upwards, and well, you know, I got over easily enough, even though it had recently been raised in height, and I then jumped down to the path below, carefully, as now it really was a long way down from the top, and I landed without making a sound. I ran pell-mell along the back of the terraced houses until I came out onto Mare Street, and then I tried to pick up his scent. I looked down Darnley Road, but he wasn't there. I couldn't find any scent indicating a cat had just wandered down the road, and I started to have my doubts that I'd seen him, so I thought that if I picked up the scent of another cat that was extremely fresh, then I may have been mistaken in my sighting of Horatio, after all. I sniffed and sniffed and sniffed to no avail. I wandered down the pavement alongside Mare Street, heading south, and I must have looked like a right sot to all and sundry as I meandered along from side to side, pausing every now and again to have a second sniff. Nothing. No scent of Horatio or any cat that had recently passed this way. I was quite confused, and in my confusion I didn't realise there was a man walking towards me. I kept sniffing, and he kept walking, until we practically collided, but as he neared me he spoke kind words.

"'Ello. Whoff we go' 'ere?" He reached down to stroke me, so I went up to him hoping to be given a sweet. I wagged my tail, and he petted me no differently than a hundred other strangers had done. He was dressed roughly, as his clothes were well-worn and rather a bit on the odorous side, thus I thought he was not from our part of Hackney but from one of the poorer areas of the neighbourhood, such as where the men lived who worked for my master.

"Luvly dog, ain't ya?" He then quickly clapped onto my collar, and before I could pull away out of his grip he had removed his belt and had slipped it through my collar, holding me tightly. "Oi've plans fow ya. You'll moike me a few bob, righ'ly so."

Hell's bells! I had not learnt a thing from the Fleet Street incident, where previously I had spent four days in the Dogs' Home, and had actually thought I would never see my family again. Now I was in a similar predicament, whereby I was suddenly in the hands of a stranger, and I found myself unable to escape. I pulled at the makeshift lead, but I was held tight. I growled at the man, but that only resulted in my being shaken until my brains shook loose and I felt dizzy. I tried to bite his leg, but his arms were long and he held me at a safe distance from his body. I gave a big, long sigh as I was led away, once again in the opposite direction of my home, my four paws dragging reluctantly upon the pavement.

"Luvly dog, ain't ya?"

At each and every opportunity I protested my capture. I tried to bite this horrible stench of a man on his legs numerous times, but he just held his arm outwards, leaving my teeth several inches short of sinking into his flesh. When he held me out like that it had a choking effect upon me, and I would gag and gasp for air, and then he would lower his arm and I would be obedient, desperately catching my breath and planning my escape. I never did get to escape from him. Eventually, after what seemed like miles of walking, we finished up at a railway station, but which one I do not know, because it was a very long way from my house and he had avoided the omnibuses and cabs whenever they drove past, forcing us to hide out of sight behind numerous bushes and buildings. As I had never been to this station before, I was, to put it simply, lost.

I hate being lost! It is a most frightening experience, and perhaps you can sympathise with me if you too have been in an unfamiliar place, with no going forwards or backwards, as all sense of direction has disappeared completely. It makes one want to cry, although I am sure you will say, "Oh, no, dogs don't cry!" Well let me tell you this. We may not shed tears from our eyes, but we still cry!

Any road, we boarded a train, third-class of course, and I have to give you my comments about the conditions. The coach was dirty, smoky and smelly, as well as being overcrowded with Sunday passengers. Nobody noticed that I had to be dragged aboard and seemed to be in a state of panic. I tried my best to act like a dog about to be butchered, but nobody took any notice. I tried yelping, but he only hit me across my face to shut me up. I shivered and cowered with fright, but everyone seemed to be minding their own business, and I sadly came to the realisation that these people didn't care about other people's dogs. After some time I simply gave in and I saved my energy, reserving it for the first chance of an escape. The train stopped at a station. It was Bethnal Green, and I could have been in Yorkshire for all the good it did me, because I didn't know where we were.

We departed the station rather quickly. I led the way, pulling hard even though I was choking myself, in the event he would let slip the lead and I would be free to go home. He was strong, strong enough to drag me to where I did not want to go.

We travelled down streets I know not where, all strange to me in the late evening gloom, as the sun had set and darkness had fallen, leaving little light to show our way. Occasionally I would see in the distance a street lit by the dim glow of a lamp, but my kidnapper preferred the darker streets and alley ways where, at times, filth was ankle deep. We stopped several times, whereby he had tried to sell me, yes, *sell* me to some other strange person for a pocketful of money. Nobody was interested, neither man nor woman, and after each unsuccessful attempt to get a little richer he set us off in a different direction. Sometimes we returned to the same street, leaving me with the feeling that we were travelling in circles, there being no intelligent sense of direction to his plans.

There was an abundance of people out that night, either walking or standing in doorways and smoking and chattering to each other. They spoke in rhymes and said strange words such as the way Pim, one of the office clerks, spoke. When they saw me, they regarded me with some sort of awe, almost as if they'd never seen a dog before. I was referred to as a "champion sort", or a "forough breed", and they wondered where I had been "nicked" from.

"Runnin' loose down the street, on 'is own plates o' meat. 'Onestly, I says, I ain't tellin' porkies," came the truthful reply from my captor. I couldn't argue with that; after all, I had been running loose down Mare Street, but that didn't give him the legal right to try to flog me. He would have been better off, both of us would have been better off, if he had taken me home and had asked the family for a reward for my safe return. I know they would have paid him well.

He seemed to know every pub in the neighbourhood, but no one was interested in acquiring a dog, they being more interested in their drink. Some of the women tried to get him to spend his money on them, for *favours*, but he wasn't interested, and they shouted their angry insults at him as he dragged me away.

We entered a pub called the Ten Bells, and it was crowded and smoky. The punters were packed in like sardines in a tin, symbolizing smelly, drunken representatives of the human race. He was acquainted with several men who came over to us, and he asked of them, "Have a tiddley?"

As they sat down they asked for "Mother's ruin".

He told them to have a "good butcher's" at me, but they weren't in the least interested and replied, "You tea leafing again?" Now, *butcher's* I understood, but not the reference to tea leaves, until I wondered if it meant thieving. Silly me, I had thought I'd already learnt the local lingo, but apparently I had not.

These geezers weren't interested in buying me, and when the fish man came over with his tray of fried fish, bread, salt, pepper and vinegar they found they were more hungry for food than in the want for a dog. My captor didn't give up, so we left the Ten Bells. It was getting very late and I was thirsty, hungry, and very tired, and not one collop or a crumb of fried fish had been sent my way. I had four sore feet to hold me up. They had never fully recovered from the damage I did to them on my journey from Worcestershire and also in Gorleston, where at the beach they had become sun-baked; they soon became sore and tender. My left hind leg was aching in the spot where it had been broken, and I wondered if it would break on me again, just from being on my feet too long.

We met up with another doubtful person, a geezer, who was well into his cups. He swayed as he stood and regarded me with a large, gummy smile.

"Gimme six shillin's an' 'e's all yors," my captor demanded in a friendly manner.

"Well, Dicky, I ain't seen ya in a lon' toime! Ow are ya, moy china?"

Dicky was the name of my captor. "Fred, you only saw me yes'erday!"

"Well, I niffer! Yes'erday, you say? Dicky, I jus' coin't remem'er back tha' far." Burp... hiccup. "I thought you 'ad yor collar touched."

"Now, Fred, a little dicky-bird. I wasn't collared, and I never saw Ol' Bill. Someone's been telling you porkies."

Fred was swaying on his feet. An impatient Dicky could sense a quick sale, and told his mate a lie. "Fred, you sais you'll buy 'im from me. You jus' did. You jus' agreed."

I was hopeful that sotty Fred would indeed provide the funds needed for me to change hands. In fact, I was very hopeful. I sat rather nicely and looked up at the stinking, wavering, cadaverous body, and in return he peered back at me, and then rather slowly and unsteadily, he reached into his trouser pocket and clumsily pulled out some coins. He looked surprised, as if he hadn't been expecting to find any coins in his pocket at all. He feebly wavered upon unsteady feet as he exhaled noxious fumes of alcohol.

Dicky eagerly said, "I'll count i' for ya, Fred. Old ou' your 'and. Yuv go' two shillin's, an' there's a tanner. And wot're these brass uns?" He went on counting, "Three ha'penni's an' a wole farvin'. That ain't enuff, Fred. Yuv come up short. Wot more do ya 'ave?"

Poor Fred replied mournfully, as he unsteadily pulled his hat from his head, "Well, Dicky, I ain't go' much more. There's m' penknoife an' then there's m' titfer."

"That's luvly, Fred; that'll do jus' foin. I could do w' a new penknoife an' a new titfer."

So, Dicky sold me for the sum of two shillings, sevenpence-ha'penny, and not to forget the farthing, as well as a penknife of unknown value, and a dirty, black, wretched felt hat. Poor Fred. I stood there with Fred holding my makeshift lead and breathing noxious fumes all over me, whilst I waited for him to walk away. He did, setting off with a drunken tug against my lead, and I set off in the opposite direction, resulting in the feet flying out from under Fred, and him falling down with a hard thud upon his flat arse. I tugged again with all my might and felt the lead come loose. I was free!

It was dark where we had been standing, but I ran for someplace yet darker. Dicky had cannily disappeared, whistling a tune as he strode away rather quickly, after pulling one over on his mate. I searched for a safe place to stop and gather my wits, all the while wondering where London City was. This place was strange and unknown to me. I knew that if I could find the city then I would be able to navigate my way home from either of the two Underground stations near the Coal Exchange. Yes, I fully intended on the eventual return home to travel via train. It had been obvious to me at the time that I was in a poor neighbourhood that awakened *after* the dark hours of the day set in, the streets being frequented by bareheaded women, though seldom alone but walking in pairs. The air smelt rank with the odour of wee and stinking privies and middens, which mingled with the scents of cooking food. An odd time of the night to be cooking, I thought. The patrons of these streets and alleys seemed to have urinated against every wall I chanced upon, and refuse and rubbish from their dwellings filled the alleys and yards, and rats abounded freely. What a feast *they* had. The rats. I thought they were probably well fed, as they boasted fat waists and were slow-moving.

Eventually, I crept away in an unknown direction, and happened to turn a corner into a street where I then quickly leapt for the safety of darkness. Even at this late time of night, when children should be tucked up in their beds, there were several of them playing in the street. Or were they playing? It seemed to me as if they were fighting, so violent their play was. Then, the rough sounds they began to make frightened me, and instinctively I turned about the way I had come. I slunk away with those ferocious sounds of play behind me. A woman's voice bellowed at their din, with no regard to the lateness of the hour. One of the children could be heard crying, and its tearful lamentations turned into shrill screams as I put as much distance between that place and myself as I could.

Sometime later, I don't know how long it was, as the time in that horrible place seemed to stand still, I saw a group of men walking towards me. The sight of them made me panic, as I was conscious of the fact that I was still trailing the belt, which was looped through my collar. I ran as fast as I could to the other side of the street, and I shot past them as if the devil himself was after me. Behind me their voices jeered, and I heard the sound of glass breaking, from the bottle they threw at my retreating shadow.

You have to understand just how frightened I was. I was frightened silly. Terrified to the point that I couldn't think rationally. I sensed danger lurking around every corner and inside every shadow, making them darker than they really were. I heard screams, mostly from women, and also there were shouting matches, rows where men seemed to shout at women and the women shouted back at them. It was as if these people were always at each other's throats. I wondered what it would be like in the daylight hours – probably quiet, as everyone would then be asleep, having been up and about all through the nighttime. In a building off to my right the sounds of a shrieking baby could be heard, and above that the loud voice of a man, obviously not pleased with the ear-piercing sounds the baby was making, and just around the corner, dogs were barking, and I assumed them to be mongrels. I did not want to encounter *them*. I suspected they were of the ignorant and starving sort, and I did not want to have to fend them off and possibly be surrounded by a large, hungry pack. All this *uncivilised way of being,* in the overpopulated dwelling houses, was intensified with the cloak of darkness, an inky veil that would not be lifted until the rise of dawn. There was a noticeable shortage of street lamps and police; I wondered where *they* were. In fact, there weren't any lamps, cabs, or policemen at all.

Occasionally I glimpsed the glow created by a candle, as it lit the interiors of various rooms and shed its meagre light onto the cobbles below – tallow. I could smell the rank odour as it seeped out through the open windows. How does one live here and remain sane? My mind was cast back to many years before, when on my journey from Worcestershire to London I had encountered hoards of ignorant cats and packs of vile dogs, and at that time their behaviour had shocked me. I now saw the equivalent in human nature.

I was lost amidst a maze of filthy streets, alleys and courts. I kept on having to retrace my steps, always after turning down, yet again, another street, which led to, yet again, another dead end. I saw no cabbies sitting patiently, waiting for a fare. Perhaps it was too late in the night for them, I wondered, or better still, unsafe. I knew there was always one cabby who would greedily wait for the late night fares without any caring thought to his horse, whose equine legs were tired from a long day's work, because it was a favourite subject of Augustus's. Many times I had heard his harsh criticisms about the subject, always in favour of the horse, as many of them led atrocious lives, and some slept between the shafts of their cabs with no stable to go home to at all, not ever. These, though, were the harshest-treated horses, their masters deserving a whipping, and not even one of those cabbies could be found this night.

I knew not where I was going in this foreign country, as alien as a far-off continent, and as I turned a corner, no different from any of the others, I saw a woman slowly making her way towards me in the eerie light cast from some nearby windows. I saw she was bareheaded (definitely not a lady of substance), and at that moment I dodged to my left, before she could see me. In that spot, there being a brick wall and a pair of open gate-doors, I thus entered a dark and lonely yard, its deep shadows being as black as my coat. I was aware I had been panting, so I clamped my mouth shut so she wouldn't hear me as she walked past, but then, out of nowhere, appeared a man. He looked to be a gentleman, as his dark coat was very long and he wore a tall, black hat. He spoke to the woman in a low voice. I wasn't very far away, sheltered in the dark of night, as no light seemed to invade the yard, so I could hear what was said between the two without my being seen.

The gentleman spoke kindly, though barely audible. "Hello, my dear. Fancy meeting you here on such a lovely night. We've met up before, haven't we? It's... Mary, isn't it?"

The woman stood in front of him with her hands on her hips, and answered in a pleasant voice, "Oh no, guv. No, moy noime ayn't Mary, but ya cun call me Lizzie, if ya loikes."

"I'm sure your name is Mary," he said, as he leaned over her.

"No. That ayn't me. But, I *can* be Mary, if ya wants."

"That matters not," he said casually. Then there were some other words spoken which were too low for me to hear. The man and woman then crossed the few feet into the yard, where I was hiding, forcing me to quietly slink a few feet in retreat.

I kept quiet.

I could dimly see her stood against the interior of the brick wall, and he was right there, in front of her, close enough that his front nearly touched hers, chest to chest. I next heard some very strange sounds, and instinctively I understood them to be sounds of someone in a state of panic. The woman was stood rigid, but the man seemed to be doing something to her. I heard her emit a stertorous, throaty sound that set my neck hairs on edge. I could feel them bristle all along my spine, and I stifled a growl. The woman, she was being physically hurt by this man and I had to do something! Her fists beat against the man's shoulders.

I leapt forward with a loud growl and I sank my teeth into the man's right leg, somewhere in the vicinity of his calf. He jerked his torso out of surprise, as well as feeling instantaneous pain, and kicked out at me with his injured leg, causing me to lose my grip, but he didn't release his hold on the woman. I lunged at him again and this time found his coat, and with it gripped between my teeth, I pulled backwards with all my might, as if I were playing tug o' war with Charles Clement. My painful feet slipped on the worn cobblestones of the yard as I tugged and tugged, and I grunted deeply with every effort.

Shales witnesses a murder.

Still, he did not let her go.

Then, in slow movement, she seemed to slip to the pavement and fall on her side, feet out towards the street, and at the same moment he reached inside his coat pocket and withdrew a dull, metal object. All of this I could see in the dimness of the yard, my eyesight being excellent at night. He made a quick movement with his hand, and I soon smelt the scent of fresh blood upon the late night air. I made another lunge at him, but nearly as quick, he slashed out at me, catching me on my face just under my left eye. I felt as if the whole side of my face had been ripped open. The knife, small as it was, glinted dully, and at that exact moment the sounds of a horse's footsteps were heard just a few feet away, as it turned the corner and onto the street. I took several steps backwards, as my face was beginning to sear with pain, something I wasn't used to, and I realised I was cut and was bleeding all over the cobbles, just like the woman was.

The horse was small, more of a pony in size, and it was being encouraged to enter the yard by its unseen master. But either the smell of fresh spilt blood, or the woman's fallen body lying just to its right, or perhaps even my own presence off to its left, prevented it from entering the yard. I shrunk further back, having nowhere else to go, and being consciously aware that the vile man was still lurking just a few feet away. He stood still as a statue, with that knife at the ready should he need to use it again on his unwelcome guest. The pony neighed, and obviously found his yard strangely abhorrent, refusing to step closer and wanting to move backwards. His master slowly reached with a stick, or something similar, and poked around in the inky darkness at the feet of the pony, and in coming into contact with something soft, he reached out with his own hands, finding the body of the woman. He then blindly dashed off into the building at the back of the yard, and raised all hell as he shouted for help. The nefarious man, the murderer, as I now believed him to be, then snatched his opportunity and very quickly slipped out of the yard, and his footsteps could barely be heard as he carefully left the scene. I, too, didn't see any reason to remain there. I was beside myself with emotion after this last tumultuous event, but I knew I had to find my own way home, as this next stranger with the horse and cart could very well keep me for himself, and I would once again be someone's prisoner.

I was in a state of shock, and needless to say blood oozed freely from the severe gash on my left cheek. It seemed to be swollen, and it throbbed incessantly. It kept me awake, though. I was also shattered and parched with thirst, and my feet were beginning to feel as if I'd been walking upon broken shards of glass. The pain was becoming unbearable. My thoughts kept going to that man, and I wondered if he was the one known as 'Jack the Ripper'. If not, then there was more than one insane murderer on the loose in London, free to prey upon women during the late hours of darkness.

I happened, by chance, to be heading in the direction of London City, but I did not know it until I began to smell the water, the familiar smell of the great winding river known as the Thames. I found myself hurrying in that direction with a renewed strength, and sometime later, when I saw the fortress of the Tower of London, I could have wept wet tears of joy, although I assure you, silent and dry ones trickled down my face.

Once at the Tower, I knew where I was, and better than that, I knew what day it was. It was Monday. I knew I could do one of two things: I could make my way to the steps of the Coal Exchange and await my master, as he would be arriving there that morning just before twelve noon, or I could go to either Cannon Street Station or The Monument, and after they opened later in the morning, I could take the train and make my own way home. I decided upon the first, because to do the latter was risky, at best, and I was very aware that I stank like an overfull privy, as well as being blood-covered from my head down to my front feet. I wouldn't have got through the doors, let alone down the steps and onto the platform, before a conscientious traveller would have hailed the station authorities, and had me taken into custody, the trailing lead making it easy for them to capture me.

My feet were so painful that I could hardly walk let alone hurry, and I left a trail of bloody footprints along the pavement and cobbles. My back leg ached so much that I thought it would snap on me, but the thought of getting to the steps of the Coal Exchange kept me going. It was still dark, but I sensed dawn was not far away. I was nithered, and craved for my spot in front of the fire. Occasionally I heard a bird chortle as it awakened from its sleep amidst the high branches of a tree. I limped very slowly around the walls of the fortress; the white stones of the central Tower built by the Norman King William gleamed in the darkness like a beacon, but I did not stop to linger. Where Spurr Gate is, I strayed to my right, and shortly found myself on Lower Thames Street with the Custom House further down on my left, and the stone steps and rotunda of the Coal Exchange staring down upon me on my right, as if I were a long-lost son. It was as close to home as I could get, but I painfully ignored the Coal Exchange and found a sheltered spot a little further on, in the shadows of the ancient church of St Magnus-the-Martyr, where I gave in to my tortured body, curled up in a tight ball, and slept from sheer exhaustion.

I awoke, sometime later, from the sounds of the now wakened city, which grew noisier and noisier as it came to life. I heard church bells ringing from all quarters, but the ones above me were especially loud and deafening. I knew it was too early, so I went back to sleep, but the pain, hunger and thirst stayed with me throughout my dreams.

Waking again, I knew it wasn't yet noon, the time for the Exchange to open, but it was close enough, so I dragged myself down the side of the street to where I had a full view of the front steps, and once there, in the shadows, I stiffly lay down at the corner, and I waited for the one carriage which would stop and empty itself of my master.

It was a busy spot. Cabs stopped and many well-dressed gentlemen emerged, some of them familiar to me but none of them Augustus. I began to wonder that perhaps there wouldn't be any necessity for him to come here on this day, but then he always came on a Monday, as well as most Wednesdays and Fridays. My heart thumped loudly as I began to tell myself that he wasn't going to come today. I didn't think I could bear the disappointment, but I made my mind up to stay there all afternoon, until the last person had left. I did wonder if I had missed seeing him, and he had arrived just that one, small moment ahead of me, unbeknownst to me as I'd patiently waited with my chin on my paws. That was it. Either I had missed seeing him, or he wasn't coming today, and if he wasn't coming to do business at the Exchange, then what was the reason for that? I feared to find out that he had become ill, or some other calamity had befallen the household, and I was not being given a second thought – that I was not missed at all.

The street was not quiet; always there was the sound of horses' hoof beats clip-clopping along, but many times the carriages did not stop, but kept on going to other destinations. Just as I was thinking about giving up waiting, more carriages came along the street. This time, however, one did slow and stop, and it came from the west, the direction of Cannon Street Station. I watched with fierce anticipation, and yes, it was my beloved master who carefully alighted from the cab with his walking-stick in hand, and head crowned beneath a familiar top hat. He paused to pay the cabby, and at that moment I limped over to him, going up several steps behind him, so that when he turned as the cabby left, he would have to see me, and see me he did. He nearly fell. He actually seemed to lose his balance, and he put out his stick to save himself, all the while with a shocked look upon his face, which had gone rather white, and he seemed to physically shrink as he saw me. Another gentleman of about Edmund's age had seen his mishap, and strode over to him, asking him if he was all right. Augustus put up his hand as if to ward him off. He used his stick to bear his weight.

"No, George." His voice wavered. "I shall be all right, but I've just had a bit of a shock." He reached down to lift my face with his left hand. "See this here dog? He belongs to me, and I can tell you something terrible has befallen him since yesterday, when he went missing." Looking over his shoulder he said, "Just now, he appeared as if from nowhere, and look at him – he's... he's nearly dead."

I whimpered and lay down on the step in front of him. I needed to do no grovelling this day, as I knew my truancy was forgiven. The man called George said, "God, man! He looks like he's been in a fierce fight, or someone has trounced him proper! He's left a trail of bloody footprints all up these steps, and his face looks as if its been slashed wide open!"

I sighed deeply. My eyes closed, and felt weighted down as if with lead.

Augustus leaned over me, and lovingly patted me, noting the belt looped through my collar, and reading like an open book that I had been taken against my will. I saw tears brimming in his eyes as he looked to and fro about the area in front of the Coal Exchange, as if looking for someone he expected to show up, but then he said to this George, "What shall I do with him? I need to go in there, but *he* can't go looking like this. He's nearly dead. Oh, George, what am I going to do?"

"Look here, man, we'll take him into my office where he can rest, and when you are ready, you come and get him." George patted my master firmly on the shoulder, as if to reassure him. "We can look after him here. That's what we'll do."

"That is very good of you. However, I'm afraid I can't accept your generous offer. No, I shall go home, and today's business will just have to wait."

The kindly young man named George said patiently, "Augustus, I shall put my foot down at you leaving. Come with me and see that he is comfortable, and while you're at it, you can have a brandy, as I think you need one." And with that he gave a tug on Augustus's arm and asked of him my name.

"Well, Shales," said George, "let's tend to your wounds, inside, and not out here on the steps in full view of all and sundry."

Oh, for the kindness of a proper gentleman. Why couldn't I have received such attention during the previous night? We walked up the steps slowly, as I simply could not move any quicker. George disappeared, but he returned quickly with another man who was instructed to pick me up off my feet and to carry me through the Exchange, the lovely floor bobbing along beneath me as I was carried to George's office. In there, both George and Augustus inspected me, and they pronounced me in a *sad state*, and in noting my thirst sent for a bowl of water. The wound on the left side of my face was examined, and George said, "That is definitely a wound caused by a knife, and one that was very thin and sharp. See how long and deep but very straight it is? There must have been more than one beastly maniac on the loose in London last night."

I drank deeply from the bowl of cool water, and then sank into a deep and safe sleep, which lasted for a couple of hours, until the Exchange closed and the sale of coal was over with for the day.

Upon awakening I found that all four of my feet had been generously bandaged. The man who had been asked to carry me into the building had also been summoned to carry me out, and he did so willingly, and gently deposited me inside a waiting cab that fortunately for us had just delivered a passenger somewhere nearby. My master shook hands with his friend George, and he thanked him for his kindness to another man's dog. George said he would only wish kindness to *any* dog, and that he had not been put out, not at all.

The cab set off, and we went to the Underground station, The Monument, where I had to then get out and walk. Oh, it hurt! My feet felt strange all

385

wrapped up in soft bandages (I remembered they had been bandaged likewise many years before). I didn't like it, and my hind leg felt is if it didn't want to work, but I managed to slowly hobble down the long flight of steps, and through the bowels of the station and onto the platform, where we received plenty of curious looks and stares.

Augustus was recognised by the authorities, and thus so was respected, so we were not prevented from boarding the train. It seemed like the longest and darkest train journey I had ever taken, and I anxiously waited for the change-over when we would board the above-ground train, which would take us to Hackney. It seemed like many, many miles as I stared out of the window as Hackney approached, but in reality it was only a couple or so miles. Somewhere out there, off to our right, was a dreadful place of wicked morality and abundant filth. I was conscious of my place in society, and I appreciated my ride in a clean and relatively empty coach.

I have said before that I was never so glad to see Hackney, but this time, my return to our home in Darnley Road meant even more to me than when Edmund had rescued me from the Dogs' Home, and you may remember how close I came then to never seeing Hackney again. This time, I had to be helped out of the cab and coaxed along the path and up the steps, my legs nearly giving out on me, as just the walk from the station platform to where the cabbies had been waiting had exhausted me. My master rang the bell as well as impatiently hammering away at the door's knocker, and Armstrong, in expecting his return from the city, had been lingering close by in anticipation of hearing the bell announce his arrival.

The door opened quickly, and she blurted, "Good afternoon, sir. Whatever is the matter? You never use the knocker in such a manner; you always ring the bell." But after uttering those words, she happened to notice me, and she cried out, "Oh, Shales!" And then, "Oh, sir! You've found him."

I was helped through the door and into the spacious hall, where there I slumped to the floor, refusing to move a step further. Armstrong had gone into the front room where we always had afternoon tea, and exclaimed to Jessie, as well as Lucy and Julia, "Excuse me, miss. It's your father. He has returned with Shales. Come quick! 'Twas him making all that noise!"

I heard the rustling of their long skirts, and then heard their exclamations of concern regarding my condition. They were all very tearful and were relieved to see me, but they immediately questioned my horrible condition. I was coaxed into the room, where Jessie then carefully removed my bandages and cared for my feet with some of her medicines. They were bandaged again in clean cloths. My facial wound was deep, and she suggested that it may need stitches, but that was something she wouldn't do herself. What of fetching a doctor? They decided against taking me to the veterinary, as I was so weak and exhausted. It was suggested that the wound be carefully cleaned, and they would wait to see if the bleeding stopped on its own. My sore ribs were noted, and it was suggested that no amount of wandering the roads and streets had caused *that* injury. The sisters also came to the conclusion that I had been beaten, and that horrid belt was soon removed and thrown away in disgust.

Both Charles Clement and Edmund were appalled at my appearance, and Charles kindly carried me all the way outside into the garden for a few moments, and then carried me back inside and into the front room where they were all seated, discussing the latest, shocking news. I crawled towards the fire, and there I found comfort with my bunny.

Jack the Ripper had struck again the previous night, or as the newspaper report said, '...in the early hours of that morning.' When, at breakfast, Edmund read out loud the account of a woman named Elizabeth Stride, and described the yard where she had been found, and that a Jew, returning to his home with his pony and cart at that late hour, had found her body with her throat cut, I then knew for sure I had encountered that evil man who called himself Jack the Ripper. From *The Times* he read, "'Two more murders must now be added to the black list of similar crimes, of which the East End of London has very lately been the scene.'"

I moaned out loud, and barked to get their attention. Edmund lowered his newspaper, gave me one long, serious look, and said, "I wonder if Shales knows something of this. After all, someone has taken a knife to him. Poor Shalesey lad."

Augustus replied, "Edmund, we'll never know. Not for as long as we live, will we ever know what happened to him last night, but I can tell you one thing."

"What's that, Dad?" interrupted Charles Clement.

"Well, son, he's very intelligent. Do you know that he was there, waiting for me to arrive at the Exchange this afternoon? How he got there I do not know, but one thing is for certain, and that is, that he knew I was going to be there, and he waited for me. More than that, he found his way to Thames Street from wherever he had been, and judging from the condition of his feet, he travelled a fair distance to get there."

He was correct. I had travelled a great distance the night before. Apparently, I had been traipsing all around Whitechapel with Dicky, as that was where the murder had been committed. After Jack the Ripper had left the dead woman Elizabeth, he had then gone off and had murdered another woman, and she, he had done a most horrible mutilation to.

* * *

THIS DOUBLE MURDER sent the city into a state of near panic. We always had several newspapers delivered each day, from *The Times* and the *Star*, to the *Hackney Standard*, as well as the *Illustrated London News*, which was a regular because Stanley frequently did illustrations for that paper and the family liked to see his pictures depicting news events. Every day, either morning or evening, someone would search the papers for the latest reports by the police. Whenever something pertaining to the Whitechapel Murders was found it was read out loud, and because of this I knew exactly what was going on, and because I had been there, in Whitechapel, I knew the conditions of the places being written about. I listened with horror. Would it never end? The Metropolitan Police had even received a postcard, in which Jack the Ripper had threatened to enter the parish of St John's, Hackney, and commit a murder that following weekend.

I imagined that he had found out my identity in some way, and it was really me he was after, and he wasn't going to murder any Hackney women, just me.

Later, the card was announced to have been a hoax, but the feeling of terror still surrounded the women of Hackney as they, too, felt vulnerable. The Metropolitan Police were highly criticised for their failing attempts to identify Jack and their inability to prevent any more murders.

Just three days after my safe return home the headless and armless torso of a woman had been found dumped at the building site of the new police station known as Scotland Yard. They said it wasn't 'his' work. Then, in December, another woman had received a minor wound to her neck by a strange man in the night hours, and then a couple of days later another woman had been found strangled. Eventually, the horrible murders either ended, or the newspapers simply stopped reporting them. I think Jack stopped murdering – either of his own accord, or someone 'in the know' stopped him. I saw him, I saw his face, and I knew then that if I ever saw him again, I would do my best to let people know his identity. Meanwhile, what could I do about Jack the Ripper? Nobody could understand me, and I have to say that it was very difficult to deal with. It was indeed a heavy burden for me to carry.

My wounds healed. I think the worn-off pads on my feet had suffered the worst infliction, and that was a most difficult injury to get over. I couldn't walk up or down the stairs, and had to be carried outside to use the loo. As for my face, the knife wound had healed quite well, after it was sewn up by G. H. A. Comyns Berkeley, a doctor, as well as a nephew of my master, leaving only a thin, bumpy scar that ran from beneath my eye and across to my cheek, which eventually became grown over with my facial hair. Like a large bucket of water thrown over a small fire, my desire for being alone on the streets of Hackney, or elsewhere, had been thoroughly doused.

It was this nightmare of terrors that would remind me of my age, not the flirtation with Florrie.

THE FOOL

BOOK V

XXIV
HERBERT

"When the evening sun is low."

AUGUST, 1889

I
T WAS A COLD, WET DAY IN AUGUST when there came a knock at the door. My fresh bone was soon forgotten – I ran to the door barking, getting there before Armstrong.

"Shales! Get back!" she ordered.

I wanted to see who it was, so I ignored her.

She grabbed my collar and pulled me back, enabling her to open the door and greet the visitor.

"Mr Rowland!" she exclaimed. "The family will be pleased to see you." She stepped backwards, swinging the door wide open. "Do come inside, sir. It's a horrible day out there."

He stepped across the threshold, dripping water all over the floor. It was raining quite heavily, and thunder rolled and beat its drum in the distance.

I strained forward and she let go of my collar. I was eager to see my old master. I jumped up and he vigorously rubbed my head. "Shales. Hello, my boy," he said.

Armstrong quickly took his things and hung them up: an overcoat, an umbrella, a tall hat, and an exquisite pair of gloves. Swiftly, she dropped his wet umbrella in the brolly stand. I danced about his heels as I followed him into the sitting-room.

Armstrong announced him to the family, "Mr Rowland is here."

Jessie snapped, "Shales! Stop it!"

I happily ignored her and closely followed Rowland across the room. He stopped to shake hands with his uncle and his cousins. The welcome was very warm.

"Well, this is a nice surprise," my master said in greeting.

"Not when you hear what I have to say," replied Rowland. He then said quietly, "I am the bearer of sad news."

"Oh, dear!" moaned the three sisters in unison.

Jessie said apprehensively, "What is it, Rowland?"

Augustus got up from his easy chair, and from the sounds and smells I determined he was pouring brandies. He passed them round to everyone, and then gently said, "Tell us. Tell us what has happened."

"I'm afraid Herbert is ill."

"Oh... not Herbert. But surely..." Jessie didn't finish. She was visibly upset.

"It has not been a secret that he has been ill these past couple of years; he's getting worse, and the doctors say he will not get better – not here, at the moment. Our English climate is killing him."

"I was afraid this would happen," said Edmund rather glumly. But then more hopefully, "We hear of it too often, but many go abroad to drier climates; they return well cured."

"I see this is most difficult for you," sympathised my master. He took a sip of his brandy as he thought about his ill nephew.

"He's going to leave the country... soon." Rowland looked very sad. He confessed, "I don't know what I'm going to do if he dies. I just can't think of a nicer person who has done so much for himself, to have to come to this."

The family became a bit frantic.

"Oh, no. Don't talk like that," said Jessie. "A drier climate will do wonders for his health. Won't it?" she asked hopefully.

Julia nodded. "I'm sure he'll get better. He just has to! But, please tell us, Rowland, where is he going?"

"North Africa. Algeria, to be precise. He'll go to Algiers, the city, and from there he'll find a house to rent – there are lots. There is even a British community in Algiers." His brandy was finished. Augustus offered him a refill.

"No, uncle. I must decline your offer. I'm catching the train home, so I must set off for the station shortly; I've left my cab waiting. But, there *is* something you can do for me, though," he said.

"Yes. Of course."

"I haven't been down to visit with my uncle George. Would you or Edmund be able to tell him, in person? Perhaps see him this week for me. I'll send him a letter, but it is better to hear it in person first. Herbert is... finding it difficult, and he is not up to calling upon everyone; there are just too many."

"Of course. I'll go down and see him tomorrow."

Edmund asked about Herbert. "When is he leaving?"

"Soon. I don't have the exact date, but soon. We were actually over at his solicitors today. He has made a new will. It's... just in case, though we don't expect anything so soon. It's just that with him going off for a long while... and Harry will see to it if anything happens."

"He certainly isn't going alone, is he?" asked my master.

Rowland was quick to reply. "No. Actually, Edmund is going out there with him, and if all is well, he'll return sometime next year. That will depend on Herbert's health."

I knew this wasn't my Edmund, who was in the room and sitting across from me, but Rowland and Herbert's brother, now retired from the army but living in Scotland.

There was a long, quiet pause where nothing was said. They were all thinking and wondering what to say next. I ran off and fetched my bunny. I shoved it into Rowland's lap. He laughed and hid it behind his back, and as I was poking for it he said, "I have an invitation for you, for all of you, and that includes Charles and Emily and their families, and of course Shales as well."

He wouldn't let go of my bunny, and I tugged and tugged. My nails dug into the carpet and I playfully growled.

"Herbert is inviting everyone over to his house on Sunday. It'll be a sort of *send-off,* but it will also give him a chance to say his private goodbyes, since he doesn't know when he shall be returning to England."

"We'll be there," Augustus said. "We'll all be there." His children all nodded in the affirmative.

"Well, I shan't linger. I have to get back to Cotheridge, to Mildred and the children."

"And to think he went all the way to Italy, and that not so long ago. It was just last winter." Edmund was talking about Herbert's holiday on the continent. I'd heard about it. He'd gone all the way to Italy, and had taken a lot of photographs when there. Once back in England, he had entered some of the ones taken in Venice in the annual competition of The Royal Photographic Society.

"Yes... well, he caught a chill and it settled on his chest. He's been worse ever since, and that and the rest, well, you all know."

Rowland left; he had a train to catch at Hackney station. It was nice to see him, but his sad news weighed heavily on the minds of everyone. They weren't sure what to think of the situation, and they all seemed to dread the upcoming Sunday. I understood it wasn't good news for Herbert, but I was being given the chance to see him before he left, and I was happy about that. Besides, it meant catching a train, and you all know how much I love trains. Boys o' boys, mmn, mmn, mmn.

* * *

THAT SUNDAY WE ALL SET OFF FOR SHORTLANDS, KENT; just us, as Charles and Emily and their families declined, excusing themselves with prior commitments. Once there, Herbert eagerly welcomed us into Glengowan, his lovely home.

"I'm glad you brought Shales," he said as he patted my sides. "I don't know when I'll see another sheepdog again. I think they eat them in Africa." He laughed, but then coughed.

Everyone found that amusing, except for me. I was still trying to understand what he'd said about eating sheepdogs, when my nose directed me to the dining-room. What a lovely time! People milled about and chit-chatted with Herbert, wishing him well and all that, and I went around looking for discarded cups and plates half-filled with tea or covered with the remnants of cream cakes and gateaux. My long tongue managed to lap up the dregs from the near-empty glasses of beer and stout. The stout I liked. However, it made me burp. Kindly people, strangers, in thinking I was starving, had offered me portions of their cakes and sandwiches, as well as saucers full of milk and tea, not to mention sherry, which flowed in copious amounts. The food was so good, the cream so fresh and delicious, that I started to clean up the plates and cups that I found set upon the various occasional tables. That was a 'no-no'. I was never allowed to touch anything that was set upon a table, only what was set upon the floor, and I knew it.

I got caught.

Edmund roughly dragged me away from a particularly good-tasting piece of chocolate gateau, and the motion of it made my stomach turn. Needless to say, I was sick everywhere, and was not very popular because of it. The dark blue dye in the carpet ran into the bright yellows and whites. The housemaid glared at me as she gently dabbed and scrubbed away at the stain; the smell of sick pervaded the room. She moaned that the carpet was ruined. Augustus offered to replace the carpet, an extravagant expense he would rather avoid making, but he had to save face.

Uncle George bellowed from across the room, "By Jove, Gus, that dog of yours does get up to some mischief!" He then added, equally as loudly, "It's a grand thing he hasn't developed a taste for ale, otherwise he'd be hung-over by teatime!"

Everyone laughed, but I didn't see the funny side to it. I could only see the blurry colours of the now devalued carpet, as I got ready to retch once again. My head spun and I felt wobbly on my feet. No one knew I'd been drinking.

Herbert was rather good about it. He said he'd worry about it when he returned from Africa, and then the carpet could go into an unused room.

"I'll keep the carpet. Something to remember Shales by," he said in good humour as he surveyed the damage. "If I change my mind then easy come, easy go." Wearily, he said, "I have more things to worry about than a ruined Persian carpet."

On that note, we left, wishing him bon voyage and a safe journey there and back. My journey home was most unpleasant. Edmund and Charles had to keep lifting me up onto my feet, and the sisters all moaned in fear that I had become poisoned, perhaps by some rat poison found in the nether parts of Herbert's house. Charles Clement kept smiling and saying, "He isn't poisoned! He's drunk! He's sloshed!"

The normally gentle rocking motion of the trains, and the repeated clickety-clack sounds the wheels made on the rails, only intensified the way I felt – ill. I was sick again – a newspaper had been provided, quickly shoved in front of me for obvious reasons. It was my own fault. I'd overindulged in all the rich foods, as well as the liquids, and I was informed by Jessie there wasn't going to be any dinner for me that night, except for some boring pieces of dry, butterless toast.

* * *

1890

ONE DAY TOWARDS THE END OF JUNE, as I was napping in front of a non-existent fire, it being too warm to have one going, a gentleman appeared in my master's office, shown in by Jules, the clerk. I knew him from a long time ago; it was Edmund Robert, Lieutenant Colonel, retired. I wondered if this meant that Herbert was home from Africa.

"There you go, sir," said Jules, as he offered Edmund some writing paper and a place at my master's desk.

I wandered up to Edmund and greeted him happily. He extended his hand and ruffled my ears. "Hello, Shales. Why are you here all by yourself? Where is everyone?"

He wrote a short letter, and then left it on the desk for my master to find. With that done he quietly left, closing the door behind him. Augustus wasn't there, as it was Monday. He was at the Coal Exchange, and Edmund was over at the depot. No matter; the letter would be noticed when my master next sat at his desk.

I didn't know the contents of the letter until they were revealed at home, in front of the family. It was before we had sat down for our dinner, and very quietly he simply said, "Herbert has died. It happened over in Algiers."

The sisters and Edmund were all shocked. The news came too soon and was unexpected.

"How do you know this?" enquired Edmund, as if the news was false.

"Your cousin Edmund has returned. He left me a letter on my desk. He must have written it there, and I found it this afternoon."

I thumped my tail loudly to let them know I knew that.

My master explained what was written in the letter. "He said he did not send word home from Algiers, that he wanted to inform his brothers, Rowland and William, himself, and not by a letter or a telegram. He had hoped to see me, but I was at the Exchange. He was in a rush to get to Cotheridge."

"What does it say about his death? And when did it happen?" asked a tearful Jessie as she pulled out a hanky.

My master sighed, then slowly said, "He got increasingly more ill, and succumbed in the night. That is all, and it happened on the 26th of May." He went on to explain, "Your cousin then caught the next steamer, as soon as he could, and made all haste back to England. Now you know as much as I do."

Our Edmund said quietly, "I suppose we'll have to wait for word of the funeral arrangements, and that will be in Cotheridge, naturally."

"Yes. I suppose so, Edmund. Do you mind informing Charlie and Emily?" asked my master. "They should know as soon as possible."

"No, I'll do it," came the reply. His voice was dull. "It's getting to be a bit of a habit. I can't believe this – he's dead."

Julia said in shocked tones, "Another death! Oh, dear, dear cousin Herbie."

They were all upset by the news, and so was I. Such a lovely man, and a member of our family. Oh, what dreadful news! I knew what was happening; another member of the family had died, there would be another funeral, and yet again it was tragic. Herbert was still young at the time of his death, only thirty-nine.

* * *

The Funeral – June, 1890

A SPECIAL COACH HAD BEEN HIRED, on one of the trains belonging to the Great Western line. Only those travelling to Herbert's funeral stepped aboard, and as we left Paddington Station early that morning the chit-chat was all but non-existent. Everyone sat still and politely stared out of the windows at the blurry view, and I lay upon the floor, there being no seats left. We were once again attired in funeral clothes. I wore my black crepe band about my neck, and the others wore black clothing and black hatbands of various widths, denoting their relationship to the deceased. At least that is what I thought, as I could see the uncles all had the same width of crepe, and the cousins different yet again. Mine was the same width as always; it never varied, but then again, I was the only dog in England who participated in funerals.

It was a large turnout. The little church in Cotheridge was filled to capacity. The service ended, and many stood by as his coffin was lowered into the ground. The coffin was plain and with no adornments of any sort. There were no brass handles or fittings; nothing to denote he was a wealthy man. I watched from my vantage point, a place not far away from the plot, it being about halfway between the east and west boundaries, but on the north side of the church, and near to the Scotch firs. There was a wild beehive close by; I could hear its humming and droning. I sauntered over and pawed at the moss-covered log. There was honey hidden beneath its surface. As I turned to leave, a bee stung me on my back leg. Obviously these ones did not know of Herbert's death; they were yet active.

Herbert.

With a sore and stinging leg, I wandered back to the grave site and peered in. The coffin was at the bottom, and the black strands of cordage used to lower it were being retrieved. The large group of mourners was leaving. They were quietly walking towards the house with their heads bowed. I followed at a timid pace, and to my relief was allowed in the house. Grace May greeted me and took me to the kitchen, where tearfully she provided me with food and water.

On a full belly, I wandered off to find my master, whom I found conversing with Rowland and the other gentlemen. I knew we would be leaving shortly. We would all be catching the train, the same funeral coach that would take us back to Paddington Station. They talked of the headstone, which was to be placed over the grave. Not a simple affair! Herbert had asked for a six-foot cross of white marble, and that to stand upon a mound of rough stone; it was imposing and in no way plain, as were the other stones in the graveyard.

I thought to myself, *"Nice, he deserves it. History shouldn't forget him and his valuable contribution regarding developing solutions. Goodbye, Herbert. You shall be remembered."*

* * *

THE TRUTH

IT WOULD HAVE BEEN NICE IF IT HAD HAPPENED THAT WAY, but the truth of the matter is that Herbert lies not in the spot he so passionately requested. There is no tall cross of white marble. Instead, he lies alone, in a strange churchyard, in a foreign land.

His brother Edmund did not, or, as I should say, could not bring him home. What with the African heat and with there being no provision of a lead coffin, Herbert had received a foreign, as well as an exceedingly hasty burial.

XXV
MAUD

*"...I don't know everything, but I shall hint
at lots."*

ONE MIGHT POSSIBLY THINK that perhaps I have neglected to mention very much about Maud, since Thomas's death in 1882. Well, we all have our places in history, and Maud's life seems to have been lived on a rather slippery incline, she ever so ready to lose her balance and slip right off the edge into an abysmal pit below. Her life should have been centred round her daughter, Mary Matilda, like most mothers are, but it wasn't always like that with Maud. I'm asking you to bear with me and read between the lines; you know, where you *have* to use your imagination. I can't give you the all the minute details, because I don't know *everything,* but I shall *hint* at lots.

Ever since Thomas's death, she had lived with us at Darnley Road during her lengthy period of mourning, and then at the house in Stoke Newington, and then later at the boarding house, with the occasional visit to her own family in Norwich. One mustn't forget that she was a very young woman at the time of her initiation into widowhood, at the ripe young age of two and twenty years, and also the mother of a small baby. Augustus wanted his granddaughter brought up in the fashion as his own children had been, with her own nurse, a governess, and a good education, and with the prospect of securing a good and happy marriage in the future, when she came of age. It all sounds wonderful, but things seldom work out as planned, and don't we all know that. We had all come to realise that Maud was not easy to live with, and she wasn't like her in-laws, having nothing in common with them except her daughter. To even just go on holiday and have her come with us was at times a strain, but then again, who isn't a thorn in someone's backside at times? She was fed up with living with her four sisters-in-law (all of whom were spinsters), two brothers-in-law who were still bachelors, and an aging father-in-law. She wanted a house of her own, or at least a place she could call her own.

In the end, in the year of 1883, she had moved out, taking Charlotte, the nurse-cum-governess, and Mary Matilda with her to the small house in Stoke Newington. There, she went back to her old trade of dressmaking, a trade she was very good at. About three years later she moved out of the house and took up residence at the boarding house, and worked alongside Mary Ann, the owner of the boarding house and also a dressmaker, that being the very same place where Thomas Rowland visited, on the night of the census, in April of 1881.

The boarding house, as I have said before, was respectable enough, although it wasn't where the family wanted little Mary Matilda to be raised. In that house Maud and Mary Ann took private orders from good, upper middle-class women who required new dresses, skirts, and accessories, and they sewed them with the help of a young female employee. Maud seemed to do quite well at it, but I know from what I had witnessed, with my own eyes, that she eagerly accepted money from my master every year, and spent it just as quickly.

The house in Darnley Road seemed enormously empty without the cheery presence of little Mary Matilda, and we all missed her a lot, especially Augustus, who still yearned for his son, her father. There were many times during that first year, after Maud had moved back to Stoke Newington, that she came with her daughter to Darnley Road for afternoon tea, or for Sunday dinner. Then she stopped coming; her visits became less frequent. So, as a result, my master took me along with him, and occasionally *we* visited Maud and little Mary. I think we went for the sole purpose of checking up on them, and not because Maud claimed she was too busy sewing to make the trip over to Hackney to see us. Quite often, though, the child would come to us and spend the entire day in the care of her aunties so that Maud could get on with her sewing, while Charlotte had her day off. Even these visits waned. They waned enough to harbour concern, and my master looked into the situation. Whatever he found, he was not happy with it. What I do know is this: he consulted his solicitors, the family ones, Charles Clement Berkeley, Comyns Rowland Berkeley and Harry Douglas Berkeley. They petitioned the courts for legal guardianship of Mary Matilda. In the end, with the threat of losing her daughter to her in-laws, Maud agreed to allow her daughter to spend holiday visits with us each year, and some of the holidays would take place at Cotheridge Court, a place where Maud herself would also come to and receive sums of money on behalf of her daughter. If she did not allow these visits to take place, then she would find herself in court, and in opposition to the family lawyers and their lawyer colleagues.

I, myself, had visited Maud on many an occasion, though always accompanied by either the sisters or Augustus. I had started to notice the odour of tobacco: reluctant to leave, but always wanting to hide its aromatic smell in the fabric of the carpets, settees, or curtains, and especially on Maud's clothes. It was a different brand than I was used to smelling, as smoking was very common amongst men (Edmund, Charles and Augustus included), and there were various brands of tobacco and cigars available at any tobacconist's shop. I merely passed it off without any cause for concern. Besides, it was a boarding house, and there were always male guests residing there who smoked either a pipe or a cigar.

Weeks went by and turned into months. The subject of Mary Matilda's future was bantered about quite regularly, and on one particular day when Maud brought her daughter to visit she voiced her opinion on the subject. *She* didn't bring up the subject, though. I have to say that my master had quietly asked *her* to speak with him, in private, in the front room. Not the sitting-room, but the small room across the hall, to the left of the staircase, with its windows facing onto the road, where visitors of an unknown category were asked to wait. It was private, and out of reach of the ears of the child in question, whilst *she* was otherwise entertained by her aunts and uncle.

"Ent it a waste of good money that could be put to better use elsewhere?" she asked with her chin held high, and looking at her father-in-law with defiant eyes. I knew she wanted the money for herself. I had heard her discuss with

William's wife, Mary, in Gorleston, her hopes of travelling across Europe, something she had never before done.

"An education is not a waste of money." Augustus was vehement on the subject. I lay unseen in a quiet corner, behind the chair nobody ever sat in. It was uninviting towards people, its horsehair seat lumpy and prickly to sit upon, and this I know because I once tried the chair myself and it repulsed me; but on that day it provided me with an innocent place to listen from. I actually remember that on that particular day Augustus wore some colour, instead of his usual shades of greys or blacks. His waistcoat was of a shade similar to clotted cream, which happened to match the colour of Maud's blouse, her lovely long skirt being a shade of brown, which complemented the cream.

"Whot sort of fogger dew yew think she'll marry?" asked Maud.

He politely coughed into his hand, before he spoke. "I should hope someone who comes from a respectable family and with enough money to live comfortably, at the very worst. If she does not marry, then at least she will have brains and a bit of intelligence to fall back on," said Augustus as he inclined his head towards her. "Then she can do as she pleases. She's my granddaugher – she will be somewhat educated."

"I dorn't know. 'Tis still too early ter be sending her away ter boarding school nor any orther fancy school, for that matter. She's ornly seven years old. We'll see in a couple ov years. I had thort she might want to be a dressmaker, like me."

"I don't see why you oppose her becoming educated," asked her father-in-law. He raised his chin. "Times are changing. She'll no doubt marry, but I want her to receive the same education as all her cousins. I'll set aside a trust fund for her education, and if she doesn't finish school, she can have it when she marries. There are some very good private schools for girls, in the vicinity as well as further abroad, and I do not see why you object to sending her to one. I must insist. I don't want her settling to be a dressmaker when there are other opportunities for her. There's nothing wrong with that, is there?" He challenged Maud, knowing full well that she would keep Mary Matilda back in life. I think he would rather have kept the granddaughter and lost the daughter-in-law.

She shook her head. "No, niver mind me. We'll talk about it again when she's older. Two or three more years, I think."

And so the subject was left to rest for a while. I didn't understand, because I wanted all the best for little Mary Matilda. I had a desire for knowledge, as you well know, so I didn't understand it when people didn't want to expand their minds. I wondered if the reluctance of Maud, regarding her daughter's upbringing, had anything to do with the fact that Maud wished she herself had been better educated. I seldom saw her read anything other than magazines, and those ones only on design and fashion for ladies. Perhaps she needed to go to school herself. I think she wanted to enjoy a busy social life and take lots of holidays, but that is my opinion of her, and I have to say, it hasn't changed over the years.

* * *

YOU KNOW I LOVED OUR VISITS TO COTHERIDGE, especially the journey to and from by train, and in July of 1888 Maud and Mary Matilda accompanied us there. At that time we were all blissfully unaware of the approaching doom created by that man who later became famous as Jack the Ripper. As for Cotheridge, I preferred to visit there in the summertime, when the grasses had grown tall and were filled with chirping crickets and springing grasshoppers, instead of in the winter months when it was less interesting. Then, in the summertime, it was a magical place to visit, with lots to occupy my mind, and I looked upon that lovely, ancient place as my second home. I was free to run about there, unfettered and unwatched by human eyes, as I roamed the two thousand odd acres as if I were its master. Toothless George was old and had become too arthritic to work a full day, so he had been retired from Rowland's old farm, and all I ever found out was that he had moved off to a little cottage, someplace up north, in Yorkshire, near to where he had been born, never to be seen nor heard from again. Occasionally, I ventured into the graveyard at St Leonard's, and tried make sense of the writing on the headstones. Some were so faint that I didn't think people could read the writing, worn away by the wuthering decades of time as they slowly sank deeper into the soft ground and tilted at alarmingly odd angles, surrounded by tufts of lush, green grass.

It was on this visit to Cotheridge, in 1888, that I witnessed another dreadful scene between my master and Maud. They were in the garden, sauntering about at a leisurely pace, and were discussing things of a financial matter. They had that look about them that said their discussion was of dire importance. I was within earshot, but I was hidden beneath the closely clipped branches of the ancient yew hedge, where I had managed to escape the heat of the sun. It was a very hot day and I was out of sight there. I listened very carefully to what they were discussing, and once again it was about money. I could have guessed it would be either *that* they were discussing, or the child. I heard Augustus tell her there was no more money. Whatever portion Thomas Rowland would have inherited from his father was now all gone.

"I have been giving you large sums of money on an annual basis since he died, and there is no more left of what would be his inheritance. Maud, you must understand this – I cannot give to you what rightfully belongs to Edmund and the others. There is but ten pounds left from Thomas's trust, and I'll give you that, but there shall be no more payments in the future." Augustus was uncomfortable. I sensed this and I wondered what sort of a backlash would be coming from Maud.

"No! Please dorn't say that! I need the extra money, orrherwise I can't make ends meet. That's why I moved back to Mary Ann's. The dressmaking ent always reliable, and some weeks there ent any money coming in."

My master stopped in his stride and turned to face her. He held himself upright with his hands clasped behind his back, and he was wearing a coat, even on that hot day, but it was a summer colour, a very light shade of grey. He was bare-headed, and the sun glinted off his sparse, greying hair. Also, he was perspiring; I could smell it upon the light breeze, which wafted in my direction. I lay there beneath the ancient hedge, intent upon the development of this situation. No more money for Maud! I thought she wouldn't like that. Boys o' boys, mmn, mmn, mmn. I tilted my head in order to better hear.

"I simply do not understand what you have done with the money over these years. My dear, I must stress that you must not have been overly careful with your expenditures. Living at that boarding house is not as expensive as running your own large household with servants. That is why you moved from the other house you had. Now, if I remember correctly, you have been receiving an income from the house in Bush Hill. That income should have more than paid for your expenses at the boarding house, including the governess's wages. Your own income from dressmaking has been an extra income for you as well as the money I have generously given to you over the years, and some of that you should have been setting aside for your daughter's future. I cannot believe you have spent it all!"

Now he started to sound angry, and he continued harshly, "Do not tell me you have wasted all that money when you should have been saving it in the bank, or you could have invested some of it in the railway or other investments!"

"I have told yew, sir, that it ent been enough. I haven't wasted it." Maud was defiant, as she held up her pretty brown head and stared at my master. "What am I to do now?" she wailed pitifully. I thought she was going to weep, as she was searching for her hanky, tucked up in the sleeve of her dress.

"Don't ask me!" spat Augustus angrily. He was offended, and I think slightly ashamed to think that his granddaughter's mother had spent a fortune, or better still, had wasted it.

"What about Mary Matilda? You'll still send her to school?" asked Maud hopefully as she dabbed at her eyes. She looked very agitated and worried, and no wonder, with her magical fountain of pounds, shillings and pence suddenly dried up, and with no hope for it to continue to spout forth as it had before.

Harshly, he replied, "You'll have to either sell the house in Bush Hill, or you simply will have to rely on the rent from it for your extra income. There are many people who would be envious of your position, in that you have a large house, which provides you with an annual income from its rent. I do suggest that if you sell it, you should invest the proceeds and keep it for Mary Matilda's future, as well as for your own." He was insistent with his advice and his tone was gruff. It was good advice he had given her, but he hadn't been ready for her response.

Forcefully, she confessed, "I *sold* the house. I sold it *two* years ago. The money's all gone." I saw her sigh, as if glad to be rid of such a secret.

"You sold it and didn't think to mention it?" There was a short pause, and then he blurted, "Incredible!" He then thought to ask, "Your solicitors? Were they family?"

She shook her head. "No. I knew they would tell you. I went elsewhere."

Augustus turned red in the face, and blustered something that sounded like, "You squanderer." He then said, "I suggest you save the ten pounds. It is a small fortune." He then looked about himself, stretched his neck, and avoided looking at her as he said, "Good day to you, madam. I think we should cease this conversation now, and let's get on... with our holiday. Oh, by the way, this is *your* last holiday; there won't be any reason for *you* to come here in the future."

He bowed his head as if the weight of the argument was too heavy to bear. He had been very polite, I think, but the point was rammed home, and he strode away in a silent rage.

I wondered whether or not to run to him and to give him some attention. He was striding towards the back of the house, so I got up from where I was listening, though before they had arrived it was where I had been resting, and I ran off and caught up with him. He was delighted to see me. I danced around him and pawed at his legs.

He sighed, and then said, "Shales, fancy a dip in the pond? I might be an old man, but let's go and see the pond, shall we? We'll sit on the bench and we'll watch the swans."

So we walked over there and he sat down on a bench, situated there for such occasions, whereby he removed his coat and carefully draped it across the back of the bench. He then undid his cuff links and pocketed them in his waistcoat, and then rolled up his shirtsleeves to his elbows. After that he removed his shoes, and then his socks and garters, and rolled up his trousers to his knees. As an afterthought, he undid his collar. This was a man who rarely took advantage of the sunshine, but for some reason, I think he needed to be at one with nature after having it out with Maud. We paddled in the water, together, looking for sticklebacks and frogs. It was a rare occasion, and I committed it to memory. All the while I wondered where this situation with Maud would lead us, as I sensed it wasn't over with. *He* was clearly upset, and knowing what I knew, I understood why. There was no money for his granddaughter as long as Maud was around. How could he make sure Mary Matilda wanted for nothing, without lining Maud's own pockets as well? Pockets with large holes in them!

He eventually calmed down, and after getting a little sunburnt we walked back to the house, where we were to enjoy the last few days of our holiday. Barefoot, he tiptoed carefully through the back, past the dairy and to the south wing of the house, carrying his shoes in his left hand and his coat slung across his right arm, with his shirtsleeves still rolled up to the elbows. One of the servants ran out, alarmed at his rakish appearance, and asked if ought was wrong. He shook his head and said he hadn't felt better in a long time. I followed him into the old house, and he, looking like he'd been at Southtown beach all day long, shouted to the walls that he was going to have a bath and was not to be disturbed.

The housemaid appeared, but nearly fainted when she both saw and heard his demeanour. "Are you all right, sir? Have you had a turn?" she asked. It was obvious that something was amiss with the master's uncle. Augustus shook his head in the negative. "Shall I fetch Grace May?" she asked.

"No, I'm fine. However, I do wish to have a bath."

She looked dismayed.

"Oh, fetch me a brandy, please," he bellowed good-naturedly as we walked through the house. The housemaid still wasn't satisfied that all was right with him, but he loudly answered back as he climbed the massive Elizabethan staircase, "I've never felt better – should have paddled in the pond with the sticklebacks years ago. Used to do it you know, when we were all lads, in Essex. Now, what's taking that brandy so long to get to me?"

"Yes, sir! Right away, sir!"

I happily followed him up the ancient staircase and down the passageway and into his room. Jessie was close on our heels. "Father! What on earth have you been doing? Are you all right? Goodness! Have you been attacked?"

He turned, shook his head in response, looked at her and said, "Thank you, Jessie."

She put her hand to her chest. "Why are you thanking me? I haven't done anything for you, have I?" She was surprised at his statement.

411

"Well, my love, you might not realise it, but you have been a wonderful daughter, and so have your sisters. I am thankful that you didn't turn out like Maud. Though heaven's sake as to why Thomas ever got involved with her. He must have been led on, and I am ashamed to think of how I spoke to him all those years ago, before they married." He shook his head with regret, and his voice turned husky. "Jessie, I wish I could take all those horrid words back. Edmund knows. He was there at Cassland Road. Those angry words I shouted at him could never be forgiven. I wonder if it would have made any difference, and he'd still be with us today, if I had just said something different. If I had allowed her to move in with us after they married, then he certainly would not have caught that dreadful disease. I feel somewhat responsible for his death." He cried, "Oh, Jessie! I can never forgive myself!"

The situation was getting a bit maudlin.

Jessie, obviously perplexed, touched her father on his arm and bade him sit down. "You've had too much sunshine, I think. Perhaps I should call for Grace."

"No, it wasn't the sun. It was Maud. She sold Thomas's house two years ago and didn't say a thing. The money from it has been spent, and she claims she cannot make ends meet. I told her, just this afternoon, that she can have the last of Thomas's money, and that it is *only* ten pounds. The rest of it she has had since 1882, and it is all gone. Spent. Wasted away on naught. Not a farthing of it invested. Comyns has advised me to cut her off, and he is correct, though I'm afraid there won't be anything for Mary Matilda. Well, not for a while."

Jessie looked appalled. She sat down on the bed next to her father and bowed her head. "If it weren't for my niece, your granddaughter, she wouldn't have had that money. I think she's led herself a grand life, but she's coming to her end. I wonder what she'll do now?"

He slapped himself on his knees and said, "She'll have to support herself. If she can't, then the child can come to us. I'm not giving Maud any more money after we leave this house. She can have ten pounds; I've told her that, and she'll have to make it last." He happily said, "Good riddance. I'll be glad to see the back of her and I hope she burns in Hell."

The wind had been taken out of Maud's sails, so she hadn't much to say for the duration of our stay. The sisters kept giving her sharp glances out of the corners of their eyes. Now that they knew about the house in Bush Hill being sold, they were not at all happy.

* * *

THERE WAS A SATURDAY IN NOVEMBER **1888** when we were invited over to the boarding house at Shelly Terrace for an evening meal, which was a rare occasion, and with my feet and other injuries having healed from that nightmarish incident in Whitechapel, I was able to attend. It was the first time a dinner invitation had been extended to us, as usually Maud came to us, unless Augustus paid her a surprise visit in the middle of an afternoon. There was quite a lot of discussion about going, because Augustus didn't think it was proper to be dining at the boarding house, as opposed to merely having a polite cup of tea there instead. Also, he was suspicious, and wondered if Maud was trying to get on his good side. He had hoped Maud was out of his life, but that had only been wishful thinking, as his granddaughter bound them together. He thought the entire situation uncomfortable, but in the end decided to go. Edmund and Charles did not attend, for obvious reasons. They had sneered at the thought, and both said, "You must be bloody joking!" So just the three unmarried sisters and Augustus and I caught the train, and it was all done in the interest of the child. Being a dog, I found it difficult to snub Maud, and like iron filings drawn to a magnet, I was drawn to wag my tail in greeting and to lick her hand. She was polite, but did not make a fuss over me; instead, Mary Ann did that, and treated me like an old friend.

At eight o'clock Mary Matilda was sent off to bed, allowing everyone to sit down and enjoy their meal. Dinner was served shortly after she departed, and though it wasn't a grand affair, the cooking was adequate and there was plenty of it. We were served a summer salad, which was rather good, as I like lettuce and cucumbers; as well, there was chicken with vegetables, and spotted dick for pudding. The subject of money or anything to do with finances was strictly avoided, with most of the conversation leaning towards fashions and the coming of the new century. My master was uncomfortable, and I knew he was hoping the evening would hurry up and get over with. I sensed his mood, which was impatient.

There were no houseguests seated at the table. It was a private do, though the owner, Mary Ann, was present. After the salad course, I went upstairs, ignoring the stares of the two elderly ladies (paying guests), and padded along to Mary Matilda and Charlotte's bedroom, where the child was getting ready for bed. Already in her nightgown, she was knelt on the floor facing her bed, with her back to me, and her thick, brown plaited hair was tied at the end with a yellow ribbon, and her head was bowed in prayer. I watched from the open doorway, not wanting to interrupt yet eager to jump up on her bed and rumple her blankets for her.

"God bless Mummy and also Daddy in heaven. God bless Auntie Jessie, Auntie Lucy, Auntie Julia, Uncle Edmund, and Uncle Charles. Oh, God bless Grandfather, and also Granddad Diggins."

She went through her list of aunts, uncles and cousins, and then she leaned towards Charlotte and whispered loud enough for me to hear, "Should I bless Shales as well?"

Charlotte smiled, and answered in a kind voice, "I suppose so. It won't do him any harm, will it?"

"Are you sure God won't mind?"

"I don't think so," answered Charlotte as she looked at me. She held her finger up to her lips, which meant "shush". I stayed "shush" and continued to watch and listen.

"God bless Shales, because I think he needs all the help you can give him. God, please keep Shales out of trouble, and keep him safe, forever. Amen."

I had to admit to myself that I did get into a lot of trouble, and after the last go, perhaps I did need a caring prayer or two to guide me. I silently trotted back downstairs, where I found a plate filled with a generous portion of meat pie set out for me alongside a bowl of water. Mary Ann's scent lingered, and I was thankful for her ministrations.

* * *

THERE WAS ONE AFTERNOON DURING LATE WINTER – I think it was a day in February 1889 – when the three sisters Jessie, Julia and Lucy called upon Maud. It was a Sunday afternoon and I was invited to go along. We hadn't heard from her in months, not since we had last dined with her, and the proper reason we went over there was to make sure Mary Matilda was all right, and yes, it was another one of our surprise visits. I was so well behaved in public that I could travel the trains with the sisters, and I did not pull on my lead and make whoever was holding the other end lose her balance and stumble. I was a true gentleman's dog, and we arrived in time for tea, as it was mid-afternoon.

Maud had mostly been nice to me since the incident in Thomas's bedroom, several years before, but I still didn't quite like her. There were times when she was irritable with me for no apparent reason. There was something I always felt that she was hiding about herself. She did always serve me tea, albeit in an old, cracked and chipped bowl. She would boast, "Shales even has his own cup sitting in the cupboard." Fair enough, I thought; at least I was offered a cup of tea – no need for the china bowl to be from the good set. That day, as I lapped it up in the sitting-room of the boarding house, just as I like it, weak with lots of milk, I smelt the stale remains of tobacco. Pipe or cigar I wondered? I narrowed it down to pipe tobacco, and once again it was a brand I was not familiar with, except for the fact that I only seemed to smell it there, in Mary Ann's sitting-room. It was always the same brand. I wondered who the man was? I wasn't jumping to conclusions, but I was simply putting two and two together and making four. Women did not usually smoke pipes; well, not the sort of women I knew, although I did see one smoking a pipe in Whitechapel on that night when I had been taken and dragged up and down those horrid, dark streets. Obviously, some women smoked, but not the gentler, more civilised sort. This meant it was a man, hopefully a gentleman (and not some down-at-heel sort), who was obviously a regular visitor to the house.

The sisters were completely unaware of the presence of this man so, therefore, they did not ask Maud any questions regarding the nature of this visitor. In fact, Maud wouldn't have revealed anything had she been asked; I know that now. She was used to being dropped in on by either Augustus or the sisters, so she was always careful of what she revealed about herself. Dear Reader, you must think my family were very snooty and strict, but no, it wasn't like that at all. It was the only way they could see Mary Matilda and make sure she was looked after properly. You must realise this by now, and if not, you'll come to know it later.

* * *

IT HAD TO HAPPEN. I suppose we could all have seen it coming from miles away, but nobody had ever thought to mention, to voice out loud, what sort of irresponsible actions Maud could do that would irrevocably affect our lives. Even you, Dear Reader, my old mate, my old china, will now be wondering, "What on earth has she done now?"

Well, I'll tell you what she did. That summer of 1888, she went to Cotheridge Court and accepted a fine holiday, and of course, some money (ten pounds to be exact), which was to be either spent on her daughter or put away in a bank to accumulate interest over the years. Yes, she did this, then had us over for a meal at the boarding house, and then right after Christmas she disappeared. The two of them disappeared; did a midnight flit without telling anyone! We didn't find out for weeks and weeks, and when no word had come from Maud regarding her daughter etc., Jessie hopped on a train and dropped in at the boarding house, in the way of a surprise visit. Well, it was Jessie who got the surprise, as well as Mary Ann Moore. There was no Maud and no niece to greet her. Mary Ann was just as surprised as Jessie, as *she* had thought that *we* had known that Maud had moved away. Mary Ann did not know where Maud had moved to, as she had been told that a forwarding address would be sent to her, by way of a postcard. No postcard had arrived, so she didn't know where they had gone. All that Mary Ann Moore knew, was that Maud had been seeing a man named Henry, and other than that, was just as in the dark as the rest of us.

When Jessie returned home that day, you should have seen the look on her face. If looks could kill she would have done so with a sideways glance! When my master and Edmund were told about Maud's flit, I thought the

416

roof would come flying off our house, as the atmosphere inside was very explosive. Here is what was said:

Jessie, seated on the edge of the settee in the sitting-room, her hands clasped tightly together in her lap, leaned slightly forward and said, "Father, you are not going to like what I have to say. You too, Edmund."

Edmund didn't even give her a chance to explain. "If it is about Maud, I'm not in the mood." He sounded fed up before he had even heard what Jessie had to say.

"Oh yes you are. You are in the mood," she said, as she nodded her head. Her face was white, and her lips were blue with suppressed anger. "If not, then I can guarantee you shall be when you've heard what I have to say."

My master ran a finger around his collar; it was obviously too tight and was uncomfortable. "I hope my granddaughter is well and she has not been taken ill?" he asked. Suddenly, he looked concerned, remembering that night many years before.

"As far as I know she is well; I really don't know," answered Jessie.

Julia blurted out, "Hurry up, Jessie. Tell them what has happened!"

"All right, all right! They are not there. They have packed up and have left the boarding house, and Mary Ann Moore doesn't know where they have gone to."

Both Edmund and my master exploded, "What!"

"I went over there today, unannounced, because we haven't heard anything since we saw them just after Christmas. I expected to find Maud there, at her occupation, or at least somewhere close by and my niece in school, but I found that they have packed up their belongings and have vacated the premises. Mrs Moore said that Maud had promised to send to her the new address, but she has received no such communication. She assumed we knew all about it, so she didn't have any cause to worry. Mrs Moore was very surprised to see me arrive on her doorstep this past afternoon."

Lucy blurted out, "Tell them about Charlotte!"

"Yes, that is another thing. Charlotte was no longer there, as Maud had dismissed her and had told her that her services were no longer required. Mrs Moore said that Charlotte remained for a week, until she found lodgings elsewhere. She had applied for a new position, and Maud had given her references, though according to Mary Ann Moore, she herself actually wrote Charlotte's references, as Maud wouldn't do it. So, Charlotte has gone as well, to some place unknown, but I doubt if even she knows where Maud is."

I looked from face to face as I tried to interpret what had happened. I understood a lot of it. It was bad news, and Maud had done something terribly wrong. This was what I had been anticipating all these years. I had known she couldn't be trusted.

My master was at a loss for what to say, but eventually he spoke words of wisdom. "I'll have the police search for her. When they find her she'll be in for a surprise! I'll have my brother Comyns follow through with a guardianship suit. How long have they been gone?"

Jessie stuttered, "Nearly... no... it is two and a half months since she was last at the boarding house. Not a word from her, and she hasn't even kept Mary Ann informed, and they are supposed to be good friends. What sort of character is she? I have to say I have *never* liked her, never, and I wonder why our Thomas couldn't see through her."

Edmund removed his coat and carefully laid it upon the arm of a chair. His white shirtsleeves were immaculate and so was the rest of him. He stood up and paced about the sitting-room, where we were all seated. We waited for him to speak.

"There's something more to this than she's just moved away without informing anyone. It's more complicated than that. It has to be. Even for Maud there has to be a good reason for doing this. When we find her, the whole story will come out, and we'll probably find she has a fancy man."

Augustus's hands shook slightly. He was enraged by the situation. "It wouldn't surprise me to find out that her own family doesn't know anything about this. I don't think she has kept in touch with them. If you ever ask her about them she always changes the subject. Perhaps I should write to her father?"

Edmund took his watch out, looked at it, put it back in its fob, looked at his father, and said, "I suppose you'll be visiting Uncle Comyns and Harry first thing tomorrow?"

"Yes. That's definite. Are you coming?"

"Yes, of course I'll come," replied his son. "We'll find them eventually. Mary Matilda *has* to go to school. It *is* the law, and unless she is being privately tutored, which I doubt, *that* is where we shall find her."

So there, now you know. Well, what you don't know is why did Maud do a midnight flit? Well, it took quite a few months to find her, and, of course, with finding her it all came out in the wash. The law of the country was that children, between the ages of five and ten, must attend school, unless they were privately tutored, so that is where the hired detectives first looked. Of course, Maud could have moved to some far-off place like Wales or Scotland, but they looked for her closer to home. They found her, but not until her feet were well rooted in her new life. They found them living in Edmonton, which really isn't that far away from Hackney, and only a stone's throw away from Bush Hill Park. Mary Matilda had been kept home and hadn't attended school right away, but when she did go to school she went under her mother's maiden name of Diggins. She became known as Mary Diggins, and her mother became known as Mary Allen, not Maud Berkeley or Maud Diggins, but Mary Allen. May was her second name but she had started using Mary, and Allen was one of her middle names, so it wasn't as if she'd used someone else's name. There was also another child, a little girl, named Blanche Evelyn Diggens: Maud had given birth to her in June of 1889, and she was half-sister to Mary Matilda. Maud's pregnancy was the reason why she took flight in secret. If Augustus had known that she was pregnant again, and not married, he would not only have *not* given her that last ten pounds, but would have demanded some of the monies previously given to her to be returned to him. She also knew that he then could easily have had his granddaughter taken away from her, and somehow I don't think she would have liked that, even though she knew her daughter would have been well provided for, as well as educated, something she could not provide on her own.

True to form though, Maud, now Mary, was living with Henry Diggens, master tobacconist, and father of baby Evelyn. If you remember, Maud's surname was Diggins (slightly different spelling) before she married Thomas Rowland, so instead of marrying Henry she pretended to be married, which was a sinful thing in the eyes of the Church, and of just about everyone I knew at that time. Boys o' boys, mmn, mmn, mmn.

Legal proceedings were started up again, and this time the family was intent on removing the child from the inappropriate upbringing she was being exposed to.

* * *

MAUD AND HENRY MOVED AWAY FROM EDMONTON, so once again she was on the run and Augustus was on her tail. They were found living in Walthamstowe, a place also not far from Hackney, where they had a joint confectioner/ tobacconist shop. Maud, who was still being known as Mary, worked in the shop as an assistant confectioner instead of working at her own trade of dressmaking. As soon as she found out the police were enquiring about her she left, taking Evelyn and Mary Matilda with her. They fled north to Yorkshire, where they settled for a few years in Bradford. The trail becomes muddied though, as Maud continued to change her names. We don't know if her 'husband' John Dixon was the same man as Henry Diggens or not as no marriage certificates for either marriage were ever found. A few years later, with the surname Dixon, they mysteriously moved across the Pennines to Ardwick, Manchester.

XXVI
My Aunt, my Uncle,
and my Cate

"...my kind and faithful friend."

1889 - 1892

EANWHILE, everyday life went on around us as it always does, full steam ahead in forward motion, regardless of the consequences. I suppose a coal strike had to happen sometime, and it did in the summer of 1889. It was a complicated affair that was responsible for Augustus and Edmund being in foul moods. It didn't last long; well, just for the last fortnight in August, but when it was over with the casual labourers at the dockyard had won a pay rise. The strikers had stopped the supply of coal coming in from the docks, and later they had even tried to prevent the supply of railway coal from coming in from the mines. The strikers had even tried to incite the coal labourers to join them, and also those employed by the gas companies. They were not as successful as they would have liked, with the coal workers and gas lighters returning to work after just a few days. Yes, there was even a night when that familiar man did not light the lamps in our road, leaving it in perpetual darkness until the sun came up. The pay rise for the dock labourers was to be absorbed by the merchants, and that meant us, and of course we the merchants, with not wanting any more losses in income, then passed it on to the retailers, who in turn passed it on to the consumers of coal, which forced up the price of coal per ton. The cost of coal was now over a guinea per ton.

* * *

I WOULD SOMETIMES WORRY that the remaining sisters and Edmund would marry, leaving the house empty with just myself and Augustus to rattle about in, leaving just the occasional presence of the cook or housemaid. Charles was to be married to Amy, but you already know that. I haven't yet got round to telling you when they finally married, but I shall do so now. It was the latter part of 1889, and it was a small affair, which was normal according to the times, and because I didn't get taken along, I can't tell you first-hand about all the details. It was obvious to everyone that Charles was in love with Amy, and even though he was a tailor, and she a schoolteacher, they would be able to live in an extremely comfortable way. They took a house in Hackney, on Heyworth Road, near to Charles's place of employment, as he now owned his own shop, becoming an employer and not an employee.

During those years there were children, other grandchildren, born to the family. Emily and Thomas had a little girl named Ruth. Charles and Amy had a baby named Comyns, as well as a baby named Dorothy, she who was born in 1890. Augustus had more grandchildren than he knew what to do with, including the four up in Gorleston.

There was the loss of Uncle George Brackenbury, near the end of 1889. That was another surprising death for the family, and once again we were plunged into mourning, twice in one year, what with the tragic death of Herbert just a few months prior.

Nearly a year later, one of Augustus's friends, who shared the same surname as us, also died. That was G.C. Berkeley.

The year of 1892 couldn't quite make up its mind whether or not to fetch sadness or joy. On one particular day during the early winter month of January the bell rang, indicating that a visitor was at the front door. Armstrong rushed to answer it, and when she returned it was with one of those looks on her face that seemed to say, "Eeh, I hope it isn't sad news again."

With a silver salver in her hand, she quietly strode over to the master and said, "Sir. This 'as just come, this very moment."

Putting down his newspaper carefully, so as not to lose his place, he reached for the message. "Oh, I see it is a telegram. I'm not expecting anything to come today. I wonder if it is to do with a shipment of coal."

Jessie looked up from her sewing, as she was doing a bit of embroidery, and was seated close to the lamp. "Dad, do you want me to open it?" she asked gently, as she eyed the small envelope. Her facial expression betrayed her fears.

"No. You're all right. I'll see what it has to say."

A moment later he quietly said, "Well, it seems my brother Charles has passed away. He died yesterday; that was the eighteenth. Oh, dear. I wasn't expecting this." There was a short pause before he spoke, "I can't believe it. Charles is gone. There aren't many of us left now; we're dying like flies."

"Oh, no," said Jessie. She rang for Annie and asked her to summon Edmund, who was in the library entertaining some male visitors, old friends of his. When he entered the room and was told the sad news of his uncle, he was asked to inform his brother Charles and his sister Emily.

"I'll walk over to Emily and Thomas's, but I'll have to take a cab to Charles and Amy's." He left the room and shortly returned. His visitors prepared to leave.

I danced about his heels, hoping to be taken along.

"Shales. Come on, we're going out."

We walked over to Emily's house at Chatham Place. The news was taken quietly. Her uncle Charles was still highly thought of, even though he'd brought shame upon himself. From near to there we hailed a cab, and at young Charles Clement's house we informed him of his uncle's death. He too had liked his uncle.

Julia and Lucy were in the city, spending a day of traipsing around museums and art galleries. They would hear the sad news when they returned.

There was to be another funeral, and once more black crepe hatbands would have to be purchased – by Augustus – this time for another one of his brothers. I was becoming concerned for my master, because I could see him aging, slowly but surely, and his siblings were passing away from old age. I wondered if he would be the next to go. I didn't want to think about that, so I told myself he wasn't going to die. Never! It was as simple as that. None of them would die, leaving me all on my own. What would I do? How would I live? No! No one else was going to die.

* * *

423

REGARDING CHARLES CLEMENT, who had recently passed away. For years the family had been in disagreement as to whether or not he was married to Susan. Well, it all came out in the reading of his will. The will was short and simple. He left everything to his 'kind and faithful friend' Susan Tomlin. Not his wife – they were not married after all. The dear man left her well provided for, as well as the children. He had loved her.

Augustus had known all along that his brother had not been married, as later, I heard him reveal it to his own children. "He was still my brother, even though I disagreed with his life. They both wore rings and pretended to be married, to keep society at bay. He knew what he was doing... he loved her very much."

* * *

BEFORE THE SUMMER WAS OVER WITH there was yet another death, on the twenty-fifth of August, and this time it was dear Auntie Emily. She had been the only surviving sister Augustus and his brothers had, and she had never married, so she had been special in all their hearts, and now she too was gone at the age of seventy-five.

I was beginning to find it eerie, how people aged as time went by. Edmund and Jessie were both going a little grey, with silver strands beginning to show here and there. Augustus's hair was thinning, and he seemed to be moving about a bit slower, and more care was given when he walked up and down the staircase. His tread was becoming ever so much heavier and yet slower, and I now saw he used the banister rail for support. He was nearly seventy-two years old, and once again I worried about more future deaths within the family.

* * *

EVER SINCE THAT DREADFUL DAY when I had thought I had seen Horatio walking down Darnley Road, and I had left the safety of the house and garden to search for him, resulting in my being stolen and taken on a wild tour of Whitechapel, and so on, I had wondered if he was dead, or perhaps still alive and safe in Essex. I sensed there was something different, but I didn't quite understand what it meant. Without going to Stanford Rivers for visits, I was unable to visit my friend, not unless I took the train, but I was reluctant to do *that* now, not wanting to venture too far on my own. I had come to realise that I had a tendency for getting myself into trouble, so an unaccompanied train journey to Ongar was out of the question. There were times when the sisters, or even Charles and Amy, went back there to visit, though usually it was just for the day, as we no longer had the farm. Edmund sometimes rode Jasper all the way out there, but on those occasions he stayed over for several days visiting with old family friends. I was envious of Jasper, as I yearned to travel with both of them, running along at their side as I had done with Thomas. I would have been able to have visited the churchyard and lie down upon the grass in front of the family vault. At times I felt that we should all go out there and pay our respects to the dead. I imagined him down there in the vault, just as I had last seen him, but at peace; still there, but neither coming nor going, not alive but dead, a state which I still struggled to come to terms with.

As it happened, I had one of those dreams, the sort that seems to be eerily strange, yet as real as if it weren't a dream at all. It started with me dreaming I was back at Wayletts, and I was enjoying a romp about Ten Acre Wood. I had been taking in the pungent aroma of the wood, and noisy squirrels chatted away in the background. There were bluebells in full bloom, creating delicate, undulating swathes of blue and green. My dream changed, as it then went deathly quiet, and I actually wondered, consciously, what was going to happen next. There he was! Suddenly Horatio, my friend, came striding up to me with his usual calculated plod and greeted me with a loud purr. He rubbed himself against me. His fluffy, upright tail wrapped itself around my face and tickled my nose.

"Shales mi mate, fanthy meetin' thee 'ere. Well, I haff to admit I knew thee were comin', so I vought to m'self, why not haff a little visit wiff him an' set vings jes to rights?"

In my dream, I said, *"Why, Horatio, mi old china, I've been worried about thee, I 'ave. I fought I saw thee walking across the street, in Hackney. 'Onestly, I fought I saw thee with mi own minces."*

"That wathn't me, lad. Nao, it definitely wathn't me; but, it wath my ghost, becauthe I was already dead by then; bewied beneave the manure pile, behind the chicken shed."

I swallowed deeply. *"Dead? Ghost?"*

"Yeah. I sowt of died of owd age. I jus didn't wike up in the usual way." And he then sat down and scratched his neck a bit, and then proceeded to clean his front paws, all the while purring away. *"I'fe been lookin' for ya, for ages."*

"Oh, my." I didn't know what else to say. There was a long pause as I thought about what he'd said.

Horatio picked up the thread of conversation, *"I wathn't sure how tha'd come out of vat escapade wiff va doctor."*

"Oh, if you mean Jack the Ripper, well then, I nearly 'ad it that noight. It must 'ave been 'im you had warned me abowt. I nearly got killed that noight, but I managed to survive it and 'ere I am. Boys o' boys, mmn, mmn, mmn."

He sighed deeply. *"Yeth. I know vat now, but at the time awl I could see wath the danger an' the vision ov a dark man wielding a knoife, wiff thee hiding there deep in the shadows. I knew it would happen to thee, but I didn't know when or where it would happen."*

"Doesn't matter." I then said, *"Wot are we doing in Ten Acre Wood?"* I was beginning to realise that the dream was too real, and questions started to pop up in my sleeping mind.

"Oh, we're here to have a roight good natter. I came to let thee know about me, becauthe I knew thee would wonder an' neffer know. I'fe had a long journey, though."

"I did wonder. I actually felt something was different, not quite roight, but I didn't know for sure what it meant."

"That was me trying to tell thee, but it's werry difficult when I'm owfer here and your owfer there."

"Can we do this again?" I asked.

"I don't know, Shales." He shook his shaggy head and his huge green eyes got even bigger. *"Thith ith the first toime I'fe done anyving like this. Oh, they're calling me, I muth gao. Shales, I muth gao now. Ta-ra, luv."*

The next thing I knew, I was waking up. I had a sensation of it all starting to slip away, and I grasped what I could, holding onto the memory of it so I wouldn't forget it. I lay there on the bottom of Jessie's bed, without moving, and went over and over what the dream had contained. It was like the one that Maud had woken me up from when I had been sure I had been talking to Thomas, who had been dead at the time. I could actually smell the scent of cat, Horatio's own personal scent, and underlying that was the faint but unmistakable odour of Macassar oil, leather and horses. I was sad. I was very sad. It had brought back a lot of memories, and I felt a terrible longing deep within my soul. I now knew my best friend was dead, and what really bothered me was that I positively knew that I would never see my mate, my cate, *alive* again. Never.

Augustus, age 70.

XXVII
These are Changing Times

"I worried about all the horses."

1895 - 1898

I N THE PAST I HAD OFTEN WONDERED why the age and health of a person was such an interesting topic for discussion, especially when that person had passed on and was no longer on this earth to hear the harsh words of criticism spoken against them, which usually referred to his or her general state of health. On this particular day it was I who was the topic of such a discussion, the point being that I was old, meaning an aged dog, and would be "going downhill" shortly, according to the words being bantered about the table. I had to think long and hard when I heard those words "going downhill", and they had been spoken with such sadness and deep emotion, resulting in the eruption of tears on many a face in the room, that I had a sense of deep foreboding that seemed to at first linger in the air, and then settle upon me, as if a heavy cloak had been placed about my shoulders. Apparently, I was sixteen years old, an age reasonably rare for dogs, though not unseen in cats. My family was apparently amazed at my longevity, especially since I had shown no apparent signs of stiffness or illness, usually brought on by old age, except for the occasional limp caused by my leg, which had once been broken. The occasional limp had now become an everyday occurrence, but I didn't mind as I had become so used to it, until it was pointed out to me by rude people, usually strangers, and then I would realise I was limping.

Edmund, who was my saviour, and reminded me so much of his late brother Thomas, gazed down at me from where he sat at the dining-room table. "You'll be with us a bit longer. You're not ready to go yet, are you?"

I thumped my tail and then trotted off to fetch my bunny in acknowledgement. I shoved Bunny into his hand, and he tugged gently on it.

"Oh, Shales," he said. "We could write a book about all your escapades and adventures, if only we knew about most of them. Put together with whatever thoughts rattle about in your handsome head, I am sure it would make good reading."

Jessie laughed and wiped a tear from her left eye. "If only dogs could live as long as people."

"He'd put us in our graves, early graves at that," said Julia.

Augustus volunteered, "I never expected him to live this long, and he has been hard work over the years, but I have to say that he has made this a happier house. I've always liked dogs, but some of them are more special than others, and there'll never be another Shales, not ever."

"I agree, Dad." Edmund was still playing a gentle game of tugging with me.

Julia wasn't so confident in my longevity, and quietly she said, "I'm afraid we shall wake up one day and he'll have died in his sleep. I couldn't bear that, but I know it will happen. We're just going to wake up one morning and find him dead in his sleep."

My master responded to this sadly, "Julia, love, it is indeed a sad event to contemplate, but we know it is coming, just as my own days are running out. You have to face up to it."

She replied, "Do you face up to it, Dad? Do you think about him dying in his sleep, or becoming so ill that Edmund has to put a bullet in his brain?"

My master leaned back in his chair, and looked at her. "Yes, I do think about it. We've had him for fourteen years, and that is a small miracle. My dad once told me that they had a dog that lived to be nineteen years old. I didn't really take him seriously, because I thought he had got it wrong, but I now wonder if he was right."

Edmund now spoke again, on my behalf. "Julia, I would take him to the vet's. I wouldn't do *that* to him. Perhaps in the country, but not here in the city."

Jessie said, "Thank you, Edmund. It is a worry, but let's hope he has another good year or so."

"I shall speak to Rowland and ask him if we can bury Shales at Cotheridge Court. It would be good to have it settled beforehand." My master then excused himself and hastily left the room.

I listened to Jessie's words as she spoke of my fate. I began to wonder about myself. Was I so different now from the time when I had first wandered into the farmyard at Wayletts? I was more intelligent, or educated, as I preferred to think of myself. Perhaps I didn't have quite as much energy as I used to have in the past, but what was wrong with that? I knew that everyone in the family was growing older, because I could see it happening, very slowly; they were aging gracefully. As for myself, I hadn't even bothered to wonder how many years I should live, nor had I known what the normal lifespan was for a dog. It simply hadn't mattered, so I hadn't thought about it. I had worried about everyone else, except for myself.

As the rest of the family got up from the table and departed the dining-room, and quietly proceeded to make themselves comfortable in the drawing-room, pipe tobacco began to circulate in ethereal wisps upon the air. Glasses tinkled as sherry and port was poured from their decanters. Augustus had returned, and now being slightly more composed, made an announcement.

"It wouldn't surprise me to see this lad live to be twenty years. He'll outlive Dad's dog. I'm sure of it."

Lucy sighed, "Wouldn't that be nice?" Then she said, "Jessie, I think what Edmund said about writing down all of Shales's escapades is an interesting idea. It would make a lovely story, especially if it were illustrated."

"I think you may be right. Lucy, let's start writing everything down, all the events that have happened throughout his lifetime, like a diary of sorts."

Julia got excited. "Then we'll always have something to remember him by, as well as recording our family history."

Edmund and his father were deep in conversation between themselves, and the sisters discussed the book they would write.

I rested my head in Jessie's lap, and she gently stroked my ears, playing with the longish hair at the back of them, and I felt loved and comforted. With a sudden surge of emotion, I knew I didn't want to leave this family behind, and neither did I want any more of them to die. Please, no more funerals, just an eternity of old age.

* * *

DO YOU KNOW THAT I HADN'T JUMPED OVER THE BACK WALL of the garden in a few years? The desire to be alone and free upon the roads and streets of Hackney and London had long since departed. These days my life existed with at least one daily walk; a morning constitutional with Augustus set us both right for the day, and if I were lucky Jessie would take me out for a stroll in the afternoons, unless the weather was unsuitable. I didn't get over to the stables to chat with the horses, not very often these days, as Augustus had retired, though he did do some paperwork at home to keep his days occupied. Edmund took me with him to work, but it was only occasionally, so if you want it in a nutshell I, too, was retired from the coal trade. Jasper was still with us, as horses invariably outlive dogs, and Edmund did exercise him regularly. He had not wanted to sell Jasper off; instead, he kept his brother's horse and provided him with a quiet and secure life. There had been the odd occasion, over the years, but not of late, when Stanley had borrowed Jasper and had ridden him to the hounds. Speaking of Stanley, we had heard that he was becoming famous for his paintings of military scenes, and that his work was greatly admired by the Queen.

* * *

SO THE YEARS GRADUALLY PASSED, and with them the completion of the bridge now known as the Tower Bridge, providing another way across the Thames. There were also strange new inventions, and one of them was called a 'motor' and it didn't need a horse to pull it along, no, it propelled itself along on four wheels, and they fed it something called petroleum. Edmund became fascinated with them, and in 1898 they appeared in London and were used for public transport. He wanted to replace the horses and coal wagons with these motor cars, but his father was reluctant to side with him.

"Yes, Dad," said Edmund, "but just think, in a few years we'll be able to shift the coal without the need of horses, stables, feed, and a stableman and boy." He went on to say, "There has been a lot of pressure to move horse stables further away from the dwelling houses and into the outskirts of Hackney, and we are not alone. It's the same everywhere. People don't want the smell and the pollution that comes with having livestock where there are paved streets and a large population of people. These cars will be able to take over and, sad as it is, the stables will be empty of horses, but the cities and towns will be cleaner places for it. There'll be no more piles of excrement to clean up, and it'll all smell a lot nicer for it."

Well! That was quite a shocking statement, wasn't it? No more horses in the city? What would happen to the coal horses and the funeral horses? Where would they go? My mind was spinning like a top as it tried to make sense of all Edmund had said. I didn't want to live in a place that had empty stables! The thought of it all was so depressing, and I wondered what would happen to all the horses everywhere. Where would they go and who would look after them? I imagined them traipsing about the countryside in small herds, grazing on the sweet grasses at the sides of the roads, but having no direction or human companionship, resulting in them becoming wild and unruly, such as a stray dog is.

Augustus had his own opinion, and in a quiet but patient voice he said, "Yes, son. I agree with you, but I shan't be around to witness it. It'll be years before people will be willing to buy one of those contraptions and get rid of their horses."

Edmund stretched out his legs and let out a long sigh. "I know, Dad, but I think this motor transportation is the way of the future, even if I myself am not around to witness it happen."

"They're very dear. I hear they're costly to run, but in a few years that may be improved upon." Augustus looked at his son, and then patted him on the arm. "You know what they say about those who stop to change their horses in midstream?"

Edmund laughed without answering his father. "Cheers, Dad. Let's hope there is still a demand for coal in the future, because it's our livelihood, and where would we be without it?"

"We'd be either solicitors, wine merchants or gentleman farmers," replied his father knowingly.

"You forgot to mention reverends."

"Yes, well, I don't think we were cut out to be those, even though my brother and my grandfather were. Way back, we even had a judge in the family."

The conversation continued, but it was focused on the nephews, some of whom had joined the various family businesses, but others were soldiers or sailors, and one was a surgeon. With the soothing, low tones of the men's voices in the background, I wondered about Jasper. I hadn't seen him in ages, and I longed for a visit to the coal yard and the stables. I worried about the horses and what would happen to them if these motor contraptions arrived in full force. Where would all the horses go, and who would look after them?

A country without horses was a place I did not want to partake of. I found it all very depressing.

XXVIII
A Reward for Service
Well Done

"Let's 'ave a butcher's at the dog."

1900

"**N**OW A LITTLE DICKY-BIRD WIV YOU, MY LUVLY CHOINA.**" A new century was dawning, and in the first few days of 1900 a letter arrived, hand delivered from Buckingham Palace. The sisters cooed with joy as the letter was read out loud by my master, as we enjoyed our afternoon tea. Dear Reader, now you will be very curious as to why the family should receive post from Her Majesty Queen Victoria, and I, too, was curious, but then astounded, to find out that it was really me who was the subject of curiosity by the Queen. In all reality, the letter was really for me, although it had been addressed to my master. What had I done to deserve this? Well, the letter was, in fact, a summons of sorts, for myself and for Augustus, to attend a ceremony at the palace, and I was to receive recognition for being 'The oldest living dog in the entirety of the British Empire'.

How did the Queen, the Empress Victoria, find out about me? Well, it all started when Augustus was at his club on one particular day (he went less often these days) and one of his acquaintances who was also a member of the Queen's own circle of personal friends had asked him if I was still living. Apparently my frequent escapades had been oft-times the subject of much hilarious discussion at the club, and there was a lot of interest about me after my Jack the Ripper incident (though nobody knew I'd encountered Jack that night). When the gentleman found out that I was indeed still alive he had broached the subject with Her Majesty, and had told her of my famous rescue of Shales at Southtown beach in Gorleston, which at the time had been reported in the Yarmouth newspapers. She had been so taken with his story, and the fact that it could be proved that I was turned twenty years old, that she decided there should be a special form of recognition for the longevity of a dog – twenty years or older, as long as it could be proved. The gentleman in question set forth and provided the documents and letters with the help of Augustus, and then weeks later the summons arrived. I had no knowledge of the secret investigations, and neither did the sisters, nor Edmund and Charles etc. It had been kept a national secret, lest nothing had come of it.

The house must have been vibrating off its stone foundations, should any pedestrian have happened by and glanced up at the brick, timber and glass facade of our house. We were all in a merry mood for days and days.

My plates of meat glided about as if I walked on air, and I ain't telling any porkies. Boys o' boys, mmn, mmn, mmn.

* * *

THE DAY TO GO TO THE PALACE FINALLY ARRIVED, after what seemed like a long wait. These days I was quite stiff when I woke up in the mornings, and many times I limped around all day long. My knees and toes didn't want to bend as I went up and down the stairs, an exercise I now reserved for mornings and bedtimes. Sometimes, if I felt like it, I would climb the stairs at dusk and watch for the lamp man to come along and light the lamps in our road. He was the same man, but he looked a little, if not a lot older these days, and I wondered how long he would go on doing his job; perhaps until a time came when *he* couldn't do it any more. Where once I had run full speed up all those stairs, sometimes from down in the kitchen and all the way up to the second floor, and sometimes further to the attics, I now could barely climb at a slow one-step-at-a-time pace.

It was nice to have the opportunity to travel by train as we journeyed to the palace, and after the changes we made, we emerged in a part of London I had never before seen. A carriage was hired, not a common cab, as Augustus himself refused to be dropped off at the palace gates such as the ways of a commoner, but a proper carriage with a well-dressed driver. Besides, he was beyond walking very far. What a sight we would have made, the two of us, shuffling along at an unsteady pace, frail enough that the wind could have knocked us down. The carriage dropped us off at the side door, and we entered the royal palace in style. My master was dressed in his most expensive suit, recently made for him by Charles, with his top hat and gloves from the best shop in London, as well as his silver-handled walking-stick. We both looked immaculate, and my collar and lead shone jet black. The name-plate on my collar glistened as if it were pure gold. This was a standard that had always been maintained, ever since I had received my first collar and lead from my master, Augustus.

We sat and waited in a small ante-room for what seemed like an eternity. Huge oil paintings mounted in gilt frames hung on the walls. I tried not to fidget, but I so wanted to meet the Queen. I wondered how she would greet us, as I had no knowledge of such events.

I wondered if she would say, "Let's 'ave a butcher's at the dog. Augustus kindly remove your titfer an' and we'll 'ave a bowler."

I hoped she spoke proper English like my family, and not the local London, or better still, cockney, such as I now spoke inside my head when I was thinking. I hadn't forgotten my original dialect, taught me by Toothless George, but I seldom thought in those Yorkshire words and accent any more.

Eventually, a door opened, and after being announced we were ushered rather importantly into a larger room, where an old lady sat in a rather large but comfortable-looking chair. This was her throne, then, and she was our Queen. She was quite elderly, and looked almost fragile. She was very small, and I recognised her from seeing her in statuette form in many villages and also in London and about Hackney. Her head bobbed about on her small, sloping shoulders.

"Come forward," she said.

We advanced forward and stopped at the appropriate distance required between her and us. We had been instructed beforehand as to what the social protocol was.

"So, this is the dog Shales," said Her Majesty. "What a lovely dog. I have been told he has spent a life full of mischief." She smiled at me with her wrinkled face. "Is he friendly?" she asked politely, and was obviously hopeful of an affirmative response.

My master bowed his greyish-white head and revealed his bald crown to his Queen. "Yes, Your Majesty. He's very friendly; he loves people."

"I have read all about his daring rescue of your grandson of the same name, and I trust the child suffered no hardships from the terrifying event?"

Augustus proudly answered, "My grandson now serves Your Majesty in South Africa."

She smiled and nodded her head. "I pray that he comes home safely."

I stared at her, this kindly, little old lady whose head bobbed about upon her short shoulders. I wanted to jump up on her and lick her face.

Then she said, "Please step closer, so that I can see Shales better. Closer, step up here." She wanted to have a butcher's after all.

So we did step up to her, and I carefully leaned forward and put my paws on her throne and dropped my head in her lap. Her thickly petticoated skirts billowed out around her like a rather large, black cloud. She stroked my head and looked into my eyes.

Her hands and head shook. Her skin was very pale and sallow-looking. She was very fragile in her old age.

"What a lovely dog," she said. Then, "I've had countless dogs over the years, but there is always just one that seems to be special, and I think this one is special, is he not?"

"Yes, he is special, Your Majesty." I turned and looked at Augustus. He was smiling broadly.

She smiled back, and then asked, "I understand that he has been painted by Stanley Berkeley?"

Augustus answered in the affirmative, and she then said, "I do admire his work and I have a copy of one of his paintings at Balmoral."

"Yes, Your Majesty, he told me so himself."

"Why, of course, you have the same surname. Are you two related?"

"Yes, Ma'am, we are distantly related."

His reply seemed to please her. She then reached across to her side, where there was a little table, and she picked up a gold medallion that hung from a blue ribbon. It reflected the daylight, dully, but I knew its worth.

"With this medal, I declare, you, Shales Comyns Berkeley, at the age of twenty-one, to be the oldest living dog in the entirety of the British Empire."

She placed it over my head and it hung there as if it were a loose but weighty collar. Augustus bowed and thanked her. I was happy and I reached up and licked her face, and she laughed and said, "Goodbye."

We stepped backwards several feet, then turned sideways and left the room. We then left the palace. Outside the door several reporters were waiting for us and they had questions for Augustus. Our photograph was taken and then we set off for the station, in the same carriage, which had been summoned, and we then slowly made our way across London and arrived home just in time for tea. It had been a long and exhausting day, what with all the travelling and the changes of trains, but I fully understood the importance of meeting the Queen, and swaggered into the house with an extra lift to my step. The gold medal bounced off my knees, but I didn't feel anything except self-righteous pride.

I had seen the Queen, and she had treated me as if I were *special*.

Celebrations were in order, and I received an extra large portion of tea along with some ginger biscuits, those of which I happened to enjoy, but before, in the past, seldom received so many at one time.

My photograph appeared in all the newspapers. It showed me sitting next to Augustus, who was standing in the doorway to the palace, and my medal was clearly seen, the ribbon hanging about my neck and the gold medallion dangling past my chest. I was a local hero, and strangers actually sent postcards and letters to our house, and the contents of such letters stated sentences such as "...saw him go down our road many a time and I wondered where he was going", or "I saw him at the train station many years ago, but I thought he was with you, and not on his own". The family was appalled at the amount of people who had written to them mentioning sightings of me over the years. They had not realised the extent of my wanderings.

A few days later a photograph of Augustus and myself arrived in the post. It had been sent to us by the palace secretary. Jessie had it framed, and placed it amongst the family photos on display on a round table in the sitting-room. It had its place of honour, and the family was proud.

So was I. Boys o' boys, mmn, mmn, mmn.

* * *

LESS THAN A YEAR LATER, in January 1901, the entire world came to earth with a shock that rocked the frontiers of the Empire, from Britain to its many colonies. Our beloved Queen Victoria had died on the twenty-second of January at the age of eighty-two. I had only just rested my head upon her lap the previous year and now she too was gone. The nation had known she would not live forever, but neither had they wanted her to die. She had been ill, but most of all she had been elderly. We had no queen, but the family said we would now have a king, and he was Edward, her son.

* * *

I WAS TWENTY-ONE YEARS OLD, and I felt every bit that age. As each month passed by in 1901, and I approached twenty-two years of age, I felt the desire to sleep longer hours, and I craved the warmth of the fireplace, even in the summer months when the house was reasonably warm. The cold would creep into my bones, but Jessie had always maintained a house free from damp in the summer months, and I was glad of it. Every morning I went for my constitutional with Augustus, but for the two of us it was a slow shuffle, and not an ambitious romp. When I slept I dreamt strange dreams, and upon waking it was as if the dream world was real and the real world was a dream. I found those instances rather frightening because I didn't understand them.

I knew it was only a matter of time for the two of us so, patiently, I began to wait.

XXIX
Augustus

*"My duty done: the house had been
alerted, and my vigil was over."*

October, 1901

DEAR **R**EADER, if there is but one word which describes my master,
it is *"gentlemanly"*. He was the epitome of that word, so kind and
thoughtful towards others, intelligent and loyal, regardless of
one's status. I had witnessed his genuine politeness towards others on many
an occasion, and perhaps he was a little too generous at times with his money.
This elderly man, who held our household together, had long since started to
show signs of old age: rheumy eyes, arthritis and deafness, but really it was
more noticeable when he appeared at times to be off in a distant world – as if
he were more comfortable with his memories of the past than with the present.
We all worried about him. He was eighty years old, and that was a triumphant
age for anyone of his generation, though his mother had lived to the ripe old
age of ninety-four. He had even begun speaking of Thomas Rowland and
William, and said his dreams seemed to be frequented by his dead sons.

Summer had passed us by this year without the annual visit to Rowland
and Mildred in Cotheridge, and we now found ourselves in the autumnal
month of October, whose chilly nights warned us of the cold winter months
yet to come. Then, he died, on the twenty-fifth, taken from us by a cerebral
haemorrhage. What can I say, but that he was gone, and that I would never
see him again. That very afternoon he had been reading the newspapers with
the aid of a magnifying glass, and had occasionally puffed on his pipe. Due
to my stiffness I lay upon some soft cushions on the floor at his side. We

440

both were close to the fire and savoured its warmth, and I half dozed in a semi-conscious state. But on that particular afternoon I had been alerted from my rest, and had known he had passed at that very moment. His pipe fell upon the floor with a small thud, and his unfinished newspaper drifted past me as if a breeze had swept it by. It landed near my nose. It was the same as when Thomas had died, and I had known then. This time I howled as loud as I could, as if I were some wild wolf in some distant forest at the farthest outreaches of Britain. It was young Charles, not so young any more, who came running, his footsteps thundering down the corridor. He had popped in at that very moment to see his father.

My duty done: the house had been alerted, and my vigil was over.

* * *

FOR THOSE LONG DAYS BEFORE THE FUNERAL TOOK PLACE, I WAS LOST. I couldn't eat and I couldn't think, but spent time wandering about from Edmund to Jessie, and then on to Lucy and to Julia. It broke my heart to see them cry, but Edmund soldiered on, as always, as the preparations for the funeral were made.

Augustus was to be buried in the family vault in the churchyard in Stanford Rivers. Until the day of the funeral he lay in his lead coffin, in the front room across from the sitting-room. The blinds were drawn and the house was shrouded in darkness. Early that morning the funeral hearse arrived, and amidst the mound of beautiful flowers and glass, the coal-black hearse departed down Darnley Road, once again pulled by four magnificent horses of the Black Brigade, with their black ostrich plumes bobbing with every step, followed by numerous carriages which made up the funeral parade.

It was a magnificent sight, and the sensation that history was repeating itself was all too strong. I, of course, was attending the funeral. A brand-new black crepe band snugly encircled my neck. I lay upon the floor of the carriage, but thick blankets had been provided to cushion me from the harsh bumps in the journey. This time I entered the church of St Margaret's, albeit I shuffled painfully and slowly along, but I still entered the church. Perhaps the favour of the late Queen had elevated my position from 'dog' to 'family' in the eyes of the vicar. He did not object to my attending the funeral, and I am glad he did not, as the little and ancient church was charming, and I greatly admired the stained-glass windows set amidst the thick walls. It was very small compared to the parish church in Hackney, which held a congregation of over two thousand. This church would hardly hold a tenth of that number, though it was a bit larger than St Leonard's. The ceiling was plastered, and I wondered, as I gazed up at it, what it would look like with all the original timbers exposed.

Many turned out for the funeral, including Augustus's brother, Comyns Rowland, his only surviving sibling who was in his ninety-first year. I saw Stanley and Edith, as well as Harry Douglas, and Algernon Cecil, who was wearing his officer's uniform and looked very smart and handsome. Edmund Robert had come up from Kent, and some of the Owen family (Augustus's in-laws) were there. Stanley wasn't well, and really should have stayed away. I didn't like the look of him and I sensed he was gravely ill. Many of Augustus's nieces and nephews were there, including George Augustus Goodrich and his son George H.A.C., the surgeon. Rowland and Mildred were in attendance with their children, and of course, our Charles Clement, Amy, Emily and Thomas White were there, and so were all their children. From Gorleston, Mary, wife of the late William had come with three of Augustus's grandchildren. Shales had still not returned home from the Boer war so, sadly, I did not get to see him.

Augustus had outlived many of his close friends, but those who were still living were there, spilling out of the open doors of the church and into the yard, where they solemnly stood and took shelter beneath the large trees.

When it became time to leave, after the service was over with, Edmund lingered at the site of the vault. One could touch the railings with one's hand, if one was inclined to do so, when walking down the path and out of the churchyard. I had time to say my silent *"goodbyes",* and then we left. Charles carried me to the waiting carriage – I was carried about quite frequently due to my feebleness. I never looked back, though I was tempted to do so. For once, I was afraid of what I would see, as I sensed *his* presence nearby. The odour of horses, leather, Macassar oil and cigar smoke was strong to my nostrils.

XXX

Forever Shales

"Is there a heaven for dogs, and another
one for cats, and yet again,
another one for horses?"

November, 1901

I was feeling very tired and weary. How old was I now? Was I still twenty-one, or was I even older than that? Augustus's funeral was over with, and had been for some time, or so it seemed to be. I was losing count of the days and weeks, and sometimes I didn't know if it was morning or evening; my days seeming to be turned upside down, leaving me with a sense of being cast adrift, or travelling on a train going to a destination unknown.

I barely had the strength to get up onto my feet from a prostrate position on the floor, and the house seemed to be awfully dark, with not much daylight or lamplight to light my way. I wondered if the family had forgotten to pay the gas bill – that would explain the frequent days and nights of darkness. The dim gaslights had gone silent, their popping and hissing sounds now non-existent. My thoughts turned to my family and to all those who had passed away over the years. It was so sad, and yet they had each one been a spark in my life as I had got to know them, and they in turn had got to know me. Did other dogs care about their human families as I did? I thought about my friend Horatio. It had been years since I had last seen him, but of late I had missed him terribly, and I yearned to visit with him again. He had seemed to care about life, and he was a *cat*, not a dog, so I think other animals did care, and perhaps some more than me, and some less. Was there any difference in the end? Once I died, would it matter what I had thought about others, and especially if they too were dead? Is that why heaven mattered to people? Is there a heaven for dogs, and another one for cats, and yet again, another one for horses? If so, would I meet up with Horatio, or would we be forever separated from each other in our separate heavenly existences?

I'd recently had a dream, one of those that seem like reality is overlapping with the land of Nod. I'd dreamt I'd woken up to the call of my name, and to my surprise I was back at Wayletts. In my dream I raced down the staircase and out through the door that led onto the drive, and then I ran through the yard and towards the fields. There, Thomas stood waiting for me, casually leaning against the bars of the gate. I sailed between the bars and greeted him such as a dog does the master he loves. His hands ruffled my ears, and he said happily, "Come on, Shales. Let's go find some rabbits. Ten Acre Wood is beckoning us."

I ran off as fast as I could, with Thomas running behind, and I thought to myself, *"He's dead, so this must be a dream."* When I actually awoke, I found it was to a feeling of deepest disappointment – surprised that I was still alive.

I would rather have stayed in Ten Acre Wood with Thomas.

* * *

MY PLATES OF MEAT – MY FEET – dragged along the pavement as I lumbered painfully down the road. I was progressing towards Mare Street and my thoughts were all about Thomas. At times I thought I'd heard him call out my name, such as now, but that couldn't have been so, because my hearing had declined to the point that I was nearly stone deaf. As I walked along I put it down to *senile imagination*. In other words, I was going barmy in my old age. I stopped to look about, as I couldn't remember how I had come to be there. I had no memory of leaving the house, and I certainly hadn't gone over the wall – I hadn't done that in years and years. Frequently of late I had found myself wandering about the house and hadn't remembered which room I had started off in.

Neighbouring terraced house, 13 Darnley Road.

"*So,*" I thought, "*Armstrong has let me outside into the street, to wander off on my own. That must be it. She's opened the door for me and let me out – I've simply forgotten; that's all.*"

I heard a team of horses coming up behind me and I turned my head to look, mostly out of curiosity. Through rheumy eyes I could see it was a lovely team of horses, and all six of them were black, and their coats glistened with the obvious care of good health and excellent grooming. They wore black ostrich plumes, which sprouted from between their ears, and I thought to myself, "*Boys o' boys, mmn, mmn, mmn.*" I thought their appearance odd, and then realised they were pulling a funeral hearse. It slowly passed me by, all black and shining, with its glass top and sides frosted with intricately etched patterns upon the glass, and it was filled with an abundance of flowers. It stopped, and as I admired all the brass fittings, I noted the smell of the horses and the pungent scent of their leather harnesses – a favourite smell of mine. My, this must be the funeral for a very important person, because *six* horses were stood there with their nostrils blowing, and they chomped on their bits as they tossed their noble, gigantic, black heads, thus creating the jingling sounds that harnesses make. Then, it glided away towards Mare Street. The road was empty of traffic and people. There was only the hearse; everyone had kept back out of respect.

I sighed. Had someone died and I hadn't been told? Had I forgotten that someone had died? I began to worry that it might have been Edmund, or one of the sisters, but just then, as I started to walk further along the road (the terraced houses were close by on my left), a carriage pulled up. The window blinds were down, preventing me from seeing who was seated within, it being part of the funeral parade. Then the carriage door slowly opened. I wondered where this carriage had sprung from, because, only a moment before, I had been admiring a hearse. Oh, my memory. It was like the cook's sieve; it wouldn't hold a thought any more. Of course! The carriage was part of the funeral parade. I knew that.

I looked for the hearse; it was still there. I could see it was getting ready to turn into Mare Street, so I turned my attention back to the carriage. *"Oh, dear!"* I thought. *"Someone has died, but I don't remember who it is. Is it Jessie? Or perhaps Edmund?"*

A gentleman leaned out towards me and put out his gloved hand. I gasped with surprise! It couldn't be... it just couldn't be Augustus, but it *was* him, and he had his familiar stick – the one with the head of a bear on the end. He spoke my name.

"Shales."

I stepped forward, ever so lightly, and clambered into the carriage and landed in his lap. I was so happy to see him that my tail wagged and wagged, and he hugged me to him tightly. I must've dreamt he had died. That was it; I had dreamt it all, or I had imagined it, and then thought it all to be reality.

Another voice said, "Welcome home, Shales."

I knew that voice, but didn't want to believe, couldn't possibly hope, but yes, it was Thomas Rowland reaching out to me and scratching the backs of my ears. I crawled over into his lap and he hugged me to him, and I knew I wasn't dreaming as I breathed in his odour of scented Macassar oil, cigar smoke and horses. I suddenly felt wonderfully alive; my aches and pains had disappeared, and I felt like I could run for miles. I cannot describe the joy I felt at being reunited with Thomas; there are no words for it. As I looked about, I could see there were others in the carriage, and I realised how crowded it had become. Why, there was William, and Uncle Charles Clement, as well as Auntie Emily, Uncle William Comyns, and Uncle George Brackenbury, and of course, Herbert – he was there. Then I smelt cat, that unmistakable scent, and as I turned my head, a familiar, soft, feline voice said, *"Hello, Shales. Thou is here wiff us now, forever. Forever, Shales."*

All the dead greet Shales, as he crosses over to the other side.

XXXI

Selected Excerpts

from Jessie's Diary

"Dear Diary,"

2ND AUGUST, 1880

Yesterday, I have to report, was a most eventful day. Uncle William's garden party was most enjoyable. It was good to see family again – so many of us together at one time, and to visit Cotheridge again. Also, I met the most lovely of dogs, and I must say, I am most envious of my cousin, Rowland. I now find myself longing for another dog, and I confess, one just like Rowland's. Also, I was pleased to see my cousins, both the males and the females, and so many of them! So many of us Jessies, Lucys, Julias, and Emilys, who share the same Christian names.

FRIDAY, 22ND APRIL, 1881

Yesterday, a very ragged dog appeared at our farm. It was sorely abused and nearly dead! Thomas carried him into the stable, and together we doctored the poor creature. It is Rowland's dog, Shales. I am sure of it, as I write this down. Even the collar has the name Shales inscribed upon it. I simply cannot see it being another dog, though the idea that Shales has come to us from Broadwas is just incredible. Thomas has written to Rowland, and we now must wait days for a reply.

7TH MAY

*Rowland's letter has arrived! It **is** Shales, and we can keep him. Rowland is so kind and generous to give up such a valuable working dog. I do not think I could have given up such a dog who has travelled so far and has endured so much. Even Father likes him. Thomas dotes on him, and one would think he had never before had a dog. Shales follows him everywhere, and together they go off into the woods at the back of the farm.*

Thomas has been acting strangely. It has nothing to do with the arrival of Shales. I have never seen my brother so interested in the White Bear. He rushes down there, then rushes back, not long enough to drink a pint of beer. I have mentioned it to Edmund, and, he has as usual, just rolled his eyes at me in response. Sometimes, I think, I could knock both their heads together! I'm concerned that this behaviour is so out of character for Thomas. What is he up to, I ask myself?

JUNE, 1881

It has been a most horrid week for us. One would not think that one of my brothers could do such a despicable thing as to get a woman with child. There has been so much rage amongst us since Father broke the news to us. Thomas's rushed trips to the White Bear were to post and receive letters from his love, not to quench his thirst in ale. We are all mystified as to where such behaviour could spring from – Uncle Charles has behaved in a similar fashion, and perhaps Thomas has followed suit.

There shall be a wedding! Thomas is to be married, and as I see it, a man who gets a woman with child has no choice in the matter. I can only wish that he will be happy, and will not live to regret his actions.

The wedding was small. I don't think much of the bride, nor her family. Nothing can be done now; it is over with.

SEPTEMBER, 1882

It grieves me to write this. Thomas is dead. I do not think I shall ever go through such a difficult time again as his funeral was. Coping with his death has been unbearable for me. I cannot get him out of my mind. Dad is still in shock and is regretting everything that happened last year, and we are all adjusting to having Maud and the baby living with us.

12ᵀᴴ AUGUST, 1884

There is lots to write regarding our visit with William and Mary, in Gorleston, but I shall keep it short, if I can. It was so good to see them – we never see enough of William, since he has acquired the hotel, and they seem to live so far away. The weather was lovely, the sun shone every day, and it was warm. On a down note, my little nephew Shales took it upon himself to go swimming in the sea, and he nearly drowned. He would have done so if our dog Shales had not rescued him! What a sight to see! People all gathered at the water's edge as Shales dragged my nephew in to shore. I could see Shales, our dog, that is, was gagging, and struggling to keep himself from drowning with his weighty load. I stood rooted to the sand, not knowing what to do. William, Father and Edmund shouted orders and gave intelligent directions. We did not know if my nephew was alive or already dead, not until he was dragged ashore. We thought he was dead, but William gave him 'air', and then Shales coughed up some water. Our dog, Shales, collapsed at the water's edge, and had to be carried to dry sand by Charles Clement. I do not know the reason, but I think that our dog is special in some strange way. There was something about the rescue that defies all logic.

OCTOBER, 1888

What is there to write about, except to say we have had a horrible time of it. Shales went missing, just disappeared, and as usual we thought he had gone on one of his 'escapades' around Hackney. Father found him on the steps of the Coal Exchange, in a horrid state. I cannot help but wonder if Shales had encountered something akin to Jack the Ripper. I find it too much of a coincidence that there were murders, and Shales was sorely abused, and all on the same night. We shall never know the truth of it all.

7TH DECEMBER, 1888

I have come across the most interesting of things. I was having a look through some of Thomas's books, all those that he'd had, growing up, and had been left behind after he married Maud. Well! There is one in particular: a small book on horse care and saddlery. And, as I turned the pages, I found to my astonishment, a letter. I could not believe my eyes and wondered how long it had been there, tucked betwixt the pages. It looks as fresh as the day it was written. There is no address or name on the front, though it is folded and sealed and signed T.B. – I wonder if I should open it – I have it in my pocket, and am not sure if it belongs to someone in this household. Perhaps it was secreted away and they have forgotten about it. I must also mention it is Thomas's birthday – he would have been twenty-eight today.

8TH DECEMBER, 1888

I suppose I should not be writing this down for anyone to see, but I must, as I am so shocked with what I have just read. I opened the letter, the one I found yesterday. Nobody else knows about it. It was in Thomas's handwriting, and I have cried much over it. The letter is brief but the message is clear:

Dear Maud, I fear I must tell you, that you and I are not greatly suited to each other. We both know that our backgrounds are as different as cotton and silk, and I feel we should part ways. My father has plans for my future, and I do not wish to let him down. I wish you every success for your own future, and should our paths cross again, please do not treat me too harshly. I'm sure you understand. I shall not be writing to you again, nor shall I visit with you.

Fondly,
Thomas

What shall I do? It is clear to me that this letter should have been delivered to Maud, but obviously he had found out about her being with child before he could address it and post it. I dare not wonder how different his life would have been, if he had delivered that letter to her before she had informed him of her situation. I shall keep this to myself, and the letter has been destroyed.

4TH NOVEMBER, 1901

It breaks my heart to write these words, but on the 25th of October, Father died, and then we had his funeral on the following Saturday, in Stanford Rivers. It was a lovely funeral, but mostly it was a reminder to us that we are all not getting any younger in years, but instead, we grow steadily older. The house is so empty without him; Shales remains by his empty chair, near the fireplace. I do not yet know what I am to do – as well as both Lucy and Julia. Shall we remain here with Edmund, or take a smaller house somewhere else? We must decide upon our future, but I think I would like to try living somewhere else for a change. This house at Darnley Road is much too large for us. There is the house in Mere, Wiltshire, which is now empty – perhaps we shall move there and leave Hackney behind. Edmund suggests another place, and that we four should remain together.

5ᵀᴴ NOVEMBER, 1901

Shales died today. I am crying my eyes out as I write, but we all knew it was coming, especially since Dad has only just gone from us. Poor Shales. He took Dad's death quite hard, and went off his food and wouldn't bother with any of us whenever we tried to give him any attention. He had gone deaf as well as nearly blind, and very well crippled as well. He died in his favourite spot, in front of the fire, with his bunny tucked under his chin: used, I think, as a pillow. I came downstairs at nine o'clock this morning and he was fine then, but later, at about eleven o'clock, I noticed he hadn't moved, and when I went up to him I said, "Oh... Shales, Shales... love." Then he passed away. There will be no reason to celebrate tonight – I dread hearing any fireworks.

6ᵀᴴ NOVEMBER, 1901

This entry is just to say that we, all of us surviving children, had to decide what to do about Shales. Charles suggested we bury him away, somewhere in the countryside: either Stanford Rivers or Cotheridge Court. At one time Father

*had suggested Cotheridge, and had even discussed it
with Rowland. Cotheridge Court is the place we have
all agreed upon, being that it still belongs to the family,
namely Rowland. This morning, Edmund and Charles
set off with Shales and caught the train to Worcester. He
has been placed inside a large crate, wrapped in blankets
with his ancient bunny, and will be shipped as baggage,
though we weren't sure if this is the proper sort of thing
to do. Never mind, it is done now. I know he would have
loved to know his last and final journey was by train, and I
am sure, am positive, that he will appreciate being buried
within sight of Cotheridge Court. Whenever I go there, I
shall always place flowers upon his grave.*

7ᵀᴴ NOVEMBER, 1901

*Edmund and Charles have returned from Rowland's, and
Shales was successfully laid to rest in the long, east field,
known as Church Field, where, from there, one can see
both the house and the church. Rowland says he shall
provide a headstone to place over the spot, to forever
mark his place of rest.*

*Just as a little note. The Hackney Post had an article
on Shales. I was surprised when the reporter asked for an
interview:*

*It is indeed a sad day, or is it? when a dog of such
extreme old age, such as twenty-two, passes away in a
peaceful slumber, in front of the family hearth. The dog
I speak of had been a common sight around Darnley
Road, as he was regularly seen accompanying his
master, Augustus Berkeley Esq. (coal merchant Berkeley
& Sons) to his place of work at the coal yard. There are
stories that the dog used to wander loose about Hackney,
and had even, yes, even been possessed to have taken
a train ride on his own. The dog, name of Shales, was*

awarded a gold medal by Her Majesty Queen Victoria, for being 'The oldest living dog in the entirety of the British Empire'. Augustus Berkeley Esq. just recently passed away at his home, number fifteen Darnley Road, Hackney.

29ᵀᴴ NOVEMBER, 1901

We are all a dither here in this large house. It is so empty without Dad and Shales that Edmund wants us to move and leave Hackney for good. Where shall we go? He, too, suggests Mere, Wiltshire, but there is also another possible place in London. Whichever place we decide upon, it is a big move for us, but perhaps it will do us some good. It is yet undecided what to do about the coal business – Edmund isn't sure if he should sell up, or take on a manager and some more men so it will be looked after, but we would then still maintain an income from it.

13ᵀᴴ DECEMBER, 1901

We have decided upon a house near London. It is a respectable house, 28 Fairfield Road, Crouch End. We shall use the Mere house for holidays. I feel we are leaving an entire life behind, all our memories, either good or bad. Perhaps it is indeed a good thing to start afresh at our ages, even though we are not youngsters any more.

20ᵀᴴ MARCH, 1902

Oh, poor Algernon Cecil. He has died. Apparently, he took a bad fall off his horse when he was practising his jumps – Brigade jumps, and the horse balked, causing Algernon to fall, with his horse landing on top of him. He had a most terrible head wound, they say. The funeral was one of the saddest I have ever attended, because so many of his soldiers were there in attendance, and they were grieving badly. It is also sad to see a horse attend his master's funeral. I couldn't stop thinking of Shales and of Thomas Rowland, and at one point I turned my head just to make sure they weren't sitting at the back of the church. The feeling that they were there was most eerie.

The turnout was grand, and according to the papers, was one of the most impressive seen in the district. His coffin was draped with the Union Jack, and was placed in the central aisle, at the foot of the chancel steps. We all placed wreaths in that spot, and there were many of them, and they even stretched all up the aisle. He shall be missed.

27ᵀᴴ JULY, 1908

We have received a letter from our niece, Mary Matilda. She has informed us of her upcoming wedding, and I gather it will be a very small do, as they have no family up north. We, that is, Edmund, Julia and Lucy have decided to not attend. It would mean travelling all that way to Manchester by train, for a few short hours, then doing the return trip. I have written to her and have explained. I hope she will be happy with her husband, a man named Frederick Skinner. She has also surprised us by saying she is keeping her surname Berkeley, and is not taking on the name of Skinner. Also, this Frederick, he will be taking upon himself the surname Berkeley – it has been done before and Cotheridge Court would not have survived without such an act. I have also received a letter from Harry D. He says Mary Matilda has asked about her inheritance and if there is any money to come to her. He has informed her, by letter, that sadly there is no money coming to her, and that her mother received regular sums of Thomas's inheritance, and that if there is no money coming to her from her mother, then it is she who has spent it. I remember Father had promised to put some aside for her, but after finding out that Maud had spent an entire fortune, he was disheartened. I shall send her a gift, from all of us; I think about twenty-five pounds – a fair sum of money to set them up with.

APRIL, 1909

Stanley has died. He had suffered from consumption for many years, and of late had been confined to his cottage. He was not old, not at what? 54 years? The funeral was quite large, as he was well respected, and a lot of the family were there in attendance. I shall always treasure the painting he did of Shales, and also, some of his pencil drawings, which he gave to me.

OCTOBER, 1915

It was nice to see Shales and his family. They sail for South Africa, tomorrow, 22nd October, on the Llandovery Castle. That puts both of William and Mary's boys in South Africa permanently, I'm afraid.

OCTOBER, 1918

Oh, how I wish this war would end. Charles Clement's son, our dear nephew, Philip, has died, somewhere in Belgium, or an area they call the Somme. There are no details, just that he has been confirmed dead. Charles had just received the telegram yesterday. Poor lad. We do not know whether he died from fighting or if it was the influenza. They say they are dropping like flies in the trenches. He had been promoted to Major, but we would all rather have had him alive and back home with us.

So far the other boys are safe; that is none of my other
nephews have been killed in this war, yet, and I pray they
come home safely. As I write, I'm not sure if there will be
a funeral, or not.

September, 1923

Sad to write, but I must, about our dearest Julia. She
passed away this summer. Now there are just the three of
us here, in Mere.

1925

Dearest Edmund has died. He has been our tower of
strength all these years, and now he is gone. There is just
Lucy and myself to look after. Thank goodness both Emily
and Charles Clement are keeping well, though I do fear
for Charles, as his wife Amy passed away just a year ago.

1925

I must also write that our cousin Rowland has died this
year. There are rumours that Cotheridge Court cannot
survive – the upkeep and the money needed to do so are
a drain upon the estate. The dear church, St Leonard's, is
also suffering from the need of wanted repairs – they say
the roof is weakening. It is too depressing to think about
– the house without the family – the church in disrepair.
Rowland did his best. God bless him.

24ᵀᴴ February, 1929

Lucy died today. She had been suffering from bronchitis
and it worsened to the point that she couldn't breathe. I
was hopeful that she would recover, but at the age of 75, I
thought 'twould be a miracle if she did. I now find myself
wondering what to do, and I think that after the funeral

in Stanford Rivers, I'll visit with Emily and Charles. I do not want to return to The Close, here in Mere, and live alone; something which I have never before done. I simply dread it.

5TH JANUARY, 1930

I am not well, and I fear my time is nigh. Even as I write, which I can barely do, I feel the worst is going to happen. I dreamt about Shales and Thomas, and they were asking me to go for a walk with them. Father was there, as well, because I heard his voice, "Come on Jessie, hurry up." Also, I thought I saw Shales out of the corner of my eye. It is silly, but I feel he is watching over me. Last night I woke up because I thought there was a dog sleeping near my feet, and I'm sure I could feel a warm spot when I moved my feet. Another thing, I have woken up several times, thinking I smelt tobacco smoke, the same brand that Dad smoked. I think these are the signs of impending death that people hint at, but do not speak of freely.

6TH JANUARY, 1930

It is I, Emily, who writes this final entry in Jessie's diary. She passed away today; she was seventy-seven years of age, and there is just my brother Charles and me left, except for the children. Jessie shall lie in the family vault, in Stanford Rivers, as she so desired. This diary of hers is quite large, as it goes back a lot of years. I think I shall read it and rewrite it as a keepsake to hand down, as the family have scattered and we only see each other at funerals. I came across the shocking part about the letter to Maud, the one that Thomas had not posted. Jessie never mentioned it, not ever! There seems to be some interesting stuff written here about Shales, and in a second volume it appears she started to write a book about him. There are many pages – it is quite thick. I think I am going to spend today reading Jessie's diary, and as well, this book about Shales. Catching up on old memories is not such a sad thing, and I am sure I shall be highly entertained. I shall sit by the fire with a pot of tea on hand...

The End

POSTSCRIPT

AUTHOR'S NOTE

When I at first began to write *Forever Shales*, before I had even decided upon a title for the book, I had no intention at all to write about genuine people who had lived in nineteenth-century England, and especially my ancestors. For some strange reason, the names of my long-dead ancestors crept in, and then I decided to use whatever historical knowledge I had of them, and to include them in Shales's story. From there the story also became *their* story, and the result is a tale of fiction (Shales's escapades), entwined with a slightly historical telling of my ancestors' lives. I have had to use my imagination in the recreation of their characters, but all the family names, dates and places they lived, as well some of the events, are accurate.

There are some exceptions to historical accuracy. They are: Eliza, the cook; I have completely invented her personal character, and perhaps it is not to everyone's liking. In real life she was the cook and house servant at Wayletts, when Augustus lived there circa 1870s. I would like to think her true personality was the exact opposite of what I have created her to be. Shales (the dog), Jasper, Florrie, Toby and Horatio are completely fictitious creations of my overactive imagination. Leo, my very own dog and companion in real life, is the model for Shales, and Horatio was born out of my cat Gulliver. Armstrong, Soames, Pim, Toothless George and some of the less savoury characters who appear are complete inventions on my part in both name and character – they are indeed works of fiction and bear no resemblance to anyone living or dead.

Augustus Berkeley is my great-great-great grandfather. The historical facts are that he did farm at Wayletts in Stanford Rivers, Essex, and before that at Blakes Mansion, or simply Blakes. Later on he was a coal merchant, with a residence at 64 Cassland Road, Hackney, while still retaining Wayletts farm. Sometime between April 1881 and Thomas's death in 1882 the family moved from Cassland Road to Darnley Road. The original 15 Darnley Road residence no longer exists – it has been replaced with a building of flats. According to my great aunt, Mary (Molly) Berkeley, Augustus had disinherited Thomas, but after his son's death was greatly grieved and tried to make it up to Mary Matilda. On Thomas's death certificate Augustus is down as being present at death, so I would like to think that the two of them sorted out their differences before Thomas passed away. The family vault of Augustus Berkeley does lie in the churchyard of St Margaret's, Stanford Rivers, just where I said it is. Augustus did in fact die of a cerebral haemorrhage in October 1901.

Thomas Rowland's lavish funeral is a figment of my imagination. However, when you look at the historical data regarding Victorian funerals of the gentry, it isn't difficult to wonder if Augustus gave his son such a gallant send-off. Lavish funerals were popular, and back then were a part of life, so I ran with the idea that Thomas would have the funeral of all funerals. Also, I have the horse-drawn hearse carrying Thomas Rowland's body from Hackney all the way to Stanford Rivers, but, in reality, the coffin would more than likely have travelled by train to Ongar, and then by hearse from Ongar's station to St Margaret's Church. Then again, perhaps my great-great grandfather received no such send-off, being a disappointment to his father, and was quietly interred with no fuss. My way sounds much more noble, and I think he would approve, just as Shales approved.

Thomas's visit to the King's Head in Ongar is only fanciful thinking on my part. However, the pub is still there today, and when I stayed there I was told the place was haunted – and things did happen there! I chose that place for Thomas to frequent because the place enchanted me so, and chances are that he had been in the bar and had sampled its ales more than once.

Thomas did work for his father in the coal trade, alongside Edmund and his younger brother, Charles Clement. As well, he did hunt, but with which pack I do not know. He did die of meningitis in September 1882, in his house on Fifth Avenue, Bush Hill Park, which was part of a new housing estate.

Maud, my great-great grandmother, did get pregnant before she married Thomas Rowland – one just has to do the math. I have painted her as a dark and distrustful character, but the facts I do know about her speak for themselves. If Mary Matilda told the truth about her mother, then Maud did spend her daughter's inheritance (which she received in instalments on

464

family visits), and she did flee north to escape the family when Mary Matilda became a 'Ward of the Court' at Augustus's behest. What I don't know is if Mary Matilda only visited Cotheridge Court before her mother ran off with her, or if she continued to take her holidays there after they fled to Yorkshire. Years later, when Mary Matilda was married, the relationship between herself and her mother had deteriorated and, when asked, she absolutely refused to allow Maud to live with her. Also, there is no marriage certificate for Maud and Henry Diggens, who is listed as the father of Maud's second daughter, Blanche Evelyn Diggens, on her birth certificate. Nor have I been able to find a marriage certificate for John Dixon, whom she supposedly married as well, this relationship producing another child, a son. As for her moving to Darnley Road after Thomas's death – I made that bit up.

Mary Ann Moore was a genuine person, and Thomas Rowland and Maud were noted down in the 1881 census at the widow Moore's address as visitors. The fact that Mary Ann Moore was also a dressmaker leads me to think that Maud knew her – so I ran with the idea, knowing that Thomas and Maud would have had a difficult time finding a decent place to have their romantic liaison.

There are two David King Fosters. They were father and son, and one of them was a witness at Thomas and Maud's wedding. They lived not very far from Shelly Terrace, where Mary Ann Moore lived. The younger also clerked for a coal merchant, so I thought I would have young David working for Augustus, in Stoke Newington, seeing that either he or his father signed himself as a witness at Maud and Thomas's wedding.

Charles Clement Berkeley, Augustus's brother, did in fact retain his servant Susan Tomlin as his mistress, and they did have several children together. They were never legally married. However, he was devoted to her, and referred to her in his will as 'my kind and faithful friend'. He left everything he owned to her. During the late 1800s this must have caused many difficulties for Charles Clement Berkeley and his immediate family, as well as with his brothers, and his legal firm.

Edmund and his sisters, except for Emily, never married, and they always maintained house together, with Jessie being the last spinster to pass away when, at the last, she had moved in with her sister Emily. Jessie left a legacy of five hundred pounds to St Margaret's Church and five hundred pounds to the London Hospital. Emily did marry Thomas White, a cutler, and they did live at 20 Chatham Place. Young Charles Clement did remove himself from his father's coal trade, and he did become a tailor and marry Amy Oswald, a teacher. William did own the Bear Hotel in Gorleston-on-Sea, but my holiday with them is completely fictitious, as is his funeral and interment. The depiction of the hotel in the illustration is genuine, and is taken from a photo circa 1860.

The actual Battersea Dogs' Home is not a work of fiction, but did exist and still does exist today, Mary Tealby being the founder, and her rule that no dogs or cats would be destroyed, but would be found an eventual home, is also factual. It seems only right that my character Shales would end up there after his traipse around the sites of London.

Rowland Comyns Berkeley did farm Butts Bank Farm and did, in fact, inherit Cotheridge Court and the more than two thousand acres that accompanied the manor house, including the church, St Leonard's. He died in 1925. Sometime later the lands were auctioned off, and then the manor house, known as Cotheridge Court, was sold and was turned into private flats and houses. Rowland's next brother, William Nichols, became a Reverend, and he ministered to St Leonard's Church, and later retired to Charlton Kings, Gloucestershire. Second brother Lieutenant-Colonel Edmund Robert Berkeley eventually retired from the army and farmed in Kent; he later married. Third brother Herbert Bowyer Berkeley did become a chemical engineer as well as being a member of The Royal Photographic Society. Also, he made a discovery to do with the developing solutions used at the time in the development of photos, and he published his discovery, but was never recognised for it. Sadly, he became ill, and at age thirty-nine he passed away in Algiers; his body was not returned home to Cotheridge as he had stipulated in his will (wanting to be buried in a plain and unadorned coffin, close to the pines, with a large cross of white marble). He, too, was unmarried. He is remembered in the Bradford Museum of Photography, in Yorkshire.

Emily must have thought fondly of her brothers, Augustus and Comyns Rowland, as well as several nieces and nephews, as she was generous to them when she died. She did in fact play the piano, and she is interred in St Leonard's, Cotheridge, where you can see the beautiful stained-glass window she had installed, with the Comyns and Berkeley coats of arms.

Stanley Tyerman Berkeley was indeed a Victorian artist, and a copy of a painting of his did hang in Balmoral (perhaps it still does), the Royal Residence, in Scotland, during the latter years of Queen Victoria. Apparently, Queen Victoria was so impressed by the original *Gordons and Greys to the Front* that she had a copy made for her own. Also, he did work for the *Illustrated London News*, and illustrated novels and magazines. As for Stanley's connection to the Berkeleys of Cotheridge, I only have my great grandmother's word (Mary Matilda) that he was family, that she met him when she was a child, and she called him "Uncle", as I can in no way find a genealogical connection to him, though I'm sure it is there, somewhere.

George H.A.C. Berkeley, the grandson of Augustus's brother George Brackenbury Berkeley, did become an obstetrician and a gynaecological surgeon. He was knighted in 1934. Shales, of the Bear Hotel, fought in the Boer War, and married and settled in South Africa. Younger brother Philip also emigrated to South Africa, but their cousin Philip, son of Charles Clement Berkeley and Amy (nee Oswald), did not return from fighting in World War I. He died at the rank of Major in September 1918 somewhere in Belgium. Algernon Cecil Berkeley became Riding Master of the 2nd Dragoons (Queen's Bays), and at age 37, in 1902, had a fall whilst jumping his horse, resulting in his injury, and the following day, his death. He was another one who did not marry.

We all know that Jack the Ripper was a reality, and not a work of fiction, and after some research and a 'Ripper Walk' around the dark streets of the East End of London, I have decided upon the likely true character of 'Jack'. Shales believes that he is a doctor, and that the knife used was a scalpel, and that the murders were not random, but were made in error – in the quest for someone named Mary. The police did receive a threat that the residents of the parish of St John's, Hackney, were in danger of Jack's murderous intentions, but it was later proved to be a hoax. I can only wonder that Augustus and his grown children must have worried, just a bit, as they went to bed at night, being as Darnley Road was in that very parish.

The "'telling of the bees' during this book was not entirely a creation of my imagination, only the way I told it. In fact it was, and perhaps still is, in some places, a ritual of beekeepers. The bees are told when their master has died and whom their new master will be, by their hives being tapped thrice with the front door key to their master's house. I thought it added an air of compassion to the deaths, in the relationship between man and nature.

Having solicitors and barristers in the family must have been convenient, as it seems they handled much of the family's legal affairs over many decades. Comyns Rowland Berkeley outlived his brothers, dying at the old age of ninety-four, and his son, Harry Douglas Berkeley, was indeed a lawyer and his name is on several of the family's wills. George Brackenbury Berkeley and his son George Augustus Goodrich Berkeley were wine merchants. I can only imagine the generous amounts of wine that flowed at their dinner tables.

A comment on the names. Many names were 'recycled', easily identifying them as members of one large family. Jessie, Julia, Lucy and Emily also had first cousins by the same names; there was even a Rowland Thomas Berkeley (easily confused with Thomas Rowland Berkeley) and a Brackenbury Comyns Berkeley. It is hard to imagine that the family was actually larger than appears in my book, and there were many more than I mentioned; too many nieces, nephews and grandchildren to mention. As for William Comyns Berkeley being worried that the family would become scattered and not know their origins; well, it did happen. There are descendants, whom I know to be living in England, Ireland, Canada, Australia, USA, and South Africa. I have found, such as in many families, that within three generations or less they have forgotten or lost their family history, and have had no photographs or documents passed down to them. I hope that this book gives them a little insight into how our family lived and died, a hundred and twenty-five years ago, and how many of them would have had a faithful family dog.

Shales's fanciful age of twenty-two years is not a far stretch of the imagination. Only recently, in May of 2008, when I was in England, I was informed by two persons who had first-hand knowledge of local dogs that were older than Shales's twenty-two years. There are records, some of them recent, of English dogs living to be twenty-seven years, and even older.

* * *

WITH THANKS

I wish to thank all those who made contributions to *Forever Shales*, no matter how small, as every contribution was helpful: Carol Myers for her valuable help and patience regarding Maud; my cousin Barrie Laverick for Darnley Road; Paul Harris for Eliza the cook; Pam Bishop and Susan Homewood for Coopersale Hall; Dennis Durant for The Bear Hotel; Constable Phil MacDonald for allowing me to use Schooner, his real-life police dog; Annie Maddern (a distant Berkeley cousin) for all her research and praise; Brian Holden for our road trips to Cotheridge Court; Jay Popplewell and her late husband, Hugh, at Berkeley House, Cotheridge Court, for their warm welcomes and for their care of St Leonard's Church; Pat Caspari for her tour of Cotheridge Court and the garden with the ha-ha; Pauline Berkeley Cherry for Herbert Bowyer Berkeley's photographs, as well as the R.P.S. magazine article on his works; Alison Maddock for her research and the obtaining of several Berkeley wills; Dr Derrill Hall for his patience regarding the technical support I needed with my home PC; Peter Walker, the local historian in Cotheridge, for providing the map showing all the fields and lands for the manor of Cotheridge; both Joe Barnes and Keith Brooks for the viewing of the ancient long barn at Butts Bank Farm (House), and also for the aerial photos; Rose Menin for her interest and support; my friend Susan Snider for the encouragement I needed over the last five years, and who cried through her first reading of the manuscript; the late Dr. Roger Berkeley for his photo of Augustus; my parents for their everlasting patience and support, and who have waited long enough to see a printed copy; Leo, my dog, who was the idea for the book in the first place; and lastly, for 'the Berkeley family', for without them there would have been no story to tell.

469

BIBLIOGRAPHY

1. The website www.gutenberg.org - *English Dialects* by Walter W. Skeat.
   -north Essex dialect words
   -selected Norfolk dialect words from *Eractics by a Sailor* written by the Revd Joshua Larwood, 1800.

2. Jeremy Alderton's site www.Aldertons.com – of cockney rhyming words.

3. Ben Judd's site www.badsey.net - Asum dialect, Worcestershire.

   For the Essex dialect I used words from *The Endo of Borley Rectory* written by Charles Benham, pub. 1890, which I found at www.foxearth.org.uk.

4. www.lillielangtry.com

5. www.british-history.ac.uk (British History on line) Details about Cotheridge Court and Hackney.

6. www.old-maps.co.uk - these old maps gave me insight as to what the streets and roads were like in the 1880s, especially Cotheridge, Broadwas, Stanford Rivers, Hackney, Gorleston-on-Sea and London City. Also the map of Hackney 1876-1882 – which also confirms the station as being on the east side of Mare Street.

7. www.londonancestor.com - a wealth of sites and old maps.

8. To confirm the location of Hackney's railway station in 1882 I used a map of Hackney printed in 1885 by Eyre and Spottiswoode, London.

9. www.victorianlondon.org - a wealth of information on every aspect of Victorian life, from articles originally published in the nineteenth century. My general source for information on coal, coal wagons, coal bays, coal horses, funeral horses, the interior of the London Coal Exchange and the descriptions of Whitechapel.

GLOSSARY

I t was suggested to me by my very good friend, Susan Cliffe Snider, that I might want to add a glossary of Yorkshire, Norfolk, Worcestershire, cockney rhyming words, and any other English words that might possibly confuse the reader who is unfamiliar with the dialect and slang of England. The interpretations and origins are to be used as a guide only – with *Forever Shales*. I claim no accuracy in their meanings, and the same goes for my usage of 'thee' and 'tha'.

Allus – Always. (Yorkshire)

Bait – Food, such as a packed meal. (Yorkshire)

Butcher's – To look. (cockney – butcher's hook)

Cate – A portmanteau word from cat/mate.

China – A good friend. (cockney – china plate)

Chuckie – Hen. Chuckie eggs are hens' eggs. (Yorkshire)

Collar touched – Arrested by the police.

Dray – Wagon loaded with barrels of beer etc.

Dew – Do. (Norfolk)

Ent – Isn't. (Norfolk dialect)

Fain – Pleased, happy. ("I'm fain to see thee here.")

Farthing – A coin with the value of one quarter of an English penny.

Fettle – To clean or tidy up.

Fettle (in fine fettle) – To be, or feel to be in good shape. (Yorkshire)

Femmer – To feel weak. (Yorkshire dialect)

Fey – Psychic.

Flog – Sell.

Fogger – A man. (Norfolk)

Gawp – To stare. (Yorkshire)

Ger agate – Get on your way! (Yorkshire)

Gob – Your mouth.

Gao – Go. (Essex)

Guinea – A coin worth 21 shillings.

Ha-ha – A mound and trench system used to keep livestock in.

"He have an ill dent." – "He is out of his senses." (Norfolk dialect)

"He'll niver moize again." – He'll never move again. (Norfolk)

Hey up! – Look out!

Int, ent – Isn't.

Ims – He's. (Worcestershire)

Kip – Sleep.

Lop – A flea. (Yorkshire)

Mafted – Feeling hot. (Yorkshire)

Maister – The master.

Midden – Refuse heap or a dunghill.

Minces – Eyes. (cockney – mince pies)

Mother's ruin – Gin. (cockney)

Mun – Must. (Yorkshire)

Nithered – To feel cold and shivery. (Yorkshire)

Northing – Nothing. (Norfolk)

Nubble – Small piece of coal.

Oss (Osses) – Horse, horses.

Ow bist? – How are you? (Worcestershire)

Ower – Over. (Yorkshire)

Ower heated – Feeling hot.

Palaver – Bother, commotion.

Peckish – Hungry, has an appetite.

Plates o' meat – Feet. (cockney)

Porkies – Lies. (cockney – pork pies)

Rammy – Pungent, smelling badly.

Rig-welted – When a ewe is heavily pregnant and cannot get up off her side and onto her feet. (typically Yorkshire, origin-Norse)

Rived – Ripped out, or torn out. (Yorkshire)

Scarpered – Ran for it. Fled quickly.

Shift – "Move over" or "get going" or to move an object.

Shilling – A silver coin with the value of twelve pennies.

Siled – Rained heavily. (Yorkshire)

Sixpence – A silver coin worth six pennies.

Skimmered – Sparkled brightly. (Yorkshire)

Strang – Strong.

Ta – Thank you. (as in "Ta very much")

Tanner – A sixpence.

Ta-ra – Goodbye. (Yorkshire)

Thissen – Yourself (Yorkshire) – pronounced "thy-sen".

Tidley – A drink of alcohol. (cockney)

Titfer – Man's hat. (cockney – tit fer tat)

Trews – Trousers. (Typically Yorkshire, northern counties, and Scots)

Um – Him. (Worcestershire)

Ums – They or them.

Whinged (ing) – Whine.

Wuthered – Wind-blown as in Bronte's *Wuthering Heights*. (Yorkshire)

Yer – Here. (Worcestershire) (Means 'you' in Yorkshire).

Yar – You.

Yew – You. (Maud's Norfolk)